BOOKS BY DENNIS SMITH

FICTION

The Final Fire
Glitter and Ash
Steely Blue

NONFICTION

Report from Engine Company 82
Firehouse
Dennis Smith's History of Firefighting in America
The Aran Islands

Steely Blue

by

DENNIS SMITH

SIMON AND SCHUSTER—New York

PUBLISHED BY SIMON AND SCHUSTER
A DIVISION OF SIMON & SCHUSTER, INC.
SIMON & SCHUSTER BUILDING
ROCKEFELLER CENTER
1230 AVENUE OF THE AMERICAS
NEW YORK, NEW YORK 10020
SIMON AND SCHUSTER AND COLOPHON ARE REGISTERED TRADEMARKS
OF SIMON & SCHUSTER, INC.

DESIGNED BY IRVING PERKINS

MANUFACTURED IN THE UNITED STATES OF AMERICA

10 9 8 7 6 5 4 3 2 1

LIBRARY OF CONGRESS CATALOGING IN PUBLICATION DATA
SMITH, DENNIS, DATE.
  STEELY BLUE.
  I. TITLE.
PS3569.M523S7   1984   813'.54   84-10627
ISBN: 0-671-44019-5

To Aislinn,
Deirdre,
Sean,
Dennis,
and Brendan

CHAPTER 1

STEELY saw her hair across the room, reflecting small sparkles in the brightness of the flames. It looked to be red hair, long and flowing down below her shoulders. A young woman probably. He wondered for a fleeting moment if she were still alive.

He looked around. He was quite alone and crouched down on his hands and knees.

LADDER SEVEN ABLE TO LADDER SEVEN CHARLIE, COME IN.

He could barely make out the squawk of the radio call amid the crackle of the burning wood. Goddamn Lieutenant Jackson, always yelling.

BYRNES, COME IN, the radio said.

Steely wondered how he would get to her. The room was long and narrow like a wide corridor, a storeroom probably or an employees' lounge, and the fire was growing fast in the middle of the room. There were tables and benches piled there, and they were burning.

He pressed the transmitter button of his radio. "All right," he said, "I'm here. Relax."

BYRNES, Lieutenant Jackson's voice raged within the static. GET BACK HERE NOW.

9

They were on the fourth floor of the Eighty-sixth Street Gimbels, fighting the store's third fire of the day. A stockboy had started them probably, or any one of a thousand employees with a bitch. The first two had been in service-hall trash bins and were easily extinguished. Small-potato fires to the men of Ladder Company 7. This one, though, had gotten into the hanging ceiling and was traveling like electricity across the rear end of the store. Lieutenant Jackson had stopped by the front elevators to harness his mask on, but something in Fireman Steely Byrnes had made him run into the dark, ballooning smoke without a mask. An impulse, maybe, a sixth sense that this was the one where a Department medal and a handshake from the Mayor lay at the other end of the run, like a glowing pot at the end of a rainbow, if the rainbow could be black.

And there she was, just the other side of the fire, lying on the tile floor, her hands by her sides, her red hair spread like a vibrance around her head and shoulders. She looked to have an appealing body, long and slender. Maybe she was still alive, even in this smoke as thick as mud. He could get to her, he thought, coughing easily, his mouth close to the floor, if only he could get past the fire. He felt good, strong. But he knew he only had seconds before he would begin to cough uncontrollably.

HEY, BYRNES, the radio belched. REPORT TO ME FORTHWITH.

He could see now that the fire was shooting out from a doorway in the middle of the room just behind the tables and benches, and burning down now through the ceiling. He would have to jump through it to reach her. Like a circus animal, he thought without smiling. Just one leap and I'll be through it, six, maybe eight feet of fire, just one mad charge. God, he thought, make her be among the living when I get to her.

As he stood he felt the smoke fill his lungs as if a valve of some kind had been opened. He coughed deeply, tilted his leather helmet toward the fire, and brought his arm up to protect his face. He began to run. Like a shot. One step, two, three. He closed his eyes. There was a brightness, and then it was gone behind his eyelids. The fire swept over him briefly, like the single stroke of a fan, and then he dropped to the floor.

FIREMAN BYRNES, RESPOND FORTHWITH. Lieutenant Jackson seemed to be screaming.

Steely moved his mouth first, opening it wide as if in a yawn. Then he opened and shut and opened and shut his eyes again, to feel if any of the skin on his face had been burned taut or crisp. It felt normal, natural. But then he coughed harshly, deeply, as he crawled toward the unmoving woman.

He began to think chronologically, as he had been trained. One, locate the victim; two, rescue, assist, or carry; three, egress safely.

Egress safely.

He looked around fast. There was *no* safe exit. He was in a corner and the only way to get out was the way he got in.

He crawled to the woman, choking, his mouth kissing the floor, sucking for clean air the way a fish sucks for oxygen in the water. Nearing her, he stopped, seeing her fully now in the jumping, reflecting light. She was wearing a tight, purplish dress, calf length. He didn't have to touch her to know that his medal was down the toilet, that his handshake with the Mayor was something to be put off.

DAMMIT, the radio squawked. ANSWER ME, BYRNES.

But he touched her anyway, pressing in and feeling her face stiff and unresponsive. He punched her then on the side of her face, just gently as he laughed and recognized the irony, and then as hard as he could. The punch made a funny sound as it sank into the face, and the eyes and the eyebrows and the nose and the mouth caved into the hollowness of the plaster shell.

FIREMAN BYRNES, REPORT.

The fire was billowing out of the ceiling now, having found an air current that flowed like a flue. He did not think he could make it back through, but he was certain he wasn't going to die either, not in a burned-out corner of a department store next to a department-store mannequin. He could hear them laughing in the firehouse, guys like Arbuckle McFatty and Whore-hickey Harrigan. After the respect was offered at the funeral, when the mourning changed with the beer and whiskey into the mirth of an Irish wake. "The dummy died saving the dummy," they would say.

Steely Byrnes wouldn't give them the satisfaction of that.

He was convulsing now with the smoke, but he readied himself to leap again through the fire. It wouldn't be three steps this time, though, closer to eight, maybe ten. The fire was glowing fiercely, and expanding very fast. He pulled his canvas turnout coat off and threw it over his head, remembering the advice an oldtime firefighter had given him when he was a rookie. "Save your head when your ass is in trouble," the old fireman had said, " 'cause you're not the kind of guy who would ever think or kiss with his ass anyway."

Steely smiled matter-of-factly, and shrugged his shoulders between coughs. He would dive through the fire, and he would try to save his head.

BYRNES, HEY BYRNES.

Just then, beyond the sound of Lieutenant Jackson's voice, Steely heard the swishing sounds of an advancing hose line, and in another moment the fire before him turned to steam. Just as if someone had snapped his fingers and ordered the fire extinguished, the men from Engine Company 5 swung their hose from side to side saturating the great energy of the fire, changing it into whimpering puffs of steam. Steely dropped to his knees and, now coughing uncontrollably, he managed to put his arms through his coat and crawl the distance of the long narrow room.

The other men of Ladder Company 7 had opened the windows, the doors, the roof door, too, and the area vented quickly. Steely bent over and, holding one nostril, blew the other clean. It felt as if all the hair inside his nose had been burned off. When he looked up again, he was face to face with Lieutenant Lou Jackson.

His face scarred by acne, the lieutenant appeared grotesque to Steely, as if he were suffering from some strange disease, of a kind that made saints like Damien.

They were by the elevators. The lights there had not blown, and Steely could see by the look in the lieutenant's eyes that he was ready to rip a room apart. Several firefighters were standing around, resting, or waiting to be assigned a specific job, and they all turned toward Lieutenant Jackson as they heard him yell.

"You are irresponsible, Byrnes," he screamed, nose to nose with Steely. "Even a stupid-johnnie fireman would know better than to pull what you pulled, runnin' in like a knight in battle. We operate as a team when we're inside, Byrnes. We have a two-man search and a team search. We don't think we're too good to be part of the team."

Steely took his coat off and threw it on the floor. He felt the eyes of the firefighters on him, and he knew he could not just take a dressing-down without comment. He didn't especially want to have a go with the lieutenant, but he had to do something. He couldn't let anyone speak to him like that, not even a chief or the Fire Commissioner himself.

Steely shoved his chest against the lieutenant's and pushed just enough so the lieutenant had to step back a little. "Real men don't yell, boss," he said, his voice low and rasping, "and they don't take it either. They put five big ones between the ivories to shut someone's mouth up." Steely stood poised with his hands folded into fists.

Lieutenant Jackson laughed spitefully then, sneeringly. "Take your best shot, Byrnes," he said, freezing his eyes on Steely. "It'll cost you charges, a trial, and a week's pay at least, and I'll be happy to do all the paperwork."

There was nothing Steely could say in return that might be adequate. The onlooking firemen turned their heads, just as Steely turned his. They were all a little embarrassed. A week's pay fine would be too much. He wouldn't be able to handle it. Not with his situation with Maryanne. He could barely pay the freight for a can of Campbell's soup at lunchtime.

He loosened his fists and turned away from the lieutenant. With nothing more to say, he picked his coat up and looked around for something to do. The fire was under control, but they still had to overhaul, to make sure there were no flames or embers in the walls, and to clean up some of the debris.

CHAPTER 2

IT wouldn't have been a problem for Steely if Lieutenant Jackson hadn't cut him down in front of so many men, and if the cop directing traffic at the Second Avenue base of the Queensboro Bridge hadn't been Irish. Murphy, it said on the ticket. *Murphy.* The traffic was five o'clock dense. Steely was peeling the Miller label in long, thin strips from the bottle between his legs, rolling the moist paper into pill-sized balls and flicking them with his thumb through the opened window. It was hot for May, and the air-conditioning was not working. "Unfortunately inoperative," the salesman had said. Steely had never owned a car in which the air-conditioning worked.

He was listening to a Mantovani arrangement of "Stardust," thinking that the violins were drunk, swaying, slurring the notes up and down the scale, making, like most drunks, a little too much of it. The music changed unexpectedly, sending the vibrations of a muffled bass drum through the car. Next to Mantovani they were playing disco. "Bag that," Steely said aloud, and he pushed the radio button to send the indicator up to the all-news station. It was then that the day's troubles began.

14

Red Hadley had relieved him early. Not that he was doing Steely a favor. Hadley had spent the day in bed on the second floor of the firehouse, massaging away the hammer blows of a hangover, and he wasn't giving away a bundle to get up an hour earlier to let Steely go. "I wanna go out and hump my cousin," Steely had said. He always said things like that to Hadley, and Hadley, a born-again Christian, usually said in return, "If you let yourself know Jesus . . ."

It had been a nowhere day at the firehouse, two false alarms besides the dressing-room fire at the Eighty-sixth Street Gimbels. "I could camp out here," Steely said to some of the firefighters who were standing around after his confrontation with the lieutenant. "Can you imagine camping out in the women's dressing room at Gimbels? And being invisible?"

"You got a small mind, Steely," one fireman had said to take the edge off.

"But I got a steel pair," Steely said, "and that's what it takes in this job."

"What about the twelve women in the fire academy?" another fireman had asked. "No balls there."

"They'll never make it through," Steely answered.

"They got a week left," the fireman said.

"They'll put 'em in the dispatcher's office, or on the ambulance, or like that."

"News for you, Steely," the firefighter laughed. "They're all going into *your* locker."

"They do," Steely answered, picking up his tools, "they better bring a vacuum cleaner and wear black nylon stockings, because I want the locker cleaned and my pipes blown."

"Wake up, pal," the lieutenant snapped in passing. "You're be-hind the times." Steely ignored him.

The traffic was pulsating, shoving forward in spurts. Like semen, Steely thought. Horns blasting in emphatic moans. Steely was sweat-ing. "Behind the times my ass," he said to himself. He wiped his forehead, and drank the last of the beer.

A radio reporter was interviewing a councilperson named Elisha Peabody-Macomber. "If the firefighters and the police officers had any respect for themselves," Peabody-Macomber was saying, "they would not come into our city every day like occupying forces, take our money, and then go out to spend it in Levittown or some ungodly place like that. They should be forced to live within the city limits, and my proposed legislation will mandate that they move into town or lose their jobs."

Steely had lived in Levittown. His wife and kids lived in Levittown, and he'd still be living there if things were just a little different. Some of his friends, cops and firemen, lived there. So when he heard those words float through the car, he punched the plastic grille of the radio loudspeaker. Hard, so that the skin scraped off two of his knuckles. But it kept on talking. "Civil responsibility from civil servants," he heard the councilperson say. He punched the radio again, shoved the gearshift into park, and jumped out onto Second Avenue. He pointed to the car, yelled at it, and stamped his feet. A tractor trailer behind Steely's car belched the bloated sound of an air horn. Steely punched the hood of his car, then pounded downward as if the wires beneath were the guts of the radio and his blows would knock the air and sound out of the car. The air horn behind belched again. Drivers on all sides began catcalling. A cop yelled. Steely raised his middle finger, thrusting it in the direction of the cop, and punched the car again, snarling as his clenched fist caromed off the wood. "You can't say that about me," he screamed, jumping up and down. "You no-good Protestant motherless piece of crap."

The cop was behind him now. "Get in the car, asshole," the cop said, grabbing him by the arm and yelling over the horns and catcalls.

Steely pulled back and yanked his fireman's badge from his hip pocket. "Where you live?" he asked the cop, flashing the Maltese cross briefly in front of his eyes. "Don't hand me no nonsense. Just tell me where you live."

The cop, surprised by Steely's aggressiveness, said, "Massapequa, why?"

"*Massapequa*," Steely yelled, stamping his foot on the blacktop. "Massapequa! You know what this bastard just now said?" He pointed inside the car.

The cop looked into the car, his hand landing naturally on the butt of his revolver as he leaned over. "I don't see no bastard."

"The radio, for God's sake," Steely said in a near normal voice. "Can't you see the goddamned radio?"

"Pull the car over to the side," the cop returned.

"C'mon. Look."

"G'wan, get in and pull it over, wise guy."

Steely noticed the vehemence in the cop's voice. He pulled the car over and parked it in front of Francesco's Italian Restaurant. He knew Francesco's. He remembered being in it when he was a kid. If they had named the joint Frankie's, he thought, they wouldn't have needed to say Italian. Like the drunken music, it was too much.

The veins danced in the cop's thick neck. "Say one word outta line and you sleep on a city mattress tonight," he said. "License and registration."

"I'm a fireman, pal," Steely said.

"I'm a cop," the cop said grimly, and Steely offered up the certificates.

Better yet, he thought, they named it Tony's. Nobody'd make a mistake about it then. A guinea restaurant for sure.

"I'm going to give you a ticket," the cop said.

"Screw it," Steely said.

"Because you're a fireman, I'm only going to give you a ticket for double-parking."

"I'm not double-parked," Steely said. "I'm parked right here next to the curb in front of this guinea restaurant."

"Don't take too much wire, fireman," the cop clicked, "because you're gonna get tangled in it. I could write you tickets here for a week's salary."

"Screw it," Steely said again, and looked at the restaurant window. Continental Cuisine, it said. Second-rate joint, one step up from a pizza parlor. Why can't people be just what they are, he asked himself, instead of posing as something better? Francesco himself should be locked up for misrepresentation.

Steely stuck his head out of the window. The cop was in the classical posture, foot up on Steely's front bumper, writing a ticket.

"Hey officer," Steely yelled, "give me a break, huh? I got the separated wife and two rabbits and the mortgage note to the Protestant bank out on the Island."

"It's just double-parking," the cop said. "I gotta do something, all the cars beeping."

"C'mon pal, I'm tapped. I can't even make the monthlies."

"You don't have to pay it, you know. Lots of people don't pay it and don't get caught."

"I don't want it to begin with, pal. Give it to some goddamn diamond-studded rich guy in a Mercedes Benz."

The cop completed the ticket and handed it to Steely together with the car registration and driver's license. "I bet your mouth gets you a lot of adventure."

"Don't lecture me," Steely said, pulling the papers from the cop's hand. He read the ticket, and it was then he saw that the cop was a Murphy. Steely's mother was a Murphy.

"Murphy," Steely yelled a third time, after the first two *Murphys* were met with a surprised sneer scratched across the cop's face. "You no-good Irish hard-on," Steely said, "giving me a ticket. If I was Italian and you was Italian, you wouldn't give me a ticket, but you're typical shanty Irish, always looking to screw one of your own."

The cop's face quickly transformed from incredulity to anger as Steely continued, "If they ever could've got your mother to stop shitting potatoes, she would've been clean enough to have a healthy baby instead of the likes of you, pal."

The cop reached the limit of abuse he would take from any civilian, fireman or not. He stretched his arm inside the car and grabbed Steely by the collar, twisting it with all his strength, forcing gurgling sounds from Steely's throat. Steely started the car as the cop tried to pull the door open, and quickly rolled the window up so that the cop's arm was caught between the glass and the metal of the door frame. Then he jammed the gearshift down into low. A voice within him said, "You're in trouble now, Steely."

The car lurched forward toward the granite bastions at the base of the Queensboro Bridge with the cop, pulled from his feet, dragging alongside the car, the tops of his shoes disintegrating as they buffed the avenue tar. The car swerved around two taxicabs waiting for the Sixtieth Street traffic to move up to Third Avenue and then stopped short behind a Baskin-Robbins delivery truck waiting for the light on Fifty-ninth Street to turn green.

Steely opened the window, releasing the cop's arm. Realizing what he had done, he laughed a strained little laugh, and said to the cop, "I guess you won't give that truck a ticket, huh?"

"You're dead," the cop said.

"If it wasn't stopped there, the truck, we'd be going to Long Island City now."

"Get out of the car, smart guy." The cop now was holding his revolver. His hand was shaking, and his voice vibrated with nervousness and rage.

Steely shook his head a little and tapped his fingers on the steering wheel. "Saved," he said, "by ice cream."

CHAPTER 3

JACK T. Haggerty, Chief of Department of the New York Fire Department, five gold stars gleaming in a circle on his shirt collar, dropped his bloodstained uniform pants to his ankles, and spoke of his wife as he leaned over the desk. "Josie is so upwardly mobile," he said, "she can't give me a tie from Sears, you know."

Dr. Henry Titlebloom, the four gold stars on his shirt improperly placed and askew, grunted in return as he looked through his bag for a spool of surgical thread.

"She's got to go to Tiffany's and buy me a money clip with a fold-out scissors. Doesn't even wrap the present for me. 'A Tiffany box,' she says, 'is better than any wrapping paper for a birthday present. Not everyone can go to Tiffany's, you know.' And she says this in front of fourteen people at my party, one of them a fireman. Made him feel lowly, the fireman. Me, the big deal with the Tiffany box, the man of means."

"So you didn't have to put it in your back pocket," the doctor said. "And you could have closed the scissors first."

"How bad is it?"

"Not bad," the doctor said, pulling the Chief of Department's underpants down to lie on top of his crumpled trousers. "Two stitches, maybe three. The scissors went in only a quarter inch or so. Maybe you shouldn't have sat down either."

Dr. Titlebloom was the Chief Surgeon of the Fire Department. He wasn't a surgeon at all, Haggerty was thinking, but a G.P. who had failed to meet the entrance requirements of American medical schools and consequently was trained at the College of Medicine in Barcelona.

He was, however, very much a chief, for the title of Assistant Chief of Department was conferred automatically with the Chief Surgeon position. It was an honorific title, to be sure, and with it came the right to wear the uniform of an assistant chief, four gold sleeve stripes, four golden collar stars, and all. Dr. Titlebloom was the first Department doctor to ever actually buy a uniform, and having bought it, he wore it incessantly, to dinner parties, to basketball games at the Garden, and to work each day. Haggerty knew that the twelve Department doctors who worked under his administrative control called him Herr Doctor, but never to his face. They were afraid of him, because he was the most fearful thing one could be in a bureaucracy. He was unpredictable.

"Ahh, for goodness sakes," Haggerty yelled as the doctor penetrated the soft flesh of his buttock with a half-moon needle.

"I'm sorry," Dr. Titlebloom said, kneeling down behind the bent-over Chief of Department. "I'll get closer."

"Yes, get closer, please," Haggerty said sarcastically. "Hurt me again and I'll break your glasses."

"It won't matter so much," Dr. Titlebloom said, leaning forward so that his breath warmed the hairless skin of Haggerty's buttocks. His nose was close to the first stitch, which was considerably off the mark and sewn into the middle of the puncture itself. "The glasses sometimes hinder more than they help."

"A million doctors in the city," Haggerty muttered under his breath, "and I am sent one trained at a blacksmith shop."

"What was that?" Dr. Titlebloom asked, adjusting his hearing aid. He had a hearing impairment that nearly prevented him from getting the Fire Department job, but the city's Chief of Personnel himself had called the Fire Commissioner to intercede. Dr. Titlebloom had friends in high places. He was also an ideal appointment for high rank within civil service, for he had a wide nose and thick features which made him appear negroid in photographs, and he had a Jewish-sounding name. A politician could not go wrong in New York with black or Jewish appointments, the only two ethnic groups in the city that had enough clout to swing an election. There was a certain irony in this, for Henry Titlebloom was neither black nor Jewish, but Egyptian. He was also a cousin by marriage to the Chairman of the Bronx Democratic Club, which is why he was in civil service to begin with.

"Just do it correctly," Haggerty said, "or you'll be treating bad backs over at the Sanitation Department."

"That threat does intimidate," Dr. Titlebloom replied, inserting the needle once more.

"Ahh," Haggerty yelled again, just as his aide, Captain Steinf, entered the office.

Steinf, a squat, white-headed man, was an administrative hold-over from a previous administration, though Haggerty wasn't sure exactly which previous administration. He was of a type in the Fire Department who, for reasons of health, family, laziness, or fear of fire, did not work the day and night chart system of the Department, and it seemed that he had been around forever. Haggerty did not much like his administrative aide, and thought him as trustworthy, perhaps, as a real estate man in Tijuana. He had known for some time that Steinf misrepresented his position to curry favor within the Department, to have men transferred, to get his relatives appointed to the Department's civilian clerical jobs, those kinds of things. Haggerty wished there was a way to get him out, but people at head-quarters, especially officers, were not transferred without their own request. It just wasn't done, for the presumption was that if a man worked his way into a headquarters staff job he had the right to it forever, or, at least, until retirement. Steinf was as entrenched as the El pillars on Roosevelt Avenue, Haggerty knew, as entrenched as any of the other officers he himself had placed in headquarters jobs. It was a system, Haggerty often thought, that insured the system.

"There's a guy on the phone, Chief," Captain Steinf said.

"Later," Haggerty said. "Have you any eyes?"

"Sorry, Chief," Captain Steinf replied. "A fireman. Says he knows you and it's an emergency."

"I'm involved at the moment in an emergency, for goodness sake."

"Fireman Byrnes, and he's at the 19th Precinct."

"What line?" Haggerty said, reaching for the phone.

22

"Two three," Steinf said, still standing in the middle of the large office, curious to hear why a fireman, the lowest rank in the Department, could get the attention of the highest uniformed rank with one phone call.

"Good-bye, Captain," Haggerty said as he lifted the receiver. He was used to Captain Steinf's curiosity.

"That's it," Dr. Titlebloom said, putting a Band-Aid over the one full stitch and the half stitch that went through the puncture. "Take two aspirins and don't call me no more." The doctor zippered his top-grain cowhide medical bag, a gift to him from a fireman.

"See ya, Henry," Haggerty said, still bent flat over his desk, his hand cupped over the telephone. "Come back if you ever need a transfer or a good word."

"I'm as high as I can go," Dr. Titlebloom said, a hint of scornful cynicism in his voice. "Just like you."

"Don't count on it, Henry. I've got a peg or two left on the board."

The doctor laughed, lit an oversized cigar, and let the smoldering match fall to the fire-engine-red carpet. "Knowing you, Chief," he said, "you undoubtedly have more than a couple left. Good day."

Jack Haggerty balanced the phone between his shoulder and ear, and pulled his underpants and trousers up as he watched the doctor close his office door.

He was surprised that Steely was calling. It had to be something terrible, and from a police station. They had been friends for nearly thirty years, ever since the first grade of grammar school, but Steely had not called him for as long as he could remember. That's the way Steely was, one of those people who never called friends on the telephone, but who was always ready to do something if you called him, to go for a meal, to a party, to a movie, anything. A loner. The kind of man who liked being around others but who would not pursue friendships. Friendships to Steely existed without any symbols like phone calls. But he was a good man, one of the best from the old East Side neighborhood, from the days of tenements and mom-and-pop stores.

"Steely," he spoke into the phone, positively, reassuringly.

"Jack," he heard Steely say, "in the sixteen years we've been on this job together, I never asked you for anything, but I need a big one now."

Haggerty felt the yearning quality vibrating in Steely's voice. If the words could be visible, he thought, there would be sweat dripping from them. All for a favor.

"Thank goodness it's just a favor," Haggerty said. "I thought if you were calling from a station house, maybe somebody from the neighborhood died."

"Forget the neighborhood, Jack," Steely yelled, "I need one now. I never asked you before."

"Yes," Haggerty said, sitting the unstitched buttock on the desk edge, feeling sorry for the desperation that would bring a man to yell at a friend. "But Steely," he went on, "the neighborhood is all we have really, the guys, the good times. Don't curse it like that."

"All right, Jack," Steely answered, his voice changing now into a kind of resignation, "what do I have to say to get you to give me one?"

"Nothing, Steely," Haggerty said, his voice soothing as a father confessor. "You have whatever it is. It has to be that way. It's neighborhood."

Captain Steinf's head appeared in the doorway a moment or so after Haggerty hung up the phone, causing him to wonder if Steinf had been listening on the extension. "Not now," he said. "I have to go up to Sixty-seventh Street and Lexington Avenue."

"It's Douglas Ratnor," Captain Steinf said.

"Tell him I'll return the call."

"He's here, Chief. Outside. Says you were supposed to have drinks, but he ain't got time."

"Bring him in," Haggerty said in an irritated voice. He always tried to talk to Steinf in an irritated voice. "And have my car waiting in two minutes."

Haggerty twisted his body to develop a comfortable position so that he could greet his visitor in a dignified manner. But no matter how he turned, or placed his leg, or sat, it was painful, except for sitting one buttock on the desk edge, like a woman would after a postpartum episiotomy. Haggerty took pride in remembering things like an episiotomy from his days as a young fireman when he had studied to be an emergency medical technician. He believed then that the Fire Department could provide the best emergency medical care available anywhere, but the city had long since sold it out to the Department of Hospitals, which knew nothing.

Now, he was at least comfortable, but since his back was directed toward the door, he decided to stand up straight, as if at attention.

Douglas Ratnor entered the office, talking like a tommy gun. "How're ya, Jack? Sit down there. I only got a minute. You know my son went into the supply business. Like military stuff. Surplus. Overseas things. I wonder if there is something you can do for me?"

Cripes, Haggerty thought, the strong arm coming from the president of the Schermerhorn Street Thomas Jefferson Democratic Club, the Brooklyn kingpin himself. The fix coming from the chairman of the Catholic Professionals in Government. The friendly request coming from the single closest confidant and friend of the Mayor himself.

Haggerty shook the small man's hand. "Anything I can do will be done, Doug, if it's within the borders of Department policy," he said, pleased with himself that he had at least inserted an equivocation.

But Douglas Ratnor, who had been around the center of city government for a very long time, quickly added, "That's right, Jack, and where would we be today if we didn't have leaders like yourself to create that policy? Have a seat. Sit down."

Sit down, the man tells me, Haggerty thought, in my own office. "I bruised my tail, Dougie, and I'll stand, thanks. I was just leaving. I have a fire uptown."

"A big one?"

"No, it just needs my presence."

"I'll sit. Just a moment." Ratnor sat on a chrome-edged chair, crossed his small legs so that his left foot ended up behind his right ankle, and folded his hands together. He reminded Haggerty of two effeminate boys he had known in the old neighborhood, one of whom grew up to be a priest, the other an editor of a political magazine. The memory was not a happy one, and Haggerty washed it from his mind.

Ratnor went on. "The mathematics are pretty simple, and my son says there's no problem. He read in the *City Record* that you're taking bids for ropes, one for each fire company, or four hundred ropes and carrying cases. He thinks he can get you those ropes for just under one hundred thousand dollars, and he hopes this will be the low bid. He's a kid. He doesn't know much. I told him there are people who always know what the low bid will be. I told him I would talk to you. Can't hurt."

Can't hurt, my old Aunt Bertha, Haggerty thought. He looked

Ratnor directly in the eyes, trying to determine just how important these ropes were in his scheme of the world. "There are certain standards and regulations on those ropes, Dougie," he said. "OSHA standards, for instance."

Ratnor uncrossed his legs and stood. "No problem," he said as he began to leave Haggerty's office. "The city government, as you know, is exempt from such regulations. The standards are good on those ropes my son has. I'll talk to you, right? You're doing a great job. I told the Mayor."

CHAPTER 4

STEELY was sitting on a hard wooden chair in a back room of the 19th Precinct, an old brownstone building on Sixty-seventh Street just off Lexington Avenue. The fluorescent lights flickered shadows on the pale green graffiti-stained walls and on Steely's forehead. His left hand was handcuffed to the dirty blond wood arm of his chair. His eyes were tired and downcast, still smarting from the morning's smoke when he had tried to save a department-store dummy. His situation, he thought, would almost be laughable if it were not for the metal around his wrist. But then he smiled broadly as he brought his head up and noticed the stars and stripes of Jack Haggerty's uniform. "Christ," Steely said to himself, gulping heavily, relieved that a way out of the 19th Precinct might exist for him. After the Chief of Department, there was not another soul he could call, except maybe Maryanne. He wanted to jump to his feet and salute his old friend.

Jack T. Haggerty, Chief of Department. It was amazing what life had brought the two of them, Steely thought. Here was Jack, old Jack Haggerty, at the top of the uniformed ladder, the chief of the world's largest fire department. One of the guys. And here I am still humping hose, still pulling ceilings, and now, God help us, handcuffed to a goddamned chair. But, Haggerty's here, dammit, here to pull me out of this quicksand, this crap I'm stuck in.

Just amazing, he said to himself, how the loyalties of the old times lingered on, like pieces of lint stuck in a hip pocket. It was the school that taught brotherhood and care for the next guy, old St. Aloysius School. No doubt about it. And they made you smart, the old nuns, if you wanted to be anyway. The opportunity was there. They really taught you how to read and write at St. Aloysius, the nuns, mean in those black satin bonnets, old Sister Alphonse there with a scowl that could stop a ship in Coenties Slip. If you didn't learn, she had you thrown out, right out, and you ended up with the dopes in public school. Funny thing was, Steely thought, Jack Haggerty or even Joey Puzzuto who became a lawyer, never got straight A's. Funny thing, really.

"It's good to see you, Jack," Steely said, unable to rise from the chair because of the handcuffs.

"Right, Steely," Haggerty said, taking a fast sweep around the detective's squad room. "It doesn't matter what happened, these guys have no right to treat you like this."

"Well," Steely said, his eyes dropping down to the short steel chain that bound the cuffs, "they didn't arrest me formally anyway, no prints or pictures or anything like that. Not yet."

"That's a small break," Haggerty said, turning then to a police detective banging at a paint-peeled typewriter. "Pardon me, officer," he said, "does the captain of this precinct know I'm here?"

"Yeah, Chief," the detective said. "He's upstairs. Be down in a minute. He's lookin' for the cop, whatsis name? Murphy. Fuckin' fireman nearly killed him."

Haggerty winced a little, and spoke a soft reprimand to the police officer. "You'll never become a sergeant," he said, "unless you improve your vocabulary."

Steely laughed quietly, presumptively. Good ol' Jack, he thought, sending it in. He can hit the communion rail every day, and then tear your heart out with his bare hands.

The police captain entered the squad room, a tall, stern-looking man. German, probably, Steely thought. Behind him was the cop named Murphy, who, Steely noticed, was now wearing a pair of glo-striped sneakers.

Steely watched as Haggerty studied the police captain closely for a moment. His serge uniform was unstained, the pants sharply creased, the gold bars on his shoulders perfectly straight. He looked to be one of the new wave of civil servants, college-educated, a lawyer probably. Strong principles would not be an issue for sure. Haggerty shook the captain's hand and, in a tone that approached a whisper, said, "I would like very much for Fireman Byrnes to leave the building with me, after his apology, of course. I don't think there is anything really to be served by pursuing this matter."

The police captain stiffened. "It is not up to me," he said, "but to the police officer who was involved. He has the legal authority to do or not do as he sees fit."

"Yes, Captain," Haggerty said, an easy, confident grin spread across his face. "I know the legality involved, for I breakfast twice a week with the Police Commissioner. The question for Officer Murphy and yourself is, is it worth it?"

The fire chief, the police captain, and Steely looked at one another. Then, they all looked toward Patrolman Murphy. There was a cold silence in the room. Finally, Murphy spoke. He said, "The fuckin' shoes alone cost fifty-two dollars."

Haggerty then looked at the patrolman in the same way, Steely thought, that the Pope would look at a seminarian reading *Penthouse* magazine, condemnation and disappointment oozing from his eyes.

The police captain held his hand up as if he were still directing traffic. The patrolman would have said more, Steely was sure, but he turned away as the captain spoke, aware of his superior's displeasure.

"Perhaps, Chief," the captain said, the tone of his voice low and acrimonious, "you think you are here with some credential, as if you have the scepter of authority to determine what happens inside of a police station."

Damn, Steely thought, goddamn it all.

Haggerty seemed surprised that the captain would take his visit personally. The captain was intimidated, Steely thought, maybe even threatened by a high-ranking Fire Department official.

"You don't, though," the captain continued, "nor do you have any rights here, Chief. Not only can't you determine, but you can't even influence what happens here. This is my precinct, and you cut no marble here telling me you have breakfast once in a while with the P.C."

Haggerty looked further surprised that the captain would speak so aggressively. "Maybe you're misreading something," he began to say, but the captain held his hand up again, interrupting.

"I don't misread," he said. "This fireman is being held for felonious assault on a police officer. He will be charged, booked, and held for court appearance in the morning."

"Okay," Haggerty said calmly, authoritatively, walking toward a telephone sitting on top of a corner desk. "You don't misread, so listen carefully."

He dialed the telephone, saying, "I'll have you working, impermanently assigned, in a precinct so far away from this one that you'll need a passport and a change of clothes to go to work. And, it will happen in the morning."

Haggerty then spoke into the phone. "Janet," he said, "this is . . . great, thanks, let me talk to the Commissioner."

The captain's lower lip fell a little, Steely noticed.

"Tell you something else, Captain," Haggerty said as he waited. "It is very possible that you'll never have another command in the city as long as I am the Chief of Department of the Fire Department."

He returned to the phone. "Bob, how are you? I'll call back later, but right now I would like you to talk to one of your police captains, the Commander of the Sixty-seventh Street Station House . . . that's the one. If you would just tell him that I don't ask for many considerations. . . ."

Christ, Steely thought, Haggerty is using his chits, calling in the credit cards. Damn, just to get me out of this mess. Patrolman Murphy, Councilman Peabody-Macomber, a goddamn German police captain—life gets so mixed up, tangled, and the Chief of Department is going way out of his way.

Haggerty held the phone out to the captain. "The Police Commissioner," he said, "would like a word with you."

"Yes, Commissioner," the captain said three times and hung up the phone. He glanced at Patrolman Murphy with a sad look, one that was pleading. Steely was certain that the captain was counting on Murphy to lessen the load a little, and finally Murphy sensed that the ball had somehow, he wasn't sure how, ended up in his glove.

Murphy stammered a little, and then said, "I have a disposition of the assault, and I know my rights as a peace officer. I'll decide if I

30

will press charges against the fireman in the next few weeks. I don't have to do it now."

Murphy left the room, and the captain simply shrugged his shoulders. The whole incident had been put on hold.

A few minutes later, Steely and Haggerty stood facing each other on the stanchion-cluttered sidewalk of East Sixty-seventh Street, just across from the grimy white bricks of the Russian Embassy. Many things were flashing through Steely's mind. He felt relieved, even if temporarily, but above all, he felt sheepish, ashamed of himself, sad that he had affected the way each of those police officers looked at firemen and the Fire Department. All of them, the detectives, the captain, even the desk sergeant, thinking that the Fire Department had people who could get themselves into such a mess. Yet it wasn't really that, not what the cops thought, that was gnawing at his insides. It was the indignity of the situation, the fact that a kind of dishonor had been brought to the Department. And then there was Haggerty, who had come up from the Municipal Building to bargain just for him. That took a lot of doing, to call the Police Commissioner like that. A big chit, and one that would have to be repaid.

"Thanks a lot, Jack," Steely said over the mufflerless roar of a passing crosstown bus. Haggerty smiled.

There was a firehouse in the middle of the block, an old landmark building that was once, at the turn of the century, the department's headquarters. Steely had been detailed there quite often to fill out the manpower minimum and he knew the firemen working there fairly well. He gestured toward the old, red-painted double doors and said, "Buy you a cup of firehouse coffee?"

"No, thanks," Haggerty replied. "I've paid my dues, and, anyway, I've got more work to do down at the Municipal Building."

"I owe you, Jack," Steely said then, in a rapid-fire staccato so fast and unreserved that it seemed to catch Haggerty off guard, to surprise him.

Steely was himself surprised, momentarily uneasy, conscious that he had made his friend ill at ease.

Haggerty looked down the street to the Third Avenue traffic. "You don't owe me anything, Steely," he said.

"Listen, Jack," Steely replied, his hands cupped and held before him. "It's like I did something to make it rain on St. Patrick's Day, you know. I feel like that, like I did some rotten thing to bring

31

disgrace to the Department, to everything that we stand for, me and you. Yet, here you are, Jack."

"I can't say," Haggerty said, tightening his mouth as he talked, "that I'm overjoyed at being here, Steely. Sometimes you do make it tough on me and tough on the Department, and you should think more about controlling yourself. Simply being remorseful does not sustain the high standards of this Department."

Steely shoved his hands deeply into his pockets. He could not think of anything more to say. A pause lingered within the sounds of passing traffic.

"Well," Haggerty said finally, grabbing Steely by the arm, walking him toward the chief's car, "we've always helped each other out, isn't that right?"

"Maybe," Steely answered, shrugging a question mark with his shoulders. "But you didn't have to come all the way up here for me, Jack."

"Small potatoes," Haggerty said.

Steely stopped as they approached the car and looked at Haggerty, a strong, serious gaze. He didn't want his friend to think he was making just another off-the-cuff remark, the kind of thing you hear in firehouse kitchens. "You have my appreciation, Jack," he said slowly. "My thanks."

"Small potatoes," Haggerty said again, trying to lighten the moment. "I guess we're not off the hook completely, but I'll do all I can to have the officer come around."

"Yeah," Steely replied, his tone of voice now a little more carefree. "Hey, Jack do you remember years ago at the Loew's Lexington?"

"You mean the goldfish pool? Lighting the lighter fluid in the goldfish pool?"

"No," Steely said. "I mean when we were sneaking in the movie that night, when I slipped."

"When you began to fall."

"Five stories up, we were, on a catwalk, the ropes from a painter's rig hanging down the side."

"I remember, I haven't thought about that—"

"I began to fall, but you grabbed me. You grabbed the rope and we fell against it and we dropped a little. You burned the skin off your hand but you held on, to me and to the rope, and we climbed back onto the ledge."

"Right," Haggerty remembered. "It could have been curtains for both of us."

"That's what I felt like today, Jack. Like I was falling and you grabbed me, except I really was falling. So I do owe you."

"No big thing, Steely," Haggerty said, opening the door to the shining blue Chrysler chief's car. "I hope it works out."

"Yeah," Steely answered, laughing. "I hope even more, probably."

CHAPTER 5

STEELY sat on an upturned garbage can in front of the firehouse eating a salami and Swiss hero. A stream of sunshine-yellow mustard pushed out from the end of his sandwich and fell onto the leg of his dungarees. "Christ," he muttered, and ran his little finger across the work jeans, picking up excess mustard.

"Club soda," he heard a thin feminine voice say. Looking up, he saw a woman, twenty-three, twenty-four, tall and shapely, though maybe a little too narrow at the hips, her hair teased and flipped over so that she was at least in the ballpark area of the Hollywood starlet look. Her lips were colored a very dark red, he noticed, and seemed outlined in silver as the sun reflected from them, a mouth shining like silver, and smiling at him. "Club soda," she said again. "It will take the mustard right out."

"Right out," he said, a little puzzled by her demeanor. She was just standing there in a solid blue dress, tight around her upper body but flowing in soft folds all the way down below her knees. Standing there and looking at him.

"Right out," she repeated.

"There's only one problem," Steely said, leaning back against the brick of the firehouse, eyeing her carefully, looking for something, anything that would explain why this woman was just standing idly before him.

"You're going to tell me you haven't got any club soda?"

He stood then, facing her. She was just an inch or so shorter than he was. Her face became less shadowed, and he could see the translucent quality of her skin. Young skin, slightly freckled skin. Her eyes were green, glittering green.

"No, uh-uh. Just that I don't care, stain or no stain," he laughed.

"Well," she said, "if you don't care, I won't care."

Steely wondered if she were being smart-assed.

She shrugged her shoulders and gestured with her hand. "Okay if I leave the car there a few minutes?"

Steely looked over and saw a blue Volkswagen bug parked in the fire zone. "No," he said, turning the garbage can right side up and dropping the rest of his sandwich into it. He chewed the last of the salami and pointed to a street sign, and then to the yellow paint striping the curb. "You can't park in a fire zone."

"But I'm on the job," she said, opening her leather bag.

"What job is that?" Steely smiled, thinking that perhaps she was a meter maid or even a cop. For that matter, she could be a toll collector. Toll collectors, too, said they were *on the job*, and they carried badges.

The woman took a small, billfold-like badge holder from her bag and flipped it open. Steely looked at it. He held her hand and put his thumb on the edge of the Maltese cross. He read the number soldered across the center, moving his lips as he read. Badge 12330, just less than a thousand numbers away from his own badge number. And that was too close, he thought.

He remembered getting his own badge, his tin, and in a moment he thought of the things it meant to him—pride, and honor, but most of all exclusivity, being a part of a very special group of men who were the best the civil service had to offer, men who had turned down the Police Department for the Fire, who had left school-teaching for the Fire, guys who had quit the father-and-son trades like the stage handlers and the wire lathers and the electricians, where it was said the only way to get an *A* card is to get the old lady pregnant.

Steely then thought of the evening of that summertime day when he had been presented with his own badge, the silver cross that came in a small brown envelope, like the ones they give you in banks. He had pinned it to his civilian shirt and worn it like jewelry through the first day of city employment, filling in endless forms, standing in lines, being lectured to and talked at.

When the day was over, four new firemen and Steely smoked some grass in someone's old and rusted Cadillac and headed downtown to a bar in the Village. They stopped for a six-pack in a deli where an old man in a soiled apron charged them three dollars. One of them, he had forgotten whom, flashed the tin and told the old man that the A&P charged only two for the firemen. The old man had smiled knowingly and taken the two dollars, a David without a sling or a stone. The old Cadillac stopped for a green light near Washington Square Park, and went through the traffic on the red. Two cops standing on the far corner jumped to the middle of the street and saw a line of badges and heard a chorus of *on the job*. Five guys, stoned, in celebration, beating the odds together, that's the memory the badge brought.

God, her eyes were green, like spring leaves in Central Park. But *on the job*. A probationary firefighter, fresh out of probie school like a kid out of kindergarten. A nothing, a zero until proven, in the firehouse and in the war zone. Let's see if she hops in the sink to do the dishes after the meals, like all the probies have to. *Like all the probies have to.* Ahh, they'll never believe that, the women. Do the dishes, and mop the floors, and wash the windows, all the old Irish maid jobs. The women will never believe the probie does those things, willingly, enthusiastically. She's not a bad looker, though, but I won't even ask her her name. *Probie* is all we gotta know. *Probie.*

Steely turned his head away from her. Ice her out fast, he thought. Get away from those green eyes.

"I wouldn't," he said finally, letting go of her badge. "The lieutenant sees you parked there, he'll eat your ass."

He thought she would react to that, but she didn't. She said nothing and she didn't move either. Steely kept looking toward Third Avenue watching the traffic move uptown. He really didn't mean it the way it came out, but he was glad it came out that way anyway. A good curse was what he wanted to deliver, to set the rules, to introduce her to the rules as they were being set, but he delivered a line that he could make a joke out of later on. "The lieutenant will eat your ass out," he would say later on in the kitchen, adding for sport, "and the firemen will get on line behind."

36

She stood there a little longer, and then said, "Sure, I'll move it."

It was like teaching children, in a way, Steely thought. Embarrass them. Make them feel ashamed, and eventually they'll feel like everyone else, that's what's supposed to be done with the probies. But this one is going to be different, whatever her name is.

Red Hadley was on housewatch duty at the front of the fire station. After moving her car, the woman walked to the housewatch desk. "Kathy," she said to Hadley, "Kathleen Ryan Angelli." She held out her hand. "I've just been assigned here to Ladder Company 7."

Steely had followed behind, curious. It figures, he thought. An Irish mother, a wop father. She could end up Commissioner, she had a little Puerto Rican in her.

Hadley jumped up and threw his hand out. "Sure glad to meet you, praise God."

"Praise God?" she asked. "They didn't teach us about that in probie school." She would learn about Hadley in good time, Steely thought, about his religious zeals.

"Well, then, they were wasting your time, Kathy," Hadley replied, walking out onto the apparatus floor, his hand still in hers. "For Jesus is the final arbiter in all things, even lady firemen."

"Firefighter," she corrected.

"That's right," Hadley replied, "even lady firefighters."

"No, just firefighter," she said firmly. "Man or woman, it covers all bases."

Even the AC-DC's, Steely thought.

"Welcome, anyway," Hadley said, "to our firehouse. And if brother Steely Byrnes will stand the housewatch, I'll take you back to see the lieutenant and introduce you to the troops."

She turned and stared at Steely for just a moment.

Steely felt uneasy, even a little self-conscious, as if a nun at St. Aloysius had brought him to the front of the class to swing a pointer over his shining gabardine trousers.

"Steely," she said declaratively.

Steely walked quickly into the housewatch partition, avoiding her gaze. "Sure, Red," he said. "I'll sit here for you."

"Thanks, Steely," Hadley said.

"Thanks, Steely," Kathy Ryan Angelli repeated, looking over her shoulder, smiling.

Steely did not answer. He picked up one of seven outdated copies of *Penthouse* magazine that lay in a back corner of one of the desk drawers and flipped through the pages until he came to the center section of eight pages of stretched and exposed vulvas. Women in the firehouse. What crap. And Red fawning over her like a missionary with a cannibal. Welcome to the firehouse, what crap.

He dropped the magazine flat on the desk, and then asked himself the one important firehouse question, will she be there? Christ, it's tough enough asking that anyway. But of a woman? *Will she be there?* And even if she grows balls under her arms, what's she going to do even if she is there? She going to carry me? She going to go through a wall or hang from a ledge to get me?

Steely picked up another *Penthouse*, opened it to the center-spread, and laid it on the desk. The next he opened and laid across the housewatch journal. He opened all seven copies to the center spread, each with legs popping out of the pages like 3-D, and arranged them carefully and evenly across the top of the desk.

Then he walked to the street in front of the firehouse and stood with his hands in his pockets. Maybe, he thought, Red will take her back to the watch desk on his guided tour of the firehouse. Won't that be a laugh? Jesus and Mary Magdalene falling over seven copies of *Penthouse*, the firehouse Bible. At least, one of three Bibles. She had better learn to read *Penthouse*, and *Playboy*, and *The American Rifleman*. She wants to come to a firehouse, she has to get used to seeing guns and flap shots in the centerfolds, that's for sure.

Christ, he thought, flipping a cigarette into the street, 250-odd firehouses in this city and she's got to end up here on Eighty-seventh Street. Maybe he should paint the firehouse door pink. Put a little Kotex dispenser in the kitchen next to the sink.

Why this firehouse? A dozen women get on the job, they should be protected. This is no game. You can get your ass chopped off in this job. They give you a chief's funeral, bagpipes and all, the city forgets about you in a week. You go to a fancy restaurant and become a waiter, you want to make an issue over jobs. Put the women in tuxedos at the 21 Club if they want to fight for an issue. The issue can get them killed in a fire department.

Steely spit in the gutter. Anyway, he thought, they're here, she's here, and the test will come. She'll be tested, they all will, because you can't fake it when the building's burning down, when the floor gives, the roof caves. You're either there or you aren't. Like Jack T. Haggerty. Maybe it wasn't a fire, but Jack was there.

Lieutenant Jackson walked down the firehouse stairs, and Steely moved quickly to the housewatch desk to cover for Hadley.

"The woman here?" Jackson asked. "I heard a female voice."

"In the back." Steely gestured toward the kitchen.

"The captain wants her in our group," Jackson said, walking past Steely and the housewatch desk. "It's the most experienced group in the house, and these women will need experience."

Steely did not particularly want to talk to the lieutenant, but he could not resist asking, "Why'd they send her here?"

"Maybe," Jackson answered, speaking out of the side of his mouth, "because we respond as far south as Bloomingdale's. The broads love Bloomingdale's."

"And maybe," Steely added, "because we go up to Harlem. We get a lot of fires in Harlem."

Jackson disappeared into the darkness at the rear of the firehouse, beyond the shadows of the red and gold massiveness of the ladder truck, and the high, squat pumper.

In our group for experience, Steely thought, still standing by the housewatch desk. Firefighter Angelli, with those green eyes, and that fresh, light freckled skin you can see through. The captain could've taken her in his group, but it's just another administrative problem to him, one that he can delegate away. So she's coming into our group, just a little more bad luck for me. I have Lieutenant Jackson to contend with, and now I have a female fireman. *Firefighter*, she said, covers all the bases. We'll see how many bases she can cover.

Red Hadley returned from the kitchen, Kathy Angelli walking behind him. Steely left the housewatch desk and stood under the high arch of the firehouse doorway. "You should sign in in the company journal, just to say you entered quarters for work chart assignment," Hadley said, and acting more like a gentleman than a fireman, he stepped back to let her enter the housewatch cubicle first. Steely saw her look down at the field of open vaginas spread across the desk and waited for her to react, to say something, maybe to gasp. But she said nothing, and Steely felt a little foolish, as he always did when the child in him was exposed.

Was it going too far, he asked himself, spreading those magazines out like that? An attempt at cruelty that was only childish? If he had a real problem with her being in the firehouse, maybe he should just say it, just go up to her and say, "Look, women don't belong in the firehouse, because you're not strong enough and you might get killed." It always came down to that in the firehouse, getting killed. It was the reason the union demanded salary raises, because men got killed every year, six or eight of them in the city, fighting fires, and every nail in every coffin was a labor negotiation. It was the reason firemen felt good about themselves, felt themselves to be more important than cops or teachers or garbage collectors, because more of them got killed.

Kathy Angelli just looked down at the magazines without expression, and Steely knew that he wouldn't say anything to her. She didn't react at all, even as Hadley reached around her and pushed the magazines to the floor behind the desk.

"Sometimes the guys do this to me," he apologized, "because I so earnestly believe in God."

Kathy sat down at the desk and wrote an entry into the company journal. "It's the *earnestly* that makes the difference, isn't it?" she asked as she put the pen down and stepped out of the housewatch cubicle.

"That appears to be so," Hadley answered, walking with her past Steely to the front of the firehouse. "It's what keeps me going, too," Kathy said, turning her head a little to look back at Steely. He knew she was wondering if he would gesture a good-bye wave.

She walked into the sunlight, her dress swaying in blue waves as she moved, and Steely thought he could see the silhouette of her long legs beneath.

"Because," she continued, "I've always earnestly wanted this job. The *earnestly* is important."

"Sure is," Hadley answered.

Kathy turned once again, and waved, her eyes sparkling like the glass in Central Park's rocks.

Steely nodded his head. It was a slight gesture, one that he hoped would not be misunderstood for friendliness.

"Since I was a kid," he heard her voice trail off, "I've always wanted this job."

CHAPTER 6

SEVERAL days had passed since Kathy Angelli signed her name in the company journal, but her assignment to Ladder Company 7 was still the fundamental focus of all firehouse conversation. "How come they put her in a truck company?" the firemen were asking one another. "How come here in this house?"

They all talked against her, McFatty, Whore-hickey Harrigan, even Lieutenant Jackson, who, Steely thought, should know better. Only Red Hadley had a good thing to say. "She's nice," he said, "a nice person."

"Everyone knows," McFatty said, "broads can't do truck work, forcible entry. They can't lift the tools."

It had been a relentlessly boring day at the firehouse. Just one alarm, a car fire in front of Gracie Mansion. "Too bad the girl's not here," Whore-hickey Harrigan commented, "so we could bet she couldn't get the trunk popped."

Steely hated all the talk. The talk did nothing but raise tempers or expectations. We'll see what will be, he thought.

After lunch that day, Steely sat in a chair in front of the television set on the third floor and fell asleep. He slept all afternoon. The sleep was an irritation. He felt cranky and mean-spirited when he awakened. He was worried about something, he realized, but he wasn't sure what. Patrolman Murphy, probably. So what if he presses charges. Worst that can happen, Steely thought, is I get found guilty and put on probation. No record in the past. Damn, I could get fired from the Department, could lose the great job.

Steely went to his locker and changed clothes. A beer, he thought, something to calm him, to take the edge off. Two pops and then home to the poverty pad on Fifty-first Avenue, overlooking the entrance to the Queens-Midtown Tunnel, where even Channel 2 and Channel 4 didn't come in clearly, and where the roaches were as big as the mice and twice as fast. Maybe three pops. Not too much, anyway, for I have the kids tomorrow. Tomorrow's my day, Dad's day. Any bar, he thought, in Manhattan or Queens, it didn't matter. Maybe out around Levittown, near Tara and Jeffrey.

In the car, Steely banged the steering wheel as he pictured his children in his mind. Tara and Jeffrey, twelve and ten, missing him, he knew, as much as he missed them.

Tara, like in everybody else's broken home, handling her parents' separation by not talking about it. Her sculptured pretty-girl face yearning, silently wishing that things would be all right again. Jeffrey, gorgeous Jeffrey, his red-rimmed eyes never quite understanding, as unsparkling as old silver coins, but alive and expectant, as if always on the brink of learning something. Poor Jeffrey, never quite certain of his father's love, yet ready always to collapse within the warmth of his father's arms. Or anyone's.

Make certain to remember that, Steely chided himself. Or anyone's. Kids need love, and they find it in the warmth of an embrace a lot easier than in an I-love-you over the phone.

The traffic snarled at the Queens side of the Fifty-ninth Street Bridge where three lanes converged into two. Like putting a big wooden pyramid into a little circle cut into a board. Steely turned the radio on and drummed his fingers to Frank Sinatra singing "New York, New York." King of the hill, he thought, as he listened to the words of the song. We used to play that game when there was a neighborhood on the East Side, before the wave of rich people and luxury towers, and Maryanne used to sit on the stoop with her girlfriends waiting for the game to be over, when the boys would find time for the girls, and for walks down by the river.

"That was old blue eyes himself," the radio disc jockey said. Old blue eyes. Steely turned the volume down until it clicked off and then he impatiently pressed the horn. It was a gesture. The Queens Boulevard traffic was moving like an oyster out of its shell. At this rate, he was still a half hour from the poverty pad even though he could almost see it.

Old blue eyes. Firefighter Angelli had green eyes, large and reflective green eyes that changed to blue, he had noticed, as they hit the kitchen lights.

Maryanne, Steely thought, still drumming his fingers against the steering wheel, used to talk about his blue eyes. "Steely's steely blues," she used to whisper when they were close, before he ever thought it possible that he might not care for her one day. "Steely's steely blues," she would whisper, looking at him lovingly, pushing his thick black hair back at the sides. She always said that it was she who had named him Steely. He wasn't sure. It was such a long time ago.

She was like a lost fawn when they first met, no one to care for her. Up from Twenty-ninth Street, she was new in the neighborhood. Her father was a tough piece of work, high up in the steamfitters' union, and rode herd on her like a mad cowboy. She had to be home at nine o'clock at night, even on weekends, when she was fourteen, and the father would beat her if she got there at two minutes after. Punch her black and blue.

"I'll kill him for you," Steely told her once. "I'll throw him off the roof." He cared for her then.

It was hard to remember when he had stopped caring for Maryanne. "I can't hump every woman I want to hump," he remembered saying in the firehouse kitchen some years ago, "and so I hump my wife without regret."

How many years ago? Was it before she stopped looking at herself in the full-length mirror in the hallway as she prepared to leave the house, a last caring look to make sure everything fit and went together?

"That sounds like a man without much choice," a fireman had remarked, a statement that he had never forgotten. Choices, he thought. There is not much excitement in life without choices.

Jesus, when did he stop?

It was *after* she got dumpy, wasn't it? *Wasn't it?*

I'll stop in Valley Stream, maybe, he thought, or Massapequa or

43

Seaford, one of those places where the cops and firemen outnumber the doctors and lawyers, across the Van Wyck, out past JFK.

He pulled off the Sunrise Highway, into the parking lot of the Long Island Cabana Club, a bar not unlike the Second Avenue gin mills where, he remembered, he learned to drink more than two beers without becoming a fall-down drunk.

The place was dark, illuminated by fluorescent fixtures that were inadequately designed for the space. Steely noticed several men sitting at the bar, along with one woman sitting in the corner where the bar met the stuccoed wall. Probably the bartender's girlfriend, he thought, but he moved next to her anyway.

She was a peculiar-looking woman who might have been pretty if she had been born with fuller lips. Her lips were thin brushstrokes that broke the lines of her face beneath her small nose, and in trying to compensate for those knifelike edges, she overly applied her lipstick so that the lip lines looked smeared, like the lips of an early-morning whore. She's a housewife, Steely thought. And a hit, if she's not the bartender's.

"Name's Steely," he said, sitting on the stool next to her, his leg touching hers.

She looked at him closely. Probably, Steely thought, determining the amount, if any, of apprehension she should feel. She gestured her head up and down a little, acknowledging him, and then she said, "I miss my dogs, I was just thinking."

"Your daughter?" Steely asked, not quite hearing what she had said.

"My dogs, the father and son. Coco and Duke."

"You miss your dogs?"

"Yeah, I really miss them."

The bartender came to the end of the bar and Steely ordered a bottle of Miller's, not offering to buy her a drink. "Where are they?" he asked. "The dogs."

"They're with my ex-husband, but I never get to see them."

"You're not the bartender's girlfriend?"

"No, I hardly know him. I'm talking about my ex-husband. He gets to see my kids. I got the two kids, but I never get to see the dogs. It's not fair."

"Why don't you go see them?" Steely asked, pouring the beer, thinking momentarily of Tara and Jeffrey.

"I can't," she answered, now turning to him. "I used to go once a week, but then Joey, my ex, used to say all the time, 'Hey Julie, the dogs don't eat for three days after you leave them.' "

"Tough."

"Yeah."

"Your name's Julie?"

"Yeah. But you said it's tough. It is. I had to give up seeing them so's they could eat. One time, though, a year ago, Joey calls me up and says, next time you're in Long Beach, come over, I have someone who wants to see you."

"The dogs, right?" Steely guessed. He didn't expect much from conversations in bars anyway, and the woman was now rubbing her knee back and forth across the inside of his thigh. He would see how far it would go with this woman.

"Just the one dog," she answered. "Coco. The son got hit with a car, but Joey never told me that for ages. Anyway, I went, but I was so afraid that the dog wouldn't recognize me, or didn't like me anymore. It's not fair."

"So, did he like you?"

"Yeah, he liked me, but he didn't eat again, so we had to end that forever, you know."

"I like you too." Steely said this matter-of-factly, in the same way he would have said, "Give me another beer." Harmless words, no big account, but she put her hand on his leg and smiled.

"Yeah?" she asked. "What's my name?"

"You said Julie."

"That's right. Julie. Hey, you're all right."

Steely laughed and touched his forefinger to her chin. "You want a drink, Julie?" he asked.

"Yeah, but let's go somewhere," she said, rising from the stool. "I think meeting you is all I want from this place."

Steely watched the soft, well-washed cotton of her dress fall over the small mound of her stomach and around her legs. Her body was evenly proportioned, and seemed firm. A better body than Maryanne's. But, she would have to travel a long way to get a face anywhere near Maryanne's, with Maryanne's bright, glittering blue eyes, and her full, wet lips as red as hothouse tomatoes. This body was nice, though, even with the lipless face. And anyway, he thought, a hit's a hit.

"Sure," he said, "anywhere you want to go. I got my flood parked outside."

He kissed her in the car. She opened her mouth and sucked his tongue into it. "I like that more than anything," Steely said. She looked at him vacantly.

They hadn't gone far, maybe two blocks down the Sunrise Highway, when she said, "I like the Soft Shoe Inn, pull in here."

They sat at the bar, Steely's worn twenty-dollar bill before them. After the sun had set over Long Island, and a new twenty was nearly gone, and then the bartender brought the tenth or twelfth Miller's and as many vodka martinis, she put her hand high up on Steely's thigh and said, "I want you to know just one thing."

In return, Steely squeezed her shoulder. He thought of driving her to the poverty pad on the banks of the Midtown Tunnel. She was now looking like a starlet to him, a young actress in a thin calico dress pushed hard against her by the wind. He could be in a movie, he thought, and he would hump her by the water pump, or by the corral. Maybe. By the dripping sink.

"What's that, babe?" he asked, letting his hand drop to the taut skin of her ass where it pressed against the bar stool.

She smiled as he tried to shove his fingers between her and the stool top. "There ain't gonna be any action here tonight with me. Some other time, definitely, but not tonight."

Steely perked up and realized he was within a beginning alcoholic haze. He felt the fullness of the beer in his head. He felt suddenly alarmed.

"Whatsa matter?" he asked. He was annoyed that she would try to cool him down after she let him kiss her and rub his hand over her ass. "You got your friend, an operation, or what?"

"No," she said, "it's nothing like that. It's only that I don't feel no pheromones being secreted, you know."

Steely laughed. "Get out of here," he said. "I'll give you a whack. Ferret bones, you got a lot of moxie."

"No, really," she protested, a touch of sobriety now tingeing her voice. "Pheromones. I gotta feel that the pheromones are being secreted so that it would be all right between us. Sex, I mean."

"What the hell is it?" Steely rasped the question through his teeth.

"I don't know," she said, taking her hand from his leg. "It's like the smell of semen. I once put semen in a cup, a measuring cup. The guy thought I was strange, but I like the smell. I can smell it a mile away, and it makes me feel good. Same thing with the pheromones. I need to smell the pheromones."

"You're goddamn crazy," Steely said, moving the remaining sum of the last twenty just a little away from her. "Not strange. Crazy."

"You don't like it, that's too bad," she said, getting up from the bar stool. "I didn't talk to you first, huh? C'mon and take me home."

"You're kidding me," Steely said, motioning to the bartender for another beer. "Let the night air soak through ya, sweetheart, it will do you good."

"You mean you're not going to take me home?"

Steely shook his head and muttered under his breath, "Not until you grow some lips."

"Of all the creeps," he heard her say as she walked away.

Steely laughed a little as the bartender took three dollars from the small pile of bills lying neatly before him. It had been an expensive night so far, and what made him laugh was the realization that the bar was filled with men, construction workers mostly, men in tee shirts and wide belts and dungarees. There wasn't one woman to look at in the Soft Shoe Inn.

CHAPTER 7

MARYANNE was sleeping, he guessed, and he quietly slipped the key into the back-door lock. He had kept the key, and he wondered in their months of separation if she had changed the locks. He never would have asked, and now that the door had opened, it seemed to him a small symbol of trust. Did she still trust him?

Did it matter?

He kicked his shoes off in the kitchen, and remembered the count-less nights he had crept like a burglar through the house, not want-ing to wake her. Often he did wake her, and when he did she would say nothing. She would just sigh and turn over, and wait until morn-ing. Then, she would speak of nothing else for the next couple of days. The dinner, she'd cry. You ruined the dinner. But they both knew it had nothing to do with the dinner.

On his toes he staggered a little through the ranch house hall until he came to the bedroom. He opened the door and looked at his wife, lying in the summer heat, the sheet kicked down off the edge of the bed, her body rounded in the fetal position, curled in the middle of the bed, her lips almost touching her knees. She lay there, he thought, like a small sculpture or a doll, something that he could pick up and carry away.

He did not stop at Tara's or Jeffrey's room. It would have been sentimental. Besides, that was for fathers who lived with their children, to study them as they slept. Instead, he went to the living room, where he undressed noisily, falling twice against a breakfront as he picked his socks from his feet. Finally, he fell heavily back upon the couch. He lay there, holding his breath for a moment, listening within the silence for Maryanne.

But he heard nothing, and he rolled over on his side and closed his eyes, the drunken half sleep turning rapidly to total blackness.

In the morning, he awakened to the smell of bacon and the sound of his son and daughter fighting over what program to watch on the television set. He had been dreaming about a dinner at the firehouse. City Councilman Elisha Peabody-Macomber was sitting next to him when the alarm came in. The councilman held on to the table, but Steely pulled him away with one quick jerk and then pushed him forcibly into the cab of the fire engine. A Harlem tenement was burning. The fire escape was crowded with waving people, each screaming frantically, each hoping to be saved. Steely rushed into the building, dragging Elisha Peabody-Macomber behind.

It was then that he heard his wife's voice. "You have a lot of nerve, Steely," she said. It was an exasperated voice. "Really, sneaking in here."

"I didn't sneak," he returned. "I made so much noise I could've woke up the drunk tank at Bellevue."

"I don't want you coming here like this, Steely."

"It was either last night or this morning. To pick up the kids. What difference does it make?"

"It's not good for the kids, you sleeping here like this, Steely."

She was standing before the picture window, and sunlight passed through the loose-woven material of her housedress. He could see the pink color of her bra and pants beneath, and the shadows of the silk as it rode when she moved from side to side. She looked so clean. He could smell the cleanliness, and he felt the stirring of an erection as he yearned to be close to her, to smell her, to run his fingers gently over the small mounds of flesh that fell over the top of her brassiere cups and the edges of her bikini panties.

"How about some bacon and eggs?" he asked, turning in toward the couch, trying to hide the embarrassment of wanting her.

"No, Steely, really."

"C'mon, Maryanne, I have to take the kids anyhow, and they have to have breakfast."

"They ate already, Steely," she said, her voice intense and frustrated, "and you can't take them until they go to church." She stood defiantly before him, her legs and thighs stuck together like pancakes.

"I'll take them to church," he said resignedly.

"*We* are going to church," she answered, her frustration turning to a sarcastic bitterness, "*my children* and I."

There was no doubt, he thought, that she meant to convey that she and the children were alone in the world, alone and defenseless.

Where did the sweetness go, he asked himself? Did it evaporate, or change into something else?

"I'll take you all, Maryanne. Relax, would ya?"

"We have thirteen minutes," she said, walking out of the sun so that her near nakedness disappeared. She now looked to him like an ordinary housewife in a sack dress, but the bottom of her legs were still something to see, curving down as they did to strong, thin ankles.

There's always something good to see in a woman, he thought, if you're looking for something good to see.

"Get the car and meet us out front, please." The word *please* smoked like dry ice, he thought, as he called into the playroom for his children. Maryanne had that way with words, that was for sure.

After dressing, Steely walked to the car which he had parked halfway down the block, the suburban streets being as crowded with automobiles as the inner city. As he slid slowly into the driver's seat, he could see Maryanne and the children walking out of the front door, Tara, adorable he thought, in a dress and white gloves, Jeffrey in a plaid polyester jacket.

God, he hated that jacket, the plaid one. It curved out at the bottom like it was starched. He always wished he could buy their clothes at some decent store in Manhattan instead of a damn shopping mall.

Steely inserted the key in the chrome ignition lock and turned it. The car coughed once, but did not start. Just then, as he was going to turn the key a second time, he heard another cough. Then still another. It was this last cough that made him realize what was happening.

Holy Good God, he thought, as he turned and saw her lying across the rear seat, her calico dress bunched high up around her hips.

Christ, what to do?

Think fast, he demanded. Do something fast, it's like the roof is collapsing.

He pressed his hand down on the top of her head, his mind racing and reciting a litany of curses. He wanted to yell, but tensed every muscle he could feel to restrain himself. He spoke in a thick, hoarse bass voice. "Julie, right?" he said, his voice high in panic, and shaking. "I'm gonna kill ya, Julie, so help me God, if you lift your head up. Roll over and lie down on the floor. Do it. Do it."

He could hear the sobbing pouring through her too-thin lips as he started the car, revving the motor as fast as it could go. Then he jammed the gearshift down into drive. "Don't move, Julie, or I'll kill ya," he again threatened as the tires spun and screeched across the suburban pavement. The car shot forward, barely missing the car parked before him, lurching past Maryanne and the children, careening just a little as he jammed the brakes and made the turn at the end of the street, and finally screeching again as he stamped down on the gas pedal to deliver him safely out of the view of his family.

He drove for blocks and blocks before he remembered that he would have to do something about the woman in the rear seat of his car. She was still whimpering, afraid to say anything at all. She must have seen the desperation in his eyes, he thought.

He took her to the Massapequa North Station of the Long Island Railroad. "Do you have money for a train ticket?" he asked her, opening the passenger side door.

Relieved, she crawled up to the rear seat. "I'm sorry," she said. "I was tired and your car was just there."

"You were drunk."

"I was drunk. So what's new?"

Steely offered her a five-dollar bill. "I got my own money," she said. "I got a good job."

Steely measured her body as she climbed out of the car. Too bad, he thought. "Listen, Julie," he called after her.

"Yeah," she said. There was a brief awkward pause as she waited for him to continue.

He smiled and gestured his empty hands, palms up.

She returned his smile.

"I hope you get to see your dog," he said. But she was just out of hearing distance. He laughed quietly then, watching her skirt sway from side to side as she walked toward the station stairs.

Maryanne was in the kitchen when he returned. The children were watching television. He was apprehensive. Did she see the woman on the floor? Would she say something if she did? Christ. The fabric of a separated marriage was thin enough without the complications of another woman.

"Are you crazy, Steely?" she said as he entered the room.

"Crazy? Maryanne, it's got nothing to do with crazy. What are you talking?"

"Crazy. Why would you ever do a thing like that? The children . . ."

"Maryanne, the lights on the dashboard lit up. You know." He sat on one of the plump vinyl-covered kitchen chairs.

"The children were so scared. You're making your own kids scared of you, Steely."

"Maryanne, would you stop it? It was the lights."

"What lights? You scare the wits out of all of us and make us miss the eleven o'clock and you talk about lights."

"The lights. You remember, I told you. You ever see those red lights go on, the oil light, or the generator light, or the fuel pump light, or any one of those lights on the dashboard go on, you go right to a gas station because you got trouble. Right? You remember me telling you that?"

"Yes," she said, confused, trying to be uninterested, yet listening closely, lighting the gas beneath the coffee pot on the stove. "I remember something like that."

"Sure," he said, gaining some confidence, "sure you do, and you talk about crazy. I almost went crazy, Maryanne. The minute I turned the key, every light in the car goes on. I know something happened. There's no oil or something, no compression, the god-damn power-steering stuff is not working. I know that if I shut it off the motor would freeze and I would have to junk the car. I have enough problems, Maryanne, I can't afford to junk the car, and I know if I am gonna save the car I have about sixty seconds to get it to a gas station, with all the lights on and no oil and everything."

Maryanne had a sad look on her face. "Steely," she said, "why do things happen, go bad, all the time?"

Steely tried to laugh. "Who knows?" he said. "I don't know."

She was weakening, he saw, her eyes were beginning to shine as they filled with tears. He hated moments like this, when she would let things get the better of her, when she would give in to tears or yelling or the need to throw things.

"Don't get mad, now," Steely said, shuffling a little in the chair. "You have your father's temper."

"Don't give me that, Steely," she said, facing him with an egg in her hand. "You always turn things around, sidestep things. The only thing I ever got from my father was his will in which there was no money or property. I was talking about us, Steely, about how everything goes bad all the time."

She turned toward the stove and cracked the egg into the frying pan, and then she collapsed. She threw the egg shells on the floor and fell into a chair across the table from him. She began to cry. "Christ," she mumbled through the tears, "even something as simple as going to church goes bad."

"C'mon, Maryanne," Steely said, halfheartedly, weakly, knowing that he was caught in a situation where he was without the strength to help, to react. Most of his life in Ladder Company 7 was spent in practice of reacting positively in negative situations, and he hated it that all he could do was to bring himself to say, "C'mon, Maryanne."

"I'm all right," she said, wiping her eyes with a dish towel. "I don't need to be consoled."

"I'm sorry, Maryanne," Steely said. It was a genuine apology, for he was saddened that he had made her cry, and embarrassed, as he always was, to be unable to support her emotionally, to reassure her. "It was just one of those freak things."

Maryanne picked the egg shells up and began to sponge the hard tiles of the floor where they had been stained. "We have to do something about ourselves, Steely," she said, one knee sticking out from her dress as she knelt.

"What do you mean?" he shot out, as if he had been accused of indecision, or, worse, neglect. He was giving her just about his entire salary check, he didn't bother her, he cared about the children. What was there to do? They might be separated and a little unhappy, but life kept chugging along. There were no real crises, anyway.

"I mean," she said, rising from the floor and returning to the stove, throwing the sponge in the sink as she passed, "that we should do something legal, get a legal separation or a divorce or something. It's crazy being married and not married at the same time."

"God," Steely said, surprised that she would even think about divorce.

He remembered he had been sitting in the very same kitchen chair when they had decided to separate. She knew it was coming, he felt, and he knew that he could not continue the months of avoiding her, of not touching, not kissing, and so he just began talking, the words, the sentences pushing out uncontrollably, like air from an electric fan. "I don't have any energy," he had said, "I don't love you, I'm depressed, I don't want to go to work, I don't like living here, I'll miss the kids but it will be worse for them if I stay, I just need some room. We can try it for a while, living separately, just a trial."

She had cried then, too, and told him that all she ever looked forward to was a good family, a good home, and a good husband, and that she had been shortchanged. She told him she thought she married a man with ambition, and all he wanted to be was a fireman fighting fires in the falling-down tenements of New York, the same tenements every decent family on the East Side had moved away from. And, she told him, he still belonged in those tenements if he wanted to leave his family.

That same evening they told Tara and Jeffrey, who cried along with their mother, though, Steely thought, they didn't know what any of it meant, and cried to support their mother in her tears. But it was just a trial, Steely told them.

It was supposed to be just a trial, only until they saw what happened.

Maryanne pried the burned-edged egg from the frying pan and put it alongside the bacon on a rose-covered Melmac dish. "We can't live," she continued, "like we're in one of those modern paintings, where you can't tell where one line ends and another one begins. It's not good for any of us without some resolution."

"But, divorce," he said, running his hand through the thick black curls of his hair. "How come you would think of that at all, Maryanne? I mean the church, and all, that doesn't bother you?"

Maryanne placed the plate before him at the table. "Does it

bother you, Steely?" she asked. "I mean, is the church really an obstacle?"

She looked at him coldly, in the way she always looked at him when she knew she was dead right. The spatula was still in her hand. "You know as well as I do, Steely," she said, "that we are going to have to do what we have to do."

CHAPTER 8

AT the twelve o'clock mass, Steely fought the urge within him to think about Maryanne and pressed his mind to think of other things, other matters that were not quite right in his life. During a drawn-out sermon that was being delivered in a gray monotone by an old, thin priest, Steely saw a phrase that reminded him of Jack T. Haggerty.

Good old Jack Silver-tongue, old Johnnie Gimme, going out of his way to be the rabbi for Steely Byrnes.

It was some time since anyone had called Jack Haggerty "Johnnie Gimme." Since he became a captain in the Fire Department, probably. It was then that people realized he was a rising star in the Department, for he was the youngest captain in the Department's history, and in consideration of his rank, Steely figured, people began to think of him in more respectful terms than a nickname like Johnnie Gimme would allow.

Steely was flipping absentmindedly through a pamphlet called *The Bible Companion* when he noticed the phrase that reminded him of Haggerty. *"Let your speech be like apples of gold set in pictures of silver,"* it said in bold letters in the middle of a page.

Christ, Steely thought, Haggerty would like that. When he wasn't being called Johnnie Gimme by the neighborhood crowd, he was called Ivory Mouth, because he never used to use curse words. "Swearing is for the weak," Haggerty said, "and I'm not weak. I can lick anybody's anything anytime."

It was true. Haggerty had the strength of a great mythological animal, yet there was a certain softness to him, too.

He was always big for his age, Haggerty was, and tougher than most. He'd like that, old Johnnie Gimme would. Apples of gold in silver pictures running from the mouth. Hell, yes.

They were twelve, Steely remembered, when Jack T. Haggerty got his nickname. It was a Saturday, and Steely was arguing on the corner of Fifty-third Street and First Avenue with Haggerty and Joe Mazzalagotta. They had been caught smoking in the bathroom of the Kip's Bay Boys' Club and were eighty-sixed there for the day. There was not much to do.

"Don't you give me no bullshit about not keeping chickie," Mazzalagotta said to Haggerty.

"Don't curse at me, Joey Guttergrate," Haggerty said. "I could split your eyebrows in half. We could of been swimming in the pool now, if you saw Mr. McNiven coming to the bathroom." His voice had a ragged edge to it.

"Don't cause no trouble, Jack," Steely said then, ready for an argument, "because me and Joey can dump you together."

Haggerty let that remark pass.

"Listen, hey," Joey interjected, always the peacemaker, the solution seeker. "I got money, we'll go to the movies."

Steely pictured Mazzalagotta, remembering his short, muscular frame, his dark eyes and shiny black curls, which he combed to a point above his nose. It was in May when that happened, and school was nearly over.

Steely remembered clearly because Joey never lived through the summer. He just died one day. He got sick, they brought him to the hospital, and he died that same day, infection or something. The guys in the neighborhood who used to call him Joey Guttergrate called him "the poor guinea" after that.

Joey had stolen a watch once in Bloomingdale's. He and Henny the Hebe, whose father owned the deli on Fifty-fifth Street, planned it all out. As the gold watch hit the bottom of Joey's pocket, Henny the Hebe punched him and yelled, "You watch what you say about my mother." They fought in the middle of the jewelry department until the clerks and the floorwalkers broke them apart and escorted them to the door of the Fifty-ninth Street exit. It was an easy diversion, and they were protected by the Bloomingdale's people themselves.

In the street, though, they argued about what they would do with the watch. Henny the Hebe wanted to sell it and split the money, but Joey wanted to give it to his father, because, he said, his father never had a watch like that. It was then that Joey got what he later described as a vision, a vision in which he realized they probably shouldn't have taken just one watch.

And so, they walked to the corner of Third Avenue, where Joey dropped the watch down the gutter grate.

Later on, he told Haggerty and Steely and everyone else, "It wasn't worth arguing about. Not with Henny the Hebe, anyway." Henny the Hebe, Steely remembered, became a rich producer of television shows. And Joey Mazzalagotta became known as the poor guinea.

Steely laughed out loud, and Maryanne gave him a hard look. The old monsignor was talking about contracts being more important when they're with God. Right, Steely thought. Joey Guttergrate had a contract with God, too. It didn't matter that he was short. He was healthy, tough as the wire on orange crates, and good-looking. Couldn't ask for more than that. Some contract.

Joey always knew how to handle Haggerty, though. He could always divert him, like the salespeople at Bloomingdale's.

"You got money for us to go to the movies?" Haggerty had asked that day they were thrown out of the boy's club. His voice had become calm, like it had been sedated.

Haggerty always liked Joey. Maybe it was because he was so much bigger, Steely thought, remembering how Haggerty always walked with an arm on Joey's shoulder, like Joey was a bar rail or an altar rail, something to lean on anyway.

"I know where to get it anyways." Joey winked his eye and smiled, the innocent smile of one who never went out of his way to be hurtful, or spiteful, or cruel.

It was great, Steely remembered. Joey Guttergrate always had an idea.

"All we do," Joey went on, "is go through the cellar of 301, on

Fifty-fifth, and we get to the storeroom of Rosen's Deli and the empties. We then take the bottles to the A&P."

Steely wasn't so sure about stealing from old man Rosen, from Henny the Hebe's father. Like Kip's Bay and the Fifty-fourth Street gym, St. John's Church and Speece's Drugstore, Rosen was a part of the neighborhood. To steal from him was something like stealing the candy money at the boys' club, or, God help us, from the poor box of the church.

"You can't do that," Steely said. "Henny the Hebe is one of the guys, and it's like pissing on him."

"Steely," Haggerty reprimanded, to the notice of no one.

"It was Henny showed me the way," Joey protested. "How you think Henny buys all those hamburgers and french fries at Riker's?"

"It's not right," Steely said again.

But they did it anyway. They stole thirty-one nickel-deposit bottles, stuffing them into brown paper bags, enough nickels to make the price of three movie tickets, with a nickel left over. "The extra nickel is mine," Joey said, "because I thought of the idea."

"Gimme it," Haggerty said. "I carried most of the bottles."

"No, I'm going to keep it," Joey answered.

"Gimme," Haggerty said, "or I'll hurt you." He leaned in close to Joey, grabbing his arm, squeezing. He was hurting Joey. His eyes were wide and unlike anything the other two boys had seen. Steely remembered how the blood rushed to Joey's face, making him the color of sunburn. Finally, Joey dropped the odd nickel to the pebbled cement in front of the Fifty-fourth Street A&P. "There," Joey said, "take the goddamn money."

Haggerty picked the nickel up and held it tightly in his fist, so tight that his hand trembled.

"I'm sorry, Joey," he said, "sometimes I just got to have things." Then he put his arm over Joey's shoulder, patting it as they walked toward the RKO Fifty-eighth Street.

At least, Steely thought, Haggerty got what he wanted, and the guy had to be given credit for that. He worked hard in high school, and then in construction jobs before he was called for the Fire Department. Harder still, once he was a fireman, studying every spare minute. He lived to succeed, that was certain. Why, Steely asked himself, didn't I?

Steely stood for the Gospel, which told him again that Eve was taken from the rib of Adam, that she was a part of him. He glanced from one side to the other of the pew in front of him. There were no young women with curved calves and round asses to look at. He turned and looked at Maryanne, the two children between them, and he smiled.

Maryanne never let him forget that Haggerty was going fast up the ranks either. At every promotion party Josie Haggerty threw, Maryanne would say to him, "This all could be yours, Steely, if you studied."

At one, when Haggerty made battalion chief, Steely answered, "What all is there, Maryanne? A colonial house instead of a ranch, a catered party instead of Velveeta cheese on Ritz crackers, a family with no children instead of two, a boy for you and a girl for me?"

She was hurt, he remembered. "I don't mean that, Steely," she said. "I mean all the happiness. The world is moving ahead for Jack and Josie."

They did seem to be happy, there was no denying that. Josie was always there helping him along while Jack beamed. She would make a point to remember the name of every fire officer's wife she met, and she would always ask about the children. She had figured out that for the firemen it was a big department, twelve thousand potential names, but it got smaller and smaller as the ranks passed. There were only eighty or so deputy chiefs, sixteen assistant chiefs, and just one Chief of Department. Knowing all the names helped get things done, helped develop a network of Department friends, for any chief who couldn't get things done was as useless as a hose connection on a horse.

And Jack always knew that he was a Department star, ever since he scored first on the lieutenants' test, but he never threw his rank around as he progressed. It was in his genes to study, Steely thought, a chemical need to know things like the fire rating of a garage door or the pounds per square inch of the water pressure of a high-rise standpipe system. It was a gift, a life dedicated to success, a gift that never came when the name Byrnes was called. Steely grinned, thinking that he got the blue eyes and the thick, wavy hair instead, a gift of a kind, but one that he never knew how to use until he was married and the father of two. It was then that he learned in some Third Avenue bar that all he had to do to win the passing fancy of a woman was to throw his head back in a certain way and angle his eyes so that a sidelong glance would say as much as a Kiss-Me-I'm-Irish button.

He had forgotten the woman's name, the first one. It had happened so many years before. Jeffrey was still an infant, he remembered. There had been a second-alarm fire and a couple of firemen had been hospitalized, burns and broken limbs, injuries that would heal, anyway. After the routine hospital visit a group from Ladder Company 57 began to drink their way from Lenox Hill Hospital to their uptown firehouse.

She was an investment analyst at a Wall Street brokerage house, or something like that, in a profession anyway that would look down on a fireman. She was very pretty, he remembered, very willing. A single woman, she lived in a doorman building on York Avenue, one of the newer buildings that a fireman, even a single fireman without a family, could never afford. She was very pretty, and she knew he was married, and that was that. Nothing more, no promises of future, no telephone numbers, no agreement except that it had been a wonderful, surprisingly wonderful hour together. Yet, as he drove to Levittown, the odor of the hour still radiating from his hands and mouth and body, he began to feel that he had betrayed everything that had been between him and Maryanne, between husband and wife, every little gesture and word and touch wilted in the scent of orgasm. He knew then that he should have stopped at the firehouse to shower before he crossed the bridge, but he had been drinking and his mind was filled with the slowly escaping energy of lustfulness. It didn't matter to him at that moment, though. Nothing mattered more than reaching home, taking Maryanne into his arms, and letting her know that he had sinned and he was sorry.

She was awake, and he undressed quickly, saying very little more than, "It's all right, baby, I'm home now." Then he sank his nose into the flesh of her neck, and into her chest and stomach. He pressed against her, body to body, and closed his eyes, losing himself in the gyrations. He held her firmly, pressing his fingers into her shoulders, until she called out his name, her voice pleading and yearning. "Steely, oh Steely," she cried.

And then, he remembered, he collapsed. He fell onto her body, caromed from it, and rolled over to the side of the bed, sweat falling from his forehead, his back bent so that his knees pointed to his chest. There were tears in his eyes, he remembered, unexpected and

61

alarming tears. I should have washed first, he remembered saying over and over to himself, I should have brought her a clean spirit with a clean body. And he lay there, without sleep, without moving, until morning.

Maryanne turned in the aisle and looked at him quizzically, and he winked his eye, just the way Joey Guttergrate winked his eye when he had an idea.

Maryanne still loved him, he thought. He could see it within the puzzle lines of her still attractive face. If only, Steely thought, he could think of an idea about Maryanne.

He wasn't really sure when things began to go bad between them. There were so many things. Being in church reminded him of when they were at a dance, in the cellar of St. Ignatius's Church, on a Friday night, the dances were always Friday nights in Manhattan, and Maryanne had called him a jerk in front of the whole table.

They had been married only a year or so. Nine people were sitting there, and Maryanne said, "You're some jerk, Steely." He was stunned, he remembered, that she would ever say that to him.

"Sticks and stones, baby," he said in reply, passing it off. Certainly, she forgot it the instant she said it. But it stayed with him always. They had been talking about religion, about the lessons they had at St. Aloysius that told them all they would ever need to know to stay faithful.

"People who are not baptized," Maryanne had said, "can never go to heaven." Jack Haggerty was there, and Josie, and they all agreed. "Limbo," she said, "that's the place, forever."

"Right," everyone but Steely concurred.

"What about the people before Christ?" Steely asked. "There was no heaven for all those people before Christ? The holy men in Tibet, the gurus of India, none of 'em went to heaven? Just the plans were made, but they never started the place up until Christ? What about the three wise men? They rode those smelly camels all that way and they never got to go to heaven because Christ never taught his cousin how to baptize until thirty years later? Give me a break, huh? You ever hear of the doctrine of invincible ignorance?"

Steely was proud, very proud that he had not only the attention but the interest of the entire table of friends. Even Haggerty had his mouth open.

"What's invincible ignorance?" Haggerty asked. He was asking because he wanted to know, a genuine inquiry, and Steely was impressed by that. Johnnie Gimme did not know something he did.

"It's when you not only don't know the Catholic way to heaven but you also have no way of knowing because of the way you live your life. Like Jews or Moslems or Hindus that live good lives."

"Or Incas," someone said. "They never knew Catholic until the spicks came."

"Right," Steely said, laughing. He really felt good.

Until Richie Conway spoke. Richie Conway was going to Iona College at the time, studying philosophy, preparing to be anything but the bus driver which he became.

"But that doctrine," Richie said, "was in an encyclical. It was not *ex cathedra*, so it really doesn't apply."

"What's *ex cathedra*?" Steely asked. It was the first time he had heard the term. They never used it in the pamphlet he had read called *The Road to Heaven*, the one in which he had learned about the doctrine of invincible ignorance.

"It's when the Pope speaks," Richie announced, "on behalf of God. From the chair, big time. It's the only thing that counts."

"Oh," Steely uttered. He felt punched, like he was sprawled on the floor.

That's when Maryanne said, "You're some jerk, Steely. You should have known that before you gave everyone a lesson."

He could still hear the ring of her words in his ears. They stood apart from the waters of his mind, like an oil rig on the ocean, popped up, distinct.

There was that, and then there was the time a year or so after when she had slapped the side of his head.

There were six of them in the car going to Rockaway Beach for the day. Tara had just been born, and Maryanne's mother had volunteered to babysit. They were acting like teenagers, drinking beer in the car, chewing gum, telling jokes. Jack and Josie Haggerty were there, and someone, a couple named O'Carroll, a guy that worked in Haggerty's firehouse on Beekman Street in lower Manhattan.

It had to be an easy firehouse, Steely laughed, remembering, for Haggerty never worked in a busy firehouse in his life. There was no time to study in a busy firehouse, and Haggerty even then had his plans laid out to study his way to number one on all the lists.

It was the only thing about Jack Haggerty that Steely resented. There was an unwritten understanding in the Fire Department that men who did not pass through the busy fire companies, the companies that worked Harlem or Brownsville or the South Bronx, had somehow cheated the Department and were trying to con their brother firefighters. Maybe it was unfair to judge men like that, for the risks were the same in the slowest firehouses, and if someone's number was up, it could be up in the fancy section of Forest Hills as well as in the garbage heaps of the ghettos. But, still, there was no doubt that Steely wished his friend Haggerty had more smoke in the cloth of his uniform.

They were on the long stretch of road between Broad Channel and Rockaway Beach. Steely was driving the car, an old 'fifty-two Ford. There were no stores, just sand and marsh on either side of the boulevard. "Give me a cigarette, Steely," Maryanne had said.

"Damn, babe," he said, feeling his shirt pocket. "I guess I forgot them, left them on the kitchen table."

It was then she hit his head, a hard slap just above the ear. "What a memory, Steely," she said, laughing. "Like the guy who bought the Brooklyn Bridge two times."

The Haggertys laughed then, too, and the O'Carrolls, and Steely felt like screeching the car to a halt, getting out of it, and running as fast as he could away from her, from her laughter.

But he let it pass. It became, he thought, just another lingering doubt about the woman he loved, and, like wishing for the smoke in Haggerty's uniform, he also wished that Maryanne was more genteel, more Sutton Place than Second Avenue. God, Josie was so restrained, so ladylike in comparison.

There were other times, too, small embarrassments, inconsiderations, uncaring reactions, and Steely could remember each of them, each stored and ready for recall. Yet he knew when he searched his conscience that those things were just small potatoes. They were inconsequential unless you had a boatload. No, it wasn't those little indignities at all that scarred the memory of their early love. There was something else that had come between him and Maryanne, something bigger, maybe, than anything he could remember, more powerful than memory itself. He wasn't sure.

He would have to probe the years of his marriage month by month, day by day, to figure it all out. It was something that would take time and concentration. But, it would have to be done tomorrow or another day, for the mass was now ending, and he had the day yet to spend with Tara and Jeffrey.

Tara and Jeffrey. How he loved them. Yet, there was something there about them that lingered. Some question. What had he done to them? Were they his children still, in the same way as when they were born? God, how he had loved them when they were infants, small balls of softness that could turn calluses to silk. Would they ever understand they were children of love, or would they, as they passed through the years, make excuses for the problems of life and pass themselves off as children of estranged parents. They were so good-looking, and bright with innocence. Maybe they had grown to be too innocent? That was always possible. Being too innocent could be like being too crazy or too stupid in that people take advantage. He could harden them a little, perhaps there was still time for that.

After church, he dropped Maryanne off at the house. She looked melancholy, like someone who had just lost her job and had the monthly bills due. Behind the sadness of her eyes, though, Steely could also see the anger and resentment that had continued to grow since their separation.

It was a clear day, cool for summer, and he noticed how fast the clouds were moving as he drove Tara and Jeffrey to the lean, confining space he was reluctant to call home.

"Why can't we stay over?" Jeffrey asked as usual when they entered the small, studio-like apartment. The building was really too old to have anything called a studio.

"There is no place to sleep, Jeffrey," he explained again. "I will not have my children sleeping on the floor. I work too hard to let my children sleep on the floor without a bed to sleep in."

"C'mon, Dad," Jeffrey said, "we can camp like in cub scouts."

"No," he said.

"I don't want to anyway," Tara said. "Susan Jasper's mother and father are divorced and she has two of everything, two beds, two TVs, two dollhouses, but she's getting too old for them now."

Steely looked away from his daughter, and around his one room, at the sagging bed he had found in a thrift shop on Third Avenue, at the single lamp he took from the rumpus room of the ranch house, at the oval early American rug he bought for twenty bucks from the back end of a hijacked truck on Greenpoint Avenue.

"You won't get such a good deal as your friend Susan, Tara," he said, finally, after deciding that his children would not look at his apartment in the same way he did, with the same kind of self-mockery, embarrassment, and dissatisfaction. "This here is just a place to lay my head."

"Until you and Mommy get back together?" Tara asked. It was something she inserted as often as possible into every conversation.

"I don't know," Steely answered, thinking of the conversation about divorce that he had with Maryanne. He was sitting on a handsome, velvet chair Arbuckle McFatty was going to throw away but gave to him instead. "Until we get straight, anyway," he added.

"You always say that," Jeffrey said, reaching under the bed for the electric football game he had shoved there the previous visit. "Like you're drunk or something."

"I am drunk now, drunk with exhaustion."

"You gonna go to sleep again?" Tara asked.

"You want to go to Central Park?"

"It's for the birds," Tara said, sniffing at the ends of a handful of hair. "How about a movie?"

"I looked in the paper yesterday. There's only R movies around. Want to go in a rowboat in Central Park?"

"The water's got garbage in it," Jeffrey said, setting up the electric football goal posts.

"Don't say *got*, Jeffrey," Steely said, remembering that his mother had reminded him not to say *got* two or three times a week. "Where else do you want to go?"

"Nowhere," Tara said, turning on the black and white portable television set that Steely bought from a factory outlet in Long Island City.

"Thank God for TV," he said, leaning way back in the velvet chair, straining his neck muscles until he felt a pain in his head.

He read the room from left to right, its gray dust-caked walls, the old-fashioned glass lamp stuck between two five-and-ten-cent-store prints of foreign landscapes, the green and white polka dot curtains that he thought were made from sheets and which at one time probably matched a tenant's bedding.

He remembered then the tenement bedroom of his youth, where he slept on the floor some nights, a wet rag tied around his neck to escape the heat, or where on cold nights, even when he was as old as Tara, he crawled in with one of his brothers to share the warmth of body heat. It was a room where his father had randomly placed on the walls decals of Captain Marvel, and Batman, and Superman, each in extraordinary ready-for-confrontation poses, feet apart, crouching slightly, hands and fingers outstretched before their color-fully uniformed and insigniaed chests. He had slept, and he had dreamed of the future, in that room, before those figures. But he had never dreamed he would end up in a room like the poverty pad overlooking the entrance to the Queens-Midtown Tunnel.

He closed his eyes and rested a moment. He surprised himself then, for, perhaps because he was so completely relaxed, a vision of Maryanne jolted his mind.

They were in Central Park. She was wearing a white summer dress, one with lace and frills, and she was walking with her arm entwined with his. They were engaged to be married. They went down a small hill and then under a bridge. The merry-go-round appeared before them, popping up suddenly like a puppet-show prop. The music was gay and boisterous, and like the sound of a passing elevated train, it was inescapable. They had to yell to each other to be heard. "Our life together," Maryanne said, "will always be like calliope music. Calliope music is never sad."

Maryanne, Steely thought as he watched the children fold pillows behind their heads, had a way of touching him that could not be duplicated, a sensitivity that was all her own. Maryanne deserved the happiness she thought she would have that day, as they rode the undulating wooden horses, laughing hand in hand. She had been so carefree, Steely remembered, so joyful. He could not tell her what calliope music meant to him, that it made him think of circuses, and departing trains, and tearful, frowning clowns.

CHAPTER 9

JACK T. Haggerty winked his eye at Monsignor Flynn as he turned the wicker collection basket upside down. The young monsignor held the worn bank bag open as wide as possible, but still a couple of dollars fell over the rim and floated to the marble floor in the back of St. Veronica's Church. "It's okay, Chief," the monsignor said, "I'll get them."

"Not at all, Frank," the Chief of Department replied, leaning over and crunching the dollar bills into balls within his hand.

Haggerty was the head usher and chairman of the Holy Name Society at the small Sunnyside parish. Head usher was not as great an honor as being a Knight of Malta, but it was at least an honor within the church. Flynn, at thirty-four, was the youngest monsignor in the Brooklyn and Queens Diocese. His rise in the diocese, a mercurial one, came in consequence of his theological training at the Vatican College, the Fulbright Scholarship that underwrote his stay at Oxford for three years, and the fact, which made the thin-of-heart in church circles smile, that his father was a fourth-degree Knight of Columbus and the Bishop's right-hand man at all official functions in Brooklyn's Cathedral. "Monsignor Flynn is so well connected," Chief Haggerty once told a communion breakfast gathering, "that I suspect his grandfather was the Bishop of Armagh."

The monsignor closed the bank bag and locked it with a five-and-ten-cent-store lock. The Chief of Department beamed, proud that he had been responsible for the collection of a larger than normal Sunday take.

"Embarrass them if you must," he told his ushers at the Holy Name Society meeting held just before mass, "but leave the basket in front of them until they drop something. They'll scramble through their pockets, pretending, you know, to look for their money, and praying you'll move on. But just smile and say, 'No hurry,' and let the basket capture their spirit."

It was important to the Chief to have a big return, for he had a favor to ask of the young monsignor, and there was nothing like a good collection to make a priest receptive to a solicitation.

"Music, Jack, music," Monsignor Flynn said, shaking the bag up and down.

"Better than anything St. Gregory wrote," Haggerty replied.

"Indeed, Jack. Now, would you have the time to breakfast with me?"

"I would. I'll just take the time to give Mrs. Haggerty money for the rolls and for the paper, and I'll be in presently."

"Don't forget to buy the *Catholic News*, Jack."

"I'd as soon forget my badge, Frank," Haggerty replied.

The Chief opened the wide wooden doors at the rear of the church, and stood like a politician trying to make eye contact with a nod at every passing parishioner, each contact bringing a note of confidence. The people flooded past in two minutes or so, a church, like the stadium of a losing football team, always being much easier to empty than to fill.

Haggerty kissed his wife on the cheek as she passed, and handed her a five-dollar bill. She looked perfectly like a Chief of Department's wife, he thought, in her mink shoulder wrap and white cotton suit, the one that came from Bonwit's and cost more than two hundred. "I'm sorry, Josie," he apologized, "business."

In the small stuffy dining room of the rectory, Haggerty saw Monsignor Flynn being distracted by the hardened calf muscles of the young Puerto Rican maid. She was reaching for a platter on the top shelf of a breakfront. "Life goes by very unnoticeable like," Haggerty said, patting his small stomach, "and the tautness of the skin becomes flab before you even know it."

"You're in fine shape, Jack," Monsignor Flynn said, pulling a chair out for his guest. "I wouldn't want to do three rounds with you anyway."

Haggerty remembered Frank Flynn's body when they were teenagers spending summer weekends out at Rockaway Beach. The best basketball in the country could be seen on Sundays in the Rockaway playground at 108th Street, and Frank Flynn was always in there with the pros, giving them a run for their money. A regular Marquis Haynes ball handler, and the best physique on the court. And handsome. He left all the neighborhood girls crying when he went away to the seminary instead of college. He always had a way with the girls.

"It's not all flab yet," Haggerty said, watching the priest walk around the table, nodding to the maid as he passed. "But the time passes quickly, nonetheless, and I'm becoming more and more aware of it."

"Lord, Jack," Monsignor Flynn laughed, sitting now directly across the oval table from Haggerty, "you're not even forty yet."

Frank Flynn was several years younger, and so not part of his own crowd, Haggerty thought, but he was still neighborhood, a man he could count on.

"Thirty-seven," Haggerty answered, "and that's exactly what I would like to talk to you about, Frank, so that you, and your father, and the Bishop can give it some thought."

"Sounds important," Monsignor Flynn said, sitting back reflectively, hands joined above his thin waist.

It was a pose, Haggerty thought, that all priests learned in Rome, where time is never a consideration.

"Perhaps," Monsignor Flynn said, "first I should clear up just a little bit of business that we have so that it needn't interfere with anything later."

"Is that the papal *we* you're practicing already, Monsignor?" Haggerty said, pleased that he was on familiar enough ground with the priest to make a joke with a church referent.

Monsignor Flynn laughed. "Except that the father in this *we* is my real father, O'Donovan Patrick Flynn."

The two men laughed together, and waited for the maid to serve the eggs and pour the coffee.

"There is a mechanic," Monsignor Flynn said, "who fixes the Bishop's automobile who happens to have a brother who's a fireman in Ladder Company . . . I have it here, somewhere." He searched within his cassock until he found a small index card and read it quickly. "Name of Garria," he continued, "Ladder Company 120 in Brooklyn, wants to be transferred to Engine Company 292 in Queens for reasons of easy travel."

Haggerty wrote the name on a wallet pad, saying, "It's done, as sure as fish swim."

The maid leaned across the monsignor to place a roll on his butter dish, and Haggerty saw her breast slide over the black cotton cloth of his cassock. He guessed that the monsignor had at one time or another played pantry games with the maid. Couldn't blame him at all if he did, for goodness sake. She was a very attractive young woman, and a priest shouldn't have to be priestly all the time with the consistency of little minds. Not at all. If a priest could cop a little something in the pantry, God bless it all, it's part of the natural law. And Frank Flynn always had a way with the girls. Seed sown in the belly of a whore is better than sowing it on the ground, so the Bible says, not that she's a whore, mind you. Still, Haggerty remonstrated with himself, it takes a tartlike attitude about the world to do it with a priest.

Monsignor Flynn flushed as the maid pressed into him, and said, "A good car mechanic is hard to find."

"We'd move the Bishop around in a hook and ladder truck," Haggerty said, "if we thought it would please him."

When the maid finally returned to the kitchen, Monsignor Flynn said, "There is a Captain Peter Petrullo who is a member of the Valley Stream Knights of Columbus, and who is said to have scored very high on the battalion chief's test. It is being said his promotion is overdue and that your office is holding up any promotions to battalion chief because you want to wait until after the deputy chief's test in the fall. I don't know what it means."

"It means, Frank," Haggerty said, holding a piece of crisp bacon between his thumb and forefinger, "that only battalion chiefs can take the test for deputy chief and Captain Petrullo very much wants to be a battalion chief soon so that he can file for the deputy chief's test. It's simple. Only, the Fire Commissioner doesn't want to make any new battalion chiefs until after the deputy chief's test."

"Why not?"

"To limit the competition among the current battalion chiefs, most of whom are Irish. He doesn't want any of those smart guineas up in the ranks."

"What a terrible thing."

"The Commissioner has no great love for the Irish, being the kind of Protestant born with an enema attached to his buttocks, but he made a deal with the Emerald Society of Greater New York. I don't know what he got in return. Something, though, you can bet your chalice."

"But that is a racist policy."

"What is racist? We live in a city, Frank, with a Jewish mayor. I have to go to a dinner tonight to honor the members of the Naer Tormid Society, a group of forty-five men, all of whom come from Forest Hills, the one district that gave the Mayor the election. Three years ago the Chief of Department would have sent a lieutenant or even a fireman to represent my office, but now I have to be there myself. That's racist, Frank, these guys, these Johnny-come-latelies, pushing around the power of their minorities just because they're suddenly plugged in."

"No, Jack, I'm afraid you can't get around the fact that to prevent Italians from taking an examination to secure the interest of the Irish is racism."

"I think you're wrong there, with all due respect, Monsignor. It's ethnocentric maybe. You want to count the number of Jewish commissioners, and deputy commissioners in our city? Nothing wrong with it. The Jews own the team, they can pick the players. Remember that the Irish used to control the school system, and still pretty much run the Police and Fire departments."

Haggerty felt the priest's stare. He seemed to be considering an argument, or at least a discussion on the level of debate, but then he seemed to resolve something in his mind, for he smiled suddenly and took a long sip of coffee. "Where does that leave us, Chief," he said, "with our Captain Petrullo?"

Goal-oriented, Haggerty thought to himself. How I love it when people are goal-oriented. "I think that Captain Petrullo will be denied an opportunity of participating in the examination for deputy chief, unless, unless . . ."

72

Haggerty thought a moment before continuing. He ate the piece of bacon in his hand and wiped the grease from his fingers with a napkin. "Unless I go way out and make a considerable trade with the Fire Commissioner. I know he has a real interest in the masks we're now testing from the Apogee Mask Company. He's got some connections with the Apogee Company. I don't know what it is, but he calls me at least twice a week about it. I keep telling him the test will take another three or four months, but I could give him the go-ahead easily enough. Maybe."

"O'Donovan Patrick Flynn would be very appreciative," Monsignor Flynn said, "for the Captain Petrullos of the world sometimes strangely and inexplicably determine the future viability of institutions as august even as the Knights of Columbus."

The priest sighed then, probably relieved, Haggerty thought, that the banality of church politics was behind him. He then began to cut into his egg when, it seemed, another thought entered his mind. He gently laid his knife and fork on the side of the plate, saying, "Ahh, just one other little thing. A young man named James Dixon from my parish here, our parish, is a fireman. Do you know him?"

"I don't, Frank."

"His wife is sick, and he needs a day job, out of the firehouse."

Haggerty wrote the name on the pad and inserted the wallet into his breast pocket. "Consider that a *fait accompli*," he said, winking his eye. "That's your language, Frank. It means it's as good as done."

Monsignor Flynn winked back good-naturedly, saying, "You're an accomplished man, Chief."

"It was the Catholic schools."

"Lord yes, we'd have an illiterate civil service if it were not for the Catholic schools."

"That's for sure, Frank."

"Now, what can we do for you, Chief?"

Haggerty, unlike the priest, did not take time to reflect, to imply that whatever was about to be said was the consequence of heavily considered judgment. He spoke very quickly in return.

"As I said, Frank, time is passing quickly."

"Well, Chief, the church moves slowly, but it does move, you know."

"I hope so Frank," Haggerty replied, leaning now, confidentially, across the table, "for I've been thinking a lot lately in terms of my future. There's another rung to climb in the Department and it would be a great benefit to me, I believe, if you and your father could mention my name in the right circles."

The priest did not respond quickly, Haggerty noticed, which was good. He knows what I'm talking about, the job of Fire Commissioner of the City of New York, an appointed post where influence is as important as ability. Sometimes more important. And now he will begin to waltz around the idea, thanks be to God for Vatican training, to find out what's in it for him.

Monsignor Flynn cleared his throat and said, "You mean, of course, my father, for I'm not quite inside the, as you say, *right circles.*"

"Ah," Haggerty said quickly, his answer already prepared, "but you could be, Frank, you could be. You know that Fire Department chaplains, for instance, are always invited for lunches and dinners at the Cardinal's residence, or to the little cocktail parties the City Council gives from time to time. And there's a stipend that comes with the job, a small one, along with other benefits."

"I didn't know that," Monsignor Flynn answered. "And a uniform, I suppose."

"With little gold crosses at the lapels," Haggerty affirmed.

"Most interesting," Monsignor Flynn said.

Wonderful, Haggerty thought. We understand each other completely. Monsignor Flynn will talk to his father who will talk to the Bishop who will talk to City Hall. And I will talk to Father Dunn from the Bronx who has already told me he will retire from his duties as Catholic spiritual advisor to the Department as soon as I can find an appropriate and advantageous replacement.

Appropriate and advantageous. Now, they are fine words, indeed, both of them being Frank Flynn's middle names.

CHAPTER 10

THE long and narrow cellar of the firehouse on East Eighty-seventh Street was a place of respite and a place to hide for Steely. He was sitting on top of a table that someone had covered with a rug remnant, a rug that had been blue and gray but was now mostly dark gray and brown from years of liquid and tobacco stains. His feet were on a narrow bench used for bench-pressing weights when there had been weights. It now gave balance and leverage to whomever sat on the table. There was oil-mixed water on the concrete flooring that came from a leaking boiler in one corner of the cellar. Next to him, on the table, was a six-pack of beer that had one can missing from the end. It was eleven o'clock in the morning.

Steely was watching the wavering brightness from the single exposed bulb in the ceiling that inadequately lighted the bare-walled room. He thought he could see the energy being forced from the bulb into all corners of the cellar, like smoke from a fire. He kept staring into the bulb. He was bright-spotting his vision, but the bulb was calming and hypnotizing, and, besides, it was at least something to think about, something to occupy his mind. He was tired of thinking about Maryanne, though he couldn't help it, and about the woman who was coming to work in the firehouse, to change every-thing, the way the men talked, and acted.

Things were not going forward for Steely, and it bothered him. Jack Haggerty, he thought, closing his eyes, was the Chief of Department, and here I am still a fireman hanging from the side step of a ladder truck. Even Pepe PeePee was a sergeant in the Police Department. "God," he said aloud, opening his eyes as he threw his head back to take a mouthful of beer, "if Pepe is a sergeant, there's a precinct somewhere in trouble."

"Whadya say?" asked a voice from somewhere.

Startled, Steely jumped from the table and turned, thinking that a man could be fired for drinking in the firehouse, friend of the Chief's or not.

"What's that?" he said apprehensively, holding his hand to his forehead.

"Whadya say?" the voice asked again.

Steely looked around, but the bright spot in his vision was as big as the sun. "Who is it?" he demanded.

"Me," the voice said. "I'm only just sitting here thinking that my prayers are truly being answered through my friendship with Jesus."

"Christ," Steely said, exasperated.

"That's right," Red Hadley said, "Jesus Christ. There ain't many other Jesuses that can answer your prayers."

Steely blinked his eyes rapidly, trying to lose the bright spot. As they cleared, he saw Hadley squatting in the back corner of the cellar. He remembered reading about religious fanatics of history, ascetics they called them, who scourged themselves like Iranians and sat on top of poles like bored college students, and he realized then that Hadley, squatting like an Indian beggar, seemed as crazy as any of them.

Hadley's real name was Hadlenski, but he had it changed when he entered the Fire Department. "I come from a family of Polish generals," he once told Steely. They had sat together at a communion breakfast, and it was the first time Steely got close to him. He had seemed pretty straight then, when he was still a Catholic, before he got those crazy ideas about being born again. "But I changed my name, even with great soldiers in my past, because everyone thinks Polack every time they see an *s*, a *k*, and an *i* together."

76

It was the breakfast where Jack Haggerty had referred to Catholic firemen as the only true saints of the age. "I don't know if I believe that," Hadley had said. "All I want to be is a good American, and a good person."

Steely looked now at Hadley. The bright spot was gone completely, and he could see the clear white skin, the high, angled cheekbones, and the deep red hair of Hadley's head. He was smiling. He was always smiling, yet the smile was not a genuinely happy one. It seemed to be more a kind of faraway look, one that begged for peacefulness.

"You can't be friends with God, Red," Steely said indifferently, sitting again on the table. "A saint, maybe, but not God."

"Jesus is my friend," Hadley insisted.

"Well, then, Jesus isn't God," Steely said. "God's too much of a big shot to have friends, you know. He's got to take care of everybody."

"Don't blaspheme, Steely. A fireman's got too dangerous a job to blaspheme."

"Look, Red," Steely said. "I don't want to talk about it. I got six here, so c'mon sit over here and we'll pop one and I'll tell you about humping my cousin."

Hadley carried the large frame of his body out of the twilight of the cellar corner. "I'd like to share a beer with you, Steely," he said tentatively, "but not if you talk like that."

Steely laughed and slapped Hadley on the back. "I won't, Red," he said. "It's sinful. So, screw it."

"Yes," Hadley said, "thank you."

The tall, thin-faced Hadley was a complicated man, but he didn't think more of himself than what he was, Steely thought, or at least didn't put on airs about anything. Steely guessed that he had replaced sex with religion, and he talked about God with the same regularity and enthusiasm that other firemen talked about sex. So he prayed openly sometimes, no big thing. He was, what they used to call in the old neighborhood, a psycho case. But a colorful one, no doubt about that, and that's what made Steely feel close to him.

Maybe they were both colorful psycho cases? Maybe there was no doubt about that either?

"How come," Steely asked, snapping the beer can ring, "you're not upstairs helping out with the committee work?"

"No reason, I just wanted to pray." Hadley sat on the table.

"Those guys are gonna be pretty mad, mopping the kitchen floor and doing everything without us."

"I prayed for them. It's all right."

"They don't want your prayers, Red," Steely said in a helpful, comforting way. "They want you to clean the toilet bowls. They want—"

Steely's words were interrupted by the harsh sound of the alarm horn, its electric vibrations wailing from the loudspeaker near the cellar stairs. LADDER SEVEN, ENGINE FIVE, FIRE REPORTED TENTH FLOOR, EIGHT-NINE-NINE PARK AT SEVEN-NINE STREET.

Steely put the six-pack of beer in a dented garbage can and replaced the beaten ill-fitting lid on top.

"Screw the Mayor," he said, which was the general toast in the firehouse.

Steely pushed Hadley before him as they reached the stairs. Going through the cellar door, he saw McFatty and Harrigan racing to the fire truck. There was another fireman, whose name Steely did not know, one detailed from a neighboring company for the day. Steely went over the assignments in his mind. Hadley had the outside-vent position, and it was his job to make sure the fire building was completely ventilated, or at least to break enough windows so that the smoke and heat could escape from the confines of an interior. The danger always existed of a buildup of superheated gases that could explode or create a flashback fire, but Hadley was a sharp enough firefighter to minimize that problem.

McFatty had the forcible-entry tools. He, with the detailed fireman and the lieutenant, would go to the door of the fire, apartment or commercial building or place of public assembly. McFatty would force the door open and the detailed fireman would use a water extinguisher for protection. And Harrigan would go to the roof, to ventilate the top of the building, to break a skylight or cut a hole with the power saw. Together, the members of Ladder Company 7 would rush a building, enter it, ventilate it, search it for victims, and tear it apart to locate any extension of fire. It was a good team, and Steely felt confident being a part of it.

Running across the apparatus floor, Steely took the computer printout of the alarm location from the fireman on housewatch. He was assigned to drive the apparatus this day, a Ward LaFrance truck with a ninety-foot aerial ladder, one that cost more than

$200,000 when it was new just five years before. He pulled himself up to the driver's seat of the truck, now scratched and dented and rusting. "At least it's not Harlem," Steely thought, looking at the address, which was on Park Avenue and Seventy-ninth Street. "No one wants to crawl through Harlem on a hot day."

Lieutenant Jackson climbed in from the other side. A goalie on a dart team, Steely thought as he turned the ignition and looked the pimply-faced fire officer up and down. Pock-faced and pock-brained. He still resented the lieutenant for the dressing-down he had to take at the Gimbels fire.

"You been drinking, Steely?" the lieutenant asked.

"C'mon, Lou," Steely laughed. "It's early."

"Don't matter the time, Steely, I'll have your ass in a sling if I catch you drinking. I smell beer, but I have to suppose it's from last night."

"The guys have a party in the fire truck last night?"

"You know what I mean, Steely."

"I don't know anything, lieutenant," Steely said, swinging the bulky apparatus down Lexington Avenue, "except when my check is late and when my horns are being broken."

The lieutenant did not answer, but picked up the radio telephone and put it to his ear, listening through the roar of the siren for further alarm information. The traffic parted before them, cars, buses, trucks, all slowing, pulling to the side, some stopping. They were obeying the laws as if they believed in a civilized society, Steely thought. Later into the day, though, things would change. The more that people became involved with the day's problems, the less traffic laws would be regarded, until the midnight hours when hardly any cars would concede the right of way to a fire truck.

As they turned onto Seventy-ninth Street, Steely noticed Lieutenant Jackson bending over so that he could see up to the top of the high-rise apartment building on the corner of Park. Jackson was a good fire officer, Steely thought, as smart and safe as they come. It was just that he had a boss's mentality. A mentality that forgot about the years when he was a fireman swilling out the toilet bowls.

Jackson's mentality and rounding to Park Avenue made something click in Steely's mind. He remembered how his father would often say, "The working class can kiss my ass, I've got the foreman's job at last." Even though he never became the foreman.

His father had worked for the railroad, the New York Central, a line that did not have a good reputation in the family. Steely remembered how his father had told them once that the modern railroad bosses made the robber barons of old look like Sisters of Charity. It was after he had been turned down for the foreman's job at the freight department. He had put on his shirt and tie, looking like he was ready for a wedding or something, and gone to the Grand Central Building, the one that is at the base of Park Avenue and is now named for a person who bought it. There, he asked an executive why he wasn't made foreman. Steely remembered the anger in his father's voice, even though he was a child, five or six at the time. "The man told me," his father had said, "that it was like all the clubs on Park Avenue. If you had to ask how to get in, you don't belong."

Steely didn't dislike Jackson, at least not the way his father disliked the railroad managers. He just wanted to keep an edge between them, between fireman and boss. And then there was the Gimbels fire, and the way Jackson talked to Steely without regard for the work Steely had done. God, he had almost killed himself, and Jackson yelled at him. Just like Maryanne yelled at him, with that tone of voice so lacking in respect for a fellow human being. It was okay to dislike Jackson for that.

How many times have I been in the presence of death, Steely asked himself, searching for parts of bodies in charred rooms? To dislike Jackson or any other person so deeply is small time in relation to those deaths. Yet, he could not cut the edge between them, no matter what. Just look the other way, Steely thought, but try to work with the guy anyway. You can never know what might come with the fire.

"You see anything, Lou?" Steely said, a little ashamed by what he knew to be a false conciliatory note in his voice.

"No, nothing," Jackson said. "Leave room for the engine at the hydrant in front of the building."

Yeah, Steely thought, a pock-brained boss all the time. Did he think I would block the hydrant? A kid in probationary school would know enough not to block a hydrant.

Lieutenant Jackson and the firefighters of Ladder 7, Red Hadley among them, ran beneath the gray canvas canopy, past the starch-collared doorman, and into the building. Steely, a portable radio strapped to his chest, was required to stay by the apparatus in case there was a need for emergency laddering. He sat on the side step of the fire truck and studied the building before him.

The gray granite blocks stacked to the sky were separated at intervals by long and narrow windows, windows made for rooms with twenty-foot ceilings. Steely knew that Park Avenue apartments bought just a few years ago for two and three hundred thousand were now selling for one to three million dollars. One-family apartments. The crazy inflation was a standing reference in the firehouse.

"Comes the revolution," Arbuckle McFatty would say, "I'm going to get a Park Avenue apartment." Steely always laughed at the reference in the same way he laughed when he heard someone say, "When I die I'm going to heaven." The heaven is here and now, Steely thought, the revolution is past. Men who worked in Manhattan, Bronx, and Queens firehouses lived in places like Levittown, Massapequa, and Tarrytown. None of them, not even the Fire Commissioner, lived on Park Avenue. Nothing really so bad about that, though, Steely thought. At least they weren't huddled any longer, families of seven or more in three rooms, in New York tenements. Like in the South Bronx. Like in Harlem. Still.

Steely came from a family of eight. They lived, when he was a child, in three rooms. The six children, four boys and two girls, were in the bedroom—it was a large bedroom, if the truth is to be told—distributed among three bunk beds, and his parents were on the pull-out couch in the living room. The kitchen was also quite large, unlike most tenements, because it was an arched courtyard building, different from the row of slate stoops of the rest of the buildings on the block. Steely's mother, when she was alive, used to joke, "If we ever have guests to sleep over, they'll have to sleep in the oven and in the sink, because I won't move the dishes to gain the shelf space."

Steely's father had passed away first, of cancer. The railroad pension was barely enough to cover the rent, and everyone worked part- or full-time jobs to help with the expenses. His mother had heart failure within a few years of that. An older brother, Pat, had died before both of them, in an automobile accident on a sandy, twisting road down at the Jersey shore. He was seventeen and drunk. Steely was a kid, just seven or eight then, and he never forgot what his father had said at the wake. "If there is a good thing at all to be found in this, it is that he was alone, that he brought no one with him."

Steely could never remember the tone of his father's voice, and he often wondered if it had been accusatory. His father, what he remembered of him, had been a cold man, and so the family was never close, the brothers and sisters going their own ways, exchanging occasional visits, but never at holidays or birthdays, never when it mattered.

The radio at Steely's chest squawked: LADDER SEVEN ALPHA TO LADDER SEVEN BETA.

Steely, the *beta* in this communication, pressed the transmit button and responded to Lieutenant Jackson, "Go ahead, Lou."

MAKE IT A TEN EIGHTEEN, STEELY, FOR A TEN TWENTY-THREE.

Steely transmitted that information over the truck's radio to the dispatch at the Department's communication center. It meant that one engine company and one ladder company at the scene would be sufficient for a food-on-the-stove fire. Crepe suzettes well done, Steely thought to himself, walking toward the doorman. In the Bronx, it might be cuchi fritos, and blintzes in Brooklyn, but on the Upper East Side of Manhattan it was crepe suzettes.

The doorman was an older man; the white bow tie around the stiff, Victorian high collar of his uniform shirt looked uncomfortable, though the man was smiling. "How ya doing, old pal?" Steely asked.

"Not too bad if the building don't burn down."

"No problem. Just somebody cooked something overdone."

"You mean a maid. The people that live here don't cook for themselves."

"Yeah," Steely smiled pleasantly, "they don't cook tea? I remember my grandfather used to say he had to cook the tea."

"I wouldn't know about that," the doorman laughed, a competitive sparkle in his eyes. "I'm of a different age altogether than to have a grandson as old as yourself."

Steely turned toward the fire truck, leaving a short aside for the doorman. "Man, don't remind me," he said.

It was then that he heard the voice of a woman, a sound that entered his memory and flashed a light of recognition in the same way the smell of roast pork would always remind him of tenement hallways.

"Is there a fire, Dan?" the voice asked. It was a finely pitched voice, Steely thought, not too high, not too low, and it vibrated with quality. He would not have turned if he had not heard the long *a* the woman used in pronouncing the doorman's name. Not that Steely was expert on the way people talked, but he did know that long *a* sound, the nasal sound that comes from New York bars and public schools and tenements which identifies New Yorkers when they used words like *laugh* or *dance* or *sad* or *Dan*, New Yorkers whose speech was stronger than anything on television.

He knew right away who she was. The high cheekbones, the full lips, the green eyes. God, eyes like Kathy Ryan Angelli's eyes. They could melt snow.

The dress she wore looked like pure silk, he noticed, probably silk anyway, and probably went for more than a week's pay. And the leather handbag she was carrying would cost even more than that. How many times while working in midtown, Steely thought, have I watched costly things burn as fast as rags and paper? It was an uneven balance, but for every ten fires in Harlem there was a fire in the fancy places of the East Side.

He could see the nipples of the woman's breasts outlined through the silk and a thin brassiere. Great body, still. How old could she be? Thirty-three, -four? Great legs, man, just great.

"Parnell," he said, not loud at all. Just loud enough so that she knew she was being addressed. "Parnell Farrell."

She looked at him a moment, but not more than a moment. If she only knew me as one of the guys so many years ago, Steely thought, she might forget, but she'll remember. Like I have remembered for so long. Nineteen years. Twenty years maybe. Man. Twenty years. Where are they, those years between holding this woman and now?

At the United Nations garage on Forty-ninth Street. The guys were playing cards, bankers-brokers, on the Forty-ninth Street pier, and she came over to him for a smoke. She was only a kid, but with a chest out to here, for her age anyway. "I need a butt," she said. And Steely remembered saying, "Nice girls ask, they don't just take."

"Well then, you got me wrong, Steely Byrnes."

"How'd you know my name?" Steely asked, offering her a cigarette.

"You can learn anybody's name in this world," she said, "but you can't always learn what they want. What do you want, Steely?"

She was only fourteen.

"I haven't thought about it today," Steely said sarcastically, playing the wise guy.

"Trust me," she said. "You want to play trust me?"

It was a game where a guy could run his hand down a girl's blouse if she kept saying yes every time he asked "Trust me?" It was also an invitation, and Steely remembered walking her down the East River Drive to Forty-eighth Street and into the side door there, and up the fire stairs to the first landing where they lay on the cold and moist cement, losing themselves in a brief awkward frenzy until he wet her leg with the warm liquid of an interrupted coitus, until she looked up at him, confused and disappointed, asking, "What happened?"

Parnell Farrell. God, she was beautiful then. It was the first time for him. And for her? He wasn't sure, but he thought so. She was great. They went steady for a while, even though she was younger.

Parnell Farrell smiled broadly and embraced him. "Steely," she said, "I would know you anywhere, even with a fireman's hat."

"It's good to see you, Parnell."

"Farrell," she said. "Everyone calls me Farrell."

"Yeah," he said, "no kidding? How come?"

"It's a story, Steely," she said, "for another time. So how have you been? Are you still in the neighborhood?" She crossed her arms, and put one foot forward and ran her eyes from his helmet to his boots.

"No, out in Queens, Long Island City. Farrell, huh, like that."

Steely felt something in the way she looked at him. She was still smiling, and she seemed happy to see him. But there was something else, a sense of knowing, one that was very strong and very secure, a kind of possessiveness. After so long, she was looking at him as if she owned him.

She laughed easily, more a twitter than a laugh. "A fireman. Steely Byrnes a fireman. Yet, it doesn't surprise."

Steely chuckled, feeling a little insecure. "You thought I went to Harvard and became a lawyer?" he said. He knew a lot of guys who went to St. John's, and City College, and Fordham, but he didn't know anyone who had gone to Harvard except for President Kennedy and a few football players.

"No," she said, touching the canvas of his turn-out coat, "just something tough. I will always think of you as tough."

"Tough as what?" he asked.

Parnell Farrell looked out of a corner of her eye at the doorman and then leaned in close to Steely. She whispered, "Tough as fucking nails."

She bent over in laughter, and held his arm. Steely laughed, too.

The firemen came out of the building then, each giving Parnell Farrell the once-over. "Springtime in the Rockies," said McFatty.

"Need help, Steely?" asked Harrigan.

"Let's go, Byrnes," said the lieutenant.

"Lookit, aah, Farrell," Steely said, holding her hand. "I gotta go, but, ah, do you work here or what?"

"I live here, Steely, apartment seventeen." She looked at him, he thought, as if she knew what he would say next.

"Are you in the book?"

"Yes." She smiled, letting go of his hand. "And I'll be in all night tonight. Call and come up for drinks."

"You're on," Steely said. "I'll spring for a telegram if I have to."

Steely climbed into the fire truck and watched her step into the street and hail a taxi.

"That is some piece of ass," the lieutenant said, as Parnell Farrell lifted the hemline of her silk dress to her knees and slid into the cab.

Steely shook his head and drove the lumbering fire truck away from the curb. You'll never know, Lieutenant, he said to himself, you'll never know.

CHAPTER 11

"WE all have dilemmas," Steely said.

"What's a dilemma?" Hadley asked.

"Well, it's like when I was in the Army in Vietnam, and went R&R in Japan. There was this whorehouse when I was in Tokyo. I was a kid. They told me if you pissed right after you came then you wouldn't get syph. But that meant I couldn't piss before I went in the whorehouse, and I can't come when I have to piss. That's a dilemma. To piss and get laid proper and catch the syph, or don't piss and screw up the bang."

"I wish you wouldn't talk like that, Steely," Hadley said, mixing a half dozen eggs into the chopped steak.

Steely grinned and poured a potful of water into the coffee machine which stood on a long counter that separated the cooking area from the firehouse kitchen table, which in turn was surrounded by a tall soda machine, a plaid couch that was ripped and in need of repair, and a television set hanging on chains from the ceiling.

He loved to needle Hadley, though sometimes it was too easy, like tripping a toddler. Like now.

"All right, Red," he said, "I'd do anything to protect the integrity of your lily-white soul."

"It's just that you hurt Jesus, Steely."

"Clean slate, Red, promise. Now, about your wife?"

"It's a great problem for me, a dilemma as you said."

"Wives are meant to be anchors, to slow you down in the waters of passion." Steely held a cup beneath the trickling stream of coffee. It was easy to be flip, he thought, but he wondered if he meant it.

Hadley began to mold the chopped steak and eggs and bread crumbs into a meat loaf. "She's leaving me," he said. He then slapped the meat and it splattered across the front of his sky-blue Department dress shirt. "She's gone already, actually, two weeks ago. Took the television set in the middle of the night, to let me know she meant business, I guess."

"No kids, though," Steely asked, "right?"

Hadley shook his head affirmatively as he repaired the meat loaf.

"Can't be too bad, then," Steely said. "It's only bad when there are kids, you know."

Steely closed his eyes for a brief moment.

"Yeah, I guess so," Hadley said. "If only she would've spoke up for Jesus, it all would be all right."

"She wouldn't soak herself in the stuff of salvation, huh?"

Hadley looked at him cautiously. "No, I don't think she thought of anything except coming home from work and watching television."

"No kidding, just like everybody else?" Steely began to cut into home-fry circles the potatoes that another fireman had peeled. "So what's the big problem? If there are no kids there's no big problem."

Problems, big problems.

Steely thought of the problem with Maryanne. She's got the kids, and they'll always think she loves them more than I do. Tara anyway. The girls always stick with the mother. That's the way it is. The mother always gets the kids, and the kids think it's because she loves them more.

Tara had cried when he carried his bags out the day he moved to the poverty pad. He didn't want to steal away in the night. He would be more honest with his children than that, more direct. It was a Saturday morning, and Tara had cried, and Jeffrey had stood by expressionless, his mouth open, caught up as he almost always was in something he did not fully understand. Poor Jeffrey.

Maryanne handled it like a strong tenement mother, one who was used to taking in wash and doing other people's ironing and cleaning other people's apartments, strong like his own mother. Maryanne said nothing, like her mother who never spoke to her father for as long as he could remember. That's what she had told him, and Steely had seen it all through the years he went steady with Maryanne. Even at the wedding of their only daughter, Maryanne's mother and father did not talk to each other. Though they loved her, they had nothing more in common. Her father had wept, Steely remembered. It was a strange thing for such a cold fish to do. He kissed his daughter, and then embraced her, hugging her for a long period of time so that people in the church began shifting their weight from foot to foot impatiently, waiting for the service to continue. She had told him that it was the first time her father had kissed her in her memory.

Maryanne was strong then, too, for she did not cry when her father left her in the middle of the aisle, just as she did not cry when Steely left her. It was as if she had resolved something in her mind, and her silence was common enough.

Just a few nights before, though, she had paced the bedroom floor, words streaming like tears and tears falling like streams, telling him all the things that she thought, that she said he did not have the courage to say. That he did not love her, that he did not want to live with her, or touch her, or look at her, that things were not as they thought they would be when they were in love.

"I saw the little marble tables," she told him, "at that bar in the Sherry-Netherland, and I heard Tony Bennett sing love songs at Radio City Music Hall, when you used to take me out, when you used to spend a buck, when you used to care. And once, we had paté at that restaurant in Greenwich Village, remember, when they came to our table and played the violins. And we went for weekends at Montauk. Not that we went *there*, not that that matters. It's that you planned it, you wanted to be places with me. Now you are just a drunk, Steely, and I think I've made you into that."

"I'm not a drunk," he protested. "Drunks drink every day. I only drink once in a while."

"*When*," she screamed, "*you have to come home to me, Steely, you get drunk. Don't come home anymore.*"

So it was good-bye Maryanne, Long Island City here I come, the poverty pad, a small studio in Queens with a view of the Fire

Department's shops, and the Queens-Midtown Tunnel, something for two-and-a-half yards a month, more than he could afford anyway, with ten roaches for every dollar.

It wasn't so much that she demanded that he leave. It was more a kind of request, a plea that he do something. *Something.* The kids can keep a marriage going for just so long, she said. She knew he loved the kids. She didn't question that. After that it always comes down to the man and the woman, and do they love each other?

"She wants money," Hadley said.

"So you give it to her," Steely replied. "Money should be the last problem. Either give her money or don't give her money, but make up your mind about it. You shouldn't ever waste time thinking, worrying about money."

Steely never had that problem with Maryanne. He held back the rent for the poverty pad, and gave her the rest.

"I give most of everything to the church group. I don't have a side job anymore."

Three firemen passed into the kitchen. "Quit your Jesus bullshit, Red, and get the meal up." The other two laughed.

Arbuckle McFatty was there, at the kitchen table. "You guys won't curse like that," he said, "with the lady firefighter Angelli around here, no sir. Things will begin to change tomorrow when she shows for the job."

Hadley shrugged his shoulders.

Steely felt sorry for Red Hadley just then. The guy really believed in something, he thought. No matter how far out and disconnected from the firehouse, the guy believes.

And things were not working out for Hadley, either.

Steely met his wife once, at a company dance. Her name was Katra. Probably Polish, too, or something near Russia. Her shiny blond hair fell invitingly over one eye, like an actress. Sexy. "I used to live in Aspen, Colorado," she told Maryanne. "There are five guys for every woman in Aspen."

The whole table looked at her then.

"So why are you living in New York now?" Maryanne asked. "You need a rest or something?"

Maryanne was great for saying things like that, for being clever. But a clever line every once in a while wasn't enough to make him want to hold her, to press his face into the flesh of her neck, and to whisper into her ear.

"She said she's going downtown to talk to the bosses," Hadley went on. "She said the bosses will get the money outta me. I told her the only way the bosses would get money outta me is to give me more to start with, but I'm not even on the lieutenant's list. The only thing she'll do is get me into trouble with the bosses."

"Why don't you take a loan?" Steely asked. "Give her a big chunk, tell her to take a walk."

"You wanna cosign, Steely?" Hadley asked.

Steely smiled. "Sorry I brought it up, pal."

Steely picked up the green plastic garbage bag that was folded over the edges of a steel can, tied it at the top, and carried it to the sidewalk in front of the firehouse. Outside, the heat was crusting the surface of the street tar. Steely dropped the bag onto a pile of similar bags near the gutter. It was noontime, and pedestrians were passing the firehouse on East Eighty-seventh Street as regularly as steel ducks in a shooting gallery, most of them in open-necked shirts, the men carrying their jackets on one finger over their shoulders. One passerby, a thin woman in a transparent blouse that covered a lacy red camisole, jumped as the voice-alarm system echoed loudly through the firehouse.

ENGINE FIVE, LADDER SEVEN RESPOND TO A TELEPHONE ALARM AT FIVE-NINE-ONE EAST NINETIETH STREET. BOX SEVEN-EIGHT-EIGHT.

Steely could smell the smoke as they reached Third Avenue going east, the particular smell of burning wood and plaster and paint that every fireman learns to identify as easily as a wine expert spots vinegar. He wished then that the woman was with them, Kathy Ryan Angelli, so that he could see what she could do. He knew there would be a job. It would be a test. Every job is a test in the Fire Department.

By Second Avenue, he could see the fish-gray smoke rising above the tenement roof, and as the fire truck bounced across the construction street coverings on First, Steely could see the front fire escape of a red-brick old-law tenement. It was filled with people.

He could not read their faces, but he knew who they were and he knew they understood the danger they were in, a crowd of people on strips of half-inch steel more than a half century old. They were the poor and the aged of Yorkville, the residue of what was once a working-class neighborhood, in the time before the Upper East Side of New York became chic and convenient for the educated and well-to-do. Pre-suburb blue-collar families, those who never got the four or five grand together for the down payment on a house in Patchogue, those who stretched out their years in rent-controlled security, and, especially among the older ones, now searched through the Gristede's, A&P, and Grand Union refuse on Friday nights before the Saturday binges, when the garbage of rejected fruits and vegetables was piled highest. Folks who could not get by on Social Security.

One thing you learn living in a tenement, Steely thought, and that is that the fire escape is the worst way to leave it.

He remembered being awakened several times in the middle of youthful nights by firemen who ushered him and his family to the back fire escape, left to shiver or sweat there until the firemen returned to tell them it was safe. Tenement life hasn't changed much. The people are still on the fire escape, their safety still unsure.

Steely saw a young woman hang from the bottom level of the fire escape as the truck neared York Avenue, and then drop the ten feet or so to the street. The hook holding the straight metal drop ladder had probably fused with age to the ladder, and the woman did what she thought she should do. Christ, he thought, doesn't she hear the siren? Christ. She got up, though, and shuffled away with just a slight limp, one without concern.

It was then he thought of Parnell Farrell, walking away from him, lifting her skirt to enter the cab, her calf muscles throwing seductive shadows down her legs. He sighed, thinking, I hope this job goes okay. I want to ride up the elevator to seventeen tonight.

Lieutenant Jackson was speaking into the radio as Steely stopped short in front of the burning five-story building. "Lieutenant Jackson, Ladder 7," he said, "transmit a second alarm on arrival at Box 788. There's a heavy smoke condition, fire in the cellar area, the fire escape jammed with people."

TEN FOUR, LADDER SEVEN, the returning voice echoed, cool and matter-of-factly.

Steely engaged the motor that operates the aerial ladder, leaped from the truck, and ran to the hydraulic panel, where he jammed the handles down and watched the heavy steel legs of the tormentors as they lowered to the street, digging into the tar, pushing down until all four wheels of the fire truck were off the ground. Beyond, he saw Lieutenant Jackson and two firemen go to the cellar of the building, carrying masks and tools.

He then climbed to the turntable and began to raise the heavy steel-gray ladder, watching its cable pull each lumber section upward.

Out of a corner of his eye he saw Hadley lifting a fifteen-foot hook to the fire escape and then climbing up on it as if he were a circus performer on a rope. He seemed to slide up, Steely thought, until he reached the fire escape fencing. He leaned over and gave the drop ladder a ferocious upward hammer with the palm of his opened fist. The ladder dislodged from its hook and fell with a crash to the pebbled concrete of the sidewalk.

I would not want to be hit by Red Hadley, Steely thought. He's got the power of a sledgehammer within. But, look at him, calming those folks on the fire escape, like a priest on a pulpit, a hand extended palm out, calming. From a long line of Polish generals, he was, as Steely watched, a poet as well as a warrior.

The smoke was pushing in spurts, pulsating, from the cellar entrance which was beneath the blue slate stoop. Every few seconds Hadley and the crowded fire escape would be smoke-hidden, and Steely could hear them coughing, choking on the thick, viscous gases which were now turning brown and yellow. Two firemen were lifting portable extension ladders to the fire escape, and disappeared into the smoke. God only knows what's burning in the basement of this old building.

Steely placed the ladder so that it barely touched the railing of the fifth-floor fire escape. Smoke was coming from several windows on the top floor, an indication that the fire had either extended up a shaftway to the top-floor ceilings, or more simply that the smoke had risen and would dissipate as soon as the firefighters ventilated the roof by opening the roof door, breaking the skylight, cutting a hole, or all three.

The ladder placement was to protect the building during the next few crucial minutes. From there he could raise it quickly to the roof, or lower it to pick up someone on a lower floor. It is never known what is happening inside a burning building until you're in it, and Steely was guessing now. He guessed the fire was traveling upward, and that the top floor was as close to hell as exists anywhere.

He leaned into a side cage on the turntable, pulled a mask out of its box, and threw the air bottle over his shoulder, clipping the harness together, as his eyes studied the building before him.

Suddenly he saw a shock of white hair appear in the smoke

flowing from a window on the far left of the building. Then he saw a hand, waving furiously, and just as suddenly it dropped, and disappeared from view.

Steely quickly moved the ladder to the window, being careful not to break it. If anyone was lying there, falling glass could take his life as surely as an out-of-control fire.

Steely placed the ladder hooks in position and began to climb the round, rubber-covered ladder steps. Halfway to the window on the fifth floor, he stopped momentarily, realizing that he had no tool in his hand, no halligan, no ax, nothing. Damn. In the excitement of seeing the white-haired figure disappear . . . no, not excitement, reaction. Spontaneous reaction. In reacting, he had forgotten a tool. It's all right, though. The white hair is what is important. The white hair, disappearing like foam on an ocean crest. Is it a man or a woman? Did he run, did he fall, was he pulled? Has the fire extended to the top floor?

There is the unknown of a fire, Steely thought, like going deep into a cave, dark blind, hearing your heart beat like thunder, as much an adventure as a risk, but always a confrontation. What's there? Is it a woman? Is it a man? Is he dead? What is the fire like? How hot? Smoky? Knife-edged, acid, boiling smoke? Got the mask, though, thank Christ for that.

He reached the stone edge of the windowsill, and stopped just below the whirling smoke pushing like an exhaust system from the inside of the apartment. This much smoke, the top floor had to be going, going good. But still, I've seen smoke worse than this with no fire showing. The smoke's got to go somewhere. Still . . .

He placed the mask's facepiece over his head, yanked the fastening tabs back, and pulled his helmet down snug on the top of his head. The bottled air seemed magical as he climbed over the top rung of the ladder and felt the floor of the apartment. He began to drop to his knees, but crouched instead and shoved a gloveless hand high into the air. It didn't seem too hot, and he raised himself, hand still held high, until he was erect. He pulled his hand down quickly then, for the air became suddenly hot above him. Fire, he thought. There's got to be fire up here. Goddamn. God. Search.

The room, as he walked into it, was night-black. A starless night. Nothing to see except black space. Empty. Like his life sometimes, he thought. Like driving home on a rainy night. Empty. Dismal.

Nothing to look forward to. Not Maryanne or the kids. Christ. Is it a man or a woman? Not by the window. Search the room. Clockwise circles. Miss nothing.

He went to his hands and knees, feeling before and around him. Over a bed, along a wall, in a closet, around a dresser, back to the window. Nothing. Under the bed. Nothing. The room was clean, but even darker if that was possible. Where was he? She? In the next room, the next car.

The next car, a phrase from youth, or more precisely from the dreams of youth. He remembered when he first learned the apartment he lived in was called a railroad flat, because the rooms, the three of them, were attached end to end. He envisioned that he lived on a train, going somewhere, always going somewhere, taking him away from the neighborhood, away from Johnnie Gimme, Pepe Peepee, Henny the Hebe, all of them. Not that they were bad guys. They weren't. Still, he dreamed his train was taking him farther than any of them could go, just a cut more, maybe a cut above. But Henny the Hebe was a rich man now, and Jack Haggerty was Chief of the Department. They had trains too, I suppose, faster ones. Christ, it's getting hot. Hotter.

Now he was in the next room, the second room in from the fire escape window. Steely recognized it immediately by feel, like a blind man. It was another bedroom. The heat was building quickly, too quickly, he thought. But the white-haired person was around here somewhere. The victim. The man, the woman victim. The dark, dank air was threatening around his facepiece. Where is the victim? *Where? Damnit, where?*

He first felt a pillow, then a narrow single bed, then a bureau, a standing metal closet. He supposed there was a mirror above the bureau, but what did it matter? He felt under the bed and rolled the mattress so that it was folded over lengthways. Another fireman would know by this that the room was given a primary search. Another fireman. Man, could it be? Did somebody get in here while I was climbing the ladder and . . .

He felt along the wall to a corner, and then along another wall. Two bedrooms, clean. The next room was the living room, or maybe the kitchen. The two bedrooms, clear. Shit. Holy shit.

Christ, the fire must be in the side walls and the ceiling. Flames had suddenly appeared before him, creating a strange flickering red

94

glow across the ceiling of the next room. Man. God. Retreat, he thought. Christ, back out.

Steely galloped on his hands and knees across the bedroom floor to the adjoining room, but he was stopped short by a terrific wave of heat that attacked his chest where his shirt and coat were opened, and his neck around the mask facepiece. It was as if he had fallen into a long and high pizza oven.

His mouth became dry, inexplicably, sexually dry, and his tongue began to stick to his hard palate as it did after frenzied lovemaking. God. Get the mask off. Things are not clear. No. Not the mask. The mask will *save* you. Holy goddammit. Save me. I'm in trouble here. Bad trouble.

He heard the crackle of the heat eating at wood and plaster. The front bedroom had burst into fire, the flames not now a red glow in the whirling smoke, but close and visible, each a torched tongue lapping out at anything and everything before it. A roomful of fire between him and the fire escape. The door. Was there a door? Is there a way out? Get something fast between me and that fire.

Steely lowered himself so that his belly was flat on the floor, and he inched himself forward, pushing his gloved hand out. He searched the side of the doorframe for a door. Thank God. Finding it, he shoved his fingers beneath the door and the floor, and pulled it as far as he could. Above him, he saw the edges of the fire leaping across the top of the door and into the room. He reached up then and pulled the door handle, forcefully, so that the door slammed, closing out the heat, if only temporarily, and stifling the hissing, the crackling, and the other murderous noises of the expanding fire.

His hand felt as if it were steaming. What now? Damn. His face was perspiration-covered and the facepiece of his mask was sliding back and forth, the smoke, just small whiffs of it, beginning to seep through. His eyes felt acid-burned, and his neck hurt where his shirt collar rubbed against it. He pulled the chin straps of his facepiece back forcefully. Fast, he thought. Gotta think fast.

The other adjoining room now had visible flames dripping like stalactites from the ceiling. Steely crawled to it and again found a door. This one opened into the bedroom, and with little effort he pushed it shut. He sat back momentarily against the bureau. The fire was dancing in each adjoining room, he knew, and he wondered why it had not yet broken through this room. A new ceiling, maybe.

The old one may have split, or fallen, and they put a new ceiling up, a modern fire-rated asbestos tile ceiling maybe. What does it matter. The walls. Feel the walls.

He moved to what he knew to be the outside wall and took off his glove. The wall was cool. Probably flat up against the bricks, without the studs. The sweat seemed to be running like water out of his facepiece. He went to the interior wall, the bearing wall probably. He felt it and jerked his hand away. Hot. But not so hot. He knew the feel when the fire was in the wall. It was hot because everything was hot, but there's no fire in that wall. Not yet.

Gotta get out. Damn, no tool. Even a screwdriver would help. An ax would go through the wall like a bulldozer.

Steely punched the wall with the bottom of his fist, but the old plaster-and-wire-lathe surface was as hard as steel, seemingly petrified with age. A pick. Something to pick with, he thought.

The air running from the tank on his back to his facepiece seemed less clear, less cooling. He felt his eyes tearing. Mother of God, am I going to buy it here, here in this old tenement where some forgotten old man, old woman, white-haired and skin-wrinkled, spent the days looking out of the windows? Oh Christ, where is that white-haired figure? The next room, probably. In the kitchen? The body now cooked beyond recognition? God almighty, how am I getting out of here?

He swept his hand across the bureau top, searching for anything long and hard and narrow, anything with a point, anything that could withstand a violent shock against the wall, anything that would pierce the formidable inch of plaster. Nothing. No scissors. No hunting knife. Damn. Knife. I have a jackknife. Try it anyway. Anything.

He opened the small knife and jammed the three-inch blade into the wall. The blade folded over into his glove. He tried to hold it open, but he had no leverage for force, and he only succeeded in scratching the wall.

Steely felt the heat pulling the energy from his body. The muscles in his arms were weakened, and they seemed deadened as he jabbed the knife into the plaster. He thought a small chip flew out of the wall. He couldn't see it, but he felt through his glove for a small indentation in the wall. Nothing.

Steely looked at the top of the doorframe and saw through the blackness that the wood was beginning to glow. It would burn through soon. He must not stop trying, banging, jabbing, kicking at the wall. He wished he could take his facepiece off. Perhaps he could see better then. Perhaps his face would cool, the sweat would dry up, become dry like his mouth. Time. The time was running fast, and against him.

He pulled a drawer from the bureau and swept his hand through it. Everything was soft and giving. Clothes. He dumped it and, on his knees now, he rammed one end of the drawer against the wall, hoping to crack it. But the wood was too thick and just caromed back. Nothing cut at all. But he kept on ramming it against the wall until the drawer fell apart, and then he took the longest piece of wood and rammed that forward. He had hardly any strength left in his arms, in his back. He wanted to lie down, to close his burning eyes, but the thought came to him that if he was going to buy it here, he would buy it kicking all the way. He would not let the fire just consume him without some movement, some violent response, and so he banged the wood against the wall repeatedly, like a madman, splintering the wood as much as shattering the plaster. God. Buy it in this old piece-of-crap tenement, this dingy old putrid room? God, no.

He listened to the blank thump each time he shoved the wood forward, and he heard between the thumps the hiss of the fire, glowing brightly now at the top of the doorframe. Then his shoulders gave out, and he realized he could not any longer put his weight behind the ramming, but he kept on throwing the wood forward, and pulling it back. The fire was now licking the ceiling above him. Nothing to look forward to. Not Maryanne. Not the kids. Ever again. Think of God, he said to himself. Think of God, goddammit, and this goddamned fire. Christ!

The heat was pressing down from above, the fire spreading across the ceiling.

It was then he heard the heavy thump, followed quickly by the cracking thump. Two extraordinary thumps and the wall came through, the shattered plaster edges smashing against Steely's facepiece like shrapnel. He fell back. It was okay. He closed his eyes, and felt the natural eye water glaze over them like a cold wet rag.

When he opened his eyes again he saw flashlight beams moving without direction through the hole in the wall. Then he felt someone grasp him under the arms and pull him toward the flashlight beams. He wasn't sure if he were conscious. He only knew that he was moving in stop-and-jerk motions, as if in a silent movie. And, he saw the fire flooding the ceiling from one end of the room to the other. He was buying it, he knew that, but he also knew he was being saved. A brother.

It was then he heard Red Hadley's voice. "I saw you go up the ladder," he said, pulling him between the upright studs in the wall. "And then I saw the room light up. But we got to you, Steely."

Steely couldn't talk. He was exhausted to semiconsciousness. But, he thought, if he could speak, he would yell, "You're great, Red, terrific."

And then he heard Hadley's voice again. "We have you, Steely," it said, "me and Jesus."

CHAPTER 12

HAGGERTY was annoyed. The hole in his buttock was smarting from the change of dressing Dr. Titlebloom had applied. He swore he didn't, but the big-nosed sneaky Arab poured peroxide on it, or ammonia. The dirty rug merchant. I wish I could transfer him up. To Surgeon General of the Police Department, maybe. I wonder if he would settle for the housing cops? Surgeon General of the New York City Housing Authority Police Department? Had a certain ring of importance to that, undoubtedly. When I become Commissioner, I'll be able to influence the Mayor toward that direction, perhaps.

Haggerty continually impressed himself by his ability to use the language, to manipulate it. *To influence the Mayor toward that direction.* A very smart-sounding phrase, he thought. He was pleased.

And any pleasure, as any port, was welcomed, for it was fast becoming a stormy day. Besides the smarting wound that he was now referring to as the Tiffany Hole, there was the Fire Commissioner. Both pains, both more than inconvenient.

Like ambassadorships to nonthreatening nations, Haggerty

thought, the office of Fire Commissioner was always a political and sometimes an economic balancing tool for the city government. It was the highest-salaried sinecure that existed among the thousands of patronage positions controlled by the Mayor. And, it was the easiest to fill, for the Fire Commissioner did not actually have to know anything. Indeed, it was a running joke around City Hall and the City Hall press room that the city had never had a fire commissioner who actually knew anything since the days of Chief Croker, who wrote a fairly accpetable essay on the courage of firemen. And that was at the turn of the century.

There are only three certainties in the world, Haggerty thought, that the sun will rise in the morning, that the dew will wet the grass, and that all civilian fire commissioners are inept jackasses, *civilian* being the operative word here. It was reassuring that Croker was a uniformed man and not a civilian, for Haggerty was a uniformed man also, and he intended to be the first commissioner in a long time who actually knew something.

And, he thought, what he knew was the inner workings of the Fire Department, the nuts and bolts of it, A to Z, for he had risen through every rank and worked in every kind of fire company from rescue to the boats in every borough, including Staten Island. Right? Even Staten Island, which was a pain in the neck to get to, where you needed a car.

Right. Not like Gore. Nicholas Gore. Neutral Nicholas Gore, attorney-at-law, the present Fire Commissioner Gore, the office-handed-to-him-on-a-silver-platter Gore. By the Borough President of the Borough of Brooklyn. The office of Fire Commissioner was always filled inexplicably and without historic reason through the machinations of Brooklyn politics. Though always through the mayor's office.

Nicholas Gore had stuck his head in Haggerty's office earlier in the day to say that he had cut a deal with the City Gas and Electric Company to approve polyurethane-lined oil tanks for the company's storage facility in Queens. In exchange for this approval, CG&E would donate five thousand balloons to be released at the next Fire Department Awards Day Ceremonies in front of City Hall.

There was more than balloons involved in the negotiations, Haggerty felt sure, for why else would he take the time to pop his phony joyful head through the Chief of Department's door?

"It will be a festive touch, and the Mayor likes pizzazz," Gore had said. "Five thousand multicolored balloons! A rainbow floating up to the sky!" Maybe now was the time, Haggerty had thought, to advance the cause of Captain Petrullo and the rest of the Italian-Americans being boxed out of the battalion chief's test. Maybe talk well of the Apogee Mask Company, too. But the Commissioner was too fast, and left him no room to develop a sensible *quid pro quo*. "So," the Fire Commissioner had continued, "we should formally withdraw the Department's opposition to the polyurethane tanks, if you would please send a letter to that effect to the Board of Estimate."

He was so polite, old Neutral Nicholas. There'll be more concentrated polyvinyl chloride poison in those tanks than anywhere else in the world, but you got to hand it to him. He did it for balloons! What any fire department or buildings department would reject right out of hand, he gets through for balloons! He just smiles and gets off a polite line, says please, and I write the letter. As if I believe that the balloons are in the best interest of the Fire Department. But he won't get the best of Jack T. Haggerty. Uh-uh. Living well is revenge enough. *Per instructions of the Fire Commissioner*, I'll write. Lot of dead cats in that bag, and I won't be caught carrying it.

The Department radio, a large gray one that sat on the cream-painted windowsill, bellowed a static message through Haggerty's office. SECOND ALARM, it announced, AT MANHATTAN BOX SEVEN EIGHT EIGHT, TIME THIRTEEN-OH-TWO HOURS. Just another second alarm, he thought, two a day every day, at least. He adjusted the small pillow beneath his Tiffany Hole and began to look through the correspondence in his in basket. Neutral Nicholas the Nabob of Know-nothingness, he said to himself, laughing beneath the shuffling of papers.

Goodness, he thought, I love what can be made of a name. Nicholas the Notable Nobody, notable implied by the word *honorable* that goes summarily before the given name of all commissioners. Or Nicholas the Neurotic. No, not neurotic. Nicholas is too vague and undefined to be neurotic. Neurotic would convey something substantive about Nicholas.

There is so much in a name. Everyone growing up on the East Side had a name. Joey Guttergrate, Henny the Hebe, Steely the Testicular, doing a jackknife off the wall of the Fifty-seventh Street park, forty-five feet, easy, into the East River. Helmet Head von

Steubal, God grant him peace, whose father had a butcher shop on First Avenue and cut Helmet Head's hair every Sunday morning before church. Frankie Stoopball, who on a good day could make as much money playing *off the point* as the neighborhood bookie made taking numbers.

Those good old names. Pepe Peepee, a sergeant today in the Police Department. What was the rhyme about him, though? Pepe Peepee peed in a pew? The last pew of St. Aloysius, right after the eleven o'clock. Oh, that was good, and the priest caught him at it.

> Pepe Peepee peed in a pew
> Phew, phew, said Father McGrew.

If he could have, the old priest would have made a Protestant of Pepe. A sergeant today, God forgive him.

The phone buzzed, but Haggerty did not answer.

And me, he continued in his thoughts, old Ivory Mouth himself, no cursing, no taking the Lord's name in vain or otherwise. Keep-it-clean Haggerty. I loved it when they called me Ivory Mouth, loved all the old names and the good sportsmanship and the loyalties that went along with them. You weren't one of the guys unless you had a name. Funny, though. Nicholas. Neutral Nicholas can have a name, but he could never be one of the boys. You can see through him. You could never see through the neighborhood guys.

The buzzer startled him this time, made him sit upright, forcing the hard edge of the pillow into the Tiffany Hole. "Ouch," he said into the phone.

"Excuse me, Chief?" Captain Steinf said. "What did you say?"

"What is it, Captain?"

"I said, 'what did you say?' "

Captain Steinf is such a nuisance, Haggerty thought, always trying to get in the last word, or butting in inappropriately, or even eavesdropping. I'm sure he must listen in on my calls. I wish I could get rid of him, get rid of all these day workers who serve at the pleasure of the Fire Commissioner. When I become Commissioner, I'll ask them all to submit their transfer requests. Better yet, I'll make it an unwritten Department policy. Just like when a new president is elected and the cabinet members and the department heads automatically tender their resignations. I'll create something called the tendered transfer tactic and get rid of the whole pack of lazy good-for-nothings. Particularly Steinf, that little bit of a pouchy, baldheaded man, going around limping, telling people he got injured at a Bedford-Stuyvesant fire when he was a lieutenant, going over to see Titlebloom every few months to secure his disability pension. I must remember to check into the record of his injury one day, just to see if I can help things along with his retirement, though he probably has it sewn up with Dr. Titlebloom already. Maybe I can find a way to get him to submit his papers early, and go push shuffleboard pucks around in Florida.

"That will be enough, Captain," Haggerty said in a stern, business-only tone. "What do you want?"

"There's a woman here, Chief."

"Well?"

"Uh, she wants to see you."

"Do you care to write me a note, Captain, or do you think you can be more communicative?"

"She's . . . well, Chief, she's got a gun, you know?"

"She's . . . is she threatening you?"

"No, she just told me she has a gun in her pocketbook, and that she's gonna have her hair all matted with blood right here in the office if you don't see her. She's got nice hair, Chief, blond."

Haggerty was immediately impressed by Katra Hadley's bosom as she walked into the office. Monsignor Flynn's maid, he thought, was an Olive Oyl in comparison. He was used to living a life without breasts, for Mrs. Haggerty was as flat-chested as they come. As flat as the palm on Palm Sunday. He never thought much about it, never complained, not even to himself. The woman before him, though, had classical breasts, he thought, shaped as if they had been molded from a new magic plastic. He could even see her brassiere clearly. She was wearing a glittering bra beneath a thin yellow blouse tightly tucked into a plain blue skirt. Each breast flashed like the nose of an airplane. Haggerty moved uneasily in his chair, causing a sharp pain from his Tiffany Hole to shoot down his leg. She smiled wordlessly, seeing his face flashing reds and pinks.

Captain Steinf had limped in behind her.

"Do you have a gun, miss?" Haggerty asked. "I'd like to see it."

Katra Hadley placed her handbag on the desk. "I made it up," she said. "Look for yourself. I went to so many offices today, and talked to so many firemen who gave me the runaround, that I had to invent something."

103

Haggerty looked through the handbag, noticed a Tampax, and guessed that she might be a little bit loony. Funny things happen to women at that time of the month. Haggerty believed sincerely that the menstrual cycle brought on chemical imbalances which made a woman think and behave erratically. In fact, he even had the Department lawyers write a supporting brief to use in the litigation the department instituted to keep women out.

There was no gun in the bag, though, and her clothing hugged her so tightly there was no place to hide a gun on her person. Between her legs, perhaps. No, she didn't look the type for that sort of business. She appeared harmless enough. Harmless enough so that it seemed safe to dismiss Steinf anyway.

"That will be all, Captain," Haggerty said.

"If I could stay, Chief, I think it would be beneficial to make me a party to this interview, until we know what the lady wants." Captain Steinf looked solicitous, and pitiful.

"Please close the door on the way out, Captain," Haggerty said sarcastically.

Katra Hadley took the slamming door as an invitation to sit. She crossed her legs and pulled the hemline of her skirt just slightly above her knee. Haggerty looked at a large photograph of his wife that obstructed his view. He moved it from one side of his desk to the other.

"Thank you," Katra said. For what, the Chief wondered?

"Why are you here, miss?"

"Mrs. I'm married to a fireman."

"Yes."

"Mrs. Rudolf Hadley."

"Yes."

"Ladder 7 in Yorkville."

"Yes."

"Katra is my first name."

"Mrs. Hadley." Haggerty wrote the name on a yellow legal-sized pad. She looked like she might have a story that would require a legal-sized pad.

"I came to see you because I walked the halls and saw *Chief* on the door. You're the Chief?"

"I am the Chief of Department, the highest uniformed rank in the Department."

"Chief?"

"Haggerty."

"Pleased to meet you, I'm sure. I've been to the Personnel Office downstairs, but they told me I have to write a letter. I need the money now. I don't have time to write a letter to some clerk in the Fire Department like they said I should do."

She uncrossed and crossed her legs. This time Haggerty saw the muscles in her thighs. Why, he asked himself, was he suddenly so interested in the thighs of a woman? Why was he thinking of sex in the middle of the business day? It was a mortal sin. No doubt about that.

"Money," he said. "What money do you need?"

"The money he's been giving to Jesus. I left him because of it, took the TV and the ironing board and all. I can't take it anymore. I mean, I don't mind putting a couple of bucks in the basket at the ten o'clock at Assumption, but this other stuff, forget it."

Haggerty hardly heard anything she said, so preoccupied was he now with her oscillating chest, swelling as she paused to breathe between sentences. "Something about money?" he asked.

"The money he gives to the Jesus freaks, to Roberto. You heard of Moses on the mountain? This is Reverend Roberto of the roof-tops. He's all the rage among your firemen, you know."

She lit a cigarette and blew all the smoke through her nose. He smiled at her as she took another puff and began to swing her crossed leg up and down. Was she masturbating, he wondered? He remembered one of the guys in grammar school saying that's the way girls masturbate, and weren't they lucky they could do it out in the open, in public?

"I'm not sure I ever heard of him Miss, ah, Mrs. . . . ."

"You can call me Katra."

"I know of no rage among my firemen."

"I was being sarcastic. Sorry."

"Are you a Catholic?"

"Went to Cathedral High School when it was on Lex and Fifty-first."

"And your husband belongs to a Protestant organization, is that right?"

"You kidding? Even the Baptists have a roof to keep the rain out. These Jesus guys meet in the park, on stoops, in the open spaces.

105

Like the Sermon on the Mount, is what they say. They're not organized enough to be Protestant."

"Is your husband a Catholic?"

"He used to be."

"Well Miss, ah, Katra." Haggerty smiled at the familiarity of calling her by her given name, and leaned across the desk toward her. "A Catholic is a Catholic, always, unless excommunicated."

"He don't care about that."

"We will talk to him about being a Catholic. Being a Catholic has special responsibilities that perhaps we can help him remember."

"Can you help him remember his responsibilities," she said, her eyebrows raising, "in terms of hard cash to me, eighty-five a week? I've got the rent and all."

Haggerty rose from his chair, grimaced a little as the skin of his buttocks shifted, and walked to her chair. Standing above her, he stared down at the the milky glow of her skin.

"Religious responsibilities," he said. "Moral responsibilities, social responsibilities, they're all the same. I'll have him down here, talk to him."

Funny, he thought. This woman has me groveling. What is it about her that has me going on like this, fawning like a teenager and leering at her like an ordinary peeping Tom? Katch-me Katra, is that it? Does she know exactly what she is doing, this woman? Goodness, what a body. Josie would kill me if she knew what I am thinking.

Katra leaned over and scratched the calf muscle of her sculptured leg. She then moved her hand slowly to her knee, and just above her knee so that her skirt was pushed back higher on her thigh.

"Will you let me know, then?" she asked. "Should I call you?"

"Yes," Haggerty answered, "call me. A week or so. Maybe you could come down, and we could go have lunch or something."

She smiled tentatively. "If you want," she said, uncrossing her legs and standing, the lines of her body curving in and out as if they had been drawn by a computer. "Or," she whispered, "you can call me. I'm at the Hotel Seville, Twenty-ninth Street."

Haggerty sat on the end of his desk, the Tiffany Hole hanging untouched over the edge, and watched Katra Hadley leave his office and then the outer office. The department's radio squawked a message: AT SECOND ALARM. BOX SEVEN-EIGHT-EIGHT, FIVE-NINE-ONE EAST NINETIETH STREET. FIRE IS UNDER CONTROL. WE HAVE ONE

INJURED FIREMAN, REMOVED TO NEW YORK HOSPITAL, AND ONE DOA, CIVILIAN, FEMALE APPROXIMATELY SEVENTY YEARS OF AGE.

But Haggerty did not hear the message. He was writing a reminder note on a pad. In attractive, self-taught calligraphy, he wrote "Hotel Seville."

CHAPTER 13

"**S**TOP it, Maryanne."

Steely was yelling into the phone, the exasperation thick in his voice. "Stop arguing with me. I'm fine. Do not call one of my brothers to drive in here. They just want to check me over, and I'll be out in the morning."

He hated the Department doctor for getting his, or Maryanne's, Levittown telephone number from the Department's notification card, and for calling her, to reassure her that her husband was not dead, only temporarily hospitalized. He'd have to remember to change that card, to scrawl *Separated* across it. Maybe he'd add *Call only if expired.*

A hobbled man leaning against the wall next to the pay phone hit Steely in the leg with an aluminum crutch. "C'mon, mister," the man said. "I been waitin' since Tuesday."

Steely put his hand over the phone and looked the man hard in the eyes. "Go pull on your pudding, pal," he said.

He continued then into the phone, "I'll call you in the morning, Maryanne. I'm going to hang up . . . Would I have this much energy to argue with you if I wasn't all right? Good-bye, no problem, good-bye."

Would he call, he asked himself? Probably not. She knows I'm not dead. She still cares, a lot, I could feel it in her voice. Poor Maryanne.

Steely walked briskly through the hall toward his room, thinking, Parnell Farrell here I come, apartment seventeen, until seven in the morning. I'm yours. The whole world knows I'm yours. I just gotta check out to check in.

The nurses' station was a little port of activity. Doctors and nurses, on the phones, banging metal charts, writing reports. It was seven o'clock. The evening after-dinner wrap-up was taking place, and one would be pilled and needled and tucked away safely for the night. And if one died without complaint during the night, at least one's record would be up-to-date for the morning check. Steely stopped at the high Formica counter, before a nurse who was evidently waiting on the end of a telephone for an answer. She seemed bored.

"How do I check out of here?" he asked.

Her eyes brightened as she looked him up and down. "You're the fireman?" she asked in return. She had a low and almost cackling voice.

"Yes," Steely said, "and there's no point in sticking around, because I feel great."

"Huh," she grunted. "You are innocent and naive."

"What's that mean?"

"It means that you were signed in by a Fire Department doctor and you'll be signed out by a Fire Department doctor. That's how you 'check out,' as you put it." The nurse conveyed a look of defiance by stretching her lips far to one side of her face and staring at the bridge of his nose.

This was a real Miss Bittercrotch, Steely thought. Not the kind who brings sunshine and a picnic basket everywhere she goes.

Steely looked at her in return as pleasantly as he thought possible and shook his head up and down. "Well," he uttered with a smile, "I think I'll just leave anyway."

"Innocent," she said again. "You'll never make it to the elevator a security guard doesn't tie a rope around you. It's the law, fireman. A doctor signs you in, a doctor signs you out."

109

In his room, Steely eyed his roommate, a post-op case, face covered with bandages. The bandages, Steely had been told, hid 180 stitches. That is what it took to repair the damage inflicted by the bullet-proof safety shield of a taxicab after the taxicab hit the concrete safety divider on the East River Drive approach to the Triborough Bridge. Steely then looked at the telephone on the small table next to his roommate's bed. He wondered if his companion was sleeping beneath the cotton strips, and if he was not sleeping, would he let Steely use his telephone?

Why ask, Steely questioned himself, knowing that he would use the phone with or without approval. The call he wanted to make was not the sort of call to be made from a public phone in a public corridor.

Steely dialed the Police Department. What name should I give, he asked himself as the phone rang? What doctor do I know?

A woman answered.

"Hello," Steely said in a feigned alarmist tone, "this is Dr. Seuss on the fourth floor of the New York Hospital, Sixty-eighth Street entrance. There is a man with a gun, threatening murder in the fire stairs at the end of the public corridor on this floor. Come quickly."

Steely hung the phone up, and heard muffled moans coming from beneath his roommate's bandages. He leaned over the gauze. "What was that?" he asked.

"A moon with a goon," he heard.

"A moon with a goon?" Steely repeated. "Oh, you mean a man with a gun." He said this very distinctly, and then he heard a shrill, muffled yell.

"Here?" the voice said.

Steely nodded gravely. "Are you Italian, pal?" he whispered.

"No," the voice answered.

"You're okay then," he said, walking to the closet where his smoke-stained clothes were hanging. "Just Italians get gunned down in hospitals and barber shops. You have nothing to fear, except the darkness."

Steely dressed and sat on the edge of his bed watching his roommate search frantically for the nurse's call button. Steely had placed the call button under his roommate's mattress.

Firemen with line-of-duty injuries, he thought, should get a private room. Right! Break your hump for this city and they put you in a room with the invisible man.

He listened to the sirens traveling down Sixty-eighth Street, and to the screeching tires as the police arrived at the front of the hospital. He heard other sirens. Maybe Patrolman Murphy was risking his life to get to the alarm, he thought with satisfaction. False alarms happen to the firemen more than seven hundred times a day. What's one to the cops? Not much. Goddamn Murphy, going to press charges over a little altercation. Maybe Murphy would be running here now. Justice.

He bent down and wrapped the thick laces around the ankles of his safety boots and tied them as he listened to the commotion in the corridor. He watched the police, the doctors, and the nurses rush by his room, and then he walked slowly, unassumingly, to the staff elevator at the end of the corridor and pressed the button. In the elevator, two physicians had suspicious gleams in their eyes. Steely nodded to them, looked at his watch, saying, "Another day, another dollar."

The physicians smiled. Mentioning money to a doctor, he thought, will always elicit the same level of interest as mentioning free soup to a starving man.

Steely looked for Red Hadley in the firehouse cellar, in the kitchen, in the upstairs commode stalls. Nowhere. He asked the fireman on housewatch duty.

"Two young girls came to pick him up in a white van," the fireman said. "They had the back filled with flowers, roses mostly."

"Jesus freaks?"

"Something like that."

"Kids, huh? Nice?"

"Chests out to the steering wheel," the fireman said, gesticulating.

"Maybe it pays off, this Jesus stuff," Steely joked, though he was disappointed that he had missed Hadley.

Steely took a shower and changed into a clean shirt and khaki pants. He rubbed an overdose of Habit Rouge into his clean-shaven face, a smoke-stained bottle he had picked up in the rubble of a fire.

He'd see Hadley in a couple days, assuming he got off medical leave. Talk to him. Thank him? No, just talk to him enough so he knows he was there. The *mark* of a man, to be there. He's that kind of guy. Let him know I know that. Enough so that we're together from now on, in everything that comes up. Together.

Steely took the Lexington Avenue bus and flashed his tin to the

111

bus driver. The driver nodded. No argument. The city will never know the real consequences of laying off a third of the work force during the financial crisis. Cops and firemen were no longer permitted to ride the subways and buses without charge. But who cared? The personal security wasn't there in any city job anymore since Father Knickerbocker let them sink or swim, laid them off by the thousands. Why should anyone go the extra yard? Days off without a mark, long lunches and sometimes longer coffee breaks to do errands, read half the applications and stamp them anyway, let them ride the buses for free, and ride the great iron snake, too, on the badges. Steal a token here, a token there, patch six potholes a day instead of sixty, bang the garbage cans and wake the kids up, run the red lights. It's hard to care about someone who doesn't care about you. Father Knickerbocker used to care, before the bankers, before the Rand Corporation and the think-tank approach to government, where the little guys got sat on and the big guys lied their way to bigger jobs.

He sat at the front of the bus, sliding down into the hard blue plastic crater, which had a "Disabled Only" sign on it, and saw the Chrysler Building in the distance. He framed the fluorescent pyramids of the building's peak between the hedgerows of three-story buildings on either side of the avenue so that it appeared to be a light at the end of a tunnel, or some bright surprise at the end of a circus fairway.

He turned and studied the faces on the other side of the bus. Mostly old, folks who no longer had the spirit to ride the subways after dark, or any time. The city's buses were for the elderly between and after the rush hours, the geriatric jitneys for the afraid.

And the blacks. In the back of the bus there were blacks smoking cigarettes or reefers, fondling cans of Colt 45 in brown paper bags, one with a ghetto guitar, tuned to a Motown screeching station, the sound four times the level of annoyance. Who cares? Not the drivers. They get a knife wound or a gun barrel when they care. He heard one bus driver say one day to a complaining woman, white, middle class, Upper East Side, "Listen, lady, if they were turning marijuana into gold like in Rumpelstiltskin I wouldn't give them a second look."

Ratty music. He wouldn't care so much if it were Mantovani, early Beatles, like that.

If a disabled person gets on the bus, he thought, I'll give up the seat. Like a good citizen.

Ride it out, four more blocks to Parnell Farrell, apartment seventeen, thirty-four years old, the sweet memories of the East Side. How should I play it with her? Parnell. Make it with her fast. Between-the-sheets time. Why else would she invite me up? She's in a different league now, though, he thought, living where she does. But there's still nothing to stop a direct attack on the pubes. Straight for it like a bee to nectar.

The elevator stopped on the seventeenth floor. The blood-faced operator pulled the brass door back, saying, "Have a nice evening, mister."

Steely wondered if there was a hint of irony in the voice. Was the man being friendly, or was he one of those Irish busybodies who squint behind curtains and through venetian blinds?

There was just one door in the hall. It was open, and behind it stood Parnell Farrell. She held both hands out to him. She wore a green dashiki, made of silk and loose-fitting. It flowed over her. The sleeves were short and wide, and he could see the skin of her body beneath as she raised her arms.

He moved in close to kiss her, but she averted the advance by sweeping her hand grandly around the room. "I hope you like it," she said.

The room, and the carpeting, were gray. The walls, from the floor halfway up to the ceiling, were fronted by Lucite shelving, covered with glass figurines, books, a micro stereo and such things, except for one wall, next to a large picture window, which was mirrored. The mirror brought the view of Central Park and the Hudson River into the room. There were two green Chinese-print couches facing each other, separated by a green marble coffee table that sat low to the floor. The green matched her dashiki. The whole looked to Steely like a department-store room, the kind you might see bordered by red velvet ropes in Bloomingdale's.

He walked to the window. "It's a great panorama, Parnell," he said.

"Farrell," she corrected. "I'm not used to people calling me anything but Farrell anymore."

"Farrell," he said, returning his gaze to the view. Farrell, huh? Right! Someone new. New name, new lifestyle. You may be wasting

113

your time here, Steely, he told himself, but be aggressive anyway. You'll find out easily enough.

"I can see where I'd want to live if I were single-o," he said.

"Where is that?" she asked, moving next to him before the window, and looking down at the wall-rimmed foliage, lakes, and ponds of the park.

"Right over there," he replied, pressing a finger against the window. "On the West Side, over by Columbus Avenue. I get detailed every once in a while to a firehouse over there just off Columbus, where all the broads go braless, big artist types and musicians, bodies like bags of basketballs, their breasts bouncing up and down when they walk, like jeeps on a rocky road."

"That appeals to you, women with no underwear?" She looked at him quizzically.

"It's all sex on the West Side," he answered matter-of-factly. "Mr. Goodbar turf. Everyone has a shrink who tells them they have to come to grips with their sex lives. You can make out there. On the East Side, here, you gotta be somebody to make out, a lawyer, a rich guy anyway, to get them to talk to you."

"Is that what's important to you, Steely? Making out?"

He turned to her and held her shoulders. "I remember making out with you, Parn . . . ah, Farrell."

"So," she said.

"It was important. It's important now."

"Is that why you called, why you're here?"

"Hey, Farrell," he said, turning from her. He felt suddenly threatened, and he looked nervously for a friendly place to sit. "I was going to go heavy after you, huh? You want to beat me to the punch?"

Parnell Farrell made drinks as Steely sat on one of the couches. She laughed easily, commandingly, as she placed a drink before him and sat on the opposite couch.

"I won't play games with you, Steely," she said, placing her drink carefully on a silver and glass coaster. "I will just tell you a couple of things, and then I will take you into my bed."

His eyes went wide and bright, and his heart fluttered. She's too sure of herself, this woman, Steely thought. But what am I going to say? No one without a major brain operation would say *no*. And, she knows it. She's got me, and I don't know what to say exactly. Keep it straight, keep it on her level.

He felt the sexual stirring within his body as she kicked off her gold sandals and placed her legs beneath her.

"I'd listen to *War and Peace*," he answered, "if I thought your bed was at the other end."

"Not that long," she beamed, picking up her glass and gesturing it in salute. "But as interesting."

She sat back, then closed her eyes momentarily, and began to talk, without pause, as if it were a practiced monologue.

"I've just had three loves in my life, Steely," she said, looking down at the drink in her hands, but then directing her gaze straight into his eyes. "You were the first, though you never knew it. The first love, the first sex."

"You could've told me that," he said. "You never told me."

Parnell Farrell grinned slightly, as if lost in a remembrance. She then continued, "The second was a man I met when I stepped out of the rain into the Bull and Bear Restaurant at the Waldorf Astoria. I was working as a secretary in a four-comma-name law office earning enough money to pay the rent on my mother's apartment on Forty-eighth Street. The man fell in love with me. I liked him at first, then loved him. He bought an apartment for me on Sutton Place. Sixty South. He sent me thousand-dollar bills for dresses and jewelry the way some men make phone calls to say hello. Then it was ten thousand a month until his wife found out. It almost made page five of the *Daily News*."

Steely began to rise from the couch, to move to her side. Better get there soon, he thought, before she changes her mind. That's big, that kind of money. Couple of gin and tonics is high enough stakes for getting it on. Ten grand is for Hollywood producers.

"Meantime," she continued, "he told me to invest in the medical technology companies. 'People will always be dying,' he told me, 'with the hope of life in their hearts.'"

"That's nice," Steely said.

"It was good advice, and it paid for the view from these windows. He also taught me which fork to use for the salad, and which dress to wear to the races. Life has different levels, Steely."

"Yeah," Steely said uncomfortably, "where does that leave me?"

"Would you care about which fork to use, Steely?"

"I was raised in a tenement. If the food don't jump off the plate I'm going to eat it any way I can."

"That's the Steely I remember."

"Who's the third, Farrell?"

She suddenly became sad, her lips curved downward, and he saw the lines at the side of her eyes extend. "He loved me like men love women in great books. A man who designed things, furniture, and magazines, clothes, machines. We did everything together, and I worshiped him. We were to be married, but he died suddenly of a virus. He began to sweat one day, the next day he was paralyzed, the following day he died."

"Like Joey Guttergrate," Steely said. "Do you remember him?"

She did not answer, but shook her head, as if to say no.

Steely wanted to kiss the tears that were building at the corner of her eyes, though he didn't. He was unsure of himself, unsure of how to comfort.

"That's pretty tough," he said.

"It was a long time ago, Steely," she said, recovering. "It's way behind."

She wiped her eyes with her little finger, and rose from the couch. She walked to him, holding her hand out, and saying, "You're here, aren't you? It's a nice surprise."

He followed her through a long hall, past several rooms, and into her bedroom, which faced east. He could see the East River and the Queensboro Bridge beyond a tufted blue silk boudoir chair.

"Now I am a date," she said, pulling the dashiki over her head. "A very comfortable, a very correct, and a very expensive date."

"What does that mean?" Steely asked as he followed the curves of her body. "You a kept woman or something?"

"Ha," she laughed, pulling the blue paisley bedspread down and lying, her head propped up by one hand, on the white woolen blanket. "Not quite. It means that I can pay the expenses of what you see around me, and that I enjoy life. Fully."

In bed, naked, Steely held her as tightly as he remembered ever holding a woman. He held her and breathed in her fragrance, the smell like a rush, a high that made his heart beat faster. She felt taut and smooth to him, like the young girls he dreamed about in adolescence. I wish I were drunk, he thought, or stoned. Yes, stoned, so my lips would get dry, so that her odor would become part of me, and the saliva would bubble like quicksand. She was so different a woman from Maryanne, or anyone else he had known for that matter. Maryanne. Christ in heaven, why think of Maryanne?

He kissed her fully on the mouth, and she licked his lips and circled the opening of his mouth, her warm, sweet breath flowing up over his nose and into his memory. Few kisses ever smelled and tasted so natural and fruitlike. Maryanne never kissed him like that, never moved her tongue out of her mouth. Never tasted as good.

"Farrell," he whispered between breaths. "Farrell."

She made him feel like a teenager again, as if awakening for the first time to the potential of the body, the moisture, the rhythms. She sat up quickly and leaned against a pillow, pulling him up gently. She kissed him softly and bent over. He leaned back against the headboard, as if ready to receive breakfast and the Sunday newspaper, remembering the way Maryanne would bounce into the bedroom on weekends, when they were just married, before there were children, and how they made love in the mornings after breakfast. He looked at Parnell Farrell, at the tracklike shadows that ran from her neck down her spine, and he received her mouth as he whispered "Farrell." He counted the seconds.

Soon she lay back, her eyes closed, her long legs undulating slowly from side to side. He kissed her mouth. "Kiss my breasts," she said, and he did. He kissed her mouth again. She held his hand and guided it down past her stomach, and he slid his fingers across the lubricated folds beneath her sparse silky hair. She sighed and repeated, "Kiss my breasts, Steely." He kissed her breasts again. She put a hand on his neck, and he thought he felt a downward pressure. He licked the flat of her chest between her breasts, and she slid her hand beneath his and caressed herself, her legs prancing faster from side to side. She was moaning. "Yes," she said, "kiss my breasts." He brought his mouth down to her stomach, wanting to kiss her fingers, but he could not. Maryanne had asked him once to kiss her there, in the shadow of her thighs, but he could not, not then, not ever. Not now, either, even with this woman who smelled so good, like sweets. Instead, he moved his head up, and watched Farrell's hand racing as he kissed her breasts once more. He kissed her breasts, and thought of Maryanne. Maryanne would never do that, never touch herself like that. "Oh, Farrell," he yelled, and he rolled over onto her, moving her hand away, inserting himself quickly into her.

The pulsing lasted just a few seconds, the thought so strong in his mind of a woman feeling and rubbing herself. His mouth dry, his breathing nearly uncontrolled, he sank his face into her neck. "Farrell," he called. "Farrell."

Farrell said nothing.

Afterward they lay looking at the ceiling. A warm towel was draped across his groin. She smoked one of his Marlboros, a cut-glass ashtray on her stomach.

"You want to talk about it, Steely," she said, just above a whisper.

"It was great," he said, "really great."

"You don't know, do you, Steely," she said more than asked. "You don't know just how few times in a woman's life she'll allow herself to be brought to that point of sexual need where she forgets or shelves just for the moment all those reservations, fears, taboos."

"Come on, Farrell," he said, "it was great."

"Do you remember the day I first laid you, Steely? Did I ever tell you that was the day my father told my mother and me that he was splitting, moving to Newark with some whore, and I cried and then walked down to the river and saw you. I always liked you, and there you were, and I needed something, someone. You were there then, at least, Steely. But now? Now, you just missed it."

Steely sat up in the bed, indignant. "What do you mean, I missed it? Missed what?"

Parnell Farrell smiled with resignation and crushed the cigarette in the ashtray. "I was at the point where I would have done anything for you, Steely, and I asked you to kiss my breasts. Three times I asked you to kiss my breasts."

"I did."

"And you didn't know what I was talking about. You didn't feel it in me."

"What?"

"Desire, Steely, desire. How embarrassing it is for a woman to be there and to return empty. I was there, Steely, at the peak."

"I did it. I kissed your breasts for chrissake."

Parnell Farrell got out of the bed and put on a blue, floor-length dressing gown. A golden peacock was hand-stitched on its back. She switched on the television set that sat on a shining brass stand.

"That's not what I meant, Steely. Women don't say it, they gesture the need. I said please, Steely, and you were not smart enough to hear it. I gestured the need, and you made love like a fireman on the way to an alarm."

CHAPTER 14

E. P. Dolan, president and chief executive officer of the E. P. Dolan and Company investment firm, reached across the table and patted Jack Haggerty on the arm. "It will be all right, Jack," he said, "God willing."

"It's not," Haggerty said, "that the church would find a need to suggest a new Fire Commissioner solely because the present one is a Protestant."

"Certainly not," Dolan said, leaning an arm on the back of the green and yellow cane chair. He opened the small, elegant Lutece matchbox and struck a wooden match, lighting a Corona Coronet.

Haggerty noticed Dolan's little finger extending out from the other four as the hand approached the cigar. The gesture of lighting the cigar was incongruous and phony, exaggerated, as if the floating finger were flashing in neon. Castle-conscious, is what the Irish in the old neighborhood called the phony actions of the upwardly mobile, the lace on their windows real or not. E. P. Dolan's family once could have been called Irish Catholic, but like many of the German Jews that found gold in New York streets, the family became something else. Not ethical culturists like the Jews who left the temple. No, the Dolans were still with the church, but they looked at it all now like Protestants. Religion was something that was done to give a good appearance, and like the extended finger of E. P. Dolan's hand, appearance was everything. The Dolan family might be Irish and Catholic, but that was a far throw from being Irish Catholic. Two different kinds of people. A sea of wealth and social status separated the two, the Dolans having risen like cardinals to the purple.

Dolan's voice was as thick and slow-moving as sludge, and, though he meant no harm, had an edge of condescension that reminded Haggerty of an English butler in a 1940s movie.

He talked and acted like a man who was heavily sedated, a little too queer and lazy to be effective at anything except what the family firm provided for him through inheritance, which was the position of social liaison with both the Archdiocese of New York and the Archdiocese of Brooklyn. E. P. Dolan and Company was the institution that handled, for three generations, the big Catholic money in the city, most of which belonged to the church, and young E. P. was sent to Exeter and Harvard so that he would be prepared to make deals with smart young priests from Fordham and St. John's, and to secure a fourth generation of Dolans within the silken red folds of a cardinal's favor.

Dolan also liked fire engines, and, like Fiorello LaGuardia and Arthur Fiedler, God rest them, was a fire buff. But it was really the communion of church real estate and financial interests that made lunch with a fireman at a restaurant as upscale as Lutece possible.

Haggerty loved Lutece, the cane chairs, the small sit-down bar, the bursting palm plants and the skylighted openness of the inner room, and especially, the extravagant prices on the menu. Two hundred easy, with the Hultgren and Samperton California red, and worth every second of it if you didn't have to reach for the bill. Not like shopping at Tiffany's, where you have to pay to be a big shot.

"Well, Commish," Haggerty said, holding his hand against the Bergdorf tie he was wearing as he leaned over the table to sip his tea, "time will tell, I suppose."

Commish was an endearing term for Dolan, who had some years before been made an honorary deputy commissioner of the Fire Department, and he grinned in self-satisfaction. "I will certainly mention it to His Eminence, the Cardinal, Jack," he said, holding the cigar out, trying to decide if the ash was long enough to flick off into the gold-bordered, cream-colored Lutece ashtray.

"Not His Eminence," Haggerty corrected, "but His Excellency. It's Bishop Donato of Brooklyn that will make all the difference. Things only happen for the Fire Department if they happen from Brooklyn."

"Yes, certainly," Dolan answered. "I once heard it said that even the Bronx companies are part of a Brooklyn fiefdom. I will speak to His Excellency, the Bishop. And, certainly too, there is always Mr. Ratnor, but a perambulation in that direction can be costly."

Haggerty was very pleased with himself. Luncheon in such a fine restaurant, the companionship of a company president, words like *perambulation* being used, none of it costing a dime. America is great, he thought, but New York is even better for getting up in the world.

E. P. Dolan would talk to the Bishop, and Monsignor Flynn would talk to his father who would talk to the Bishop. The Bishop would be talked to, and that is what counted. Let the Bishop call the Mayor. Only one person should call. Two becomes badgering. One right person. Ratnor could do it too, but there were no guarantees with Ratnor. His son wants to sell us ropes, no big deal. Ratnor would not go out on a limb for me, ropes or no ropes. But still, goodness, he is a connection to be preserved.

"Yes," Haggerty said, "I would prefer to walk behind the Bishop at the moment."

Clever. Just right. Dolan understands perfectly. Ratnor's got nothing for Dolan, but the Bishop has the portfolio, God bless him for that. "The Bishop is the leader, and I'll get behind him, reading his breviary aloud for him if I have to."

"He will get the message, Chief," Dolan said, signing the check.

Haggerty envied him the signing of the check. It is very classy. No credit card. No cash. These guys in business, they just sign the check and never think about it again.

"In the meantime. . . ." Dolan said.

I knew it, Haggerty thought. Had to be. Luncheon at Lutece would not come about because E. P. Dolan wanted to let me ask him to do me a favor.

"There is a building," Dolan continued, "on Essex Street, 945 Essex Street to be precise, given to the Archdiocese of New York by one of the city's larger corporations, for tax reasons as well as within the human spirit of giving. The Diocese has an opportunity to sell it, but we find there is a standing order to retrofit a complete sprinkler system, which makes the building much less attractive, financially speaking."

Haggerty leaned back against the tightly woven green and yellow cane of the Lutece chair and searched through the inside pockets of his Johnny Carson blue serge suit for a piece of paper on which to write the address.

CHAPTER 15

THE Coronation Room at Leopold's of Great Neck was filled with firemen and their wives. There were several civilian guests, friends of the Department and politicians, mixing unobtrusively into the Department's affair. The round dinner tables were like scalloping that rimmed the dance floor. It was the annual Holy Name Society dinner, held outside of the city limits because most city firefighters and almost all Brooklyn firefighters lived on Long Island, and the Knights of Columbus Hall in Sheepshead Bay was not large enough to accommodate the most popular of all the Fire Department's fraternal dances and dinners.

Through the heavy, beer-scented haze, Jack Haggerty was delivering the affair's keynote speech with the same sincerity as a president delivering a state of the union address. It was the speech that kept him close to his constituents, the firemen whose morale was always a touchy subject at City Hall.

The newspapers talked of low morale among the city's firefighters. The presidents of the Department's unions and organizations warned that the consequences of low morale might be an increase in the number of fire fatalities among civilians and firefighters. Haggerty believed he could raise the morale of firefighters and decrease the fire mortality rate simply by being appointed Fire Commissioner, and so his speech was prepared specifically to outline a Department policy that would come about if he were. He was standing at a podium in the middle of a raised dais. The officers of the Holy Name filled the white-sheeted table.

Steely only half listened. For it was the first Fire Department racket he had attended since he and Maryanne had separated. He wasn't going to come at all. He had been off all day, and he sat in the poverty pad, flipping through old magazines that he had brought from the firehouse, sweating in the June heat. And he had worried the day long about attending a Department affair without his wife. He had not bought one of the tickets at the Ladder Company 7 table, which was no problem, for he could always pay at the door. But he did worry about being there without his wife, wondering who, if anyone, he would dance with, who he would talk to.

He had called Maryanne. She wasn't at home the first time he called, but he had called again. He wasn't sure of what he would say until she answered, and then he realized there was only one thing to say if he was not to lie. "Maryanne," he said, "do you think you'd want to go to the Holy Name dance tonight? I mean, I'm going, and I thought maybe you'd like to come along."

There was a long pause on the other end of the phone, a frightful pause during which Steely felt the gases in his stomach bubble. He shouldn't have called, he realized then. He wasn't even sure he wanted Maryanne with him so much as he wanted not to be alone at a Department affair. Of course, he had thought, there was always the option of not going at all, but it *was* the biggest dance of the year, and everyone who really cared about the Department would be there. And now that he had asked, he was in up to his knees, and he would have to drive out to Levittown to pick Maryanne up and worry about what he would say to her on the drive home afterward, about how they would leave it for the night.

But Maryanne said, "No."

"It's inappropriate, I think," is what she said. Damn, he thought, how could it be inappropriate? It wasn't like asking her to go away for a weekend on Montauk Point, but just a dance. "I think there's a lot of water under the bridge," she said, "and a lot more will have to pass before we can even think about talking about the things that have to be talked about before we can go dancing."

Steely felt like ripping the phone off the wall, but instead he dressed in the afternoon and went from bar to bar until he arrived at the Holy Name dinner dance, where he sat, half listening, at a table set in a corner of the huge banquet hall.

He had made the gesture, dammit. Not that it was so much of a request to get together. It was a simple thing, and she said no right out, didn't even beat around it trying to be polite, careful not to hurt his feelings. It wasn't like Maryanne to say no like that right off the bat. Not like her at all.

"And so we are gathered here," Haggerty was saying, "all of us friends of the Department . . ." Steely squinted through the crowd at Haggerty, wondering why the Chief paused. He couldn't see that Haggerty was looking down at one table where Douglas Ratnor's son Marvin was sitting, and next to him Monsignor Frank Flynn, who had given the opening blessing.

". . . and members of the Department . . ." Haggerty was now looking down at another table where he saw Dr. Titlebloom, wearing a new Rolex watch, one that he had been bragging about as costing more than ten thousand dollars. It was also one that Haggerty suspected came as a consequence of giving a tax-free medical disability pension to a fireman who had complained of a constant earache caused by the yelping of the new electronic sirens. He looked down at the Department's leadership, all in uniform to distinguish themselves, the assistant chiefs of department and the deputy assistant chiefs of department, their gold collar stars making their tables gleam like a staff luncheon at the Pentagon. Out of a corner of his eye he saw Captain Steinf sitting at a side table with other low-rank officers.

The Fire Commissioner himself, Gore, was conspicuously absent, the Board of Directors of the Holy Name Society having chosen this particular date for their annual dance. They made the choice only after consulting the Mayor's calendar to make certain it coincided with the date of the Mayor's annual commissioners' dinner at Gracie Mansion. It wouldn't do to make too much of a Protestant fire commissioner at a Holy Name Society dinner, and so it was easier to schedule it on a night on which he would be predictably unavailable.

". . . to give honor," Haggerty continued, "to our city's Catholic firefighters. Of course it is our intention to give honor to all firefighters, both . . ." He paused momentarily, and counted the seconds for effect, just as he had practiced.

"I would bet," he went on, "that you thought I was going to say Catholic and non-Catholic firefighters, but actually I was going to say . . ." Here, he paused again before saying, "both men and women."

Haggerty's audience tittered a little, unsure if they were meant to laugh. Steely, sitting at a back table in the shadow of a corner, began to talk to the fireman next to him. Having drunk too much scotch and water, he spoke in a voice that was loud enough so that the men and women at the surrounding tables turned to look at him.

"The broads," he said. "I knew he would talk about the broads. We've been working with men all these years and they expect us to look at a pair of tits in the same way we'd look at a pair of suspenders."

"Shh, pipe down," several of the firefighters said.

"Disgusting," a woman said.

"He's right," another woman said. "There shouldn't be women in the firehouse. It's not safe."

"Wrongo, wrongo," still another woman said, this one, Steely thought, frail and pug-faced and an obvious woman's lib type. "Every woman has a right to a job, no matter what it is."

"Then go to the NHL," a firefighter said.

"Macho, macho, firelady," another firefighter began to sing.

A small, shapely woman rose from her chair not far from Steely and yelled to the frail one across the table, "I hope it's your husband, Toots, that some woman sleeps next to in the firehouse."

"I wouldn't care at all," the frail woman said.

"Your husband bangs you, he'd probably bang anything," Steely said.

He thought he had whispered.

Suddenly Steely was on the floor, holding the side of his face. A large man, the frail woman's husband he supposed, was being pulled away by several other large men. "Listen, pal," Steely yelled after him, "I wouldn't poke her with a tightrope walker's balancing pole."

"Gentlemen, gentlemen," Haggerty kept repeating toward the

corner commotion until quiet again controlled the room. "Football weddings and firemen's rackets," he said when attention was once more directed to the podium, "always seem to have unpredictable diversions."

"*Firefighters'* rackets," someone corrected.

"Firefighters," Haggerty acknowledged, "a wonderfully generic, amorphic, sexually indeterminate word."

"Firemen stoke fires on locomotives," Steely said, this time just loud enough for his own table. "Firefighters have tits and save lives."

"Just get me out of here," a woman across the table said to her husband as she rose from her chair. "Take me home if you have to."

"Good evening, madam," Steely said, half bowing and gesturing his drink in salute.

"Whatever the word," Haggerty kept on without interruption, "the issue of women firefighters is at last resolved. They are now in the firehouses, and they will meet the standards expected of firefighters in this great city."

"The Island," someone called out. "We're out on the Island."

Haggerty paid no attention. He knew perfectly well where they were.

"New York has a history of great firefighters," he continued. "Chief John Decker fought the mobs when they tried to burn down the colored orphanage on Forty-second Street during the Civil War Riots. Elisha Kingsland, our first chief of department, resigned rather than go along with a military structure imposed by politicians on the Department. Smokey Joe Martin led attack after attack in burning factories, warehouses, high-rises, and smoky cellars, the toughest chief, maybe, in the history of the Department. He was there, always, with his men. Now we are in a different era. I can't say with *my men* anymore; I can say, though, with my firefighters, and I will always say it with pride and with humility, for there have been 687 men killed in the performance of duty since this department was created, little more than a hundred years ago, and this department will always have at its head a leader who will be sensitive to the honor those fallen brothers bring to us all. We hope there will be no new names added to our bronze honor roll at headquarters, male or female names, but we know what this job is, and we are forced from time to time to think the unthinkable, to prepare

127

ourselves for the sudden tragedy that brings simultaneously profound sadness and great honor into our lives."

Steely felt the redness and the sting leave the side of his face and the moisture building at the corners of his eyes. He thought, as Haggerty talked, of the funerals and the widows and the children he had seen through his years in the Department. "Am I gonna cry for some broad, the first one who goes down?" he said, talking, he thought, to himself.

"Not if she don't bite it," a fireman sitting next to him answered, winking an eye. The fireman didn't catch on, Steely thought, he didn't get it. It was a serious question, and not a set-up for a smart-ass firehouse one-liner.

"Christ," Steely said, getting up and walking across the dance floor as Haggerty continued to speak. "I could've got a good seat, I got here early."

Haggerty stopped talking momentarily as Steely passed. Oblivious to the eyes in the room that followed his small stagger, Steely waved casually at the dais. Haggerty grinned familiarly.

Steely saw an empty seat at a table that edged the end of the dance floor. He sat and scanned the faces across the table. Crap, he thought, recognizing the faces of the Department's brass. Bosses. I sit with the bosses, and a priest with the red monsignor trim. The only two hierarchies in a fireman's life.

Two assistant chiefs smiled politely but uncomfortably. A drink, he thought. In crisis, to help me say hello, how do you do, excuse me please. Damn. He looked about the table for an empty glass. Not finding one, he took a half glass of beer, emptied it into the water pitcher, and reached for the scotch. Hope they don't mind me drinking their booze, he thought.

"Hello, Steely," he heard a voice whisper. God. It was Josie Haggerty, her sparkling ivory whites overhanging her lower lip, smiling that kind of half-honest smile he hated from the first time he met her. She smiled only because she thought it would make her more easily accepted by others, when in fact Steely thought her smile was as distracting as bad breath. Large Chiclets sticking down from the roof of her mouth.

Why didn't he like Josie? Phony, he thought, the kind of woman who worries about what kind of jewelry she'll wear to the beach. Even when they were back in the old neighborhood, Josie put on airs. She ate lunch in a restaurant every Sunday after church, and had her friends and Jack Haggerty meet her there like fans at a stage door. She bought milk shakes and hamburgers when they met after a Saturday night movie, when everyone else had only enough for a soda and shared french fries. She always wanted to be a big deal, at least bigger than what was around her, and she flaunted everything because her father was a bartender at the Waldorf and had money to burn.

"Many things are changing," Haggerty continued, "and will continue to change in the future. Among other things I would like to establish is a new Department policy on headquarters jobs, so that a new administration is not saddled with the personnel of the old."

Even now, Steely thought, Josie was overdone, too much makeup, too much jewelry.

"And we should create a new tradition, that of the tendered transfer . . ."

"How're ya doing, Josie," Steely said, pouring the liquor.

The room filled with applause as Haggerty concluded his speech. "The Catholic firefighters," he had said, "have always been the bulwark of the faith and the protectors of the citizens in this great city."

"We're out on the Island," two or three people yelled, this time in unison and above the applause.

"I'm fine, Steely," Josie answered, raising her fingers a little in apprehension as he poured a full glass of scotch, no ice or water or soda. She looked around the table to see if anyone was watching.

"I wanted to thank you," she continued, "for coming out to the Chief's birthday."

"It was good, thanks," Steely said, wincing as the sting of the drink hit his palate.

"It's too bad Maryanne wasn't there."

"That's the way it is when you're separated. You don't go out much together."

"You're the only one in the old neighborhood crowd that's separated, Steely."

"C'mon, Josie, look at Hermie the Helmet Head and Ritzie."

"Hermie is dead, Steely."

"Well, they're separated, right?"

"He died of cancer when Ritzie was eight months pregnant with little Ritzie. It's not the same thing, Steely."

"What is it you want to say to me, Josie?"

"Just that you have a good Catholic family, Steely, and you should be here with your wife."

Steely looked over Josie's shoulder and saw Red Hadley eating a dessert of strawberries and pound cake. He seemed to be alone, the seat on his right being unoccupied, the one to his left filled by Arbuckle McFatty, who, like Red, was gobbling the dessert.

"Know what I mean?" Josie pressed.

The loneliness and the apprehension of the afternoon again swelled within Steely. He sighed, looking away from Josie for a moment, looking into an empty space. He had made the gesture. He did try. What business is it of Josie's anyway, he thought, and attempted to change the subject.

"I guess I'm sitting in the Chief's chair, huh, Josie?"

"Just stay there, Steely," Haggerty's heavy, gregarious voice interrupted. "I'll pull up another chair."

Steely felt captured. He looked through the smoky air that hung like a sheer film across the room, and beyond the bobbing heads of the crowd to where Hadley was sitting. He wished he could get up and sit in the empty chair next to Red, but it was like Jack Haggerty had him in a headlock and pinned to the floor.

Haggerty introduced Steely around the table. "One of our finest firemen," he said about him, and then he referred to the assistant chiefs as Department stalwarts, Monsignor Frank Flynn as the Holy Ghost's confidant, and Mr. Marvin Ratnor as the Department's newest purveyor of ropes and son of the Mayor's best friend.

There was no one at the table willing to correct the Chief of Department, Steely thought. He could say *fireman* to the brass and the friends of the Department and there would be no one there to correct him. Fireman, firewoman, no one cared.

"One of our finest," Haggerty said again in reference to Steely. Steely took a large gulp of the scotch, and the alcohol attacked his mouth and throat. It made him want to heave it all out. And he would have, he thought, if Frank Flynn wasn't there. He remembered Flynn vaguely from the old neighborhood. He was younger, but Steely remembered him mostly as the head altar boy at Sunday masses. A gentle kid, and it figures he became a priest.

Anyway, Steely thought, priests should not come to the Department's rackets. Not to be heaved on or cursed at. Priests and wives.

It was then Steely saw Kathleen Ryan Angelli walk through the smoke waves and sit in the empty chair next to Red Hadley. She was wearing a short blue dress, low cut and tight around her hips. Goddammit, what's she doing here? Not even a real part of the company yet. She has no right to be here.

He saw briefly, between tables, the bulging form of her calf muscles. Like a dancer's. She looked good, good enough to take out, or even to run after.

Though, Steely thought, it wasn't right. Ask anybody. Anybody would be more than a little distracted that she was here. She doesn't belong. No way. Not yet. Hadley must've dragged her along out of special charity, but she wasn't even really on the job yet, not in any big fires anyway. She hadn't been tested yet.

Steely watched as she sank into the seat next to Hadley. Christ. In my seat, he thought. Goddammit. *In my seat.*

He looked around the room from table to table, searching for another place to sit, but he saw only one empty chair, at Dr. Titlebloom's side. Better to pass on that table, Steely thought, until the time was right to get to the Chief Medical Officer. A tax-free disability pension is all right when there's something to look forward to, a job, travel, a vacation home, but not when there's nothing ahead. When there's nothing ahead is when you need the Fire Department most.

"Mr. Ratnor," Haggerty said, "is marketing the new roof rope. He knows a great deal about ropes and rescues, Steely."

Steely swilled down the scotch and reached for the bottle. "I heard they're still testing that rope," he said.

"That's right," Ratnor announced. "In Brooklyn."

"I heard Engine 383 was moving a piano up the side of the firehouse and the rope broke, and the piano played Sousa's 'Stars and Stripes Forever' on the sidewalk."

Haggerty laughed. "But a piano, Steely. Moving a piano, for goodness sake."

"The rope still broke, Chief."

Ratnor took out his handkerchief, blew his nose, and looked away from the table. Monsignor Flynn, noticing an awkward pause, changed the topic of conversation by asking Steely if he were a member of the Holy Name Society.

"I used to be," Steely said, "and of the Emerald Society and the Anchor Club and the Third Alarm Association. Now I'm lucky the city takes out the dues for the union, otherwise I wouldn't belong to the union either."

"Tough times?" Monsignor Flynn asked sympathetically.

"It's what happens you get separated, Father," Steely said.

Overhearing this, Josie said, "You shouldn't be separated, Steely, you from a fine Catholic family. You should be with your wife and children."

"Fine Catholic family your ass, Josie," Steely said, fondling the half-empty glass of scotch, thinking he'd had as much of Josie as he could take.

"Now just a minute, Steely," Haggerty interjected, throwing off a hand that was on his shoulder. Steely fell into a half-reverie, half-stupor daydream.

Catholic family. She don't know Catholic family. He remembered when he was eight years old and his father had been laid off from his job at the New York Central Railroad, forced off the job because the railroad needed to save a few bucks for a month or two. And, it was just before Christmas. Layoff always came at the end of the year, and a few times they got far enough down the seniority list to reach Steely's father.

He had been lying in his bunk bed, a boy listening to the quarrels of his mother and father, trying to sleep, like his brothers and sisters were trying to sleep, all of them together in the one room, sharing their own silences.

"I can get a job, Paddy," his mother said. She had a soft, high voice, like a singer's. "Marie Costello said she can get me a job at the stapler factory in Long Island City, right across the bridge."

Steely remembered that he heard a hand slap against the hard wood of the kitchen table, and then his father's rough voice. "No wife of mine will ever work," his father replied, snarling. It was the angriest voice Steely had ever heard.

"I will," his mother said. "The family needs the money and I will work."

"You'll do as you're told," Steely remembered hearing, and then another loud crack, this one as if a crate board had split, and then a thump as his mother fell to the floor, hitting her head against the porcelain of the refrigerator door. He remembered her crying. And he, like his brothers and sisters, was too afraid to get out of his bed and run to her side. Crack, like a splitting crate board. A good Catholic family. He prayed, that night, and every night thereafter for several years. "Oh clement, oh loving, oh sweet Virgin Mary,

132

please take the sickness away, please make him well so that he will be good to my mother."

The man tugging at Haggerty's shoulder was Captain Peter Petrullo. "I just want to thank you, Chief, for freeing up the battalion chief's test. I already thanked the monsignor, and told him if I pass the test I'm gonna build a church and name it after him."

Haggerty didn't hear the captain. He was waiting for some response from Steely, who seemed unaware of anything but the glass of scotch in his hand.

"Well?" Haggerty said, demanding Steely's attention.

"Well, what?" Steely said.

"Apologize to Mrs. Haggerty for using that language."

"What Mrs. Haggerty?" Steely replied. "You mean Josie? What's this with Mrs. Haggerty?"

"Apologize, Steely. I insist on it."

"C'mon, Jack, it's me, Steely, from the neighborhood."

"That's correct, Steely, and I recently got you out of a terrible jam just because of the old neighborhood, and you're not out completely yet either."

"So I owe you, Jack."

"It's more than that, Steely."

Steely spread his arms out in front of him, a gesture that reminded him even in his drunkenness of the illustrations he had seen of Jesus at the Sermon on the Mount.

"You always make such a big thing about the neighborhood. Jack, you gotta take friends as they are rather than how you remember them."

"Just apologize to Mrs. Haggerty. . . ."

"It's okay," Josie interjected. "I understand about Steely."

Captain Petrullo backed quietly away from the table. It is a general rule that it is better to be forgotten in the Department than to be remembered for the wrong reasons, so no one noticed him as he moved away.

"You don't understand shinola, Josie," Steely said, getting up from his chair, the scotch glass still in his hand.

"I understand," Josie snapped, "that you should be with your wife and family, and because you're not, you are under a strain."

"You had better reconsider leaving this table without an apology," Haggerty said.

"Oh, I'll apologize, Chief, because you're the boss."

"Not because I'm the boss, Steely, but because you're out of line. We're from the same block, remember, and you don't pull this stuff and get away with it."

Steely placed the glass on the table. How many times, he asked himself, had he gone head to head with Jack Haggerty, with Johnnie Gimme, arguing, disagreeing on sports, betting, shoving one another? How could he not remember?

He fought him once, in the old lots of Fifty-fourth Street and Sutton Place, but it wasn't much of a fight. It was the Radishetskys that caused it. Steely smiled as it passed through his memory.

Raymond Radishetsky and his brothers stole the candy machine, all six feet of it, out of the lobby of the Parson's Design building, and threw it over the six-foot wall that enclosed the lots. Steely and Johnnie Gimme and Henny the Hebe, two or three others, were playing blackjack on a large piece of packing cardboard when the machine crashed down into the discarded bricks and refuse of the lots. It was like pennies from heaven, and when they saw the Radishetskys running up Fifty-third Street, being chased by two security officers, they knew they had a good thing going. It was like a ship had broken up and the goods were floating into shore. "The machine's mine," Haggerty said. "I saw it first."

"You can go spit on your mother you think this is yours," Steely said. It was then that Haggerty, a head taller, had taken him in a bear's hug and pulled him to his chest. Steely had felt powerless, he remembered, like a roach in a matchbox. It was dark, so dark, close in to Haggerty's body. Haggerty began to screw his chin down into the top of Steely's head. The pain was sharp and constant, like a tie rod was being hammered down into his cranium. Steely had no choice, he thought. He would've taken Haggerty punch for punch, but he was unable to move his arms, as they were pressed into his sides, like in a vise. Dark, and dank-smelling. He thought hard at first. He was confused, and he didn't see any other way. He had no choice, he believed, as he then drove his knee fiercely up into Haggerty's crotch. The grip loosened. It became brighter as he was freed. He was sorry he did it, then as now in his memory. But, it freed him.

Steely now looked at Haggerty. "You can have the machine, Chief," he said. "It's yours."

"What?" Haggerty replied. "What's that?"

134

Steely looked at Josie, the scotch finally making waves on his brain fluid bubble. He was whirling. "I'm sorry, Josie," he said. "Really."

Steely's eyes got suddenly red. It wasn't the scotch. They got red and filled with moisture until a tear fell from one eye.

"It's okay, Steely," Josie said.

Steely didn't want her feeling sorry for him. He felt like spitting. "But you don't know a thing about me, Josie," he said, "about me and Maryanne. All you know is a picture, Josie. You got a picture in your mind, and everything in the picture stands still. You can't see anything move. You can't see the life in it."

"I don't know what you're talking about, Steely," Josie said. Monsignor Flynn, sitting next to her, put his hand on top of hers for comfort.

"Don't matter, Josie," Steely said. "I'm sorry anyway."

Steely stumbled a little and walked over to the table where Red Hadley was sitting with Kathy Angelli. Kathy, with the beautiful green eyes. She was sitting there, her chair out to the side, her shapely legs crossed, nylon glittering like tinsel, the fine light silk of her dress up over her knee. Her arm was draped over her chair. A cigarette placed elegantly between two long, thin, sculptured fingers gave no doubt to her femininity. How did this woman ever pass the fireman's exams, Steely asked himself drunkenly, this woman with great shoulders, with great breasts, smoking a cigarette? How could you smoke a cigarette like that, gentle and womanly, and pass the fireman's exam? This was not a construction-site woman, broad and rough-skinned. She wasn't a firefighter type. And what was she doing here in this hall, at this racket, with all these firemen? Paid nothing yet, she hadn't. There were no dues. There were no fires.

"Sit down, Steely," Hadley said.

Kathy looked at him in the same way she'd looked at him in the firehouse. A strange, unsure look. He felt something. He knew that she wanted to say something, the kind of look that when two people are alone certain things can be said. "How're you doing, Steely?" she asked.

Steely paid her no mind. Ignoring her, he grabbed Hadley by the shoulder. "What're you doing at this dance, Red?" he said. "With a fireman with tits?"

Hadley jumped up fast. "Now wait a minute, Steely," he said. "Now you just wait a minute."

"A fireman with tits, Red, a fireman with great legs and great tits."

Hadley grabbed Steely at the back of his neck with one hand. He braced the other hand across the front of Steely's mouth, pulling him close, so that their noses were less than an inch apart. *"Now just a minute, Steely."*

A thousand things ran through Steely's head. He could punch Hadley. His arms were free, and he could push him away. Or he could bring his knee up, hard and straight, to come out of the darkness that he had felt against Johnnie Gimme's chest. He could do that. Oh, Christ, he could do that again.

"Just one minute, Steely," Hadley yelled again. This time it seemed even the band stopped playing music, and all eyes turned toward the table against the side wall.

Steely fell momentarily into Hadley's neck. His eyes went dark. Christ, he admonished himself, what am I doing here, going at it with Red Hadley? He remembered the hammering sounds as Hadley clawed through the wall to drag him out of the fire. He then pushed himself away and his eyes opened as Hadley loosened his grip. "You have no right to take that woman to a racket like this, Red," he said.

"She came to the racket with me, Steely, just like in the same way you would come to the racket with me, or anybody else we work with."

"It ain't right, Red. I got nothing against her, but it just ain't right."

Steely then began to back away. As he did he bumped into an empty chair from the table behind and stumbled, almost falling to the floor. He grabbed the side of the table and regained his balance and walked toward the door of the banquet hall. Groups of firemen and their wives crossing back and forth to the rest rooms stopped to let him pass. At the revolving door that led to the street, he heard someone call his name.

"Steely," the voice said. "Steely Byrnes."

He stopped and turned. It was Monsignor Flynn. "You remember me from the East Side, Steely?" he asked.

"Sure I do," Steely answered. "The only altar boy that didn't have holes in his shoes." He staggered a little, closed his eyes.

The priest handed him a calling card. "You're troubled," he said.

136

"I'm drunk, pal," Steely said, taking the card. "When I'm just troubled I can handle it."

"Call me sometime," Monsignor Flynn said, an assured, understanding smile on his face. "I'm going to work with firefighters now, maybe work my way up to Department Chaplain."

"Sure thing, Monsignor," Steely slurred as he began to push on the revolving door. "I've never been one to turn my back on the voice of God."

Steely stopped the door's movement, turning to the priest momentarily. A comforting, sober thought passed through his mind. He liked Flynn, liked the looks of him. He could trust him maybe.

Laughingly, he added, "God or his reps."

Once on the sidewalk outside of Leopold's of Great Neck, Steely felt the night air surge through him, and he began to reel. His head a cloud of images, he saw Josie Haggerty, confused and forgiving, and the Chief of Department, the blood filling his face like air in a balloon, angry, defending his wife. Damn, Steely thought, what else could he do but defend his wife? That was a man's job, a husband's job. And Hadley, damn, goddamn Hadley. He was there when I needed him. *There*, right there, through the wall.

Steely felt the liquor come up through his throat. It was as if there were a piston in his stomach pushing everything upward. Keep calm, he said to himself, leaning over a manicured hedge that rimmed the sidewalk of Leopold's. He closed his eyes then and retched, thinking, things will be all right, goddammit.

CHAPTER 16

STEELY sat in his car, drummed his fingers on the steering wheel, and looked at his watch. It was not yet midnight. There was time for some action, to search for the near occasion, to travel the bars of Second Avenue looking for the stray nurse, the lonely stewardess, the drunken, unmarried, used-to-be-married thirty-five-year-old.

A man passed by, briefly holding the fender of Steely's car for balance. A fireman, probably, Steely thought. Jacket open, tie loose and half unknotted, reeling more than staggering drunk, his arms flailing. It was then, looking at this man zigzagging aimlessly through the parking lot, that Steely remembered Haggerty's reprimand outside of the 19th Precinct house. "You should think more about controlling yourself," Haggerty had said.

What the hell does he know about it? Steely thought. A man needs something to hang onto, someone to point him in the right direction. And what have I got? Nothing.

He started the car then, and began to think of the joints he could prowl. There was Malachi's and Doran's and Kennedy's on Second

Avenue, and Moran's on Forty-eighth Street, the ritzy singles joints on Lexington. His mind wandered in the possibilities.

As he began to pull out of the parking space, his back bumper, which had been distorted by a previous car scraping, ripped a two-inch scar across the back panel of a metallic recreation van. Goddamn, Steely thought, stopping the car.

He knew he had done some damage, he wasn't sure what, and he wondered if he should leave a note. There was no fireman's sticker on the window, or Maltese cross. He didn't think long about it, a second or two. Some kid probably owns the van, he figured. A kid at one of the other parties at this racket heaven. Only a kid would drive a piece of square crap like that anyway.

He turned the wheel a little more and accelerated, thinking that the insurance company would make things easy for the kid in the long run, and it's not going to make anyone less unhappy to receive a note. Anyway, if he was certain of anything, he was certain that there was no pen in the glove compartment, on the floor, or between the seats of the geriatric, vein-popping bomb that he was driving.

He turned downtown on the Manhattan side of the Queensboro Bridge and drove to Fifty-second Street, double-parking in front of Eamon Doran's Fine Irish Food Establishment. He went inside and had a beer and a ball.

It had been years since he'd had a beer and a ball. Somehow the scotch he had been drinking on the arm at the Holy Name racket seemed out of place in a joint like Eamon's Fine Irish Food Establishment. Too fancy, maybe. There was no such thing, Steely reflected, as a Fine Irish Food Establishment. That's like guinea pizza parlors, where the check goes up a thousand percent when you call it something like Umberto's Fine Northern Italian Cuisine. Or Francesco's. Tomatoes and garlic are tomatoes and garlic, no matter what the price.

Steely looked at the glass of beer with the small shot glass sitting almost like a support wall next to it. He remembered his old man once sitting in a bar in Sunnyside, Queens, where the family had gone after a First Communion or a baptism or an Easter Sunday, he couldn't remember which, and his father picked the shot glass up and dropped it right in the middle of the glass of beer. "A boilermaker is a boilermaker," he said, "and it's somethin' you should never be afraid of."

Steely picked up the shot glass and dropped it in the middle of the glass of beer. He stared at it, a depth charge. The bartender, who was standing in front of the computerized register totaling up the tab, looked through the mirror and watched Steely. He turned, wiped the bar in a polite gesture, and said, "You all right, pal?"

"I'm all right," Steely said, laughing. "Just like the traffic on Second Avenue outside is all right. If you leave it alone, it goes along all right. But if you put a driver from New Jersey in the middle of it, you're gonna screw it up for sure."

The bartender nodded. "Gotcha," he said, and walked toward the other end of the bar.

It was then he saw her enter the bar's vestibule from the never-ending stream of passersby on Second Avenue. Tall, pretty, long red hair. What was it about redheads? Why did red hair mean wild? Anywhere a redhead shows up, he thought, heads are sure to turn. Like a passing fire engine with the siren blasting, a woman with red hair is noticed. This one had red hair that flowed down over her shoulders, with lipstick that matched her hair, and lips that were the focus of her thin and lightly freckled face. She had a body like a gymnast's, long slender legs and thin waist, though her breasts were larger than a gymnast's usually are. She wore a light cotton dress, white with thin red stripes. It wrapped around her body and tied at the waist. I've seen her before, Steely thought, as he picked up his boilermaker, shot glass clinking in the middle, and followed her to the end of the bar where she had taken a bar stool.

Steely put his glass down on the bar next to her. *Ping*, one glass hit against the other, and she turned just as she put a ten-dollar bill on the bar.

"I'm just a visiting fireman," Steely said.

She smiled at the bartender when he approached with what looked like a martini. So she knew the bartender, Steely thought, so what? So she's a regular.

"Visiting from where?" she asked, looking around the room, anywhere but at Steely.

"From Harlem, the South Bronx, Yorkville," Steely said, lifting the glass and reeling backward just a little. He caught the edge of the bar, and noticed that she had seen him.

"From the bottle, I would say," she laughed.

"Havin' a good time," he said defensively. "Trying to, anyway."

"Good," she said. "Me too."

"Buy you a drink?" he asked.

"No, thanks," she said. "I'm a reporter for the *Daily News* and I can buy my own."

"Hey," Steely said, "that's where I know you from."

"From the *News*?"

"No," Steely said, proud of his memory, "from all the Sunday mornings of my life. You're Brenda Starr, right?"

"Brenda Starr?"

"Right," Steely said, "hot for the guy with the patch on his eye and the orchids."

"Oh," she said, connecting, "the funnies."

"Right," Steely said, putting his hand on the small of her back. "Red hair, and beautiful."

"Beautiful, huh," she said, sitting up a little straighter on the bar stool.

"Name's Steely," he said, "and meeting you made my day, maybe my year." She was good-natured, Steely could see that in her eyes. Green eyes, not as green or as glowing as Kathy Angelli's, not like hills of wet grass, but nice enough. He rubbed her back a little. "What's your name?"

"Prudence Potter," she said, sipping the martini.

"Prudence, huh," Steely said, his hand now fully around her waist. "You'll always be Brenda Starr to me."

She turned and looked at him close up, as if she were trying to find something in his face. "Are you really a fireman?" she asked. "I love firemen, cover all the fires."

"I'll show you my badge," he said, now squeezing her waist. "But a little later. Want to go out to my place, Brenda, out in Long Island City?"

"Maybe," she said, "but you'll have to look at my one breast first."

Steely thought she was joking, teasing him, pulling him along. "You carry it around in your pocketbook?" he asked.

She became very serious. "I'm not kidding," she said. "I've had an operation, cancer, and if you don't know that first thing, we might not be on the same track." She smiled and cocked her head a little, waiting for a response from Steely.

Steely squeezed her tighter, and then put both hands on the bar in front of him. "All right," he said. "I'd like to see it now, this one breast."

"I only said that," she laughed. "I wasn't really going to show you."

Steely turned and put both hands around her waist this time. "Brenda, look," he said, "it's a serious thing and I guess you learn to deal with it in a way that works for you. One breast, two breasts, it's still you, right?"

She leaned over and kissed him then, lightly on the cheek. "Steely?"

"Right," he answered.

"Where'd you say we're going in Queens?"

He began to make love to her in his apartment, their bodies piston-like, back and forth, in and out. Cars and trucks could be heard in the distance, backed up at the Midtown Tunnel tollbooths. She let him keep the bathroom light on, after a small discussion, and in that thin, veiled light he could study the long, smooth flowing lines of her body, and watch her eyes as he kissed her all over, even on the small scar that ran in a straight horizontal line beneath the reconstructed nipple on one side of her chest. The other side was a mound of soft delicate flesh that lay seductively flat and normal and moved with her body's movement like a jellied mold.

Panting and sweating, they brought their lovemaking to a furious level. He kept looking at her in the vague light, wanting to consider every movement, every sound. She brought her voice above a whisper, tightening the wild grip she had on him. "Steely," she cried.

He called her Prudence, and kissed her fully on the lips, losing himself for the moment in the moisture of her mouth, the warm wind of her breath. The alcohol and the dizziness had been purged completely from his body.

He climaxed as she screamed. It was not a piercing scream, but a high "Ohh" that trailed off into silence.

Steely brought his head down and kissed her in the middle of her chest, on the sternum. He felt the vibration of her heartbeat with his lips.

She brought his head up in her hands, and looked at him innocently. "Do you think I do this all the time?" she asked. "Meet someone and hop into bed with him within the hour?"

Steely rolled to the far side of the sagging bed. "I don't know," he answered. "Do you?"

She did not move, did not say anything.

It was not the right answer, he thought. She needed to be reassured, someone to say, "Look, I understand that this is a very special, once-in-a-lifetime experience."

Finally she moved and reached for the specially made bra that lay on a wooden chair next to the bed.

Steely watched closely as she sat up and wrapped the bra around her body and slid her arms through the straps. He tried to gauge what he was feeling. He didn't want her to leave, he knew that. Was she leaving, or was she simply covering up the nakedness of her operation?

"It's like I'm in a new neighborhood," he said, "and I guess you are too."

She lay back then, and smiled at him.

"And," he continued, "I'm trying to figure out the lay of the land, you know. Where's the Chinese laundry, the A&P, the dry cleaners, the church, that kind of thing. How do I get along here?"

She then reached for her dress and climbed out of the bed. As she stood in the bathroom light, he saw the silhouette of her gymnast's body. "I don't want you to leave," he said, his voice a cracked whisper.

"I must," she said, covering herself with the thin red stripes of her dress. "Don't take it personally."

"How else could I take it?" he said, trying to hide the frustration he felt. He was not angry, or even resentful, for he had shared something memorable with this woman. But he felt disappointed that she did not want to cling to him the night through.

"Well, Steely the fireman," she said, her pleasant, happy tone of voice bringing him some relief, "we'll see each other again sometime. I stop in at Eamon's quite often."

It was obvious she did not want to give him her phone number. Steely shrugged his shoulders a little and got out of bed. Naked, he walked to the phone. "I'll call a cab," he said, "unless you want me to drive you somewhere."

She approached him, put her arms around his neck, and kissed him. "A cab will do fine," she said. "And I want you to know that you are a warm, gentle man. I enjoyed being here."

"Warm, huh?" he said, his smile disappointed and forlorn. "Just ask Josie."

"Who's that?" she questioned, leaning back, still holding him around the neck.

"And Johnnie Gimme," he said, "ask him, and Red Hadley."

143

Then his voice almost a whisper, he added, "Ask Maryanne."

"Whoaa," she said, pulling herself into him. "Who are those people, what's going on?"

"Nothing," Steely said, squeezing her, looking deeply into her eyes. "Can we leave it like that? Nothing much, just that?"

"Sure," she said, for the first time looking a little distant to him. "Sometimes there are things I don't want to think about either, don't want to remember."

They sat on the side of the bed, and Steely stroked and kissed her vibrant red hair until the cab arrived. They kissed then and he closed his eyes until he heard the door open and click softly shut.

Lying on the bed, Steely tried to sleep, but a loneliness began to filter through his thoughts. He sat up, groped through his shirt for a cigarette and, finding one, lighted it and leaned heavily back against his pillow.

There he sat, motionless, the smoke rising silently from his cigarette, listening to the lonely, oscillating sounds of the Midtown Tunnel traffic.

CHAPTER 17

"**Y**OU were never there anyway," Maryanne had said, when it didn't matter anymore, "never there when they needed you, never there when they fell down and got hurt, never there when they broke a bone, never there when the homework questions had to be answered, never there when the teachers had to be talked to, never there when the parents came to complain. You were never there, Steely, you were never there as a father, you didn't care as a father, you didn't care about them."

Steely was changing into his work clothes at his locker on the second floor of the firehouse. Photographs of Tara and Jeffrey were pasted to the locker door. On the inside of the door so that every time he opened it to change his clothes or get his toothbrush or get an extra pack of cigarettes, he saw Tara standing, tentatively, as if someone were going to tell her to stand differently, in her white confirmation dress, pretty, but not too pretty, looking like a painting that might be called innocence. And Jeffrey, Jeffrey in comparison, in a snowsuit, his arms around a standing-up sled like he loved it. Like it could love him back.

She was wrong. It wasn't that he wasn't there because he didn't care. He wasn't there because he was working to make it all into *something*, to make it work. He was working at part-time jobs, stocking shelves here at a grocery store, bartending there at a gin mill on Saturday afternoons, driving a cab Tuesdays and Thursdays, and a school bus when he thought it could be a good deal. It wasn't easy. It was never easy. It was all one big pain in the ass.

But it had seemed worth it. Worth it when they moved into a new house out on the Island. Worth it when they went to Department rackets and danced, and drank, and laughed, and stopped on dark roads on the way home, and kissed and hugged. And worth it when the kids got older and they went to school and they began to read and talk about things they didn't fully understand, when they looked to him to answer questions. He did care, he thought to himself. And Maryanne probably would never know just how much.

She was never much good at figuring things out. Oh, she was smart, smart as a fox, and never missed a beat. She could smell a strange drop of perfume or see a foreign hair a mile away. But she couldn't figure out the big things, the things that acted like hinges to keep the lid on. She always went frothing at the mouth about the things he didn't do. She never talked about the things he did. Had no respect or concern about them. She didn't care that he was doing the best he could, the best he knew.

Other firemen were dressing, preparing for the day's tour of duty. Steel locker doors were swinging in the small aisle space. Pasted on the locker doors, according to the personality of its occupant, were centerfold nudes with paper creases across their stomachs, faded stories about firefighters and fires from local newspapers, photographs of girlfriends taken on vacation trips to islands in the Caribbean with unpronounceable names. There was just Tara and Jeffrey on Steely's door. Tara and Jeffrey were all there was, the pair, the only real focus in his life.

God, he thought, I love them. Yet, I wish they were more like the kids I grew up with, kids like me, maybe. They are so straight, so plain, like faces you see in the stands at the Saturday football games on television. Plain and middle America, people who grow up without oceans. I wish they could have grown up tougher, prettier, maybe smarter. They were just kids, but not even the kind of healthy, rosy-cheeked, vibrant kids that he remembered on the old *Saturday Evening Post* covers, the dirt-road, back-lane, small-town New England American kids. His kids had no real definition. They were not country kids with daisy-field innocence and a sense of adventure. And they were not city kids, with tough edges and a plan. They were suburban kids who went to a school with orange hallways, where the success of the eighth-grade soccer team was as important to the school's future as the Friday night bingo games. They were kids with a colorless suburban innocence, who stood in line quietly when they were told to, because there was never a reason not to.

They were like their mother, nice, consistently pleasant. Like most people in the suburbs. The cops and firemen as well as the doctors and the lawyers. Living there in Levittown, though, came with a price tag. It made them gray, the suburbs, took the colors out of their characters, the rainbows out of their personalities.

Steely stared at the photographs momentarily, and then he kissed his finger twice and touched the image of each child, lightly.

He then searched through the top of his locker until he found an old picture of Maryanne, one that was taken when she was seven or eight months pregnant with the firstborn, Tara, one that would win a contest for happy faces. Steely held the photograph flat in his hand, and studied it for a long while. Whatever her faults, he thought, the fundamental goodness that radiated from her face could not be denied. She was pictured in a heavy, salt and pepper coat, a long colorful scarf wrapped twice around her neck, posed in front of the pagoda-like entrance to a Chinatown restaurant, her hands clasped beneath the mound of her belly. They had loved going to China-town, before the baby came, before their expenses began to demand his whole paycheck. Even afterward, after Tara and Jeffrey, Mary-anne would ferret money from the household till, and they would go out for Chinese or Italian. She was so thoughtful then.

Maybe she was still thoughtful, Steely said to himself as he slid the photo into the small space between his locker mirror and its frame.

He had forgotten why he had ever taken the photograph down, why he had thrown it casually to the back of his locker shelf. But now, he would leave it up on his mirror, at least for a while.

Maryanne had a lot of goodness within her, a lot of love, but she needed a lot of care to make things come alive inside for her. One of her favorite sayings was, "I need squeezes, lots of Steely squeezes," but for some reason, the squeezes stopped coming. Maybe if I cared more for her problems, Steely thought, things would be different today. She is what I asked her to be just by moving her out to Levittown. It was the right move, the kids needed a house, a yard, good schools. So what if they had orange halls. Maryanne became a mother with a car, like all the women out there, but God, look at her now, the situation I've put her in. No husband, no job, no real skills except the ability to organize the lives of a family. No money, except the bare minimum to get the essentials paid for, and no money on the horizon either. Damn, what a deal I dealt, to her, to the kids. No calliope music in the background, that was for sure. If only I *wanted* to pay more attention.

He looked hard at the photograph, and thought, no more smiles like that either.

Hearing the rapid, hollow clicking of narrow-heeled shoes, he turned and saw beyond the locker doors the passing image of Kathy Ryan Angelli. Broads, he thought, on my tour of duty, in my firehouse. Christ. They should send them down to Greenwich Village where the fire hydrants are purple. Steely shook his head, and closed the lock on his locker door.

It was an easy morning. The firehouse committee work had been done quickly, each firefighter going from task to task picking up the slack wherever needed. Hadley was an exception, Steely thought, for he was out of sight, probably in the cellar, praying.

Steely mopped the kitchen down, while Kathy Angelli, a small half-inch hose in her hands, in turned-over fishermen's boots, knelt by the apparatus floor drain and scrubbed the company tools with a pad of steel wool. McFatty had shown her what to do, and how. She had a halligan tool in her hand, gliding the soapy steel mesh up and down the blue steel shaft and over the large fork end, and down to the adz and the slightly curved pull point. An ax with a grimy wooden handle sat on the floor next to an equally stained six-foot hook, the tools having been used by the company at a fire the previous tour.

Cleaning the tools was one of the more tedious jobs in the firehouse, one traditionally assigned to the person with the least amount of time in service. That was Kathy, Steely thought, and she looked better than any probationary firefighter he had ever seen.

He placed the mop handle across the threshold of the kitchen doorway, a symbolic detour that would safeguard the wet floor from the dirty soles and heels of rubber boots.

Kathy had a nice style about her, Steely thought, even as she

148

grabbed and rubbed the handle of the six-foot hook. Her body gyrated gracefully, the muscles in her arms hardening and softening with each stroke. "The qualifications oughta be," he remembered a fireman saying when the courts mandated the appointment of women into the Fire Department, "that the curly canal is big enough to make firemen babies who will grow up to be laddermen." It was the kind of remark that spread quickly from house to house, racket to racket.

Lieutenant Jackson passed by several times, a lieutenant supervising a firefighter's work, a low-level boss making sure no waves were being made. It was common knowledge in the Department that the division commanders were told there would be major transfers with the first women-in-the-firehouse incident that made page five in the *Daily News*. Close supervision, the officers were told, in all things.

"Even in the commode stalls," one firefighter had said. "The boss has got to supervise the eight o'clock dump every morning." It was a predictable remark, and Steely didn't laugh with the others. None of it mattered to him, the remarks or the slurs. Just as they weren't really funny, they weren't really important either. What got to him, though, angered him, was the command instructions themselves, the fact that command decisions were made, had to be made, about a woman, that orders about women specifically were promulgated, that the women were made so special, so different, that they were being made to stand out as individuals in a world that was made up of teams.

Still, he thought as he stood by the kitchen door, Kathy Angelli was graceful and nice to watch. He couldn't deny that.

An alarm came in for the north side of Ninety-sixth Street and Lexington Avenue, the Maginot Line that separated the downtown elite, the white and leathered and perfumed, from the blacks and the browns of lower Spanish Harlem. Could this be the fire that would test her, Steely asked himself as he ran to the truck?

It wasn't. He could see that as soon as they turned onto Ninety-sixth Street. There was a row of garbage cans lined up neatly in front of a bodega on the Lexington Avenue corner. It was burning briskly, blowing snakelike fumes toward the sky, like votive candles, Steely thought, in homage to the uptown gods of the ghetto.

Arbuckle McFatty was driving the truck that day, and Steely had the irons, the forcible-entry tools. In one hand he carried an ax, in

149

the other a halligan tool. Kathy was assigned to the two-and-a-half-gallon water extinguishing can, and the six-foot hook. Her back was as straight as an iron pillar as she carried the tools and approached the cans of fire. She moved with authority, Steely thought, as he watched her press the handle of the extinguishing can and move the small hand-held hose from side to side. Still, it was no fire. Not a fire to speak of, anyway.

Back in the firehouse, Arbuckle McFatty was preparing the firehouse lunch. His real name was Arthur McFadden, but he had the rotundity and the good humor of the silent-screen idol, and there was no point in calling him anything but Arbuckle. He had spread before him on the kitchen table, on a large sheet of waxed butcher paper, twenty or so pork chops. Each was slit down the side, and into the pocket he was inserting a mixture of chopped sausage, wet bread, and parsley. Kathy approached, a dish towel in her hands, and said, "I finished doing those pots. Is there anything I could do now with the meal?" She had taken her boots off and looked more like a woman again.

McFatty laughed, throwing his bald head back, and said, "Come on, Kathy, I already have enough role reversal in the firehouse than to deal with you putting your hand in the meals here."

Kathy herself laughed, but it was a nervous little laugh, Steely thought, a twitter. She then commented, "Lucky for you, because my mother always told me that in exchange for my good health God kept me from knowing the difference between ketchup and salt and pepper."

She held her head high for a moment, defiantly, braced for a retort. Steely thought she was trying too hard to be one of the guys. When he was a probie, the firemen wouldn't let him talk at all, like a plebe at West Point.

"I don't believe you can't cook, though," McFatty answered. His voice was friendly, but Steely was sure he heard a hint of sarcasm. "But then again, there's a lot of things I don't believe, like the Mayor really likes firemen, oops, sorry, firefighters. The only thing I know for sure, Kathy, is that as long as you're a probationary, you'll always wash the pots and the pans in this firehouse."

Kathy threw the dish towel over her shoulder and sat down on a hard wooden kitchen chair. She looked serious for just a minute, and said, self-mockingly, "You know, I bet if I could get a class-action suit on behalf of all probationary firefighters, we'd never have to do another pot or another pan in another firehouse in this city ever again."

Steely was sitting in a corner of the firehouse kitchen, reading an old issue of *National Geographic*. He looked at Kathy, and bit his tongue slightly, keeping himself from saying the reams of things he would have ordinarily said in response to such a remark. She could never have gotten on this job without a half-fag judge, he thought, who wouldn't know whether to fondle a hose or shove it in his mother's ear. It was the wrong thing for her to say, he convinced himself, a small storm brewing within his mind. It was an absolutely wrong thing to say. In the wrong place, in the firehouse kitchen, where there's no sympathy for stupidity. This woman was still playing games, he thought. She thought the whole thing was a game. She didn't know, none of these women knew, that there was no game here. That there were jobs and people's lives right on the line, right at stake.

Steely got up, fighting to restrain the anger within him, clenching his fists until his fingernails were pink. He walked briskly out of the kitchen, saying as he passed Kathy, his voice hissing, "You've got as much goddamn brains as you have pecks, as much understanding as biceps. Goddamn broad."

McFatty jumped toward Steely. "Hey," he yelled. McFatty was posing, Steely knew, no doubt about it. McFatty was never charitable.

Steely brushed past him. "Sue the whole Department," he snarled at Kathy. "Sue your old man for stickin' it to your mother!"

Kathy was silent, but Steely saw the blush cover her face, the veins at her temple pulsating.

He walked out onto the apparatus floor. McFatty was behind him. "Hey, creepo," he called. He called everybody creepo.

Steely stopped at the housewatch desk and looked at McFatty. The thing about McFatty was that you never knew what he was thinking. Steely once told him that he was like Daniel Webster, only he would be called "The Great Deceptor." McFatty lied, but because he maintained an even sense of humor he got away with it, always. In the same way that people put up with small crying children, they put up with McFatty's lying, because he made them feel good once in a while. And, people got used to him, as they got used to spoiled kids.

McFatty had perfect teeth. Like an illustration, they were, for a dentist's advertisement, white, as even as a ruler's edge, and not a single cavity or mar. Every spring McFatty made up some lie to suit his wife, and used his teeth to advantage, taking a room for three days at the Concord Hotel, high up in the part of the Catskill Mountains he called the Jewish Alps, registering as Arthur Fadberg, DDS. At the pool, he would get the attendant at the loudspeaker, the Borscht Belt Bugler, he called him, to page Dr. Fadberg every half hour for two hours. Two hours the first day was enough to score the best in the house for the following three days. "I have a special touch-and-go surgery case," he told everyone around his beach chair, in a voice loud enough so that whatever woman he was baiting would hear, "and they have to keep me informed."

The women loved him, no matter how rotund and balding he was, and were only slightly disappointed when they learned he was a dentist and not a medical doctor. His perfect white teeth convinced them that he knew what he was talking about.

He smiled now at Steely. "You can't let them get to you, Steely, because you'll end up transferred. Staten Island, creepo. You'll be in a firehouse with a view of Hoboken."

"I don't care about that," Steely said. "You know, these women are now suing for a make-up lieutenant's test on the grounds of past discrimination."

"Sheer audacity, Steely," McFatty said, "but don't get mad at them. Let's just glue her boots to the apparatus floor."

"That's kid stuff, Fatty," Steely said, lighting a cigarette. "People are gonna get hurt, die maybe, and you want to glue her boots to the floor."

"It's something, creepo," McFatty said, searching for a tube of instant glue in a paint locker by the apparatus floor bathroom. "It gets even a little."

Kathy's boots stood, ready to be entered, at the side of the ladder truck. McFatty turned each one upside down and squeezed a glob of instant glue onto each sole, replacing each boot then firmly on the concrete floor.

"Kid stuff," Steely said, climbing the narrow stairs to the second-floor bunkroom, shaking his head slightly. He could hear McFatty laughing in the background.

The room was filling with the aroma of burning pork. He was hungry, and his stomach was gurgling. He sat on the edge of the newly made bed, and then lay back on the pillow. He had not been eating regularly, he remembered. Living alone in the poverty pad had its drawbacks. He was not interested in cooking. He could, of course, broil a chicken or fry a hamburger, but it took too much effort, too much commitment to the very idea of living in the poverty pad. He wouldn't let himself believe that he could possibly do anything there except drink, screw if he ever got the opportunity, and maybe suffer his thoughts.

Maryanne's face entered his mind. It was a mad, bitter face. He tried to think of how the lines on Maryanne's face moved when she was happy, like in the picture on his locker mirror, but he couldn't. He couldn't remember that far back.

CHAPTER 18

LADDER SEVEN ON A SPECIAL CALL, the voice-alarm loudspeaker called. Steely arose quickly from the bed. FILL OUT THE ASSIGNMENT AT BOX ONE-ONE-SIX-SIX, PARK AVENUE AND ONE-OH-SIX STREET. Steely watched for Kathy as he slid the pole to the apparatus floor. He saw her run from the kitchen, kick her shoes off, and step into the folded-over rubber hip boots. She stepped into the right boot without event, and then, as she moved to step into the left boot, she realized that the right boot was not moving and it threw her off balance. She fell forward and grabbed onto the fender of the ladder truck, holding herself up as she stepped out of the boot. McFatty laughed and yelled, "You really got your boots firmly planted in this firehouse, Angelli."

"What's goin' on here?" Lieutenant Jackson said as he opened the door of the apparatus room. Steely ran over to Kathy's boots and kicked each one hard at the base of the heel, forcing it loose horizontally. "We have a goddamn job to go to," he said as he stepped into his own boots and climbed to the side step of the ladder truck. The truck, its siren walloping, sped up Park Avenue. Over the high

154

electronic sound of the siren, Kathy called to Steely, "Hey, thanks for helping me out with the boots there."

Steely looked at her and shrugged his shoulders, as if to say that he didn't do her any favors.

"They told us in probie school," she continued, "that things went on to give the probie a bad time. But I'm just thinking here, what in God's name would I have done if you hadn't come and kicked the boots loose?"

Steely grinned slightly and said, "You would've responded in your shoes, or even in your bare feet, if you had to. Because you never miss a run in this job. Missing a run is like punching your mother in the face. It just isn't done."

Kathy looked at him sitting there in the makeshift side seat next to the truck motor, and he looked back at her until they were staring at each other. Suddenly Kathy said, "Oh my God."

Steely got up from the side seat, looked up Park Avenue, and saw the smoke pouring from a window on the third floor of an old-law tenement building, the kind of building that would be abandoned after one or two fires. He could see, as he looked at Kathy, the tension in her eyes, the apprehension. "Just stay close to us at all times," he said to her reassuringly.

"Are you sorry you cursed at me like that?" Kathy asked.

"You'll learn to take it, like everybody else."

The apparatus stopped in front of the burning building. A bunch of teenagers were standing around the front of the building, cheering the fire on. "Hey, hot stuff, do your thing," one of them said in a Spanish accent as the firefighters rushed by. Two or three middle-aged people, squatters probably, stood by with quickly filled shopping bags. They looked forlorn and hopeless.

Walking up the cracked concrete of the front stoop, Lieutenant Jackson said, "All the El Barrio companies are out, and it'll be a couple of minutes before we get an engine company here."

The smoke was lead-heavy, and the firefighters could smell the cutting, putrid gases as they maneuvered their way up the falling-apart interior stairwell. The third floor was dark as a cloudy night, the smoke swirling freely. Lieutenant Jackson stood aside as Steely put his ax on the floor and hit the apartment door with his halligan tool. The door didn't budge. He put the fork end of the halligan tool at the door jamb, saying, "Kathy, take the ax and give this a whack."

155

Kathy put the water can down and picked up the ax.

"We better put our facepieces on," Lieutenant Jackson said. The three stopped what they were doing, took their helmets off, put the facemask pieces over their heads and adjusted the straps securely around the back of their heads, then replaced their helmets. His voice now muffled, Steely yelled through the facepiece, "Give her a good one, now, Angelli." Kathy hit it, but there was nothing.

"Again," Steely yelled, "harder."

Kathy hit it five times, as hard as she could, each blow driving the fork end into the door jamb, giving Steely a healthy bite to pull on.

"That's good, all right," Steely said, pulling hard on the halligan tool until the door popped open, silently pleased that she had done as he asked, that she didn't panic. As the door opened, new, even thicker black smoke rushed over their heads. And the heat came, too, in waves that hit their ears.

"Get down, get down," Steely yelled, worrying about a flashback fire where the heat sucks in the oxygen and the fire flies out toward the air.

They couldn't see, but Steely figured there was a long hall before them, and a room off to the side where the fire was. Lieutenant Jackson crawled down the hall first, followed by Steely and Kathy. In the front of the building, McFatty, Steely knew, was raising the ladder to one of the smoke-filled windows, giving them all a second way of escape. The farther down the hall they went, the more they could see a red glow coming from a room off to the left, and as they got to the door, Steely pulled Kathy past him and pushed her before him.

The fire was coming from a corner of the room, Steely could see. It was a couch or a bed, and had not yet extended, it didn't seem, into the walls or ceiling. "Easy now, Kathy," he said, urging her forward toward the fire. This was a probationary firefighter he had beside him now, one that had to be trained, one whose hand had to be held in the midst of the battle. They were on all fours, hands and knees inching forward, closer and closer to the heat. Kathy stopped and hit the handle of the water can she was dragging, sending a thin spray of water surging forward.

"Not yet," Steely said, his hand down beneath her coat on the top of her thighs, urging her forward. "Wait till we get a little closer." His muffled voice filled the room. As she moved then, he realized his

156

hand was on her thigh. It would have been normal in this situation for any firefighter. He would not have thought about it if it were a man. But it was not a man. It was Kathy Ryan Angelli, and he had his hand on her thigh. It was a firm thigh, and he sensed it was smooth. He pushed harder as they inched nearer to the fire.

"Now?" she asked, almost pleadingly.

"Not yet," Steely said, bringing his hand up and pushing her just a little further toward the red glow. His hand was now on her buttocks, right in the middle of her buttocks, beneath her coat.

Christ, Steely thought, I've got her ass, I've got her ass here in my hand. Here! Here in the fire. God, what an ass. Kathy Ryan Angelli has such a beautiful ass, and has such beautiful green eyes, and looks so great. Christ.

Suddenly, Kathy stopped and turned her head toward Steely.

It was difficult to talk in the mask facepiece, and so Steely yelled, "What's the matter?"

Kathy reached back and grabbed Steely's wrist, pulling his hand from under her coat.

Steely felt his face flush, and he hoped that Lieutenant Jackson had not seen what she did. Christ, he said to himself, feeling a little like a teenager caught at the Saturday matinee with his hand in a girl's blouse. What's wrong with me, that I have to try for a feel even in a fire? Christ.

"What's up," Jackson yelled.

"All right, Lou," Steely yelled in return, his hand now on Kathy's shoulder, prodding her forward even closer to the fire.

"Now?" she yelled. She had stopped again.

"Yes, Kathy, now," Steely said. He could see the mattress and the wooden bedframe before him, alive with fire.

"Spray the water sparingly, Kathy," he said, his hand now moving to the center of her back, pressing, urging her on. "You only have two and a half gallons, and you need every drop. Get as much of the fire out as you can." Steely was yelling now at the top of his voice, trying to forget for the moment that she had taken his hand from her ass. "An extinguishing can," he yelled in explanation, "can actually put out a whole room of fire if you use it right, so you can get this bed and mattress, completely."

The heat was oven-hot, sinking deeply into the inch-thick plaster walls. Kathy moved the small nozzle of the extinguisher from side to side, from one end of the bed to the other. Back and forth, back and forth, just as she had been taught at probie school, just as she was urged now by Steely.

Soon the fire was out. The windows were all broken out of the room, the smoke and the heat were dissipating into the hot afternoon Harlem air. Steely and Kathy were joined by Arbuckle Mcfatty and Red Hadley. They picked the mattress up, now smoldering and stinking wet, bits of spark still glistening, and shoved it out of the tall and narrow window opening, and together they watched it fall to the street, hitting the concrete there, and breaking out again into flame. But at least the fire was outside now, and not inside. Steely and McFatty and Hadley overhauled the room, taking the window out completely, stripping it bare, poking holes in the walls. They took their masks off, and then they broke the bed apart and threw it too, together with the springs, out the window. They worked quickly, with the precision of a computerized machine, swinging a tool, cracking the wood, pulling, lifting. They worked together, naturally, as a practiced basketball team that picked moves instinctively, without language. Kathy wasn't sure what to do, and she picked up some garbage that was lying at the side of the room and threw it out the window.

"Leave the garbage there for the next time," McFatty said. "They're gonna need something to burn."

In the street, Steely placed his tools on the side step of the apparatus as an arriving engine company pulled parallel to the still-burning mattress. Kathy approached, and secured the empty water can in its harness. "I did all right?" she asked Steely, a tentative quiver in her voice.

"You stopped. Hesitated."

"I didn't know how far you wanted me to go into the fire."

"You got someone like me behind you, you don't have to worry. You forget?"

"Forget? How could I forget you were there?"

Should I say something, Steely thought, about being in there in the fire, my hand going like a buffing rag, from her thighs to her ass? Sure as hell, she won't say anything to me about it.

"You gotta get pushed, the first few fires," he said.

"I know," she said. "No problem. I can take anything I have to take."

What's she telling me? Steely thought. Is she telling me she can take more than my hand going from one side to the other? Is she telling me that she'll take whatever I want to give?

"Let me tell you something, Kathy," Steely answered, determined now in his mind to change the course of the conversation, to change the control. "Anytime you finish the water in a can at a job like this, you don't put the can, empty, back into its harness."

Kathy looked surprised, and raised her eyebrows. "What am I supposed to do with it?"

"You take it over to the engine company, you take the top off it, you put the hole underneath the hose, and you put water in the can. When you finish that you take it to the air hose at the side of the truck here and you put air in the can."

Steely said this in such a rapid-fire, direct, mean-spirited way that he could see Kathy felt assaulted. She took the heavy Nomex fire-coat off and threw it on the ground next to the apparatus, and unharnessed the pressurized water can. "All right," she muttered, yanking the can from its place. "I'll learn soon enough, Steely, faster than you think."

CHAPTER 19

IN the firehouse, later in the afternoon, Lieutenant Jackson gathered the members of Ladder Company 7 around the kitchen table for the afternoon's drill. Engine Company 5 was out on the street, performing building inspections, and so the firefighters of Ladder 7 would drill as a single unit.

Lieutenant Jackson stood at the head of the newly scrubbed table before Steely, Red Hadley, Kathy Ryan Angelli, Arbuckle McFatty, and Whore-Hickey Harrigan. "I would like to discuss," he said, "the elements of the small job we had a little while ago, as we should recapitulate the elements of every job we have, the teamwork, et cetera, et cetera."

Oh, man, Steely thought, it's hard enough to take Lieutenant Jackson just sitting around saying nothing, just looking at him, but to have him lecturing is more than any man should be asked to take. Steely then raised his hand, saying, "Lieutenant, could I leave the room to go to the bathroom or to clap the erasers, or something?"

The gathered firefighters laughed, being receptive, Steely knew, to any diversion.

"Can it, Byrnes," Lieutenant Jackson responded. "I don't want to hear any lip as we go over this job the way we are supposed to. Now, it was Probationary Firefighter Angelli's first real job."

All eyes on the table focused on Kathy, singling her out, making her feel fairly uncomfortable.

"Firefighter Angelli," Lieutenant Jackson continued, "operated fairly well in a small but very smoky job. She operated the can efficiently and extinguished the fire enough so we could dispose of the burning mattress by dumping it out of the window and into the street and thereby saving the building from further ruination and deterioration."

Steely lit a cigarette and took the opportunity to steal a glance at Kathy. She had changed her shirt, and her breasts seemed larger as they pressed against the stiff, newly starched material.

Lieutenant Jackson went on. "Firefighter Byrnes forced entry efficiently and quickly into said burning apartment, and Firefighter Hadley vented the roof area in his roofman assignment in a fairly proficient manner."

"More better than fair," Hadley interjected.

"You're right," Lieutenant Jackson said, "I used the word merely as a figure of speech to get through the drill period. If you would prefer to exchange the word *fair* for *superior*, I would be happy to say that his functions were performed in a superior manner."

"Praise the Lord," Hadley laughed, and the others joined him in the small joke.

Old pimple-head is developing a sense of humor, Steely thought.

"Firefighter McFadden," Lieutenant Jackson said.

"McFatty," Steely insisted.

"Got us to the fire safely," Lieutenant Jackson said, ignoring him. "We never got a scratch on any of our fenders and so he functioned well as a chauffeur of the apparatus. And, finally, Firefighter Harrigan performed adequately as the outside ventilation man."

"You mean, outside ventilation firefighter," McFatty said, gesturing toward Kathy.

"You got it," Lieutenant Jackson replied. "Firefighter Harrigan performed well in the outside vent firefighting position."

"Which means," McFatty said, "that Whore-hickey Harrigan broke the windows when he was supposed to."

Whore-hickey Harrigan was so named because no one in the firehouse, least of all himself, was able to fully accept the reason for his recent divorce. Everyone loved the name, Steely thought. Whore-

161

hickey Harrigan had a wonderful ring to it, especially when it was pronounced with a New York accent, as in "Who-a-hickey Harrigan." It had happened just two years before, at a First Division promotion party, the night they stopped the Brooklyn Bridge traffic on the Manhattan side so that two firemen from Rescue One could have a Manhattan-to-Brooklyn foot race at two in the morning, and four sheets to the wind. It was a stag racket, and three fifty-dollar prostitutes were invited to dance on a makeshift stage at the back of a Battery bar called Barnacle Jim's, a place that was said to be owned by the local precinct captain. The three hookers had set chairs on the stage and asked for volunteers. Elmore Harrigan was, without a doubt, Steely thought, the most drunken firefighter in the audience, and naturally arose with a staggering wit to join the women. "All I wanta do is smell yez," Steely remembered him saying as he crawled onto the chair set in the middle of the stage. "That'll be enough to get my cookies."

Elmore Harrigan then leaned back in the hard wooden chair and fell unalterably asleep. The women had a great time with Elmore in his drunken oblivion, sucking on his neck and his thighs. And when Mrs. Harrigan saw the blue-gray blotch of skin at the side of his neck the following morning, she promptly packed her bags and left the Harrigan apartment without a single question. Harrigan never heard from her again.

It was a particularly regretful story for Steely to remember as he sat at the kitchen table, looking across at Whore-hickey Harrigan. What had happened between him and Maryanne, he remembered, was not much different, the circumstances that led up to the collapse of their marriage as crazy. He laughed then, as he remembered Harrigan relating to the firehouse how he would have run after his wife and tried to save the marriage, but knowing that she had not even seen the hickey on the inside of his thigh yet, he realized it would all be fruitless.

"It was only a whore's hickey," Harrigan used to say relentlessly, as he explained the absence of his wife at all the Department rackets after that.

Lieutenant Jackson held the end of a rolled fifty yard roof rope in his hand, saying, "We're going to drill today on the use of the new roof rope, a roof rope that all the ladder companies in Manhattan and the Bronx have been issued, along with new guidelines for the single-slide rescue, and the two-man lowering rescue technique."

162

"Two-person technique," Harrigan said, hoping to make the group laugh.

Lieutenant Jackson grew suddenly stern and angry. His voice became bitter. "This is too life-and-death serious for goddamn word or symbol games," he said. "This is a good rope. The information with it says it's tested up to five thousand pounds per square inch breaking pressure, and it also says that it is used by the navy in sending over a breeches buoy from one boat to another."

"Nothing's ever certain," Hadley said, "except the final judgment."

"There's only one more, Red," McFatty interjected, "and that is that all creepo firemen are so cheap they can suck the shit out of a buffalo on a nickel."

Steely felt suddenly protective, and held Hadley by the wrist. "Watch the things you say in front of our man Red here. He doesn't deserve our ridicule, you know."

McFatty had first a surprised look, and then a defiant one, but just for the moment.

"All right, you guys, uh, firefighters," Lieutenant Jackson demanded, trying to control his anger, "let's get down to business here, and cut the crap. This rope is important for us to understand. Now, I want somebody, one of you to tie a bowline-on-a-bight knot for me." He looked up and down the table and saw that there were no volunteers.

Kathy raised her hand, saying, "I can do that."

Sure, Steely thought to himself, sure. She can do that, and everything else, too, I suppose. Except fill the can right. Time will tell about the rest, though.

Lieutenant Jackson handed the rope end to Kathy, saying, "Talk us through it as you go, Firefighter Angelli."

Kathy took the rope in her hands and moved it so that twelve inches stuck out of the end of one hand, and then she threw her arms out wide so that the rope stretched from one hand to the other. "Take an arm's length," she said, "and leave a twelve-inch overhang for measure, and then take another half length, fold it over, at the fold take one more half length, turn it under, pull it through, take the two overturns inside, pull it through, there you go."

Lieutenant Jackson held the rope up and studied the two circles that hung down from the line, the two circles that were the leg holes for the larger rescue knot. "That's great," he said. "Now I just need somebody that Firefighter Angelli can harness into the rescue knot."

He again looked at Steely, knowing that he would be as unco-operative as anybody else in the crowd, and said, "You'll do great, Fireman Byrnes, thanks."

What the hell, Steely thought, getting up from the kitchen chair and walking to Kathy, standing there with the bowline-on-a-bight knot dangling from the end of the rope. He stood in front of her. She knelt down before him on one knee, and Steely thought for a moment to say something cute, but decided it would be too easy, like all the jokes about women in the Fire Department. She held out one circle of rope and he put his foot into it, and then she held out the second circle of rope and he put his other foot into that. She wriggled and pulled the ropes upward until they went as high as they could. And then she went to the back and pulled each rope circle high up to the top of his thigh. Steely felt the rope being pulled up on his crotch as she swung it into a half hitch and placed it over his head and under his shoulders and tied it. She then tested the knot by pulling up on it very hard, and as she did that she was face to face with Steely, and he could feel her breath brushing his face. She really knew what she was doing, Steely thought, for she handled that rope like an old pro. She was great-looking, right, but there was no doubt that she was something else, also. She knew what she was doing, sure of herself, too. It was then that Steely began to worry about Kathy Ryan Angelli.

CHAPTER 20

THAT afternoon Jack Haggerty had several meetings scheduled. The one that was meant to reevaluate the Management by Objective System the Department had recently initiated was canceled because of the time he had spent at St. Joseph's Hospital, where he visited a fireman who had been buried and injured in a building collapse in Brooklyn earlier in the day. It was just as well it was canceled, though. The MBO System was his doing, and no reevaluation motivated by Nicholas Gore would undo that system's acceptance by the Department. Was Gore beginning to undermine him? Goodness, after I wrote a very positive report on the Apogee Mask Company? Did someone tell him I've been moving the little pins around to see if I could get them to fall in the direction of the Commissioner's job? Did E. P. Dolan call him, perhaps? You could never tell with Dolan. Rich guys like that would cross their brothers and sisters to gain a little more influence, to go a little further forward.

Haggerty was restless during the regularly scheduled personnel grievance committee meeting. He kept thinking about the rest of the afternoon. It was an extraordinary coincidence that he had arranged to meet Katra Hadley for a drink in a small Greenwich Village restaurant on the very same afternoon that his secretary had penciled in the name of Katra Hadley's husband on his daily calendar.

At this particular moment he did not care that one captain with less longevity was receiving more overtime pay than another, or that a particular firehouse in the Bronx was overrun, so the grievance said, with rats and mice and roaches and lice. Grievances were something that could be handled, always, by somebody at a lower rank. One of his deputies, or maybe even Captain Steinf himself, could handle any one of the grievances.

But Firefighter Hadley, that was something quite different. He had a very special interest in speaking to Firefighter Hadley.

When, after countless dispositions, consents, and holdovers, the meeting was adjourned and his office was once again cleared, Haggerty pressed the intercom button and said to Steinf, "Send in the next appointment, Captain."

He knew very well who the next appointment was, though he refused to say the name.

Red Hadley walked into the Chief of Department's office with his uniform cap in his hand. He had no idea why he was there, Haggerty was sure. Firefighter Hadley knew only that he had received an order to arrive at a certain hour at the office of the Chief of Department. And there was nothing that would stop him from keeping that appointment, for, like the captain of a ship, the Chief of Department can bury you if he wants.

Haggerty did not look up from his desk at Hadley, but studied a piece of paper before him. The paper was simply a copy of the typewritten order summoning Hadley down, but it was, at least, something to look at other than Hadley's eyes.

Hadley was at attention, military style. He saluted the Chief of Department, but unlike the military, he did not wait for the salute to be returned. Haggerty did not look up, but said, "Are you a Catholic, Fireman Hadley?"

Hadley shuffled a little, seemingly uncomfortable in his rigid position before Haggerty's desk. Haggerty could have called him at ease, but in such situations it was always inadvisable to put a person at his ease. The rule of thumb was to keep somebody as rigid and as tight against the floor or flush against the wall as possible. It was, after all, a paramilitary organization.

"I'm a Christian," Hadley said. "A Christian in the Judeo-Christian ethic."

Haggerty looked up and smiled benignly. "Is that to say there's a little bit of you Jewish inside and a little bit of you Christian inside?"

"No, sir—"

Before Hadley could complete his sentence, Haggerty interrupted. "The question to you, Fireman, was, are you a Catholic, and you give me the fundamental philosophy about how you live your life."

"I'm a Christian."

"Did you go to Catholic schools?"

"Yes, St. Columcille's, in the Bronx."

"If you went to a Catholic school, I assume you were christened in a Catholic church?"

"Yes, at St. Benedict's. We moved."

"Well," Haggerty said, sitting smugly back in his chair, "if you were baptized in a Catholic church and went to a Catholic school, then you are still a Catholic, unless you've been formally ostracized by the Bishop. Did you know that, Fireman Hadley?"

"No, sir, I did not know that."

"The Catholic religion, Fireman, is not like other religions where you can come and go as you please. It's not like we can just tear the buttons off your uniform and send you on your way, or tear a piece of cloth from your vest, and that ends that, case closed. Oh, no. The Catholic Church is much more serious than that. Yes. The Catholic Church is much more serious than that."

Hadley began to walk away from Haggerty, but hesitated, unsure of what to do. He stopped then and turned, and stood again before the Chief of Department.

"Stay where you are, Fireman," Haggerty said, looking carefully at Hadley's eyes now, wondering if he was stable or unstable. He had to be unstable, if he was a Catholic and decided to become a born-again Christian. Stable people don't do things like that. In fact, he realized, the firefighter before him might be thoroughly unpredictable, unsafe. "Just stay where you are," Haggerty repeated. "This interview hasn't even begun yet, and you're not going anywhere."

Hadley put his hands behind his back and spread his feet a little bit, as if at ease. "I believe under the union rules," he said, "I have the right to have a union representative in all official Department interviews. Is this an official Department interview?"

Haggerty relaxed somewhat. The man before him was not, it seemed, going to be violent.

"Why don't you have a seat, Fireman," he said in a conciliatory tone. He was worried that Hadley might make this interview something more than he intended it to be, might make something official out of it, when he was simply trying to do someone a favor.

"No one is going to create any kind of stir that you would need any official or legal representation here, I assure you," Haggerty said. "In fact, this is an information-gathering meeting only and so it doesn't require the union at all."

Hadley sat on a hard wooden chair before Haggerty's desk, and put his cap on his lap. "If you would give me permission to speak, Chief," he said tentatively, "I would like to say that you have no right to discuss my religion in a Department interview, or even in an interview at a neighborhood saloon on a Sunday afternoon."

"Ah," Haggerty responded, "I must tell you that you are wrong there, Fireman, for Section 132, Paragraph 132.8.4 says the Chief of Department is responsible for the maintenance of good and proper behavior of all personnel in the New York Fire Department to ensure the best interest of the New York Fire Department."

"But you have no right to discuss my religion, Chief."

"But I do have that right," Haggerty smiled. "And also the responsibility, for as one Catholic to another I must tell you that we have an obligation to preserve what is good in the world, to foster behavior that is in the best interests of the Catholic Church. But I will go no further than this. Your soul is in grave danger, and I want you to believe that I am here to help you."

"But it's not that you are here, Chief," Hadley argued, "it is that I am here, because I was ordered here by a piece of paper that ended up on the desk of the company commander, Ladder Company 7."

"Yes," Haggerty answered, folding and unfolding the paper before him into squares. "And I will get to the point about that right now. You have an obligation to save your own soul, and if you cannot see the light of day, then we must trust in the power of our faith that you will be soon put on the right track again." Haggerty then rolled the piece of paper in his hand into a ball and threw it into a wastepaper basket at his feet. "In the meantime, though, I want to ask you about your negligence in conveying to your wife, I believe her name is Katra, a sufficient amount of resources so that she might lead a normal life."

Hadley arose from the chair, saying, "Now I do know that you're

168

out of bounds, Chief. My personal life has nothing to do with this Department."

Haggerty stood up himself and slammed his hand on the blue blotter cardboard of his desk set for effect. "I have full and complete authority over you, Fireman," he said, "and if you want to trade in your uniform for some job out there on the streets doing whatever you can do, and cash in your badge for whatever it takes for you to walk out of this office at this moment, why then you go ahead and do it. But I'm telling you right now that I can garnishee your salary without the authority even of a justice of the peace or a court clerk. Or I can have you working in the rural end of Staten Island on a Tuesday and in the north tip of the Bronx on a Wednesday, and then on Thursday you'll end up in the bowels of Brooklyn. You will play by my rules while you are in this office, and don't you forget it. Now, if you're quite ready to give this job up, you can just continue on your way out of this office."

Haggerty sat back in his chair, perhaps a little too heavily, for the healing wound in his buttock smarted. He watched Hadley carefully.

"I need this job," Hadley said softly, his words just at hearing level. "And you should not threaten me with the loss of it. It is not a Christian thing. Jesus would never do any such thing."

"Don't talk just about Jesus to me, Fireman," Haggerty said, "unless, of course, you're going to talk about the Father and the Holy Spirit at the same time."

"Jesus will see me through everything," Hadley said, sitting down again gingerly on the edge of the hard chair. "He will see me through the rest of life. I see signs of that every day. Even while walking through the streets this morning, after a Sanitation man had flushed the grime of Church Street with a fire hydrant, I saw a small circle of glistening water, parts crowded into one, like mercury, reflecting just a small patch of blue sky on the cold black steel of a manhole cover. And what I saw there in that small patch of blue sky, in that reflection, was the infinite, everlasting love and protection of Jesus. It is never-ending."

"And you take that as a sign from Jesus?"

"Yes, sir, I do. For Jesus is in all things, particularly in the blue sky."

Haggerty picked up a pencil and flipped it a couple of times in little circles so that it dropped and then bounced on his desktop blotter. He then picked it up again and began to bend it, harder and

169

harder, until it snapped in two. He threw the pieces in the waste-paper basket, making small, tinny reverberations.

"I am not going to argue that point of view, Fireman." Haggerty smiled. "But I would like you to know that there is a symbol right here in this room, and it's as big as a billboard, and I'm not sure if you are prepared to see it. It is a symbol that says simply, your wife does not have enough money to sustain herself because you have been remiss in your duties as a husband."

"I have not been remiss. I love her."

"Love is something that ought to be backed up by caring and responsibility."

"There is nothing to give her. After the rent and a few dollars for the commissary fees at the firehouse, everything goes to the church."

"But you should give to God what is God's, and to Rome what is Rome's, and in this case, Rome is your wife. She has her rights, to be supported by her husband."

Hadley looked at Haggerty briefly and then into the distance. "Well, there comes a time when every man must determine how much is properly God's, and I have determined that Jesus needs what I have more than anyone else, for there are so few people in this city who are doing Jesus's work, who are giving up some of their worldly things to share with God's poor and afflicted. Most of us would be perfectly willing to help the poor if the poor were clean, and to help the afflicted if they were not scabbed."

Here, Hadley took a handkerchief from his pocket and wiped his forehead, though Haggerty thought he saw a tear welling in the corner of his eye. "The shopping-bag people," Hadley went on, "the bums and the mental cases are desperate for people, like Francis of Assisi, and Father Damien, and the great Protestant missionaries and the Catholic missionaries of Africa and China, who are willing to give things up for the sake of the work of Jesus. But they're not around this decade or this year, so I have determined it to be just to give what I have to Jesus and to the church."

"And what church is that, Fireman, what kind of church is that?"

"It's just the church, it does not need a name. It is just the church. It has no building, structure, director, statues, or candles. It has only people."

"That is the kind of thing that people go to Guyana for, and end up dreaming false dreams and drinking pineapple juice."

"No," Hadley said, looking now directly at Haggerty, "the work

170

has no dreams. Just as the diseased, bug-ridden poor who live in doorways and cardboard tents, and under warehouse loading docks, and in subways."

The buzzer of the intercom interrupted what Haggerty took to be a coming reverie from Hadley. The intercom buzzed, a very ugly, belching sound. It was Captain Steinf. "Mr. Ratnor is here."

Haggerty pressed the intercom button down, saying, "Have him wait just a minute. I'll be right there."

It was then that the door of the Chief of Department's office opened and Mr. Douglas Ratnor and his son, Marvin, appeared. "I only have a minute, Chief," Ratnor said, "and I won't take any more than a minute of your time, with apologies for the interruption."

Haggerty rose to his feet, and so did Hadley. A fortuitous interruption, Haggerty said to himself, turning then to Hadley. "You will send to your wife one half of your salary every payday," he said directly, with a strong authoritarian ring in his voice, one that he had practiced for years. "And then you will seek a court settlement. You will send her one half your salary until you get a court settlement. And if you do not, you will not have a salary, and I guarantee you that."

Haggerty stared sternly into the eyes of Hadley, who said nothing. He had an ethereal face, Haggerty thought, there was no doubt about that. Crazy, and ethereal. "That will be all, Fireman," he said, as he turned to greet one of the most powerful political forces in the city, and his apprenticing son.

Douglas Ratnor did not waste any time and got right to the point, speaking as Marvin sat down on the hard chair vacated by Hadley. "My son is very, very pleased, Chief, with the result of the tests of the New York Fire Department on the ropes that he has, through his own sensible investment, provided to the Department. Also, the Schermerhorn Street Thomas Jefferson Democratic Club is pleased to make you its important honoree at next month's all-county luncheon, and you'll get a beautiful plaque that says 'The Thomas Jefferson Civic Leader of the Month.' You'll love it, Chief, you'll love it."

"That is indeed an honor," Haggerty said, sitting down, picking up another pencil, drilling it again against the porous blue blotter of his desk set. "Quite an honor, really. Will the Mayor be there?"

"The Mayor always says he will be there, and comes to about a third of them, but you never know which ones. But there's no doubt in my mind that we can inspire him to come to the luncheon honoring you, Chief, for he loves it when we take a hard look at the great work his staff people are doing."

Ratnor then walked over to his son, who was silent, putting a hand on his shoulder. "Yes, sir, Marvin and I are very pleased that the testing procedure showed that we met the OSHA standings, and that the rope stood up to your best tests. It is a source of great pride for us to know that every fire truck in New York is carrying this great new rope, coming through the industry and intelligence of Marvin here. Yes, sir, things are really beginning to happen. Marvin also has, while we're here, a new product he'd very much like to show you. Come on, show him, Marvin. Show him the rescue-V-rig."

Goodness, Haggerty said to himself, the Ratnors are industrious and unstoppable. He then sat back in the big leather chair and waited for Marvin to go through the briefcase which he had carried in with him and placed beside his chair.

"Come on, Marvin," Ratnor was saying, "we don't have all day here."

Finally, Marvin pulled from his bag a cellophane package in which was wrapped a folded-up series of what appeared to Haggerty to be parachute harness straps. Marvin handed the package to his father, who tore the wrapping off and placed the apparatus on Haggerty's desk, unfolding it. It was very much like a parachute harness in that it had two strips of nylon webbing that came up from a center belt in a V-shape that were meant to go around each shoulder. There was also a buckle at the belt's center where it was meant to cinch around the waist, and an aluminum hook hanging from that. Haggerty had seen many such items before, though this design was a thoroughly unique one. Still, the Department did not have a need for a new life belt system, for the life belt system that had been in place for the last twenty-five years was quite sufficient and reliable, a kind of heavy cloth webbed belt that tied around the waist and had hanging from it a large metal hook on which a rescue rope could be tied and turned. Haggerty held the rescue-V-rig up in his hands. "It certainly looks interesting, Dougie," he said, "and I'll send it out to our Division of Research and Development to have it tested."

"Yeah, yeah, that would be just great, Chief," Ratnor said. "It comes with an instruction pamphlet and everything. The guys out there at Research and Development will have a real incentive to take a close look at it. You'll send that one out, and the Fire Commissioner will send one out too, because we just came from his office and asked him to take a look at it, just in case you weren't in today."

Covering all bases, Haggerty thought, the runty Ratnor, diligent Dougie the deal-maker.

But, he considered, I sure don't want him in debt to Nicholas Gore. No sir.

"I'll certainly send it out there," Haggerty added quickly, "with a note that conveys to them in no uncertain terms my interest in seeing the research done on this right away."

"That-a-boy," Ratnor said, rapping his son on the upper arm. "We really appreciate that, don't we, Marvin? Let's go, Marvin, for the day is getting behind us, and we still have the Police Department to see about those fantastic new ankle holsters you can import from Taiwan."

Haggerty determined then that he had some quick thinking to do. What if E. P. Dolan and Monsignor Flynn don't come through? I've got to solidify my ground forces if I'm going to fight this fire successfully, and make maximum use of every resource. Ratnor is here now, and no telling how long it will be before I get another opportunity like this one.

"Can you wait, Dougie," he said, "for just a minute?"

"Certainly," Ratnor replied, his hand on his son's shoulder, pushing him back down into the hard wooden chair.

"About that luncheon next month."

"Yes," Ratnor answered, a pleased expression running across his face.

"Let me be direct, Dougie," Haggerty said, now standing. "Is it possible that you can guarantee the Mayor's attendance, and further guarantee a short, say ten-minute meeting with you and hizonner before lunch, so that I can personally pitch a few ideas I have?"

Ratnor was still smiling. He was very accustomed to this kind of conversation, Haggerty thought.

"Guarantee," Ratnor said, "is a very strong word in these circles."

Haggerty then picked up the phone and dialed the number of the Director of Research and Development. His eyes never left Ratnor's as he talked. "Chief Haggerty. Give me Chief Johnson," he said, and waited a short period. "Tony," he continued, fast-paced and authoritatively, "I am sending something called the rescue-V-rig for your evaluation, made by the company that made the new ropes. Since the ropes met all our standards, I would like you to move very quickly on these rescue devices so we can get them in the field as quickly as possible."

"The lunch is guaranteed," Ratnor said, pulling up on the arm of his son, as Haggerty replaced the phone gently on its cradle.

Wonderful, Haggerty thought, as he watched the door close behind the Ratnors, the rangy, rakish, ravenous Ratnors.

What Dougie will now learn is how the chiefs stick together. The uniformed force, as opposed to the civilian force, always has the ongoing responsibility for the past and the future of the Fire Department. Chief Johnson and I will completely box out neuter Nicky Gore.

Two hours later, after a long meeting with the Department attorneys about litigation the Department had instituted against a certain Republican real estate family whose corporation did not meet the letter or even the spirit of the recent high-rise building code law, and two boring, tedious, number-citing meetings with the Department Director of Budget, Haggerty, now in his civilian clothes, walked through the etched glass doors of the Watercress Club, an American-nouveau-cuisine, art deco restaurant. It was hidden on a side street one block over from Washington Square, at least a mile north of City Hall and the Municipal Center, a restaurant that Haggerty knew was discreet and safe enough. There, at a far table, against a wall that was glossy black and streaked with silver lightning bolts, he saw Katra Hadley, sitting in a plain white cotton dress, with a small yellow satin tie at the collar. He could see the outline of her brassiere under the dress, and he smiled as he began to walk toward her.

She had a martini in her hand, and she sipped it as he sat before her.

"Did you talk to him like you said you would?" she asked, even before he had a chance to say hello.

"Yes," Haggerty said, inhaling the delicate aroma of her perfume. "I think it will be all right, Katra."

"Good," she said, relieved. She took another sip—more like a gulp—of her drink, and said, "Now, what would you like to do?"

174

"I don't know," he said, looking around for a waiter. "Get a drink, I suppose."

"I got a better idea, if you want," she said, somewhat more demurely than he was used to.

"It's just nice being here with you, Katra," he said. It was an understatement, for he had been looking forward to this meeting since he had called her a week before, since he had sent her a bunch of calla lilies the day after that.

"It's nice for me too, Jack," she replied, taking a cigarette from her bag and lighting it. "Nice to be near a man who isn't trying to get me on the train to heaven, 'salvation.' "

Haggerty laughed, and reached over and patted the top of her free hand. "What was your idea?" he asked.

"Let's just go to my hotel room," she said, her eyes beginning to sparkle. "I need an apartment, maybe you can help me. I have no friends here, all alone. Maybe we can get to know each other better."

"Yes, Katra," Haggerty said, "I'd like to get to know you better."

"Would you?" she asked, as if she were genuinely surprised.

"Sure," he said, reaching over and holding her hand this time.

She took two puffs on her cigarette, and snuffed it in the ashtray. "Well, then," she said, "we should go. Maybe we can sleep together, Jack." She pulled her shoulders back a little.

Haggerty took her glass and sipped the martini. His mouth had become very dry as he watched her. He didn't say anything at all. He was afraid to say something that might interfere with the flow of her thinking.

"I haven't been with a man," she then confessed, "in ages, and I really like you, Jack."

The waiter, in a short white serving jacket, came to the table and stood before them, a pad and pen in hand. "And for you, sir?" he asked.

"Just the check," Haggerty said, squeezing Katra Hadley's hand.

CHAPTER 21

IN his civilian clothes, loafers, khaki pants, and his favorite green shirt, Steely leaned against the pay phone in the corner of the firehouse locker room, fingering the tarnished silver buttons on his blue cotton blazer. "Come on, Parnell," he was saying, "just one drink."

He hated the whining he heard in his own voice, the pleading. It was a kind of desperation, he thought, born of loneliness or just plain sexual need, he wasn't sure.

"Please," he added.

He lit a cigarette as he listened to her soft, musical voice. "I'd love to have a drink, Steely," she said, "but not tonight. Perhaps we could have lunch soon."

Steely hung up the phone. "Lunch, huh," he said in an angry whisper. He remembered her then, as she looked at him boldly, like a boss might look at a worker about to be fired, when she told him he made love like a fireman on the way to an alarm.

Let's have lunch, he thought again, laughing now, just a little, to himself. Sure, if she comes to the firehouse to have lunch. Let's have lunch is something an advertising executive might say over the telephone, not something that should be said to a guy with a bulge in his pocket.

"Who's she kidding?" he asked aloud as he contemplated the telephone coin-return lever, wondering if he should hit it once, just to make sure.

"What's that?" Kathy asked. He hadn't heard her passing.

"Money in the bank," he said.

"Oh," she said, and walked down the metal stairs, her high heels clicking on every step. She was wearing a red dress, tied at the waist with thin white cords, and held up by equally thin shoulder straps. Her shoes were red leather, and probably set her back a few, Steely thought. He followed her down the stairs and out of the firehouse, waving casually, matter-of-factly, to Whore-hickey Harrigan, who was on house watch.

No one else was around. All the other night tour firefighters were in the kitchen watching the news, and he and Kathy were the last of the day tour to leave the firehouse. He would be a mocked man if anyone saw him following behind.

Where is she going? She looked juicy from twenty feet behind, her hips pushing out softly from her waist, her legs shooting down like stakes into her red shoes. Should he make a move now, he asked himself? The opportunity was right, if not once in a lifetime. What would he say to her? That he couldn't throw the memory of feeling her ass in a smoky hallway? No, he thought, that wasn't it, not really. The truth of the matter was that he wanted to hold her close, he told himself, to learn more about her, who she is, what movies she likes, who her friends are, where she goes at night. Be honest, he chastened himself. He wanted to kiss her, too, and breathe in her full breath as he felt the warmth of her skin.

Even at lunch today, in the firehouse, he couldn't hide it. She was washing a pot, the one McFatty used to make a tuna salad, and her shirt top fell forward as she leaned over the sink just as Steely was placing the dishes in the tin cabinet next to the sink. She was wearing a plain white bra, no lace, no ribbons, but what he saw of it preoccupied him for the whole of the afternoon.

He had to act, he knew as he followed her, do something. Here she was, Kathy Angelli, walking down Lexington Avenue, probably going to the Eighty-sixth Street stop on the iron horse, the northern

177

end of the line for Manhattan's white people. She didn't have her car, which Steely thought was a stroke of luck. No car, nothing to hide in.

He walked faster and caught up to her as she was passing a street-corner flower man. "Hey, Kathy," he yelled, stopping now next to her, by her side. "Let me do this, huh?" He shoved two bucks into the vendor's hand and picked out an American Beauty rose. It was deep dark red. Almost a purple. He knew it wouldn't last as long as one from the regular flower shop, but it was something, and it looked like velvet. He was pleased as he watched the surprise overtake her face, and then as he saw her smile and accept the flower.

"Peace," he said, "among all firefighters."

"I'm for that," she said, standing now in the middle of the passing crowds of people, either Upper East Siders rushing to their apartments or to local restaurants, or blacks who had traveled down to any one of the five movie theaters on Eighty-sixth Street, movie theaters being uneconomical in Harlem because of the security risks.

"Have time for a drink?" he asked quickly, trying to hide any tentativeness in his voice.

"Not really," she said, smelling the rose. "Sometime soon, though."

Steely reached out and held her by the arm just above the elbow. "Kathy," he said, squeezing just a little bit, "just one drink. It can't take very long, not as long as it may take between the Number 4 trains downstairs."

He pointed then to the Gondola Restaurant, a place he knew, an old Yorkville joint made modern by putting cloths on the tables and using stemware for water glasses, little changes that permitted the owner to get twice as much freight for a drink.

"All right?" he said, tugging her a little.

She laughed and shook her head, saying, "Just one, Steely, because I really have to be downtown in a half hour or so."

"Great," he said, ushering her toward the restaurant. "You'll really like the Gondola, you know. It's one of the few restaurants in the neighborhood that hasn't become a Mr. Yakitori Sushi House."

The doorway to the Gondola was filled by bright fluorescent lighting, and he thought as they passed through the doors, just for a moment, that he saw the lines of her underwear beneath her dress.

178

She was wearing, it seemed, underwear like the brief jock shorts that men wore. It sent a flash of electricity through his body to see the outline of her underwear for that one moment, just like when he saw her leaning over the sink.

There were few people in the place, since it was early evening, and they sat at a small table for two near the bar. The waiter brought them drinks, a white wine spritzer for her, and a bottle of Miller's for him.

He peeled the label in small strips from the bottle as they talked, or he smoked a cigarette, or he chewed at the nails of his pinkies, the only nails he bit.

They talked about New York, and she told him about being born in Brooklyn and raised in Queens, where she went to Catholic schools and became the fastest female runner in the history of her high school's track team. She laughed when she told him that her father kept a collection of her trophies on top of the refrigerator so he could remind himself of how important it was to be athletic every time he went to make a sandwich, and that his daughter was the only thing that kept his body trim and his heart healthy.

Steely told her about growing up in midtown Manhattan, and about swimming off the dock by the United Nations building, and a hundred other things that had nothing to do with what he was feeling for her then.

From where he was sitting he could see the hair on her arm, so fair and delicate, move like tiny bristles in the air currents made by passing waiters. He wanted to slide his hand up and down her arm. He wanted to kiss her green eyes, her eyes that seemed like spotlights that were warming his face as they gazed across at him. He wanted to tell her the thoughts that were in his mind as they crawled together through the dark smoke toward the mattress fire. What could he say, he thought to himself, that would endear him to her, that would make her look at him as something other than a man in the firehouse?

He ordered another beer and began to finger the label off, looking away, saying, "Listen, Kathy, do you think we could maybe go to a movie, dinner, or something like that, anything that's a little different from stopping for a drink after work with the guys, you know?"

She looked at him with what seemed to be a desire to understand, and then she glanced down at her hands, which were folded in her lap as if she were in church on a Sunday saying the rosary. "Aren't you married, Steely?" she asked.

"Yeah, I am," he said quickly, "but I don't live with my wife or anything. I mean, that's over. I live in Queens now, in Long Island City."

"But you're still married, Steely," she said, "and that's important. I mean, even if you were divorced, you would still be married in the Church and all."

"God," Steely said with some exasperation, some disappointment, "you're talking like Sister Mary Teresa of the sixth grade."

"Oh, Steely," she said, in a voice that was very much like the sounds of consolation he had heard at a hundred wakes. Her eyes were sad, and lines developed at her temples. She turned her head a little to the side and leaned closer to him, saying, "What is, is, and always will be. You know that, Steely. Not that it matters, though. Look, you're a nice man, Steely, at least I guess you probably are. You don't know anything about me, or about where I'm going this evening for instance, or that maybe I'm going to see a friend that I've been seeing for a long time, and that I'll marry someday, or even next week. You don't know that, Steely."

She drank the little that was in her glass, and ordered another spritzer.

Steely rolled all the strips of label before him into little balls and dropped them in the ashtray. "Is that where you're going?" he asked. "To see some guy you're in love with?"

The drink came, and Kathy took a sip and then put the glass down on the table with what Steely thought was exaggerated determination. She held her fingers against the glass as she said, "Look, Steely, that's a question I don't feel I have to answer. That's a question that I should never be put in a position where I'm asked. The fact is, all I want to do, Steely, is my job. All I want to do is to be a firefighter."

Steely reached over and placed his hands on hers as she held the glass, just briefly. "I'll let you in on something, Kathy," he said, "just because we're talking private here, and that is, they'll never let you."

"Never let me? What does that mean?" She drew her hands away.

Steely sat back and put his elbow on the table and laid his head casually, maybe a little too casually, into his palm. Was she rejecting him, he wondered, or was she just covering her bases, just making sure that things at work wouldn't happen as they were predicted to happen, that every woman firefighter was going to be the object of every male firefighter's desire?

Did he still have a chance with her, or was she boxing him out completely? He wasn't sure. He was sure, though, that he wasn't going to get her to a movie or to a restaurant, or especially out to the poverty pad, in the near future. He wasn't going to lie with her and kiss her eyes, and the rest of her.

"It means," he answered, "that you'll never get the support of the people you work with, and I tell you this now from the bottom of my heart, because I know it's true. You'll get what we called in the old neighborhood a continuous hand job, which means it's never completely satisfying. People will say all kinds of things to you, but yet when it really counts, they won't be there. They'll tell you you're great, but they'll never do anything to really help you, and they may even set you up."

Kathy grabbed the end of the table with her fingers. "Set me up? You mean, like the cops set up Serpico in the movie, to take a blast?"

"Christ, no," Steely said, taking a swig from the bottle of beer. "Nothing like that. You could get set up at evaluations, or the way you are sent out on inspections, and you must sign your name on an inspection card where there are real hazard problems, toxic wastes, that kind of thing. Or they could set you up by writing little accusatory letters downtown to headquarters, letters that you'll never know about, except that somebody downtown is on your case for no good reason."

"I don't believe that, Steely," she said, relaxing now a little bit. "I don't believe that men will go out of their way so far to do harm to me just because I'm a woman. The real question firemen seem to ask is the one that says, 'Is a woman going to be there, in the fire, when it comes time to carry a man out?' I'll prove it someday, but you know what, Steely, it's a pretty stupid question."

"Yeah," Steely answered, "it may be, but it's the same question that's asked of men, too. The question is, what happens in the fire? Who's got the smarts to be where they're supposed to be, and the muscles, and the strength of determination, to do what has to be done? Man or woman, it doesn't matter."

For a moment Steely thought of Red Hadley breaking through the wall and carrying him out, Steely Byrnes, all 171 pounds of him.

Could she have done that, he wondered? More important, would she have been there trying?

"Except that the women," Kathy answered, bringing him out of his reverie, "are made O's in a world of X's, and if you looked at everybody the same, there would be no problem. Treat me exactly like you treat any other firefighter, and I'm happy, you know, because then I'm an X in a world of X's. But I'm not an X sitting here in a restaurant having a drink with you, Steely, and you know it."

"But I look at you like a new firefighter," Steely insisted. "Now I do. Look at the last job we had. I'm sorry that I . . . for that little problem we had, but after that I got you down the hallway and right into that mattress fire, the way any firefighter would take a probationary firefighter into a fire." There, he had done it, he thought to himself, he apologized in his own way, if that's what she was looking for.

Kathy finished her second spritzer and then searched through her pocketbook. "Right, Steely," she said, "that's all I want, to be treated like any other firefighter."

She smiled at him, just a brief, understanding smile. He knew then, for the first time, that he would grow to love her, but in the same way that he loved the job, the Department itself. Kathy Angelli was all right.

She put a five-dollar bill on the table and got up. "I'll do my share, Steely," she said, looking at her watch. "See you around."

He noticed then that she had left the dark red rose he had given her on the table next to her empty glass.

CHAPTER 22

JACK Haggerty got out of his car and walked to the double arches of the Municipal Building. The month of July was nearly over, he thought, wiping his brow with a handkerchief. It had been a month of record degree days, and almost all of the Department's outdoor activities had to be canceled. The training schedule was behind, but much worse was that the building-inspection program was almost six weeks out of whack.

When I was a fireman, he said to himself, we did our inspections no matter what the weather. The unions will be the downfall of the city yet, controlling things as they do, everything from in-law mortality leaves to wind-chill-factor-level determination and approval. A sin, a real sin.

In his hand he carried a little Lucite square, attached to a small wooden stand. Etched into the plastic were the words that certified the Chief of Department as The Thomas Jefferson Civic Leader of the Month. It was a significant liberty, Haggerty thought, that they took with Thomas Jefferson's name. As far as honors went, it was simply a piece of cheap plastic thrown together by a group of local political hacks, but at least Dougie Ratnor kept his word. Or, half his word anyway. The Mayor had shown at the lunch, but his schedule was too crowded for even a five-minute conference.

Well, Haggerty thought, the Mayor is a busy man, and perhaps it's just as well. I don't want to expose myself too much until I see some movement from the Bishop, or from Ratnor. Dougie said he'd talk to the Mayor "at the right time." There's never a right time, not unless Nicky Gore has a brain aneurysm and the city has to search for a successor.

In the ornate, red and gold elevator, Haggerty pressed for the sixteenth-floor Department headquarters. A firefighter ran for the elevator as the door began to close, and Haggerty tried to reach the door-open button, but he was too late. He shrugged his shoulders and gestured apologetically to the closed door before him.

"Dr. Henry Titlebloom is waiting in your office," Captain Steinf said as Haggerty passed his assistant's desk in the bright, fluorescent-lit anteroom of his office. A secretary behind the captain looked up briefly, then resumed typing.

"Well," Haggerty said, stopping momentarily, "is that all?"

Steinf looked at a steno pad at the side of his desk. "Chief Black of Repairs and Transportation called," he said. "The first five of the twenty-three new pumpers arrived, and they're fitting them with equipment. Be in the field in a week. Captain Peter Petrullo called again, to thank you for something, no message. Commissioner Kedozeris stopped by, wants to schedule a meeting on the retroactive sprinkler legislation. Also, public hearings should be announced in the *City Record*. Mrs. Haggerty called, wants to know if you're at a racket tonight, or be home for dinner."

"Tonight's the Naer Tormid dinner, isn't it?" Haggerty asked.

"Seven-thirty cocktails," Steinf replied.

"Did you tell Mrs. Haggerty?" he asked, knowing that Steinf had not. Steinf never did anything that saved time or that could be helpful.

"Sorry, Chief," Steinf answered. He seemed to have a smirk on his face as he continued, "Correspondence is on your desk, phone messages too, and the weekend operations report is in. And, oh, don't forget you have the Harlem Chamber of Commerce meeting at three-thirty. Better leave soon."

"Thank you," Haggerty said as he continued into his office to greet the Department's Chief Medical Officer.

"How's the old dorsal rump?" Dr. Titlebloom smiled without

rising from the small couch that sat against the side wall of the office. Before him, through two adjoining windows, was a view of the World Trade Center towers, lower Broadway, and the statue of blindfolded Justice that sat on top of City Hall's dome.

Haggerty brought his hand back and patted the wound. "It managed to heal," he said, "despite your attention." He was feeling very pleased with himself. The day was going well, and no doubt he'd make a few friends up in Harlem later. They were a good group to be friendly with, those Morningside Park bankers and merchants, a group with a voice loud enough so that it's always heard in the Mayor's chamber.

"Eh," Dr. Titlebloom uttered, "what's that?"

"Forget it," Haggerty said a little louder.

"I stopped by, Chief," Dr. Titlebloom said, pressing down on the hearing aid that was behind his left ear, "because of interesting news."

Haggerty sat back in his chair and wondered what Titlebloom wanted. The doctor's reputation was as well known in the Department as the Metropolitan Museum was among art lovers. It was said that the Buick he drove came as a result of a fifteen-second piece of advice he gave a firefighter applying for a lung-impairment disability. He told the man, as Haggerty remembered, to smoke nine cigars before seeing a certain lung specialist. The car came in return for the phone call he made to the specialist and the cigar advice was free. He was cagey all right, Haggerty thought, and he would not be in my office unless he wanted something.

"Interesting, huh?" Haggerty grinned as he looked at the small pile of correspondence on his desk. "What's that going to cost me?" He was deliberately avoiding the doctor's gaze, hoping to make him a supplicant rather than a negotiator. It was an old political trick, proven many times over.

"You know, Chief," Dr. Titlebloom continued, indifferently, "my brother-in-law the lawyer is chairman of the Bronx County Democrats?"

Haggerty became suddenly interested, relieved that whatever Titlebloom had to say, at least it wasn't about some internal Department matter, something to upset the delicate balance of Department management. "I thought it was a cousin-in-law."

"Doesn't matter," Dr. Titlebloom said, rolling his hands out before him, "the genealogy. He's a director of the City Gas and Electric Company, which board met this morning to discuss the sudden unexpected resignation of the company president. Long story short, they want Gore as the replacement." The doctor rose to his feet then.

Haggerty beamed. Talk about brain aneurysm, he thought, picking up a pencil and drumming it quickly. This is so much better. Have old neuter Nicky promoted out of the Fire Department. So clean, clean like a laser beam. Up past the Peter Principle.

"The thing is," Dr. Titlebloom continued, putting both hands into the pockets of his uniform jacket, "that the Mayor, because of CG&E's tax deal with the city, has to approve the selection."

Haggerty also rose to his feet and said, "I appreciate that you told me this."

"No big matter," Dr. Titlebloom said, waving in departure. "You have more irons in the fire than me, so better to tell you sooner than later. It's all hush-hush, you know?"

Haggerty slouched down in his chair. That Titlebloom, he laughed, what a hustler. He knows I want up, and he just secured his whole future with me, giving me time to think, to act. Well, as long as he keeps low he'll be okay. Undoubtedly, letters have been dropped on him. I even received a couple of unsigned complaints, but no allegations have ever surfaced. As long as old tithing Titlebloom keeps his tracks hidden, if there are any. Have to guard always against bad press, that's the first rule in politics. Have the *New York Times* on your side, or watch out.

Haggerty reached for the phone and dialed a number, thinking of an old Tammany Hall ward boss who saw his opportunities and took 'em. Yessir, he said to himself as the phone rang, a man can't be out of the office when opportunity knocks and expect to get ahead.

He heard Douglas Ratnor's voice then, and apologized for any interruption his call was making. "Listen, Dougie," he said, "it's no problem at all that we didn't meet with the Mayor, none. I wonder now if you can help me out in another way, though."

Captain Steinf entered the office just as Haggerty was concluding his conversation. He had simply informed Ratnor of the CG&E situation and asked that he speak directly to the Mayor on behalf of his good friend Nicky Gore, the present Fire Commissioner.

"The Harlem Chamber, Chief," Captain Steinf said. Probably

made plans, Haggerty thought, to leave the office early, pushing me along like this.

"Right," Haggerty said, throwing the correspondence into his attaché case. "Make sure the car is in front."

As the chief's car went around the Brooklyn Bridge entrance to the East River Drive, Haggerty lifted the attaché case to his knees and opened it. He went through the pile of correspondence, mostly reports on manpower and leaves of absence from the personnel division, until he came to what he was searching for, the weekend operations report. He held it in one hand and began to read. It had been a normal Saturday and Sunday in New York, just under four thousand alarms, two third alarms, seven second alarms, and eighteen hundred false alarms. Two civilian deaths, he read on, and twelve injuries requiring hospitalization of firefighters. Not so bad, he reflected, considering the heat spell. He shifted the paper into the bunch of other papers he was holding in his left hand and began again to peruse the pile. He stopped when he saw a report signed by Anthony Johnson. It was more a memo than a report, and he wondered why Chief Johnson was communicating with him. He hadn't asked for a report, any specific information.

The radio blasted then into Haggerty's thoughts. He liked to keep the radio loud, for it reminded him of the days he worked in the firehouse as a lieutenant and captain, the radio screeching, the siren screaming on the way to each alarm.

They were just approaching the Ninety-sixth Street exit of the Drive, he noticed as he listened. A SECOND ALARM HAS BEEN TRANSMITTED, the radio squawked, FOR BOX ONE-OH-EIGHT-TWO, LEXINGTON AND NINE-NINE STREET.

Haggerty looked up and saw the large black cloud rising over the tenements of El Barrio. "Pull off here, Eddie," he said to his driver, replacing the papers in his attaché case and closing it. "We'll go crosstown on Ninety-sixth Street instead of One-twenty-fifth and pass that job."

The gleaming blue Chief of Department's car began to travel west on Ninety-sixth Street, moving with the rhythm of the traffic. Suddenly, as the car approached Second Avenue, the red dome light on the roof began revolving, and the wail of the siren shot piercingly through the neighborhood. Department Car Number 5 then fell out of the line of traffic to respond to an alarm.

CHAPTER 23

THE only thing Steely remembered from last night, just before stopping at Clancy's gin mill on Masssapequa Avenue where he had six straight whiskies and smoked two packs of Marlboros, was Maryanne's parting words. "From now on, Steely," she had said, "don't ever do that again."

Why does she get like this? he asked himself, searching through his firehouse locker for a clean Ladder 7 sweatshirt. They had just returned from an oil-burner fire and his shirt had been covered with soot. Why does she rush to judgment so quickly?

He had taken Tara and Jeffrey to Central Park in the afternoon. They wanted to stay in his apartment to watch a rerun of one of the Star Wars movies, but he had read that there was a young people's concert in the park. "You'll go to the concert," he told them, "and learn something about the music. There'll be more music in your lives than trips in space."

He hated the concert.

It was a hot, end-of-July day, and the sun beat down in waves around the bandshell. The orchestra was filled with teenagers, probably a high school orchestra, he figured, or maybe college jayvee.

Tara and Jeffrey sat on the wood slat benches and put their fingers in their ears to let him know what they thought, in case he did not already know.

"A bunch of Chinks playing violins," Jeffrey said.

"Who's this Mahler guy," Tara asked, "and what did I do to deserve this?"

"You win," he said finally, and then led them off to the Bethesda Fountain, where the children threw stones into the paper-strewn rowboat lake and he leaned back against the carved stone buttress and thought about Maryanne.

There was no doubt in his mind that he was less happy without her. Like when there is a death in the family and it has to be accepted eventually, maybe he just had to accept that it was not in the cards for him to be happy with Maryanne, not in the cards for him to be in love. It could be a lot worse. At least he didn't have a real tragedy on his hands. Suppose she had leukemia, or a spine disease, and was laid up immobile, able only to move her head. Christ almighty, that would be tough.

But she was a good woman after everything was said and done, and if she was good underneath everything, maybe he could bring the goodness out. Maybe he could work on it. Maybe.

There was no doubt that he had to get things on the right track again. It seemed that nothing was working out, as if in heaven some great saint of bad luck and disillusion took him on as a special project. He had the thing with the cop, Murphy, still hanging over his head. He couldn't get to first base, not really, with Parnell Farrell, and not even up to bat with Kathy. Even a low-key guy like Hadley had something to fill his life, no matter how off-the-wall the religion was. All he had was the time in the firehouse and his view of the Midtown Tunnel where he could watch the multitudes throwing their quarters into the buckets so they could get into the big time.

"Could I sit and talk to you?" he had asked when he returned the children that evening.

"If you have to," she said.

Maryanne was dressed in an old dark blue flared skirt, one that pressed into her skin around the waist. She wore a thin white blouse that had yellowed a bit from overironing. Her hair was done specially, perhaps just for him, he thought, pulled over to one side of her neck and tied with a dark-blue ribbon, combed out like a velvet scarf over her shoulder. They were facing one another, he standing near the kitchen table, and she leaning against the finger-marked and food-stained white enamel of the refrigerator door. The room was dimly lit, for one of the two fluorescent bulbs overhead had blown out.

The children had fled to the living room to watch television. Steely grabbed his wife around the waist, then, and pressed his lips against hers. She turned her head away quickly, and pushed him back as hard as she could. "I'll scream, damn it," she threatened, her eyes wide and raging.

Steely sat on a kitchen chair, his insides shaking, as if he had swallowed some terrible toxin. He didn't expect her to react with such anger.

"Maryanne," he said, "I just want you to know that I miss being here, that we should begin to talk together, to some priests, or marriage counselors, like that."

Maryanne took a dish towel that was hanging on the refrigerator door handle and began to wring it in her hands. "You've got more than a hell of a nerve, Steely, to think you can come in like I'm a pushover, like some blow-up punch-me doll, and kiss me or screw me or do whatever you please. Don't you know how late it is for anything to save this marriage?"

Steely rose from the chair and began to approach her.

"Don't do it," she warned. "This is so unfair of you, so just leave me alone, Steely."

He found the sweatshirt, finally, but it, like all the clothes thrown haphazardly into the bottom of his locker, needed washing. He just couldn't get it together. He just couldn't remember to gather it all up and take it out to the poverty pad, and to a laundry four blocks from the Midtown Tunnel tollbooths.

Maybe Maryanne would come around, just talk to him about a possible reconciliation. Just a *possible* one, that's all. Maybe there would be an end to all the clutter one day, the sloppy, uncaring clutter of his locker. And the clutter of his life, too.

He changed into the soiled sweatshirt, and grabbed the newly issued rescue-V-rig that was thrown over a wire hanger. He put his arms through the loops of parachute rigging, and buckled the rig around his waist. It looked a little strange, but felt all right, and not uncomfortable in any way. He fingered the aluminum snap hook that fell from the base of the buckle. Smaller and lighter, but not very much different from the life belt the Department had been using for more than fifty years.

At least, Steely thought, they didn't make us pay for these things like those ugly drip-dry uniform shirts I had to buy and wear until the Department discovered that they burned like sulphur-soaked hay. "Makes sense to me," Arbuckle McFatty had said about those, "a fire shirt for firefighters."

McFatty, his cavityless teeth almost glowing in the shadow of the ladder truck, smiled as Steely made his way to the kitchen. There, the men of Engine Company 5 were sitting around a half-empty box of doughnuts which was placed in the middle of the worn and scarred wooden kitchen table. Sitting at the table, too, waiting for the afternoon drill period to start, were Red Hadley and Kathy Angelli.

Harrigan had signed out to shop for the evening's meal since he had been assigned to work overtime for the following tour of duty. Just as Kathy had worked last night.

He looked at her for some sign of her mood. She had every right, he thought, to be angry. The guys working last night weren't used to her, used to working with a woman, and they tried to be funny by leaving a pink pillow on her bed and hanging a size 46 C-cup bra from the metal headboard.

She had been quiet all day, and so he smiled at her. She nodded to him as he walked through the kitchen, but that was all.

He had deliberately kept her at a distance since their conversation at the Gondola. It was better for them both, he believed, to keep any interaction at a formal, very impersonal level. He had exposed himself with her, brought his nerve endings to the surface, but it didn't fly. She was polite enough, but it was plain there would never be anything between them. He couldn't help the way he felt every time he looked at her. That would never change, he guessed. But now they were just two firefighters doing their jobs, as far as he was concerned. She was all right. It would just take a little time for the rest of the guys to find that out.

He noticed as she was replacing the lunch dishes in a cabinet that the back strap of her rescue-V-rig had a twist in it. It was a new piece of equipment and nobody was yet used to wearing it all the time. Some of the men refused to wear it, and only buckled it on as they stepped into their boots to answer an alarm. McFatty was one of those. "I don't carry my ax or my halligan tool all the time," he commented when the rigs had first arrived, "so I'll wear this rescue brassiere only when I go to fires."

Steely reached over and straightened the twist in Kathy's rig. Mc-Fatty spotted him. "Hey, Byrnes," he called out, "don't touch the merchandise."

Kathy turned, curious, her hand on her back. "Thanks," she said.

Embarrassed, Steely tried to divert the attention of the other firefighters. He began to massage Hadley's shoulders back and forth, rhythmically. "Is this heaven, Red?" he asked playfully.

"Heaven," Hadley said with great earnestness, "is salvation, and the answer to our prayers. It feels good, Steely, but it's easy to feel good in this world."

"Will it be hard in the next world?" McFatty asked.

"Not with my luck," an Engine Company 5 firefighter said, which made everybody but Hadley laugh.

"Feeling good," Hadley replied, "will not be an issue in the next world, for pain and suffering cannot exist when you're with Jesus."

Steely interrupted a firefighter who was about to say something, probably something cutting, he thought. "Let's save the important discussions," he said, "until after the company drill period."

Lieutenant Jackson entered the kitchen then with a piece of Department letterhead in his hand. "Drill's canceled," he said, an annoyed look spread across his face. "I've got to go through the company journal for the division. They want a report on line-of-duty sick leaves for the last six months."

The men relaxed back in their chairs, or flopped across the table. "The price of authority," one man said.

"They want it in tonight's mail bag," Lieutenant Jackson said, leaving the kitchen and walking to the housewatch desk where the company journal sat. Hadley followed the Lieutenant out of the kitchen, and Kathy moved wordlessly to the couch that fronted the television set.

Steely climbed the stairs to the second floor to look again for another shirt to wear. The sweatshirt smelled of dried fuel or motor oil or something. He saw Lieutenant Jackson at the housewatch desk at the front of the apparatus floor, writing on a Department pad beside the company journal.

On the second floor, as he was walking to the locker room, he saw Hadley standing over the office desk. "What's up, Red?" he called as he passed.

"Look here, Steely," Hadley answered. "It don't seem too fair."

"What's that, Red?" Steely asked, entering the office.

"Just read this," Hadley said, handing him a piece of paper.

It was an evaluation report, Steely saw right away, a monthly report that the supervising officer must make out for every probationary firefighter under supervision. It was Kathy Ryan Angelli's evaluation, and it stated, briefly enough,

> *Firefighter Angelli performs the*
> *duties of a firefighter inadequately*
> *and needs further training.*

It was signed by Lieutenant Jackson, and endorsed by Captain Esposito, the company commander of Ladder 7.

"Doesn't surprise me," Steely said, handing the paper back to Hadley.

"Well," Hadley said, replacing it on the desk, "it doesn't seem fair. Why is she so inadequate, do you know?"

"Because she's a woman, Red," Steely said, slapping Hadley on the back. "They're all scared to say anything good, so they'll all say something negative and pass it up the ranks until it gets to the Fire Commissioner."

"You mean they'll all lie?" Hadley asked, unbelieving.

"The courts ordered them on the job," Steely said, lighting a cigarette and choking a little bit, "and the union is fighting against them. The firemen, even you and me, and all the captains and chiefs, have molded their lives by believing that only men, and special men at that, can do this job. No one wants to crack those molds, or even chip them."

Hadley sat on the edge of the plastic-covered desk and stared vacantly out of the high office window. "You know, Steely," he said, "I hate the authority people have over us in this job. Like Chief Haggerty telling me what to do, forcing me to send money to my wife, or like Jackson here making things tough for Angelli."

"You can't fight the Department," Steely answered, choking again on the cigarette. The booze from the night before, mixed with the heavy smoke of the oil-burner job, had tightened his chest and throat so that the cigarette smoke seemed rough, like a steel file. "It's like fighting City Hall."

Hadley jumped off the desk enthusiastically, an idea seemingly in his head. "But you can resist authority, if you can find the right ways."

Hadley walked to the window then, and sat on the sill. "My great great grandfather," he continued, "was killed in the Polish Insurrection of 1863, when the Poles fought the Tsarist army. He believed fighting was the way to resist. But his grandson, who was my grandfather, found a way to resist the Russians by demanding that everyone speak only Polish in the Polish schools, for the Russians had forced them to speak Russian. Soon, my grandfather had all the students of Poland speaking only Polish, and then they went on strike. He found a way to resist, you see, with the language."

Steely laughed. "You really like your Polish connection, don't you?"

"Proud, Steely," Hadley answered. "Proud of it. Do you know that Poland had free elections as early as 1573, that they had a free public library in 1747, and a public theater in 1765? That's all before America was even a country, Steely."

Hadley, Steely noticed, developed the same faraway look that he had when he talked about Jesus, a kind of haloed look.

"We could find something in the Department to resist," Hadley went on, holding the evaluation report in his hands, "if we looked hard enough. Like Jesus, and Francis of Assisi, and Gandhi, and Martin Luther King. They all found something to resist."

Steely was interested in what Hadley was saying. "They were all killed, though," he said, "weren't they?"

"Yes," Hadley answered, "except Francis, who went blind. You always have to give up something to resist, Steely."

Steely coughed again, and threw the cigarette on the floor. "I'll give up smoking, Red," he said, "if you can find the thing to resist in the Department."

"Well," Hadley said, but he was interrupted by the shrill buzz of the voice-alarm loudspeaker. ENGINE FIVE, LADDER SEVEN, RESPOND TO BOX ONE-OH-EIGHT-TWO, REPORTED TO BE A FIRE IN A VACANT BUILDING AT ONE-ONE-SIX EAST NINE-NINE STREET, BETWEEN PARK AND LEXINGTON.

"Let's go," Steely said, running to the thick brass pole that went from the ceiling of the locker room to the apparatus floor below. Hadley was right behind him as he slid down the pole, bouncing off the rubber mat at the base.

Arbuckle McFatty was already in the driver's seat of the ladder truck as Steely ran to his boots and Nomex firecoat which were laid out on the side step of the apparatus. Lieutenant Jackson was sitting in the front of the cab, his helmet pulled firmly down over his head.

Kathy was in her boots, helmet on, and throwing her coat over her shoulder as she jumped up onto the side step of the truck, a six-foot hook in her right hand. Hadley raced around to the other side of the fire truck, where he put on his gear and stepped up to the side of the truck. Steely stood next to Kathy. He was holding an ax and a halligan tool.

The pumper of Engine Company 5 was first to leave the firehouse, followed by the long apparatus of Ladder Company 7. Both fire trucks went down Eighty-seventh Street and turned up Third, sirens and air horns blasting cruelly through the hot July afternoon.

CHAPTER 24

STEELY could smell the smoke at Ninety-sixth Street. It was the smell of burning wood, and he knew they had a job. There was only one smell like that in the world.

Engine 5 and Ladder 7 turned into Ninety-ninth Street, going up a small hill, across Lexington, and then down toward the New York Central Railroad trestle. Steely was looking over the top of the cab of the fire truck at the smoke, and the yellow leaping flames shooting out of a window on the top floor of the abandoned building. He could see that the building that once stood next to it had recently been torn down, for the pinks and purples and oranges and blues and greens of the rooms were still attached to the standing building, like a garish quilt of plaster and paint, a series of rectangular colors that, if they were on a small canvas, could hang in one of the fancy museums downtown.

"Better take a mask," Steely said in a quiet, steady voice to Kathy as he pulled up his boots, and as the apparatus screeched to a halt and the air horn blasted furiously. It would be a tough job, a good job as they say in the Department, and he wanted to convey a sense of calmness to her.

Steely looked over the cab to see what was wrong, for they had stopped more than half a block from the burning building. A purple van, like the one he had ripped open after the Holy Name racket, a scene of the Grand Canyon at sunset painted on its side, was double-parked before them. There had been just room enough for Engine Company 5 to get by, but there was no way that the much wider ladder truck could inch its way forward. "Damn," Steely said, picking up a halligan tool and an ax.

"Leave the extinguisher there," he called to Kathy as he watched Lieutenant Jackson and Hadley run toward the burning building, "and take the power saw, because we'll have to cut a hole in the roof before the fire takes the whole top floor."

Steely gave the building a quick study as he followed the others up the street. It was a six-story H-type building, probably built just before the Second World War, he thought. Built of sand-colored brick, it had two wings connected by a corridor. There were no fire escapes on the front of the building. The fire escapes would be in the center court area on the side of either wing.

Kathy was on his heels as he turned into the center court. He saw Hadley drop the ladder of the fire escape to the cracked and crumbling concrete of the courtyard. Hadley had the outside vent position today, and would ventilate the fire wherever possible from the outside of the building. Steely was assigned the forcible-entry tools, and Kathy the extinguishing can, which she wouldn't need now anyway. The only part of the team they were missing was Whorehickey Harrigan, who had been assigned the roof-man position. Signing out to shop for dinner, Steely thought, was a kind of blatant and not easily acceptable excuse to get out of the afternoon's drill period. It didn't matter anyway, Steely thought, because most of the doors of the building were probably forced open anyway, abandoned buildings being as valuable to building strippers as diamonds were to Harry Winston. Running up the interior stairs, Steely saw that he was right, for all the doors in the large interior corridors were open or missing completely, no doubt like every lead and copper pipe and plumbing fixture in every apartment. Abandoned buildings were like a carcass for the strippers to pick at like vultures and crows.

Lieutenant Jackson was on the sixth floor, kneeling on the rubble-covered marble of the landing way waiting for them. The smoke was thin and wispy, for the fire, Steely remembered, had vented through the rear windows.

"The fire's in the end apartment," Lieutenant Jackson said, "in the rear corner. The Engine Company will be up soon, but we better go to the roof and make a trench cut just to make sure."

"Right," Steely said, following the lieutenant up the stairs to the roof. If the fire were traveling across the ceiling from one end of the building to the other, a trench cut across the center of the roof would force it out into the open air, like steam coming up through a grating on the street.

Steely turned to check on Kathy, and laughed a little as he saw her struggling with the forty-pound portable circular saw. How many times had he struggled with it, too, he asked himself? Hundreds, he answered.

On the roof, the smoke and fire were dancing up toward the sky wildly, like a reverse waterfall of gas and flame. Lieutenant Jackson was standing in the middle of the roof, pointing to the soft, bubbled tar of the surface. "Better start a cut here, Steely," he said.

"Angelli carried the saw up," Steely said, "so let her do it."

"Because I said for you to do it," Lieutenant Jackson answered, ending whatever uneasy truce existed between them.

Steely threw the ax and the halligan forcefully against the bulkhead brick of the roof and turned to the lieutenant. "Look, I don't really want to have it out with you," he said, "but as long as I've been in this job, the guy who carried the saw used it."

"Listen, Byrnes, I'm the boss at this job, and you'll cut the trench just as I say."

Steely remembered then the evaluation report he and Hadley had read earlier, and realized that Lieutenant Jackson was not going to give Angelli an opportunity to perform adequately, not if he could help it. It could become an issue, he thought, easily. All I have to do is start the saw and give it to her to operate. There's nothing he could say then, not over the roar of the saw. But why should I? Why should I go out of my way to give Angelli an opportunity to perform adequately? All I wanted to do was to take her to dinner, maybe a movie.

Was this the kind of thing Hadley said we should resist? Hardly

198

seems worth it, not here in the middle of a fire, not over something as small as a trench cut. So he's acting out his own part, playing the boss. There's nothing to gain by fighting him here.

Steely, without saying a word, went to the saw and bent over it. He primed it a little and pulled the rubber T-handle, once, twice, and then on the third time the large circular blade began to revolve and the motor roared like a World War I fighter plane. He picked the saw up, and yelled at the top of his lungs to Kathy, "Just stay behind me, for safety. Put your hand on my back, and hold it there."

Steely walked to the edge of the parapet wall, where it met the roof, and began to cut deeply into the roof. He noticed that it had become a little more spongy, a little more bubbled. There was no doubt that the heat of the fire, if not the fire itself, was directly below them and traveling across the cockloft, the space between the top-floor ceiling and the roof itself.

The saw rumbled through the inch or so of tarring, then through the tar paper, and then through the wooden slats of the roof itself, the plywood and the planking. Smoke began pushing up, like from a machine, as soon as he was all the way through. He continued cutting the line, bending over, Kathy behind him, her hand held firmly against the Nomex material of his coat.

Suddenly, Steely felt a hard slap on his back, and he took the saw blade out of the roof. He looked around and saw Lieutenant Jackson, who was yelling at him over the sound of the motor. "I think we should back off," Jackson was saying. "The roof is getting very soft, like sand at the goddamned beach."

"I don't think so," Steely yelled in return. "I know these roofs, and we have a few minutes left easy before it begins to shift and wobble."

"How many minutes?" Kathy yelled, alarmed.

Steely realized that this was the first time she had ever been operating above a fire this way.

Just then, a message was transmitted over Lieutenant Jackson's portable radio. It was a loud, squawky message from the lieutenant of Engine Company 5. ENGINE FIVE TO LADDER SEVEN, it said, WE HAVE HAD A BURST LENGTH IN THE HOSE AND IT WILL BE SEVERAL MINUTES BEFORE WE HAVE WATER ON THE FIRE.

"All the more reason to get this hole done," Steely said. "Otherwise we'll lose the building completely, and we'll be here for the whole day."

"Right," Lieutenant Jackson said, coughing now in the smoke that was beginning to get thicker and heavier as it pushed up from the cut.

Steely finished the first cut, about twelve feet long, and then returned to the parapet wall to begin a parallel cut just twelve inches away from the first. The motor started to fade down and then rev up in the swirling smoke, as it lost and then regained the oxygen it needed for combustion. The roof seemed to sway every now and then, and it felt to Steely as if he were walking on a barge.

"How much longer?" Kathy yelled, her hand still firmly planted on Steely's back.

"Just relax," he returned, "just relax."

Finally, the second cut was completed and Steely returned again to the parapet wall to make a cross cut at the end. That done, he killed the motor and told Kathy to take his ax and begin to pry up the roofing with its head.

Steely picked up his halligan tool, and using its adz end, began to lift the plywood and the slats and the paper and the tar. The smoke billowed up in chimney-like puffs as the trench hole was made, forcing Steely and Kathy to step back every few seconds to look for cleaner air to breathe. Both of them were coughing and choking now. They pulled and pried as quickly as they could, and Lieutenant Jackson stood just behind them in the escaping smoke, trying hard not to cough as much as he was coughing.

Suddenly the smoke disappeared and a large, bright ball of fire shot up through the trench cut, as if someone below had ignited a tank car of gasoline.

"Bail out," Steely said, running quickly toward the roof stairs, pushing Kathy before him. Lieutenant Jackson was right next to him, puffing in exhaustion.

"I dropped the ax," Kathy said.

"Don't apologize," Steely answered, still holding on to his halligan tool.

Steely opened the heavy metal roof door and was hit with a blast of heat. "I think the fire must be out in the hallway," he said.

"We can take the fire escape down," Lieutenant Jackson said, heading toward the gooseneck steel that led to the courtyard fire escape.

Just then they heard a loud call coming from the front end of the building, more a screech then a call. *"Jeesuss,"* it said, the voice cracking on the final long *s*.

"That's Red," Steely said, running back toward the fire, over the soft, lumpy tar, and past it to the parapet wall at the front of the building.

There he looked over the four-foot-high wall and saw Red Hadley, his face covered with fear and anguish, standing on the top floor window ledge, wedging himself as far to one side of the window as he possibly could. God, Steely thought, how'd he get there? Must've been venting when the fire blew back at him.

Behind Hadley was the fire. Rushing out furiously from the adjoining window, and lapping quickly from the top of the window frame where he was silhouetted, the flames of the fire were just inches away from him now.

He was being burned, Steely thought, there was no way he could escape it. No way except to jump the fifty feet to the sidewalk below.

"Hold on, Red," he yelled. That goddamn van, he thought. If only we had the truck here, McFatty could pick him off in seconds with the aerial ladder. Goddamn burst length, with no water coming. What to do? God, what to do?

"Hold on, Red," Steely yelled again. "I'm here."

What good does that do, he thought. Being here does no good at all. Action. What is the action? Red has seconds, just seconds.

Lieutenant Jackson was now beside him. "Think if I held your wrists he could grab your legs?" he asked after peering over the parapet wall.

Steely looked at him with disgust. There was an easy fourteen feet between the top of the parapet and the top of the window frame, and any fool could see that even the length of a basketball player's body wouldn't be long enough.

"Jesusss," Red Hadley yelled again. He was being burned now, Steely knew. He didn't have to look.

"Call for a roof rope, Lieutenant," Steely said, beginning to rush away. "I'm going down and try to reach him from inside, maybe through a wall."

"For God's sake," Lieutenant Jackson said. "The room is on fire."

Steely moved away.

"I've got a rope," Kathy said then, bending over in a burst of coughing.

Steely stopped as if he had hit an imaginary wall. The fire was now shooting with furnace energy from the trench cut, and they were enveloped in smoke and barely able to see one another.

"What rope?" Steely yelled, grabbing her arm.

"Here," she cried, pulling a plastic bag from the oversize pocket of her Nomex coat.

"I don't like it," Lieutenant Jackson called. "That's nylon, the new navy utility rope."

"I don't give a damn what it is," Steely said, grabbing the package violently from Kathy's hands. "How long is it?"

"Seventy-five feet," she gasped, leaning over again in a coughing fit. .

"That'll make it," Steely said.

But there was no point in just dropping the rope to Hadley, he thought, for if he's burned he'll never have the strength to hold it. I'll have to drop. Christ, with the fire like this, I hope the roof holds. He pulled Kathy to the vertical surface of the parapet wall. He could see that she was scared, but who wouldn't be? *I'm* goddamned scared.

He quickly made a bowline knot at the end of the rope and snapped its open circle into the hook of the rescue-V-rig tied around his waist. He handed the other end of the rope to Kathy. "Tie this around that vent pipe and then lower me down," he said, putting his leg over the parapet wall.

"*Lord, Lord*," came the cry from below, and then a fierce scream. Steely looked down quickly, hoping that Hadley had not jumped. "Hang on, Red," he yelled. "I'm coming."

Lieutenant Jackson edged Kathy back with his forearm. "I'll lower you down, Steely," he said. "I got it."

Steely looked at him, and then at Kathy. At least the lieutenant had experience, he thought to himself. At least he had been here before, and could hold the weight of two people on a rope.

Did Kathy know how to do that? What if she slips? What if lets the smoke get to her? I'm on the end of the rope, for chrissakes.

The seconds were speeding by. Steely looked hard into the eyes of Lieutenant Jackson, and then back to Kathy. Finally he said, "She has the rope, Lou, and she'll lower. Got it?"

There was no mistake about the threat that was thick in Steely's voice, and Lieutenant Jackson just nodded his head.

Will she be there when I need her, Steely asked himself? It's her rope, and that answers that.

"Put three turns of the rope around your rescue-V-rig hook," he said as he began to swing over the parapet wall. "And buttress the hook up against the wall itself. Then let the rope down steadily, until I yell. Hook goes on top of the rope."

"I know how to do it," Kathy said as she turned the rope into the snap hook.

"*Lord Jesus*," Hadley yelled as the fire now began to wrap around him like burning cellophane.

Steely dropped over the roof wall and descended, first in jerks, then steadily, until he was lowered just to the left of the window parallel to Hadley, coughing all the while in the smoke, feeling the radiation currents of the heat. "Stop," he yelled when he was level with Hadley. The rope stopped short, and just then Hadley jumped at him. Grabbing him.

"I'm here, Red," Steely yelled, remembering then how Hadley had chopped through the wall to pull him out of the fire on Ninetieth Street. I owe you plenty, Red, he thought.

"Steely," Hadley yelled in return as he pulled himself into Steely's neck.

"I got you, Red," Steely said, wrapping his arms around the Nomex coat, looking down and seeing that Hadley's dungarees had been burned away just at the top of his boots. The pain, Steely thought, the pain he must feel. Steely felt the great heat coming out of the large figure that was now clamped to his body. "I got you, Red," he repeated.

Hadley screamed again in pain as his weight transferred fully onto Steely's body, and Steely saw the fire, felt it lick at him, lapping through the window opening.

He looked up at the roof edge, yelling, "Okay, Kathy." His voice carried through the smoke. A command, a crucial life-and-death command, yet he tried to make it a request. Kathy was there, damn it, just like Red. "Lower," he yelled, "lower easy."

Then, just below the now murmuring sound of Hadley's agony, Steely thought he heard a rip, like a rough zipper violently pulled. Was it a tear, he wondered, or something cracking? It happened so fast, in tiny parts of a second, and then there were Hadley's cries.

Suddenly, there was a jerk and Steely's mind began to flash. He thought of Maryanne first, on their wedding day, so lovely she was in that long, full gown, the one she had to carry in her arms every time she walked, like royalty. And he thought of his children, Tara and Jeffrey, kicking a soccer ball to each other across the backyard grass in Levittown. He heard their voices, giggling and laughing, the sweet voices of children.

Steely and Hadley had been swinging, and now they were falling. The rope that had hung between them, Kathy Angelli's utility rope, attached to the hook of the rescue-V-rig, was gone, and they were falling. Christ, Kathy, Steely thought, you were there, *there*. But what did you do? God. God help us.

"*Jesus*," Hadley yelled. "*Steely*."

They fell to the ground in two or three seconds. Hadley held furiously onto Steely's neck with one hand, and held the other hand up, as if reaching for something, reaching toward heaven. The weight of the coupled men had shifted just a little bit with his raised hand, but enough to change the angle of their feet in relation to the ground. It was as if they were beginning to move in a circle now, like the hands of a clock, and then they hit the ground. Hadley struck the pavement first, almost perfectly flat, like a hamburger thrown on a grill. His helmet was knocked away, and his head splattered as it hit forcibly against the concrete, the rough-stoned, cold, and indifferent concrete of New York's Spanish Harlem.

Steely felt his chin go into Hadley's shoulder, sinking deeply into his skin, and his eyes falling hard against his neck. Then he felt his wrist hit the concrete, the wristbone flattened inside the skin, and he felt his ankle, too, hit the concrete with a thud sound.

The pain shot through him like venom. And he felt his whole body surge into Red Hadley, pushing every bit of oxygen out from within. His helmet, too, had flown off, and as he felt his chin go into Hadley's shoulder and eyes into Hadley's neck, he felt an ear being pressed forcefully in against the cheek of Hadley's face. And now, as he caved into Hadley with his full body, he felt the blood that was forced up from the body of the man below him splatter against his face and his neck and drip down his shoulders and beneath his shirt to his chest.

Then he heard Hadley attempt to say something, but all he heard was a gurgled, blood-choked sound of despair. They had fallen, and they had hit the ground, and he felt the pain leaping like electricity through his wrist and through his ankle, but he heard Hadley's gurgle. He was *hearing*.

He tried to move his head slightly, fearfully, and found that it moved with little effort. He raised his head away from Hadley's cheek and neck and shoulder, and turned toward him, wondering why he could move at all. He looked at the face of his friend, a face that was oozing blood from the nose and from the mouth and from the ears, almost floating in a pool of blood, and he saw that Red Hadley was smiling.

CHAPTER 25

THE Chief of Department's car got as far as Ninety-eighth Street and Lexington Avenue, where a dozen or so fire and police vehicles were parked, double-parked, and triple-parked. Haggerty was out of his car even before the wailing sound of the siren stopped. Eddie, his driver, opened the trunk of the car, and Haggerty reached for his white canvas firecoat. He then grabbed his dented and scratched chief's helmet, the same white helmet he had bought when he was promoted to battalion chief and carried with him through the ranks of deputy chief, deputy assistant chief, assistant chief, and finally, Chief of Department. Through all of those ranks in only five years, the helmet was his symbol of achievement.

Haggerty ran to Ninety-ninth Street and turned west toward Park, noticing an ambulance and a ladder truck blocked by a double-parked van. A policeman was writing a parking ticket, his foot high up on the van's bumper. The scene was a panorama of flashing red lights and scurrying firefighters. Haggerty walked into the middle of the street, and noticed Deputy Chief Joe Tierney directing fire operations from a command center set up before a large H-type building.

The deputy chief was surprised to see the Chief of Department at a second-alarm fire. Even with injured firefighters, the Chief usually does not respond before the fourth alarm.

Haggerty casually returned the deputy chief's salute, while at the same time looking at the crowd of firefighters and ambulance attendants huddled on the sidewalk before them. A stretcher, more a stretcher bed with a mattress and wheels, was being lifted over a parked car. "Any woman?" Haggerty asked. He thought to himself, all I need is a smashed-up female firefighter. The newspapers will swear we endangered them recklessly to prove a point.

"No, sir, there are two firefighters, one of them in very serious shape, the other is a miracle."

Haggerty looked up and saw the fire burning through the roof of the building. There had to be a lot of pressure on Tierney, he thought, with two injured firefighters, and a fire raging through a cockloft of a building as big as this one. He had to deal with the injuries, and at the same time think about the safety of all those working on the top floor, on the perimeters of the fire. It was no easy job being a command chief in the field, that was for sure.

"Do you want to take command?" Tierney asked.

Haggerty knew that he was asking out of respect for his rank, and that the Chief of Department did not take command of second-alarm fires. "No, Joe," he answered, "just fill me in about this." He gestured toward the crowd of firefighters and EMTs before them.

"The fire began on the sixth floor rear," Tierney answered, "origins still unknown."

"Not the fire, Joe," Haggerty interrupted. "Tell me about this, how did it happen?" He had been at hundreds of similar fires, and they always got extinguished, one way or another. What was important here was that two firefighters had fallen a distance of more than sixty feet, and the question was, why? And then, how?

Tierney seemed suddenly a little nervous, Haggerty thought. He knew Tierney, and knew that it wasn't like him to be anything but direct and authoritative. Did he know something here, I wonder, that will have to be pried out of him?

"We're not sure yet, Chief," Tierney said, adjusting the volume of his portable radio so that he could listen for messages as he talked to Haggerty.

Probably, Haggerty thought, Tierney is just unsure. We're always so sure of everything in the Fire Department, sure what to do in

207

every emergency. It's just natural to be nervous when you're not so sure. "I'm not asking for a formal report just now," he said, sticking his hands into the pockets of his white canvas coat. "I just want to know what you feel about it."

"I think there was a failure somewhere," Tierney said, moving just a little so he could get a better view of the injured firefighters being lifted onto the stretchers. "I have a battalion chief in the building now, asking some preliminary questions, but the fire's not under control yet, and so the big questions will have to come later. Something happened, though. One of the firefighters was being lowered from the roof to pick up the other on a window ledge and maybe the rope snapped, or burned. It was a nylon rope, I guess. Not even sure of that yet. Or the rope could've sheared on the corner of the roof, because we know for sure they didn't use a roller to guide it over the edge. Or maybe the rope wasn't secured properly in the first place. We don't know yet, Chief."

Haggerty started to walk toward the ambulances, where firefighters were lifting the stretchers. He stopped, turned toward Tierney, and said, "Just get me some preliminary facts, Joe."

Tierney made a half salute and went into the fire building as Haggerty continued toward the ambulances and the injured firefighters. He looked down at the first firefighter and saw a mass of blood starting to cake around the side of his head and ear. He did not want to look and fought the impulse to turn away. He noticed the shape of the body of the man on the stretcher, wide shoulders and heavy-muscled arms, placed over a thin waist. Such a strong body, Haggerty thought, and to think that just a couple of minutes ago he was fighting the fire, using the strength that God gave him. I wonder what he ate for breakfast, or for lunch today? Haggerty then slapped his hand gently against his knee. It was a gesture of powerlessness and frustration. I had lunch with the Mayor of the City of New York, enjoying myself with all the big shots, making points, and consolidating a future. I suppose he ate hamburgers in the firehouse, or maybe tuna fish salad. He doesn't look good at all, this fireman. If I had a son, if Josie and I could have had a son, I would dissuade him from coming near the Fire Department, anywhere near it. Like the Irish say, "The world is made up of gay fights and sad songs." The Fire Department has only humor and tragedy to offer. My son, if I had a son, would never be caught dead sprawled out on a sidewalk in Harlem. I wouldn't permit it.

He was then joined by a battalion chief whose name was unknown to him. "What hospital are these men going to?" Haggerty asked him.

"I think," the battalion chief replied, "that the ambulances came from Central Harlem Hospital."

"That's not good enough," Haggerty said, walking toward the second ambulance, where firefighters were preparing to secure the stretcher to the floor of the vehicle. "These men will need neurosurgical care probably, and the best bone men available, and so you better send them down to Lenox Hill."

The battalion chief was right on his heels, helmet in hand. "Yes, sir," he said, turning to look for one of the ambulance drivers.

Haggerty stopped a passing EMT, and he had to yell to him in the midst of all the excitement to be heard. "Give me a prognosis on these men," he said. "Just off the top, if you please." He did not want the medical technician to feel he was being asked an official question, one that would have to be backed up by interviews and transcripts later on.

"Watch it now," a firefighter yelled in the background. "Let's get these ambulances moving."

The EMT put down the suitcase-size medical equipment container he was holding and gestured toward the ambulance right behind him. "This guy's unconscious," he said, "but he's not so banged up. The other fireman is going to be touch-and-go all the way, and he'll need life-support systems."

As the EMT picked up his medical case, the door of the first ambulance slammed shut, and with its siren screaming, pulled away toward Park, making a left and going downtown against the traffic toward Lenox Hill Hospital.

Just as the doors of the second ambulance were closing, Haggerty noticed that the face of the stretchered firefighter had turned and was lighted by a beam of afternoon sunlight that reflected from the ambulance wall. "My God," he said aloud.

"What is it, sir?" the battalion chief asked as he was passing by.

Haggerty did not answer, but ran quickly to the ambulance just as the EMT was pulling its door shut, and grabbed the door handle. He climbed up on the back step and took a look, a careful look, at the unconscious man sprawled on the stretcher. He only whispered then, closing his eyes. "Steely," he said. "Steely."

Haggerty watched the second ambulance speed off before he returned to the command podium. He looked up at the fire and saw that the flames had turned to dark smoke. He next noticed splashes of water shooting out of several windows from the interior. He knew that the firefighters had made their way from the hallway through the burning apartments on the top floor.

Tierney exited the fire building holding a portable radio to his ear. "Ten four," he said, pushing the transmitter button as he approached Haggerty. "Have the two additional ladder companies pull the ceiling, and get some relief for the engine companies. I'll call the fire under control."

Haggerty again pushed his hands into his heavy canvas coat, but this time without a flare of authority. He felt sad as he pictured Steely's face in his mind. He had been in command of a lot of fires where great tragedies had taken place, and he had experienced many New York deaths that never made the newspapers, the suicides, the suffocations, the burns, the murders. He had watched stretchers and body bags being moved from the scene of a fire hundreds of times in his career, yet he never felt quite the emptiness in his stomach that he felt now, the yearning that things could somehow be different. Steely Byrnes, one of the few great friends from the old neighborhood, there, unconscious in the ambulance, a miracle, Tierney had said. God, how this job brings the living so continually close to death. Steely, the old roughhouse, irreverent, pain-in-the-neck Steely, unconscious on a stretcher.

He turned to Tierney, saying, "Okay, Joe, tell me what you found out, and make it clear. I know one of the men quite well."

"One of the injured firemen?" Tierney asked.

"Steely Byrnes," Haggerty replied, "from Ladder Company 7."

"Yeah," Tierney returned. "The other one's last name is Hadley, also from Ladder Company 7. He's very, very broken up, inside and out. The other guy, Byrnes, evidently fell right on top of him, being cushioned completely. It looks like he's got a concussion and a wrist fractured and smashed pretty badly. But not much more, an incredible thing."

"What about the why, Joe?"

Tierney took his helmet off and placed it on the thin metal podium. He then took his coat off and laid it on top of the helmet. His white shirt, the gold eagles gleaming on the collar tips, was wet with sweat and stuck to his body. "Evidently," he said, wiping his forehead with his hand, "Hadley must have heard a victim crying or something. There was a report of a derelict in the building, a squatter, and Hadley went after him, got caught in a flashback fire on the top floor with no fire escape. The officer and two firefighters of Ladder 7 were on the roof, and it was decided to lower Byrnes down on a three-eighth-inch utility rope to pick Hadley out of the window. The eyewitnesses said that when Hadley was picked off, something happened so the rope 'jerked.' That was the word the officer on duty used. Something malfunctioned."

"It was witnessed in its entirety by the officer?" Haggerty asked. He took his own coat off now, and let it hang on two fingers over his shoulder.

"No," Tierney answered. "He had a female firefighter in the lowering position, and he said he was supervising her as much as watching what was happening below. He says the jerk happened as soon as Byrnes picked up Hadley, and they began to lower together. It was then it happened and they plummeted."

"A female firefighter," Haggerty said. "Was everything done correctly, according to the procedures?"

"We're not sure, sir," Tierney sighed. "Both firefighters were wearing the new rescue-V-rigs, but the officer says he isn't sure if the female firefighter put the hook on top of the rope and took the turns, or put the rope on top of the hook and took the turns. If she didn't have the hook on top, the rope would have snagged with the sudden increase of pressure of two men hanging on the end of it. Which could have caused the rope or the rescue-V-rig to go beyond its breaking strength. But it wasn't the rope that ruptured, sir. It was the rig. The hook tore off."

Haggerty looked at the small columns of black smoke still rising to the sky, and shook his head. "Just what we need," he said in a low, cynical voice. "Women in the heat of the job. I'm going to take off, so have the field communications unit relay all and any information about the job, or Byrnes or Hadley, over the city-wide frequency."

"Right, Chief."

"And Joe," Haggerty added, "what about the derelict?"

"Roasted," Tierney replied. "They're bagging him now."

Eddie, an old black man who had been driving Haggerty and the previous chiefs of department for as many years as anyone could remember, was standing by the open trunk of Haggerty's car. Haggerty handed him his coat and helmet. Eddie folded the coat and placed it with the helmet in the corner of the trunk. In the front seat, Haggerty leaned down and turned the air-conditioner on. The afternoon seemed much hotter as it grew toward evening.

"Where to?" Eddie asked.

"Let's see," Haggerty said, looking at his watch. "I suppose we've missed the Chamber of Commerce meeting altogether, so let's just head back downtown to the office. I don't feel much like giving speeches or socializing anyway."

"I know just how you feel, Chief," Eddie said. "Every time one of the brothers gets hurt, nobody feels like doing much of anything. I saw a fireman, one of the guys I guess from Ladder 7, sitting on a parked car crying his eyes out."

Haggerty then thought of a speech he had given some years before at a promotion ceremony out at the Department's division of training at Ward's Island. "Emotions may work on a stage," he had said, fully believing it, "but never at the scene of an emergency. We cannot do our job in protecting the public with anything but the dispassionate facts needed to save the life of another human being." He remembered that the firefighters and the officers about to be promoted and their families had applauded him. "Your idealism is only good for firehouse chatter," he went on, "and you should always remember that. The only thing that works on the fire ground is cold action."

"It's tough on the men," Haggerty said. "Like a tragedy in the family."

The blue command car went across 101st Street, under the Grand Central Railroad trestle, and down Park.

"Should I take the Drive, sir?" Eddie asked.

"Stay on Park," Haggerty answered. "We don't want to get stuck in five o'clock traffic."

He thought of Steely then, and of the ambulance as its door shut and it sped away from the Harlem tenement.

Funny, he said to himself, remembering, it was such a small thing. And, why do I think of it now, after so many years? We were eleven, maybe twelve years old, and it was a lonely Sunday afternoon. Just Steely and I walking up Third Avenue. Me, not a penny in my pocket. And then there was that delicious smell in the air, that aroma of chicken chow mein coming from the upstairs Chinese restaurant on Fifty-ninth Street. "What a smell," I said to Steely.

"I could eat Chinese food right now, even if I knew for sure that cats were in it."

Steely laughed, that great, wide-faced grin he had. "I have three bucks, Jack," he said. He had been saving for something, a baseball glove, a football jersey, something like that. But he said, "You want Chinese food, Jack, let's go." How generous he was, how natural and generous. Everything I've gotten in my life I've had to work for, and no one ever gave me anything. Except Steely Byrnes, who gave me chicken chow mein on a Sunday afternoon.

They were at Fourteenth Street and Union Square when the radio blasted through the car. CITY-WIDE COMMUNICATIONS TO CAR FIVE, it squawked.

Haggerty picked up the worn black telephone handle receiver, saying, "Car 5 to city-wide, go ahead."

CITY-WIDE TO CAR FIVE, THE MIXER IS OFF. WE HAVE A FIREFIGHTER FROM THE SECOND ALARM AT NINETY-NINTH STREET DOA AT LENOX HILL HOSPITAL.

"Jesus, Mary, and Joseph," Haggerty sighed, again closing his eyes.

"I'm sorry," Eddie said. "I'm real sorry, Chief."

"Ten four," Haggerty said, replacing the telephone gently, dispassionately onto the fixture screwed to the dashboard.

He stared absently before him. "That would have to be Hadley," he thought, and he remembered Katra Hadley, lying in her hotel bed, her head propped up by two pillows, looking as beautiful as any woman he had ever seen in his life. Then he remembered the blood-matted hair and the blood-caked ear of her husband as he lay near death on a stretcher. He felt something give in his stomach, and in his chest, and he threw his head back on the car seat. "Turn around, Eddie," he said. "We'll go to Lenox Hill Hospital, and spend an hour there, or so."

It was a sad day for the Fire Department. That was the first thought that came then into Haggerty's mind. He wondered, also, if it were even sadder because it was Hadley who was dead. Each day a firefighter dies in the line of duty is a sad day. The signal 5555 was communicated from firehouse to firehouse over the Department voice-alarm system, the message then printed out on the computer, a simple signal that said, Lower your flags to half mast in front of the firehouse, for a firefighter has fallen, and he will not rise again. It was something that Haggerty as the Chief of Department was used to. It happened eight to ten times a year, and eight to ten times a year he would talk to the widows, commiserate with them, promise them that everything humanly possible would be done to alleviate the great stress that occurs during family tragedies, a great loss in the family. He would try to engage the children in soft conversations that had nothing to do with their fathers, nothing to do with the idea that their fathers would no longer be with them, forever and ever. If he knew anything, he knew how to handle a hospital scene, or a widow at a wake, and children at a funeral. It was an awful skill, a skill that he hated, and today it was a skill he would have to practice with Katra Hadley.

Katra Hadley. Goodness, what a strange thing to happen in a world as large as ours. Twelve thousand men and it is Hadley's wife who comes to see me, Hadley himself that I dress down. An awful thing, this coincidence, this tragedy. All caused by a female firefighter on the roof making the wrong turns with the rope, causing a snag, a rupture. Who is she, I wonder? What does she look like? Is she one of those militant sue-'em Suzies, or one of the others, the ones who are really trying to do the job? She must have panicked, must have been scared of the roof. There's always so much smoke on the roof of a top-floor job. Everything we taught her, all that training, must have gone up with the smoke. What are these women doing on the job anyway?

"Do you want the siren?" Eddie asked, interrupting his thoughts.

"No," Haggerty answered curtly. There was no reason to rush to the hospital. Nothing could change between now and the time he got there, traffic or not. He picked up the car radio phone and pressed the transmission button. "Car 5 to city-wide."

CITY-WIDE TO CAR FIVE.

"Have all notifications been made on the death of a firefighter?"

YES, CAR FIVE, THE BATTALION CHIEF, SECOND BATTALION, HAS GONE TO PICK UP THE WIDOW AND THE RC CHAPLAIN IS ON HIS WAY. DIVISION OF SAFETY HAS BEEN NOTIFIED. THE CHIEF OF PRESS RELATIONS IS ON HIS WAY TO THE HOSPITAL. THE SIGNAL FIVE-FIVE-FIVE-FIVE HAS BEEN TRANSMITTED.

"Ten four."

In Lenox Hill Hospital on Seventy-seventh Street, Haggerty walked amid the hectic activity of people, doctors and nurses and orderlies rushing from one room to another, from one corridor or elevator to another. In the Emergency Room waiting room, he saw

214

the Chief of Safety stride through the doors, and the Chief of Press Relations sitting on a blue plastic bench, his knees crossed, writing on a yellow pad attached to a clipboard. A couple of reporters were already asking questions, and a photographer was sighting his camera. It was not a new scene to him. It was a scene he had experienced too many times before, except in different hospitals, in different emergency rooms. He nodded greetings to those he knew in the room and walked through the double steel doors marked HOSPITAL PERSONNEL ONLY. At the nurses' station inside, he asked for the doctor in charge. A long period of time passed before an older man, a stethoscope hung over his right shoulder, approached him. Seeing the authority of the chief's uniform, he said, "I'm Dr. Azenberg, can I be of some assistance?"

Good, Haggerty thought, that's why I had them sent to this hospital. Experience. No young kids here, fresh out of medical school, and foreign medical schools at that. My firefighters take chances enough in the field without taking chances in hospitals.

"I'm looking for Firefighter Byrnes," Haggerty said.

"He's upstairs," Dr. Azenberg said. "He may have a small concussion, but nothing very serious."

"Do you think I could see him," Haggerty asked, "talk to him?"

"Tomorrow, perhaps," Dr. Azenberg replied. "His left wrist and hand have multiple breaks and fractures, and they are working on him now. The anesthesia won't break for ten hours or so. But you know, that fireman is one of the chosen. That he should survive such an impact, even thrown on the body of another man, is nothing short of incredible."

"And the other man?" Haggerty asked.

Dr. Azenberg shook his head. "He was dead when he got here. There was absolutely nothing we could do."

Haggerty pushed open the heavy steel doors and again entered the Emergency Room waiting room. Chairs had been pushed aside from the middle of the room, and sitting there in a circle, cross-legged on the floor, were three men and one woman. Their eyes were closed, and they were holding hands. Each was wearing a white shirt and blue gabardine pants.

"What's this?" Haggerty asked his press officer.

"They're praying, Chief," the press officer said, "For Hadley. The news is on the media already. Hadley was one of their church group."

"Get them out of here," Haggerty snarled.

"I don't think we can, Chief," the press officer replied. "I think they probably have a right. I mean, it's hard to force people to leave if they don't want to."

Just then, Katra Hadley entered the room. She was wearing a red plaid skirt and a white ruffled blouse, and except for her blond hair, she looked like a Scottish noblewoman. She saw Haggerty talking to the press officer, and ran to him, throwing herself onto his chest.

Haggerty held her as the photographer snapped pictures. It was an awkward moment, as if he had been photographed dancing with another woman in a night club, instead of comforting the wife of a firefighter who had been killed in the line of duty. He felt his face flush and perspiration build on his forehead.

"Oh, Jack," Katra said, her eyes filled with tears. "Was it very painful for him?"

"She's the widow," he heard a reporter in the background say. "That's Hadley's wife," he heard from another.

"No, Katra," Haggerty said gently, putting his arm around her and leading her to a far corner of the room where they could share a few moments of grief and solitude together. It was something he had done many times before. "It all happened in just two or three seconds, in just two or three seconds it was over completely. I'm told he lived for another half hour or so, but he never was conscious, and everything possible was done to try to save him. It's over now, Katra, and you must think about the future, about yourself. The death of your husband is a great tragedy for the New York Fire Department, and it's a tragedy for you, too, but everything will be all right now."

She held a handkerchief to her nose, blowing it, and she was crying so forcefully that it was hard to understand her. "Why will everything be all right now, Jack?" she asked.

"Because you'll have the pension, Katra," he said softly, reassuringly. "And you'll have all the insurance policies, twenty thousand dollars from the state, fifty thousand dollars from the federal government, line-of-duty firefighter's death benefit, and you'll have the union insurance policies. A full year's salary also. Things will be all right, Katra, just you wait and see."

"The money doesn't matter, Jack," she said, falling again onto his chest. "All I ever wanted was for him to take care of me, and he didn't want to do that."

216

Her scent went deep into his nostrils, and he closed his eyes. He opened them quickly when he felt her being pulled away from him. One of the men from the prayer group had her by the arm, leading her toward the other members of the group. "Mrs. Hadley," he said rapidly, "we are from the church, your husband's church, and we are praying to Jesus for his soul. We will give him the burial that he wanted, the burial that will bring him into the arms of Jesus, who waits for him with great sadness in his heart, and with tears in his eyes. We will handle everything, everything from the selection of the coffin, to the buying of the burial plot. We will carry him to the arms of Jesus. . . ."

Haggerty could not control his anger. He grabbed the man's wrist and squeezed it as hard as he could until Katra's arm was freed. "Get me a police officer," he shouted to the press chief. "I want these people out of here right now. The Catholic chaplain is on his way and he will take care of everything. So get these people out of here this instant."

It's sacrilege, Haggerty thought, a sin that people like this were allowed to roam free throughout the city. He again held Katra around the shoulders to console her.

When two hospital security guards appeared, the prayer group left the waiting room without protest, and Haggerty decided it was time for him to leave too.

"Can I call you if I need to know something?" Katra asked.

"I'll see you at the wake," Haggerty replied softly. It was an ambiguous reply, he knew, but there was no point in having her think she could call him at will either.

"Do you know what caused the accident, Chief Haggerty?" a reporter asked.

"We understand one firefighter fell on top of the other," a second reporter said.

"I cannot answer your questions at this time," he said, pushing open the waiting-room doors. "We are presently preparing a full report for the press."

Goodness, Haggerty thought, sitting again in his car traveling downtown on Park Avenue, what *will* we tell the press? It's bad enough when a firefighter is killed in some accident that nobody could have foreseen or prevented. But this. All of this caused by a woman wrapping a rope wrong on a hook. It had to be that. The rope was sound, all the tests proved it. And the rescue-V-rig was

217

overstressed by the snag. Johnson said the initial tests on the rig were fine. *Johnson*, right? Didn't I see a memo from Johnson?

Haggerty placed his attaché case on his knees, opened it, and lifted the batch of papers in his hands. He went through them, casually scanning each page until it was familiar to him, until he came again to the memorandum from Chief Johnson. He picked the memo out of the pile, and dropped the other papers back into his attaché case. The memo was dated, he noticed, on Thursday of the previous week. I must get them, he thought, to route the Department papers faster.

He read the memo, its style so familiar that he did not think anything of its formality, even though it came from a good friend and associate.

TO: Chief of Department
FROM: Chief, Research and Development
SUBJECT: Rescue-V-Rig

We have found problems in the secondary stages of testing.
A 170-pound man hanging from rescue-V-rig can create a
stress load on webbing near 1200 pounds. Rig should test
safely at 4,000 pounds, but has ruptured on several occasions
at 3000 pounds. We do not feel there is sufficient safety factor
poundage in stress load to permit use in field.
    Respectfully submitted,
    Anthony Johnson, Chief in Charge

Haggerty felt stunned, but only momentarily. He read the memo once more, studying the figures. The rig ruptured at 3000 pounds, after all, which was more than enough to hold two men. Perhaps the safety factor wasn't as great as it should have been, but everybody knows those standards are completely unrealistic. That rig would have held up fair enough if the procedures were followed correctly, no doubt about it. It was the woman who caused the rope to snag, creating a jolt. No wonder it came apart. No wonder.

Haggerty put the memo back in his attaché case and stared blankly out of the window. It is a great queer thing, he thought, an extraordinary circumstance that I get this memo, now, after this fatal fire. Johnson himself called me when they did the preliminary tests. "Looks good," he said. I remember. He was just waiting for the lab tests on breaking strength, but they had used the rope and the rescue-V-rig in more than fifty simulated rescues. "It worked out fine," he had said, "it's a good rescue system." Goodness, why did I end-run Department policy to get this V-rig out in the field? Just to move in tighter with Dougie Ratnor? Perhaps I should have waited until all the tests were in, but what's done is done. Anyway, it was not a failure in the equipment so much as a failure in procedure.

Haggerty realized his fingers were drumming madly on the side of his leather case. He clenched his fists.

This fire is going to create a problem for me, and the Department, especially when the press learns it was a woman that caused the accident. Two firefighters down and a dead derelict. It will be a feast. They love anything about women in the Fire Department, the press. Like cheese to the rats, they go into a frenzy. This fire will have to be handled with velvet gloves all the way. A pity it had to happen just at this time, with Gore moving out and me, in all likelihood, moving up. There will have to be an official inquiry, no doubt, and that's always bad publicity for the Department. But now that I think about it, it might not be all that bad for me. A chance to get my name in the papers, maybe even an opportunity to demonstrate my qualities of leadership, warn the city about these women in the Department fighting fires. It's a misfortune, there's no doubt about it, and I feel sorry for the girl. But bad luck for some can turn into good luck for others. That's the way it is, the way of the world.

Back in his office, Haggerty walked directly to the telephone on his desk. He dialed the Division of Research and Development and asked for Chief Johnson. "Tony," he said, "we've just had a line-of-duty death of a firefighter, and the rescue-V-rig is implicated, but I'm sure not at fault."

"Yes, sir," Johnson said, "I heard the four fives come in, but I didn't know it had anything to do with the equipment."

"It didn't have anything to do with the equipment," Haggerty said. "A woman firefighter lowered the man, and she put the rope on top of the hook, and not the hook on top of the rope before she took her turns, and you know how that can snag the rope. So when the one firefighter picked up the other in the rescue, a much greater stress was placed on everything, on the rope, the rescue-V-rig, everything, because the turns weren't taken right to begin with, you understand?"

"That could happen, yes, sir," Chief Johnson replied.

"And, Tony," Haggerty said, in a tone of voice that conveyed friendship and confidentiality, "I received the memo you sent me on the rig, which is, of course, not at all germane now. Certainly, we'll pull out of service all the ropes and all the rigs pending further evaluations, and go back to the old systems, but I want to know if you made a copy of that memo, if there's another copy around?"

"No, sir," Johnson replied, "it was only an informational memo, and not a formal report, so there was no copy made."

"Good," Haggerty said. "Then for the time being, we'll just go with the initial testing results, which were satisfactory. Can you handle all of that on your end?"

"Yes, that's correct, Chief," Johnson said, "the initial testing was satisfactory. The fact is that the secondary testing is not yet fully completed, anyway."

"Okay, Tony," Haggerty concluded, "we'll leave it there. What we know about the rescue-V-rig is that it tested satisfactorily in the initial testing."

After he hung up the phone, Haggerty opened his attaché case and pulled the memo out of it. He tore it into little pieces, thinking, the real problem is not with testing, the ropes, the rescue-V-rig, our training procedures, none of it. The problem is with the courts and the way they kowtowed to the suits of these women. It's the courts at fault for a firefighter's death. The courts forced these women into the job, and it's too bad some judge is not now laid out in a hospital bed up in Lenox Hill, and not Steely Byrnes.

CHAPTER 26

WHEN Steely awakened, he thought for just a moment he was in the first apartment he and Maryanne had rented after their wedding, the three-room flat up on Bainbridge Avenue in the Bronx. They had painted all the rooms there white, for white would make the place look clean, anyway.

He looked around. Everything was white here, too, the ceiling, the walls, the doors, even the blanket. He realized then, as his eyes tried to focus on things, that he had a headache. Whiskey, probably, he thought, boilermakers. And his mouth was dry, too, terribly dry. He narrowed his eyes a little in a squint, and found the window. It was a bright, sunny day, but what was that? he thought. What's that track on the ceiling, and the curtain? Christ, oh Christ, yes, he said to himself. A hospital. Red. God, Red. What . . . ?

Steely panicked, realizing he was completely alone. Move your legs, he told himself, and he looked down at the protuberances that were his feet below the blanket and watched them move. There was a slight pain in his left ankle, but only slight. The supports in the rubber boots, he thought, must have cushioned. Like Red. Oh God, Red, he cried in his mind, are you dead? No, you can't be. I've seen that much blood before, scraping pieces of people off the Triborough Bridge, people who lived through it.

Try your arms, Steely, he said then, and your fingers. The right-hand fingers were working, but nothing in the left hand. Not even any feeling. Jesus, take the covers down, pull the covers quickly.

With his right hand he pulled the blanket down to his waist, and then the sheet. He saw the cast, lying against his body, propped up by square gauze pads, white plaster from just beneath his elbow to the very tips of his fingers. The fingers were stretched apart, as if he were trying to measure the longest distance between his thumb and pinkie. He tried to lift the arm, but couldn't. The weight of the cast was like a vise grip. He moved his shoulder then, up and down, and saw the arm being dragged and then pushed against the sheet. Finally, he raised one knee and then the other, feeling again the stinging pain in his ankle. At least he could move everything, he thought, at least I'm together. He brought his right hand up and felt over the skin of his face, like a blind man would. No bandages, no scabs. But what's this, he asked himself, feeling the large bump on the right side of his forehead? Christ, no wonder I've got a headache. What happened? What the hell happened?

He remembered completely, then, picking up Red Hadley, falling with him, like two dolls wrapped around one another until they smashed into the pavement, pressing into him as if pushed by some great force, his chin going into Hadley's shoulder. You saved my life, Red, he said to himself, just like at that fire on Ninetieth Street. And I was supposed to be saving you. Oh, Red, what did I do to you?

I was there, Red, he repeated to himself over and over, his head throbbing. I had you. It was the rope. Something happened to the rope. Kathy, he said, shaking his head to clear his thoughts. Kathy, he said again as his awareness grew. Where were you, Kathy? I gave you the chance, and then . . . I should have given that goddamn rope to Lieutenant Jackson. How did you screw up, Kathy? What did you do?

Steely dozed off then, and woke up again when he heard a commotion in the hall. Turning his head, he saw Kathy standing just outside the door. Two nurses were barring her way into the room. She had flowers held in one hand, and her badge in the other. Her voice was reassuring. "I'll just watch him until he wakes up," she said. "We work together."

"It's okay," Steely yelled so that his voice carried into the hall.

The nurses were surprised, and ran in to him, fluttering around his bed, studying him, his cast, pulling his sheets and blanket up. One poured him a cup of water, which he drank in one gulp. She refilled it. "Do you feel like eating something?" the nurse asked.

Steely stared at Kathy. Her eyes and eyelids were red and pink and wet. She looked tired, beaten.

"Forget it," he said to the nurse, and they left the room.

Kathy pulled the flowers from the wrapping, four red roses and some angel's breath, and put them on the bed table. "Remember the flower you gave me on Lexington Avenue?" she asked, not waiting for an answer. "Now we're even."

She smiled, but it was a posed smile, he knew. He continued to stare at her, and thought he saw in her eyes the look of a frightened little girl, a little girl who knows she has done something wrong.

"It's terrible, Steely," she said then, turning her head away from his stare, hiding her face in her hands.

"Right," Steely said. He didn't know what else to say.

"With Red gone, and you here," she said, "I didn't know who to talk to, who could possibly understand."

Steely closed his eyes. He had sensed it all the time, he thought, but he didn't want to hear it, to know for sure. He's gone, he said to himself, dead. Jesus. Jesus Christ help him.

Steely's mouth was very dry, but he would not ask her to give him some water. He could not ask her to do anything for him. Not now. He opened his eyes and looked directly at her, his face distorted in pain and anger. "Where the hell were you?" he exploded. It was a reprimand, not a question, for his voice was cracked and harsh. "*Terrible*," he continued, not giving her a chance to reply, "terrible is not the goddamn word. What did you do? Everything was going great, until you did something. You blew it, Kathy. Shit!"

She was startled and drew in her breath in a gasp, as if he had struck her in the face. But then her expression changed and her green eyes seemed to shoot sparks of light. "I was there, Steely," she answered, slowly, deliberately, making certain he heard every word. "I knew what I was doing. Everything was done right."

"How do I know that, Kathy?" he asked.

"Because I'm telling you," she answered quickly.

"What about Jackson? What does he say?"

"Jackson's a jerk."

"That's not good enough."

Kathy turned now away from him, and folded her arms beneath her breasts. She was breathing heavily, to keep in control of herself, Steely guessed. When she turned again, she looked at him searchingly as if she were trying to find something in his face. "Look, Steely," she said finally, "it's important that you remember everything on the roof, before I lowered you."

"Why?"

"It's just important. Tell me how the procedure went."

"Christ, I don't remember. I thought it was okay when I went over the roof."

"How about connecting the rope on the hook, Steely? Do you remember that?"

"It was okay, I guess." His ankle was beginning to smart, he noticed, and he moved his leg a little. But then he was startled by her voice.

"Think," she yelled. "*I guess* isn't good enough for me either."

"Christ," he said, his tongue almost sticking to the roof of his mouth. He had never seen a woman so angry, not even Maryanne.

"I know what happened, Steely," she said more calmly now, "and I don't want to put words in your mouth. But my future is hanging on all of this."

Steely closed his eyes, trying to recollect the scene on the roof. "I remember you brought the rope out," he began, "and Jackson said something about how he didn't like it."

"Right," she said, urging him forward.

"But I didn't give a damn what kind of rope it was. I grabbed it and hooked it to my rescue-V-rig. And you tied the other end to a vent pipe and hooked the rope to your own V-rig."

"Do you remember what you said then, Steely?"

"Yes, I went over the procedure. 'Hook on top of the rope,' I said."

"What did I say, Steely?"

Steely pictured her face in the smoke. She had been calm, self-assured. "You said 'I know how to do it.' "

"And then you made Lieutenant Jackson let me lower the rope, Steely. You trusted me, I know it. Or you wouldn't have gone over the side."

"I did trust you, goddamn it!" This time it was Steely who was yelling. "But you must have done something wrong."

Kathy moved the straight-backed hospital chair up to the side of his bed and sat down. "I know I put the hook on top," she said softly, gesturing with her hands. "I just know it, because that's the way I like it. Are you my friend, Steely? Can I tell you this? It's the way I like it. With sex. On top. So the hook was on top, the rope was below. It's the way I remembered the evolution. I got a hundred in all those exams, using things like that to remember. The rope was hooked on right. It was something else that malfunctioned, not me. You've got to believe me, Steely. You've got to remember."

Steely closed his eyes. He didn't want to remember. The sound of Hadley's screams, his desperate lunge, the fall. The noise of their bodies hitting the pavement. The blood. He didn't want to remember any of it. But it came clearly into his mind then as if he were watching the scene in slow motion. He was holding Red, and Red was holding him, when suddenly there was some kind of a jerk. "I felt something give," he said.

"So did I," Kathy said. "One second the rope was stretched tight over the parapet and the next second it went slack."

"It broke," Steely said. "Christ, we didn't use a roller to feed it over the side, or something smooth for the rope to glide over. I should have known. It was my fault. Jesus, I was the one who killed Red."

Kathy reached out to touch his hand. "No, Steely, it wasn't the rope. For a second after I felt it go slack, I didn't know what to do. I didn't know what had happened. I looked over the parapet and I saw you and Red lying on the pavement and I guess I probably screamed, or at least I think I did. And then I saw the rope. It was just hanging there over the side. If it had frayed on the parapet, I would have seen it. You know that, Steely."

Christ, he thought, one minute I'm laying the whole load of blame on her, not even thinking that it could have been my fault. She could have blamed me, too, but she didn't. I can't figure her out.

"You want to know something else?" Kathy asked, laughing a little, trying to make him feel better, Steely thought. "I did a single slide. Right after it happened. I threw the rest of the rope over the parapet and slid down, rappelling. Jackson tried to stop me, but I went ahead anyway. I just wanted to get to you, to you and Red. You were right about the length. The rope just reached the side-walk."

"Well, that's something anyway," Steely said. He couldn't help but smile. She's crazy, he thought, sliding down the outside of a building in an emergency. That's the kind of thing the Department gives medals for. She must have never lost her head. She was all right. Smart.

"Faster than the stairs, at least," Kathy said.

"So we're both big heroes," Steely said with grim humor. "But Red is dead. We can't change that. Why? How did it happen?"

"Don't you remember anything else?"

He shook his head. It had all happened so fast. Red had grabbed him and then there was that zipper-like sound, a ripping, a tearing, not something a rope would do. A rope would just split, hardly any sound, maybe a little pop.

"I do remember something else, Kathy," he said, "a ripping, like a seam was bursting. It was the V-rig. The V-rig ripped apart."

"That's what I think, too, Steely. You picked up Red and the system couldn't take the added weight. But that's not the story that's going around." She took a deep breath. "The whole job is saying that I'm responsible for Red's death, that I connected the rope to the hook wrong and caused a snag. Even in the paper this morning, the *Times*, it says there was reason to believe that an error in rescue procedures had been made."

"Screw that," Steely said. "I saw what you did. Jackson must have seen it, too."

"I don't know what he saw, if anything. And I don't know what he'll say. There's going to be an official inquiry."

"Okay, then, we've got the rope and V-rig. Where are they?"

"That won't do any good, Steely. They know the V-rig tore apart. The question is why. It must have passed all the Department tests. A woman firefighter is the most logical explanation, don't you see that? That's why I had to talk to you. You know what Jackson thinks of women firefighters. You were the only witness, Steely. Will you swear I performed the procedure right?"

"Yeah," he said, "yeah."

Steely threw his head back deeply into the pillow, and thought of what was happening. Then he said quietly, reflectively, "It's not going to matter much what I say, but I'll tell them what I saw. Jackson will say what the Department wants him to say. And if it's in the *Times*, it means that the Department didn't work overtime to clamp a lid on information."

Steely again felt his ankle stinging, and tried unsuccessfully to shift his weight. "The worst thing is, Kathy," he said, "that once the damage is done to your reputation in this job, it will linger forever, no matter what the truth. They'll always question you."

"Not if you fix it," she said.

"Maybe," he said. It was a noncommittal maybe, he knew. She did too, he thought.

"Oh my God," she said. "I just realized something."

"What's that?" he asked, suddenly feeling like a prisoner in his hospital bed. He wanted to get up, but he knew he didn't have the strength, that the strength had been knocked out of him. He looked at her, feeling sorry for her, knowing that her eyes were pink from not sleeping, from the tears. She was in a tough situation, no matter how it was sliced.

"How hard it'll be for you," she said, "to go against Jackson, or the Department."

Steely smiled. She was right, of course. Unless they had something concrete.

Kathy got up suddenly. "The flowers," she said, looking around. "Do you have something to put the flowers in?"

He did not answer.

She then fell back into the chair. "I'm so glad you're here, Steely, that you're alive."

He shrugged his shoulders, unable to speak. Finally he said, "Everything will be all right, Kathy. All we have to do is tell the truth of what happened."

Suddenly, they were interrupted by the loud voice of the Department's Chief Medical Officer, who entered the room in his worn and wrinkled deputy chief's uniform like a tank crashing through a picket fence. "Good to see you're up, and in shape to take visitors on, but that will be all. Good day, miss. I'm afraid that visiting hours are in the evening only."

Kathy got up and left the room.

"See you," Steely said. "Call me. I'll have a phone put in later."

"Now," Dr. Titlebloom said, "tell me what's the matter."

Steely knew the doctor only by his reputation, and he did not think highly of him. He could be gotten to easily enough, it was said, but he would as quickly be an adversary if it wasn't in his interest to help you. There was the story Steely had heard that Titlebloom had once gotten a doctor to write an unsympathetic analysis of a firefighter's injury, and the doctor, a Pakistani, wrote it in Urdu. Titlebloom made it part of the official record anyway, and often referred to it though no one knew what the Pakistani doctor actually said. "A thoroughly negative report," is all the Chief Medical Officer would say.

Steely could not see how Dr. Titlebloom would or could help now in any way. "You know what's the matter, doctor," he said.

"Tell me," Dr. Titlebloom said, pulling at Steely's lower eyelids as if he were making a judgment.

"The roses need a vase, doctor," Steely said, "or they'll never last the day."

"A vase, huh," Dr. Titlebloom said indifferently. "The roses will be in the hospital longer than you, Fireman."

"How come I can't feel my arm?" Steely asked, giving in to the urge to ask.

"Like novocaine with the gums," Dr. Titlebloom said. "Another six, eight hours, you'll feel it itch."

"An itch is something, anyway," Steely whispered.

"It's broken and fractured, the wrist, and the hand is as bad," Dr. Titlebloom continued, taking Steely's pulse. "The records show you're right-handed, so you're lucky there, but the left hand maybe could never heal right, maybe never be good enough to get you back to full duty."

Steely pulled his wrist out of the doctor's hand. "You mean I may never go back to work?" he asked.

Dr. Titlebloom smiled. "Didn't say that," he replied. "Just that it might never heal *right*, and only the Chief Surgeon determines if it's healing right."

Steely was silent. If this was the doctor's way of asking him to buy a tax-free pension, there was not much to say. What the hell would I retire to anyway, he asked himself? Even with a tax-free, I still wouldn't be able to make the rent on the poverty pad. I need a goddamn raise, not a pension, and it's too bad the Chief Surgeon doesn't have raises to sell.

"How are you, Steely?"

The voice was a complete surprise to Steely. Of course, the Chief of Department visits all hospitalized personnel. It's part of the job description. Yet, it was still a surprise to hear Haggerty's voice.

Dr. Titlebloom left the room, saying, "He's a strong man, Chief. Probably be out in a couple of days."

Haggerty shook Steely's hand and sat in the chair that Kathy

228

had pulled over to the side of the bed. "Close call," he said, smiling.

Steely shrugged his shoulders. "Hadley's dead," he said.

"He never regained consciousness, Steely, never felt any pain. The Department is arranging everything now for his funeral."

Steely saw the humor in the situation. Things are always funnier when you know something other people don't know. "He didn't like the Department, Jack," he said. "He thought the Department took him over the coals, had too much power over him. He hated it."

Haggerty crossed his legs and threw an arm over the back of his chair. "It's not always easy, Steely," he said, "running a department of twelve thousand firefighters."

"You're a good friend, Jack," Steely said. "You're here, you came to Sixty-seventh Street to bail me out."

"Did he ever get back to you," Haggerty interrupted, "the policeman?"

"No," Steely said, remembering Murphy's snarling promise to decide about pressing charges. "Maybe he forgot about it."

"I hope so," Haggerty said. "Be just one more thing less to worry about. How's your arm?"

"It's supposed to wake up soon. I'll tell you then."

"Your head looks like you were hit by a barstool."

"Feels big too," Steely said, putting his hand to the lump on his forehead. "Like a blimp. My head went into Red's jaw, I guess."

"No point talking about that," Haggerty said.

"We've got to talk about it," Steely said. "What happened, Jack? What went wrong?"

Haggerty shifted his weight in the chair. He seemed a little uneasy to Steely. But almost everyone seems uneasy in a hospital, he thought.

"We're not sure, Steely," Haggerty said. "There's an investigation on now. I can't say anything for sure."

"But you must have an opinion?"

"Sure, Steely," Haggerty replied. "It seems on first look that there was a failure in procedure."

"There was no failure, Jack," Steely protested, although his tone was friendly. He and Haggerty went back a long time. He could be down-to-earth with Haggerty. "I was there, I saw everything."

"The lieutenant on the scene," Haggerty said matter-of-factly, "says he thinks the procedure wasn't one hundred percent."

"Then he's wrong, Jack," Steely insisted.

"The investigation will get to the heart of it, Steely," Haggerty said.

It was an evasive answer, Steely thought. An investigation, hell. He's not listening to me. He looked at the five gold-braided stripes on Haggerty's sleeve, and realized that his old neighborhood friend had answered him in the voice of the Chief of Department.

"That's it?" Steely asked.

"That's it for now," Haggerty replied.

"Is the Department of Investigations investigating, or is it a Fire Department thing, an internal thing?"

"I've appointed a board of inquiry, Steely," Haggerty said, "and it will report to me."

"What about Kathy Angelli?" Steely asked.

"Kathy Angelli?" Haggerty repeated.

"The woman who lowered me down," Steely said, raising his voice a little in impatience.

"Yes," Haggerty said, "what about her?"

"She connected the rope to the hook right," Steely said. His voice was now just above a whisper. He was growing tired. "Get your investigators to ask me about that. I want to be asked about that."

Steely closed his eyes then. He had done what Kathy had asked him to do, told the truth. And he could relax now, get some sleep. Everything would be okay. Jack Haggerty would take care of it, just like he always did.

"You're in need of a rest," he heard Haggerty say. "I'll stop by to see you soon."

"Great, Jack," Steely said without opening his eyes, his voice trailing off into a murmur. "Ask the nurse to bring me a vase, will you, and a newspaper."

Steely slept then, for most of the rest of the day. And the room was different when he awakened. It seemed livelier, almost like a motel room on a traveling vacation. A vase sat at the edge of the bed table, and Kathy's flowers had been arranged into a small, cheerful burst. A copy of the *Times* also lay on the table between the vase and a tray of food, light food, a bowl of bran flakes and milk, and juice. A phone had been installed, he noticed, and made the bed table appear crowded and disorderly. But, the room glowed as soon as he saw the children. The television was tuned to a cartoon program with the sound off, one of those Japanese-made cartoons that always seemed to Steely to be joyless and without character.

Jeffrey saw that he was awake and ran to the side of the bed. "We're the only ones allowed up," he said, kissing Steely matter-of-factly on the cheek. "Even the firemen downstairs, they aren't allowed up to see you. Mommy went to get coffee."

Tara hugged him. "Look, Daddy," she said, opening the newspaper, "here's a picture of you, but it doesn't much look like you."

Steely held the newspaper up with his right hand and saw the old photograph that he had taken for the official personnel file when he was a probationary fireman. It was next to a similarly posed head shot of Red Hadley, and both pictures appeared underneath a headline which read: DOUBT CAST ON FIREFIGHTER DEATH. He looked at the byline and saw the name, F. X. Burns. Like his but spelled differently. Francis Xavier Burns, probably. Every F. X. he had ever met, anyway, was a Francis Xavier.

Firefighter Death, it said. They didn't even mention Red's name in the headline.

Steely pondered the photograph of his friend, a stiff and formal Department photo, yet it still conveyed the feeling of warmth and kindness that emanated from Red's eyes, a look he would never forget. Red, he thought, a stand-up guy, a guy they can't replace, a guy whose absence will be felt.

Tara sat on the bottom edge of the bed and put her hand on the little hill of blanket that was his knees. He diverted his attention to her for just a moment, thankful that she was near. Renewal, he thought. All of life is renewal passing from parent to child, one life to another. Only Red didn't have any children so he passed his life on to me. And now that I have this other life, Red's life, I wonder what God means for me to do with it? Funny, thinking about God now. Hardly ever think about God, but death brings Him out, no doubt about that. Funny too, that Red thought and talked about God all the time in life, and I never took him seriously until now, in his death. Christ, it's all pretty hard to figure, to cut out the meaning of his death.

Steely let the reverie pass and began to read the *Times* story, which, even in the lead paragraph, implied that the woman firefighter on the roof of the burning tenement had made an error in rescue procedures. "What crap," he said, throwing the newspaper down on the bed.

"Feeling better?" Maryanne was standing next to the bed, a container of coffee in her hand.

She did not kiss him, embrace him, or even touch him lightly in a gesture of friendship. It was good to see her, though, he thought. At least she came, one of the corporal works of mercy being to visit the sick. He wondered how long she had been there, trying to keep the kids quiet until he woke up.

"Just okay," he said. "Not better."

"Can we turn the TV up now, Mom?" Jeffrey asked.

"No," Maryanne said. "Go down to the solarium at the end of the hall. You can watch TV there."

The children left the room, Tara chasing after Jeffrey. Maryanne sat on the chair next to the bed and there was a short, awkward pause during which they just looked at one another. Finally, Maryanne spoke. "Does your arm hurt?" she asked.

He could feel the arm now, and it felt swollen. But neither it nor the hand hurt. "Small potatoes," he answered.

"Compared to what?" she asked quickly. "Dying?"

"I suppose," he said.

"You've got to say what you feel, Steely," she said. "What you know. You can't keep things inside you."

If I could only talk to her, Steely thought. Jesus Christ, I can talk to women in bars easier than I can talk to my own wife. Anyway, we always have this conversation. But that was before. Maybe now, things will be different. There has to be a bigger meaning for everything. God, she looks pretty there, like she was as a teenager again, sitting on a wooden bench in the Fifty-first Street park.

"Right," he said, "say what I feel." Was she ready for what he really wanted to say? "It's like a coin was flipped and Red Hadley won," he said. "How come? How come Red didn't fall on me?"

"There's no answer to that, Steely," Maryanne said, "except to say it's God's will."

He tried to sit up in bed, but he felt a pain shoot through his left arm. He grimaced, and she reacted, leaning toward him. But then she stopped, and they both remembered the existing apprehensiveness between them.

"Maryanne," Steely said finally, "I just want to get close to you for a moment. To . . . you know. To thank you for coming."

"Oh, Steely," she said, her voice almost a sigh. "This is a sad time for you, and I want to share it with you, be a part of it, because you need somebody to share it with you. But I'm not sure, Steely, I'm not sure about anything else between us."

"I'm not sure either," he said. "Maybe we're not supposed to be sure. Maybe that's God's will, too. I only know that when Red Hadley and I were falling, I thought about you. I thought about you when I woke up in this room. Goddamn it. I can't *stop* thinking about you."

"I know," she said. "I can't help thinking about you either."

"Well, then, what's the problem?"

"You have to care, Steely. Not just about me and the kids. You have to care about yourself."

He put his head back on the pillow. "I do care, Maryanne," he said.

"Do you?" she asked. "Do you? I used to think the only thing you really cared about was yourself. Steely Byrnes, Firefighter. Rush in, smash the windows and break down the doors. Do whatever you had to do to put out the fire and get out alive. But now I'm beginning to wonder. Did you hear what you just said to me, Steely? You said you felt like a coin was flipped and Red Hadley won. *Won.* He's dead, Steely. He lost. How can I love a man who acts like he doesn't even care whether he lives or dies? If there's a future for us, Steely, it has to be built on life."

He wasn't sure what she meant. It was hard for him to concentrate on her words. But she was wrong about one thing. He was scared as hell of dying. Scared to death of death, that was funny. But maybe he was scared of living, too. Scared of the future because he thought he didn't have one. Hell, it didn't used to be like that. He used to care. But, Christ, if that's all she wants, it's not much to ask for. She was here, anyway. That was the important thing at the moment. And they were talking.

CHAPTER 27

THE early morning sun shot laser-like beams from the brass handles on the end of Red Hadley's coffin. The coffin, draped with the flag of the City of New York, was placed on top of one of the new pumpers just delivered to the Department. There was not a scratch or a mar on the fire engine, Steely thought, just like Red's soul. Muffled drums of the Department's bagpipe band beat a constant, eerie rhythm that broke through the silence of the funeral parade. The pumper stopped before the small, red-brick Catholic Church, and six firefighters of Ladder Company 7, Harrigan and McFadden among them, shifted the weight of Red's body and coffin onto their shoulders. Steely watched from the small group of dignitaries, a kind of review squadron, that stood just before the church steps. A wave of blue uniforms could be seen lined up and down the narrow Queens side street. A couple of thousand men had shown up, Steely guessed, some, he had read in the morning newspaper, came from as far as Chicago. Several television crews were walking up and down the street, between the blue-uniformed multitudes, taking their silent footage.

He heard the shuffling of feet as the drums throbbed, da da dum, bang, da da dum, bang. The pallbearers of honor lined themselves in front of the church, its red-painted Romanesque doors opened wide. Limousine doors began to open and shut, open and shut, and the gathering of Hadley's in-laws stood in uneven formation behind the coffin. Steely saw Red's wife, dressed in black, and he wondered if she was weeping. He couldn't tell, for her eyes were obscured by a black net veil that came down to her mouth. She had a full red mouth, he noticed, slightly thick lips that were shining with gloss.

Poor Red, Steely thought, no family at all, just the relatives of a wife who left him. All we can do now is hope he will find some peace in the great and final loneliness.

The Department's Chief of Personnel was in charge of the funeral, and Steely watched him, standing alone at the church doors, like the head altar boy at high mass, making sure that everyone moved when they were supposed to. He had asked Steely to stand in the platoon of dignitaries, with the Mayor and the deputy mayors, with the Fire Commissioner and the deputy fire commissioners, and with the brass, the Chief of Department and the assistant chiefs.

Steely watched the rest of Ladder Company 7 get in formation behind the relations. He saw Katra Hadley at the head of the civilians, and Lieutenant Jackson at the head of the firefighters just behind. And he saw Kathy among them, trim in her dress uniform and standing straight as a plumb line. There was a larger space than normal, he noticed, between her and the firefighters on either side. Were they giving her some room, he wondered, or was it something else? She looked a little uncomfortable, as uncomfortable as he was anyway.

He wished he was somewhere else, anywhere but here among the bosses. The Chief of Personnel, though, said it was more appropriate for him to be singled out as a "courageous firefighter." It was more an order than a suggestion, Steely thought, and he hated the idea of being singled out for anything. He was the reason they were all there, lined up in military fashion, no doubt about that. If things turned out the other way around, they'd all be lined up out in Levittown, and Maryanne would have a veil on her face, and people would weep for his children. Thank God there were no children here. Children are the saddest thing in a firefighter's funeral.

"So this is St. Bart's," he heard Jack Haggerty say to a fat, red-faced assistant chief standing next to him. "I've heard a lot about this parish. Great choir. They had a record done and it made more money than the bingo one year."

"Good idea," the assistant chief said.

Steely was standing just behind them, watching the gold stars on their shoulders gleam as if they were wired like Christmas tree lights. Does anyone here, Steely asked himself, know anything at all about Red Hadley? They just know he's a dead fireman, and respect has to be conveyed, the widow and the Department have to be propped up with the ritual. Doesn't matter if it's St. Bart's in Queens or Immaculate Heart of Mary out in Levittown, good choir or not. Doesn't matter who the fireman is, just as long as the funeral conveys the right message, which is that the Department takes care of its dead.

God, Red, Steely said to himself as the honor pallbearers began to carry the coffin up the steps, I would change places with you if I could.

Suddenly, a chant began ringing through the air. *"Give us Brother Hadley. Give us Brother Hadley."* And Steely saw a dozen or so white-shirted men and women across the street, behind a formation of firefighters, their arms locked together as they chanted. Large video cameras began bobbling up and down as the television crews ran toward the commotion. A few firefighters broke rank and started to push and pull the chain of people. The end of the chain broke then, and a small, bearded man ran to the front of the church. "We are the Street Congregationalists," he yelled, his voice just a beat lower than a scream. "And Brother Hadley would die if he were alive and knew you were going to bury him in a Catholic Church."

Steely watched the Chief of Personnel's face flush a bright pink as he grabbed the bearded man by the arms and pushed him backward.

"Get rid of those nuts," Haggerty commanded, and Steely saw him look over at the Mayor for approval. But the city's highest-ranking executive was staring straight ahead at the family that was beginning to enter the church. The Mayor seemed to shrug his shoulders a little, Steely thought, crazy protest situations not being unusual in a city as large as New York. The bearded man was still yelling as the Chief of Personnel handed him over to several assisting policemen.

The procession continued and Steely again heard only the sounds of the muffled, vibrating drums and the shuffling of feet as the

236

contingent of dignitaries turned and followed the members of the fallen firefighter's company into the church. That was the order of entry, the status of bereavement. First, the family, and after them, the fire company, the dignitaries, and the Department. There was no room for friends, if there were any friends. Red's friends were being hustled out of sight by the police.

Steely limped slightly. His left ankle was like a topographical map of swollen veins and discolored masses, but there were no bones broken requiring a cast, and so the doctor had wrapped it tightly with a stretch bandage. The hospital orthopedists wanted Steely to use a cane, which he took without argument and then discarded in a corner of the poverty pad. It made him feel uneven when he walked, but now as he turned, the pain was just barely endurable.

Steely saw Kathy pass through the opened church doors. Her green eyes were still inflamed and framed in red and pink, although her head was held high, high and determined. The men before her and after her were walking in twos. Kathy had no one beside her.

It will always be tough on her. Steely thought. Even if he signed a notarized statement that explained the truth of the accident, the men would think he was trying to make things easy for her, covering things up. He had heard what they were saying. There were two firemen at the Queens Boulevard diner where he had stopped for breakfast earlier, and one of them said, "Even if that damn rig was soaked in acid they would have made it, if she had only threaded the rope right so that it didn't jam."

Steely had looked up from his eggs and toast. He didn't know the men. Probably from some Brooklyn or Queens fire company. They had stopped for containers of coffee and were simply talking casually. Like him, they were in uniform and on their way to the funeral. They nodded at him in acknowledgment. He had felt the blood rushing through his head, he remembered, and he wanted to grab them, yell at them. But what was the use, he asked himself? Here were two firemen saying what twelve thousand firemen were thinking, and straightening them out, changing their minds, would be like trying to change the tide of the East River.

In the church he again found himself behind Jack Haggerty, who was in the front pew. He looked over his shoulder and saw, behind the family on the other side of the middle aisle, Kathy, three pews back, an eighteen-inch space between her and the firefighters on either side. Lieutenant Jackson was on the aisle, smiling, looking across at the Mayor and the Fire Commissioner. Steely could see he was pleased to be so close to such famous men.

The mass began and the mourners rose as the three priests and nine altar boys entered the altar proper from the side sacristy. The church organ vibrated as the procession broke into parts, everyone taking his assigned place, preparing for the mass. Steely saw that the celebrant was Monsignor Frank Flynn, his first line-of-duty funeral, he guessed, since becoming a Department chaplain.

The choir sang. It was a powerful choir, and the voices seemed to wrap around him like a cool sheet. They sang the *Dies Irae*, the funeral hymn that Steely had learned as a child. He mouthed the Latin, the voice in his mind going high and low with the modulations of the Gregorian music.

Steely watched the mass progress, straining his neck to see through the openings between the profiles of the men in the aisle before him. Every now and then, Commissioner Gore would lean over and whisper something in the Mayor's ear, and the Mayor would nod silently. The Mayor, it seemed, thought it improper to talk in church. Maybe because he wasn't Catholic, Steely thought, he had a stronger reverence.

"Greater love hath no man than this," Monsignor Flynn began his sermon, his first official eulogy, "that a man lay down his life for his friends."

What crap, Steely thought. He's missing it. Blowing the goddamn sermon. I don't want to hear that. Firemen don't give their lives *for* anything, so much as they give their lives because it's expected. A certain number of men are going to die because dying comes with the job for some people, just as leukemia or twins or blue eyes comes with some families. The courage is there, constant, going into any fire, live or die, searching for victims, live or die. But it's not something to sing songs or write poems about. It's just part of the picture, like some men put wrenches on pipes for a living, or some women scrub floors in downtown high-rises.

Steely turned and looked at the wave of faces, mostly white and male, behind him. Men don't die in this job, he thought as he turned his head toward the pulpit again, because they trade their lives, one life for another. They die because of *accidents*. Red didn't trade up to some special hero status. It was an *accident*. A crazy, stupid accident in which he died, and I lived.

Steely put his hands up to his face and covered his eyes, pressing in lightly so that the pressure relieved the stress he felt building in the muscles of his forehead and his cheeks and his temples. Oh, Red, he said to himself. A crazy goddamn accident, and you're dead. Dark and airless forever, dead in the silk of your coffin. Christ.

The small neighborhood church was filled completely. Blue-uniformed firefighters, caps held in their white-gloved hands, packed every pew, up and down the side aisles, even in the small spaces in the choir loft just behind the choir. Loudspeakers were set up under the supervision of the Chief of Personnel so that the thousands in the street outside could listen to give them a sense of being part of the ceremonies.

"And so Firefighter Hadley lives on in our memories," Monsignor Flynn concluded, his voice floating through the army of men standing at rest, and up through the leaves of the trees that lined the street. "And the things that he stood for, courage and dedication and dignity, will live on in the lives of all firefighters."

Christ, Steely said to himself again. All Red wanted was to be left alone to be dedicated to his own thing, his own born-again groupies, and here he is in church, the dedication of his life being shut off in death like a faucet, the talk and the ritual and the choir being turned on instead, not for Red, but for the Department and everybody else. To keep them all going, to kind of pump them up with ritual until the next time. What crap. Courage. The man was being burned and then the goddamn rescue-V-rig tore apart. A terrible accident. So what if he was in there up on the top floor looking for some drunken wino? That's all part of it, being there. Doesn't matter that the drunk was roasted. Red was where he was supposed to be, doing what he was supposed to do, and being there is the only thing that's ever expected, just being there. Courage? It's not courage, but knowing what to do, knowing the job.

The communion was just ending. Six priests had joined the celebrant in administering the hosts, and the line of firefighters moved quickly. Steely sat back and let the others pass through the pew space.

All in the church stood at the end of the mass and left their pews in the same order they had entered, except for the honor guard around the coffin containing Red Hadley. The first to enter the church, Red would be the last to leave it. Red would have left the job faster than they let him leave the church, Steely thought, and that's about all that could be said about his dedication. Did he love the job? I wonder, Steely answered in his mind as he placed himself in line among the bosses and politicians to leave the church.

The morning sun now seemed to be steaming, rising in waves from the hoods of the cars parked down the street, and from the tar-covered street itself. Red loved the job, but I think he loved his church work, and being American and Polish, more. He would have left it in a second if he had something else to go to. But, Steely thought, the skills of a fireman are important to a society like those of a ukulele player are to a symphony orchestra. No, there's no great market out there for driving through red lights and climbing ladders.

Outside, he watched Katra Hadley join the family of Red's in-laws lined up across from the contingent of dignitaries. Together the two groups formed a passageway. Next to the family were the members of Ladder Company 7, and next to them the Department bag-pipe band, led by a very tall, plaid-covered man with a gray goatee.

Kathy was there, Steely saw, in the first row of the company contingent; the space between her and the man on either side was now very wide, leaving her isolated in the ranks, alone in the still, hot air. That space wasn't accidental, Steely knew now. It was too much. They didn't have to shun her out in public like this. They should not have. It's not right. And Red was her friend. He took her, Steely remembered, to the Holy Name racket. What kind of dedication would Kathy Angelli ever have for her job when this is over?

The fire truck that was being used as a hearse pulled in front of the church, and the honor pallbearers carried the coffin down the steps. Suddenly, the drums rapped heavily through the morning heat, and the high, shrill sounds of the bagpipes broke the quiet like a burglar alarm in the middle of the night. The music seemed to Steely to be deafening. It was a tune he thought he remembered from his teenage years, when folk music was popular. A Scottish tune. A *Scottish* tune, for chrissakes, being played for Red Hadley, the final ritual that would carry him out of the Department forever. "Will Ye No Come Back Again," that was it. Yes, a song about Prince Charlie, Steely thought, a loser who never did come back, a *Scottish* song for a man who loved being Polish. God, what dignity are we going to remember of Red's? His dignity was in the fervor with which he believed in his church group, the enthusiasm he had

240

for his past, and now the Department was taking everything from him, soiling all of it. Dignity? Where is the goddamn dignity for Red Hadley? We must remember him in his own dignity, in the way he lived, in the way he was *there* when he was supposed to be.

Steely looked hard at the bandmaster, and took a step out of formation to move toward him. The pain shot through his ankle like electric volts, but he kept on. He wanted to reach the tall bandmaster with his mouth open above his gray goatee, to swing his cast in the white linen of his sling, to rush him, hit him so that his brass-topped staff would drop as he fell against the bass drummer behind, to fly into the bagpipers, limping, pushing, grabbing at the plaids of their uniform shawls, pulling them down, fighting until the music stopped, until the bagged breath expired, until the melody celebrating a failed prince turned to squelches as painful and unforgiving as the surging blood through his ankle. Where is the goddamn dignity for Red Hadley, he yelled out in his mind?

But he stopped and, turning, saw the row of firefighters from his company, from Ladder Company 7, Jackson and McFadden and Harrigan and the rest, still standing slightly apart from Kathy Angelli. She had dignity, he thought. Just look at it. Sad and confused and unsure, maybe, but her head was high, her back firm and erect, because the dignity was there, there inside of her, standing alone and apart, maybe, but she was taking it, and that's a strength, a dignity that radiates with the power of a generating plant.

He continued now toward Kathy, past the hard glare of the Chief of Personnel, whose ceremony had gone askew, a firefighter breaking ranks at a formation, here at a funeral, in front of the TV cameras, everybody, even firefighters from as far away as Chicago.

Kathy looked strangely at him as he approached and stood before her for a brief moment, putting his right hand on her arm, moving her over just slightly, decreasing the space on one side of her and increasing it on the other. Then he turned, limping, and backed into the formation of the dead firefighter's company. Standing at her side, he didn't look around at the TV cameras pointed at him, or at Haggerty or the Chief of Personnel. He stood stiffly, at attention, and raised his right hand so that it was rigid, touching the tip of his cap in salute, just as Red Hadley's coffin was raised to the hosebed of the pumper and thousands of arms were lifted in salute to the strains of Scottish war pipes.

CHAPTER 28

THE following afternoon, Steely led Kathy up the curved marble stairs of City Hall and into the large city council hearing chamber on the second floor. A long table had been set up in the front of the room for the announced press conference, and several television cameras sat on tripods in the center aisle. Thirty or so people, mostly reporters and Fire Department personnel, sat in the first three or four rows of the chamber. Steely and Kathy went to the far side of the room where they would not be noticed.

Behind the table, sitting in three neatly arranged rows of chairs, was the brass of the Department: the Chief, the assistant chiefs, the borough commanders, the deputy commissioners, all except Gore himself, who was said to be attending a fire-prevention seminar in Boston. It looked to Steely like a promotion ceremony, or some happy event where everybody turns out in gleaming gold and braid to congratulate themselves for something.

Haggerty was standing, holding the end of a nylon rope in one hand and the torn rescue-V-rig in the other. "You see, ladies and gentlemen," he said, "how the hook connection tore away from the harness itself. To answer the question of Mr. Burns from the *Times*,

I can tell you with great assurance that this would not have happened, it *could* not have happened in normal procedures."

At least, Steely thought, they are admitting that the V-rig itself failed.

A red-headed man in the first row rose, saying, "Does that mean your procedures during this fire were not normal, Chief?"

"No, Mr. Burns," Haggerty answered, "but we do have a Department inquiry being conducted to ascertain the procedures that were followed."

So that's F. X. Burns, Steely said to himself, remembering the name from the *Times* byline.

"Then why did the thing, this rescue-V-rig fail?" Burns asked.

"We are not certain yet," Haggerty replied, a dozen or so heads behind him nodding in agreement, "but there may indeed have been a failure in procedure. The Department inquiry will determine that."

"Which you will make public when it concludes," Burns said, in an affirmative way.

"Which we will make public," Haggerty agreed, "when it concludes."

"There is some talk, Chief," Burns pressed on, "that one of the women firefighters in your Department is involved, that she may have been in some way responsible for this accident."

Kathy reached over and dug her nails into Steely's forearm.

Haggerty cleared his throat, and several of the brass behind him put their hands to their faces, gestures Steely thought that probably indicated they were hoping this particular question would not come up. "The Department cannot make a statement on that at this time," Haggerty said.

Sure, Steely thought. No denial. That means Kathy will take a beating on this thing. But why not just blame it on the rig? Would they go that far to get women out of the Department? It didn't make any sense.

"Why not?" another reporter asked.

"The board of inquiry will be the more appropriate body to comment on that," Haggerty said. "Now you are all free to examine the equipment, to photograph it. We have it displayed here on green felt for your convenience."

"Let's get out of here," Steely whispered to Kathy. It had become obvious that Haggerty was not going to say more than he had already said.

They left City Hall and crossed the parking lot toward Broadway, the summer heat radiating from the pavements. Steely noticed that the blood seemed to have flowed from Kathy's face, and that her cheeks had turned white.

They sat in a dingy booth in a restaurant called La Petite Coffee Shop, in the basement of the union building across from City Hall. An old Chinese woman brought them coffee. Kathy played with her spoon, circling it within the cup. "So that's it," Steely said, dumping a spoonful of sugar into his coffee. "There's just so much bullshit you can be asked to take, and then you have to do something. You just can't keep taking more and more."

"I can handle it," she answered quickly. "Doesn't matter."

"But it's a team, Kathy, and it's hard work unless you're part of it."

"Things will lighten up," she said, "after the truth is known by everyone."

Steely wanted to believe her. But he knew it would not be easy to take a position in the firehouse, and in the Department, defending a woman. It reminded him of the stories he had heard about black firefighters in the thirties and forties. Separate bunks were maintained for them then, and anyone who thought that was not right, or unfair, was called a nigger lover. It took a long time for that attitude to change, Steely thought, and it might take as long for the men's attitude about women to change too. Even within himself, he thought. He wasn't really sure what his attitude toward women in the Department was, but he was sure of one thing, and that was that Kathy was there, she had done her job.

"What I can't figure is why the Department is trying to lay the blame on you," he said. "Usually they bend over backward to protect their own, unless some guy really screws up."

"That's easy," Kathy said. "I'm not some guy. I'm a woman. And it's just our word against theirs."

Steely nodded. "Well, at least we know where the rope and the V-rig went."

"The Department confiscated all of them," Kathy said. "The Division Chief himself came over to pick them up."

"You mean they took the V-rigs out of service?" Steely asked. "That means they found something wrong with them."

"Not necessarily," Kathy corrected. "They said it was for reevaluation only. Meanwhile, we're back to the old safety belts and manila ropes."

"Dammit," Steely said. "So they'll stick to the story that it wasn't used right."

"But what if something is wrong with the rigs, Steely?" Kathy asked, a note of hope entering her voice. "That could explain what happened. Should we go to the fire marshal, or the Department's Inspector General?"

"And tell them what?" Steely said with a gesture of his hand. "That it was used right, that it ripped for no reason except that it couldn't hold the weight? You know what they'll say? They'll tell us to take a walk."

"But what if we could prove it?" she insisted.

"They'd still tell us to take a walk," Steely said. "Everybody would try to protect himself. There would be suits, and no one is going to admit blame for the death of a firefighter."

"Well, I'm not going to let them point a finger at me," Kathy said with sudden defiance. But as suddenly then, she became sad, terribly sad, and Steely guessed that she realized her position wasn't going to get any better simply by telling the truth. "It's unbelievable," she said. "The only group of people in the world whose whole function is to protect what we value, and we value everything but honesty."

They left the restaurant and walked back to Steely's car in the City Hall parking lot. "Can I give you a lift somewhere?" he asked.

"Thanks, but I think I'll take the snake home. The Brooklyn Bridge station is right around the corner."

"Look," he said, trying to generate some hope between them. "I'll make a few calls. Maybe I can find out something about the rig anyway. Things don't operate in a vacuum in the Department. I'll just have to do a little digging."

"Okay," she said softly. "Is there anything I can do?"

He shook his head. "No, you'd better stay out of it."

"And what if you can't find anything?"

"Then I'll go to the newspapers, the television people, the Mayor even. I know the Chief of Department. Jack Haggerty and I grew up in the same neighborhood. He came to see me in the hospital and I told him you wound the rope right. I can tell him again."

Kathy bent her head a little, and he saw the look that crossed her face, a quizzical look, as if she wondered whether he would really do all the things he said he would do. Or maybe she thought he was still making some kind of a play for her, talking big, hoping to win her gratitude, and maybe even something more.

"Thanks, Steely," she said and turned away from him without even a smile. He watched her walk toward the Brooklyn Bridge subway entrance and realized he could not just let her leave him like this, sad, suspicious. It wasn't right, for her or for him.

"Hey, Kathy," he called after her. She turned, and he limped toward her. "Make believe just for a minute," he said, his voice strong with enthusiasm, "that you're caught in a job, trapped in a railroad flat, the fire coming at you from both directions, nothing but walls and the fire lapping through the doorways. You got it?"

Her face, he saw, was beginning to fill with interest. She nodded her head. "You have no tools," Steely continued, "and there's no way out. You're going to buy it, taps, the Mayor will come to the wake, right?"

He paused, forcing her to nod her head once more.

"You have maybe a minute," he went on, tapping her just once, and lightly, on the forearm, "but now you remember you're a firefighter. You have to believe that someone in this job is going to come crashing through the wall to get you out. Someone is going to be there. And you know what, Kathy?"

Steely paused a third time, but just for a moment. "What?" she said.

"If you don't believe that," he answered himself, "you don't belong on this job."

It looked to him as if she were holding her breath. There was a very long silence, filled only by the noise of bridge traffic and a distant siren. Finally, she touched his arm, the one encased in the cast and sling, and her face exploded into a smile. "Thanks, Steely," she said again. And this time he felt she meant it.

Standing beside his heap in the City Hall parking lot, Steely wondered what the hell he was going to do next. He *was* talking big, giving her false hope. And he realized then that it wasn't a simple thing at all, this problem that caused Red's death. Things are never simple when they get to City Hall. But at least he could ask some questions, call a few friends. Maybe he was making promises he couldn't keep. But he had to do what he could for Kathy. And not just for her. He had to do it for Red.

He found a public phone booth in Suerken's Restaurant on Park Place, the kind of booth where he could sit down to ease the pain in his ankle. There weren't many booths like that left in the city. He dialed a number, looking up at the small squares in the tin ceiling that was probably more than a century old. They were the hardest ceilings to pull down in a fire, the high tin ones.

He was calling Jerry Ritter, a firefighter he had worked with some years ago in a firehouse on the west side of Harlem, in Ladder Company 57. Nifty Fifty-seven they used to call themselves, back when he was a probationary fireman and things were exciting and gay-spirited in that firehouse, where the firefighters were always joking and laughing, before a roof caved in and sent five of them down into the middle of the fire.

"Hi, Jerry. How'ya doing, pal?" he said. "How're things now that you're answering phones in headquarters instead of answering alarms in Harlem?"

He listened to Ritter's reply, and laughed. "They wouldn't let you up because all the nurses have your number, Jerry. It's not bad, left arm that's all, but I appreciate that you came to the hospital. Listen, Jerry, you hear anything down there, I mean at headquarters, about the fire and all?"

He listened again, this time for a longer period, as Ritter told him about headquarters gossip. Talk of a shakeup was in the wind and the men in light-duty clerical jobs were scrambling for places in companies that did not require full-duty status, like the mask service unit, or the ambulances, or field communications units, or the medical office, or even the fire prevention bureau, where all of life is spent carrying a black briefcase and inspecting light commercial establishments.

Finally, Steely said, "I'll talk to Haggerty for you. You know we grew up together. Maybe he can get you a job backstage at *A Chorus Line*. Theater patrol, you know."

Then Steely took over the conversation and told Ritter what was on his mind. But he found it hard to talk about the fall, to say Red Hadley's name. To think it was one thing, but to say it aloud, even to a good friend like Ritter, was something he found difficult, maybe because he still didn't want to believe that Red had been killed. "Her name's Angelli," Steely said. "Kathy Angelli, and I know she wound the rope right around the hook. I saw her do it. You think I'm going to go over the side of a six-story building on the other end

247

of a rope that isn't wound right? I think it was the rescue-V-rig that couldn't take the weight. It's a new piece of equipment, Jerry. We never used it before. Where the hell did it come from? Did it pass all the Department tests?"

Ritter told Steely there were just two people in all of the Department who could be counted on to know everything. The first was a battalion chief, Vic Bollon, who ran the Department's mailroom and attended every dance, dinner, racket, promotion party, fraternal installation ceremony, retirement party, bachelor party, company picnic, wake, wedding, and funeral. "The only thing he doesn't do," Ritter joked, "is baby-sit. But you can count on him to know everything official and unofficial." Ritter then promised to talk to Chief Bollon in the next few days. The second man, he told Steely, was the Fire Commissioner's driver. It was a joke in headquarters that Scott Elvino was the only person in the Commissioner's office, including the Commissioner, who could remember the chiefs by name. Elvino was a good man, it was said, and one who kept Department things together when the Commissioner became unglued.

Steely appreciated the effort Ritter made on his behalf, even when he called the next day to say that Chief Bollon was a dead end, that he had heard nothing at all and knew only what he had seen on TV or read in the newspaper. Steely was sitting on the edge of his bed in the poverty pad, the phone between his ear and shoulder, going through his mail. He wondered why he ever took an interest in his mail, for he had not received even a postcard from a traveling firefighter since he had moved to Queens. Only bills and flyers.

"Thanks, Jerry," Steely said. "I'm waiting now for Elvino to call me back. We'll meet soon for drinks, huh? I owe you a pour from the top shelf."

Lying forcefully back on his pillows, his cast heavy across his stomach, Steely closed his eyes and wondered where all this would take him. He had Elvino calling him back. He had Ritter asking questions, snooping around, and he had Kathy, who had seemed pretty dispirited when he called her earlier that morning. "Whatever happens will happen," she said. She's probably ready to leave the job, Steely thought, pack it in. Just so much bullshit a man, or a woman, should have to take.

It was Elvino on the other end when the phone finally rang. Steely was smoking a cigarette, leafing through an old copy of *Reader's Digest*. The television was on, but it was unwatched. The Fire

Commissioner had an appointment scheduled at the City Gas and Electric Astoria plant, Elvino told Steely, and perhaps he could meet the Commissioner's driver there, just past the bridge to Roosevelt Island?

"Sure thing," Steely said, crushing the cigarette in an already-filled ashtray, the ashes spilling over the sides and onto the top of the end table next to the bed. The room was a wreck, Steely thought, but maybe he'd have a chance to clean it, a one-arm cleaning anyway, after meeting with Elvino, after knowing what he knows. He wouldn't ask me to meet him unless he had something solid to tell me. Wouldn't waste my time or his.

Steely drove through Long Island City and out along Twenty-first Street to Astoria, thinking of the things Elvino might tell him, the possibilities that existed in a large organization like the Fire Department. Maybe the Commissioner himself wanted to blame the death directly on a woman, which would make it tough for all the women in the Department, all twelve of them. The Commissioner was never for them anyway. No one in the Department was, really. He drove through the industrial area, block after block of two-story buildings with high neon signs and empty streets, and then past the low-income projects built in the fifties to move the blacks and Puerto Ricans out of the congestion of Harlem to the open spaces of Queens. Or, he thought, maybe something really stupid happened, like a clerk bought those rescue-V-rigs without anyone's approval, and the brass needs to cover it up. Or maybe someone took a big kickback. You never could tell in New York. It isn't like being in Duluth or some small town where everyone knows each other and risks are hard to take. In New York, if you can't make it on one block, you can always move to another and start over. Even the whores who can't make it on Eighty-sixth Street can always turn a trick on Thirty-third.

Steely drove past the barbed-wired linked fence that rimmed the City Gas and Electric plant, and saw the dark blue Oldsmobile parked at the curb in front of the plant entrance, its plate, a bold Maltese cross with the number 1 in the center, attached prominently to the rear bumper. He left his own car in the employees' lot and walked to the sedan, limping a lot easier now that he had rested the foot almost a full day. He opened the front door. Sitting, he shook Elvino's hand and said, "This where the Commissioner himself sits?"

"When I permit it," Elvino joked. He was not a typical boss's driver, younger than most, and his words were precise and clearly spoken, unlike the shortened speech of firefighters. It was known that he had gone to law school for a year, but had dropped out when he was called for the Fire Department appointment. He had dark hair and dark eyes, was probably Portuguese or Greek, Steely guessed, maybe Italian.

"It's good to meet you," Steely said. "Thanks."

"Well," Elvino replied, "you said you lived out this way and there was the appointment here, so it was convenient. Anyway, we would always try to do everything possible to help out someone who's been through what you've been through."

Steely didn't like the idea of anyone thinking of him as being any different since the accident. Red's different, he thought. Red is no longer alive. But I'm here, and I'm the same. Would Elvino have helped me out a month ago? Like Haggerty did? It's a funny thing about getting rabbis, about getting the favor of influential people. You have to be unique in some way to get their attention, stand out, be anything but normal and productive and one of the crowd. So I fell six stories on top of Red Hadley, and I'm unique. Christ.

Something inside of him told Steely to open the Commissioner's door, leave the car, and forget it. Why should he be doing this? What difference would it make to him if Kathy had to take heat, even if she was forced out of the job? Hadley was dead, nothing was going to change that. But then, he was here anyway, he thought, and Elvino was just trying to be brotherly.

"I'm just wondering," Steely said, "what the story is on these rescue-V-rigs, informal you understand, just between us."

"I understand, Byrnes," Elvino said, putting both hands on the steering wheel. The air-conditioning fan whirred, and the Department radio reported a false alarm in the Bronx. "You have every right to look for answers, but all I know is that they were bought, tested, and put in the field, right through regular channels."

"What's regular channels?" Steely asked.

"Approvals of the chief officers of Purchasing and Accounts and Procurements, and the Chief of Department," Elvino answered. "Everything was standard procedure. Look, Byrnes, I'll level with you, absolutely straight arrow. There is no question about these things, except for the woman."

"You mean Angelli?" Steely asked.

"So she made a mistake," Elvino said casually.

"She didn't make a fucking mistake," Steely said forcefully. "She did what she was supposed to."

Elvino held his hands up. "I'm not investigating it, Byrnes," he said. "It's just that it's an open question. The boss wants everything to go smooth the next few weeks, I'll let you in on that. He's in here now with guess who?" Elvino pointed to a new blue Chrysler sedan parked up at the end of the sidewalk fronting the plant.

Steely shrugged his shoulders. It was just a car.

"It's the Mayor's car," Elvino said. "The boss is in there with the Mayor and the bigwigs, talking about taking over the top position in City Gas and Electric. So he wants things to be straight, no complications, everything standard and routine. A big fire, a catastrophe, a scandal, anything could blow this job for him."

Steely sighed. It was an exhalation of frustration. "What the hell did I drive over here for," he asked, "if you don't have anything to tell me?"

Elvino threw back his shoulders. "I had to give you the courtesy of meeting with you, and not simply putting you off on the phone. You've been through a lot. It demands courtesy."

"Right," Steely said, opening the door. He got out of the car, then turned to Elvino, putting out his hand. "Thanks, anyway," he said.

That evening, he heated a serving of frozen baked macaroni and spooned it out on a chipped china plate, one of a set he had bought in a Manhattan thrift shop. He remembered the sign in the window: "Items priced especially for divorce and separation emergencies." It was a shock to realize after he and Maryanne had separated that he needed a duplicate of everything, even little things like a sugar bowl and salt and pepper shakers. He would have been without utensils and lamps and appliances if it wasn't for those thrift shops on Third Avenue.

He lay back on his bed, the plate of macaroni on his lap, the television tuned to the evening news. He ate slowly, leisurely, for there were no alarms looming through the dinner, no fires or emergencies. He was lonely. If his arm were not swollen and heavy with plaster, he would go out for a few pops, maybe a boilermaker or two. But he was also tired, and disappointed. Again, he realized there was nothing special in his life. Red Hadley was dead, the funeral was over, in the past. It had to be in the past. He would be on medical leave from the Department for some time, and there weren't even the alarms to occupy him, divert him, focus his energies. He was still in the poverty pad, alone, listening to the traffic of the Midtown Tunnel.

And then there are the days ahead, he thought, days that have to be filled. Filled with what? One dead end after another? I told Kathy the Department doesn't operate in a vacuum, but I still don't know anything useful about the accident. Does Gore's wanting a big job at CG&E have anything to do with it, I wonder? Did he order someone to trash Kathy, so that . . . what did Elvino say? So that things would be straight, no complications, nothing that might blow an opportunity. Christ. Maybe I should use a big credit card and go down to Haggerty, tell him he's got to do something, say something public? But how many credit cards do I have left? And if there's a big shake-up coming at headquarters like Ritter said, Haggerty's not going to want to listen to my violins. Christ.

The telephone rang then. "Hello," Steely said.

"Fireman Byrnes?" the voice said. It was not a smooth voice, or an understanding one.

"Yeah," Steely answered, "who's this?"

"You don't know me, Byrnes," the voice said, "but my name is Steinf, Captain Steinf."

CHAPTER 29

IT was near lunchtime. Steely was sitting in a booth at the rear of the Shamrock Bar, a neighborhood tavern on a narrow street off Coenties Slip. It was one of the few neighborhood joints still in business since the Chase Manhattan Plaza was built and real estate prices rose like a moonshot.

"Just meet me," Captain Steinf had said before hanging up. He wouldn't say anything else, except that he was part of the headquarters staff. If only Jerry Ritter had been in, he could have told me about Steinf, Steely thought. Once a month he goes to therapy at New York University, and this has to be the day. I wonder what Steinf wants?

Maybe he could answer a question about Hadley's death, whatever that question might be. There is always a question surrounding the death of a firefighter. Line-of-duty deaths are always caused by some malfunction, something going wrong, some accident. A roof collapses because of an oversight in the building code and some merchant has placed a four-ton air-conditioner on it, or a mask has a stuck valve that was never tested correctly, or the walls fall in because someone didn't see the bricks coming apart at the mortar points, or a floor gives way because it has been rebuilt so many times over the years, each time adding a new and unsafe weightload. All accidents because someone didn't look close enough, think hard enough. Any number of deaths. Any number of reasons.

The waitress came and asked if he wanted to order. She reminded him of Maryanne, same curls at the side of her head, same pleasant, round face. "I'll wait, thanks," he said.

He thought then of Maryanne, and of what she had said in the hospital. He had talked to her once on the telephone since then. He had asked to see her. "Could I come out, maybe have lunch?" he had asked.

"No," she answered. No beating around the bush, no gentle let-down and meager excuse. Just "no."

"Why not?" he had pressed.

"It's not time, Steely," she said. "I'm glad you're okay, and I'm glad you're out of the hospital. But I need time to get my own act together, to think about my priorities."

Damn, he thought. My priorities. *My*. Not *our*. Things were really changing with Maryanne. She's not the same, at least not completely, anymore. She's on a little different road, but not so different I can't find it. A road that's maybe straighter, and more orderly, and maybe going somewhere.

"Fireman Byrnes," the voice said. It startled him out of his reverie. A man in a captain's uniform was standing next to the booth. Steely put out his hand.

"I don't want to shake your hand," Steinf said, sitting down across from Steely in the booth and taking an envelope out of his uniform pocket. "I answered the phone when you called from the 19th Precinct, remember? I work for Chief Haggerty."

Steely put his hand in his lap across the arm cast that he had placed on his thigh. He looked at Steinf suspiciously. It was obvious there wasn't going to be a friendship growing between them. "Right," he said, "I remember a little."

"Doesn't matter," Steinf said, shoving the envelope across the table at Steely. "I don't want a drink, and I don't want a prolonged conversation."

Steely reached for the envelope. It was stamped but unaddressed. Peculiar. He opened it with his one good hand. It was a photocopy of Chief Johnson's memo to the Chief of Department.

"I was going to mail this to you last night," Steinf said. "Even stamped the envelope. But I figured you might take it more seriously if I gave it to you in person."

Steely read it, uncertain of what it meant until he looked at the date . . . almost a week before Red Hadley was killed.

"God almighty," he uttered.

"I copied this for no good reason," Steinf said, waving the approaching waitress away, "except that I don't like some of the things the Chief has been doing lately. He wants to change the staff jobs, and a lot of people like me have nowhere to go but put the paper in. I have another five, eight years before I want to put the paper in."

"Christ," Steely said, reading the memo again. He felt a chill across the back of his neck. "Then he knew those rigs were defective. He's known it all along."

"That's not for me to say." Steinf replied. "But you tell anybody you got this from me and I'll deny it, mark you a rat, and have you transferred. I'm only giving this to you because I heard in the halls you were looking for information. And it's a little piece of justice for me to keep it in the job like this. You can take it from here."

Steely studied Steinf quickly. He had met many captains like him before, stern-nosed, even Nazi-like, the kind of man whose pride would let him kill whole populations on principle if he had the power. A short man, homely, probably not ever good-looking, his stomach bigger than he ever expected it to be. He was of a Department type, that was for sure, and he was doing what he wanted to get done, which was to pass the burden of this incriminating memo to somebody else.

"I met the firefighter who was killed," Steinf said, rising abruptly from the booth. "Hadley. I heard the Chief chew him out." Then he was gone.

At first Steely laughed, thinking that Steinf wasn't what he had in mind when he told Kathy that someone would come crashing through the wall. But white knight or not, Steinf had knocked down a big wall.

Then Steely sat back against the hard wood of the booth and looked again at the memo. What the hell, he asked himself, am I going to do with this? Haggerty *knew*, he knew all the time that the rescue-V-rig was a problem. Shit. Maybe he didn't lie to me, or to the reporters at the press conference. Maybe he thinks there really was an error in procedure. That Kathy screwed up. But he knew there could have been another explanation, and he kept quiet about it. Why? Who is he trying to protect? Why didn't he just recall the damn things? That would've saved Red. Red would be here today if Haggerty had simply given the order not to use the rigs. But he didn't. Not until they were all taken out of service. And then it was too late.

Getting up, Steely left two dollars on the table and then picked up the memo. He folded it, shoved it into the envelope, and stuck it into the back pocket of the chinos he was wearing.

It was a cool day for August, and a breeze was blowing in from the East River, carrying with it the fish smell that lingered in the old Fulton Street market. Steely began to walk then, limping slightly but not feeling any discomfort in his foot at all. He had too much to figure out, to ponder, to waste time thinking about his foot.

He looked up at a street sign. Duane and Broadway. The city's old fire museum was just down the block. He had walked from Coenties Slip to Canal Street and back down Broadway. It was like he had walked in a horseshoe, a living horseshoe filled with lunchtime hordes, and he was now just two blocks from the Municipal Building and the office of the Chief of Department. He had walked without any real direction, past the old Civil War era buildings in the east side harbor district, up and across Canal Street, where a carnival of hawking Israelis and Arabs worked side by side, selling their Japanese sound and video equipment, on the street that once was the hardware capital of the world, and then down Broadway in the shadows of the cast-iron buildings that went higher and higher with the invention of the elevator.

Why me, Steely asked himself over and over, taking the envelope from his back pocket, opening it, reading the memo again? Who can I talk to? Used to be, he thought, I could talk to Maryanne if I was in trouble. Used to be even Jack Haggerty. Christ, I was going to call him today, try to see him and ask what he knew about the V-rig. I thought maybe he was covering for Gore, or someone in the Department had screwed up and he ought to hear about it. But he knew. He knew. What would he have told me? More evasive answers? And now I have this memo. What does it mean? It means that no matter how you look at it, or who screwed up, Haggerty is responsible. The Chief of Department is responsible. But how can I talk to him now? How can I go against Haggerty? Christ, he helped me with that cop. He thought enough of me to go out of his way, put his own authority up front. For me. Small potatoes, Johnny

Gimme said that night. He had gone way afield for me, and he called it small potatoes. Anything to keep that old neighborhood thing going, to keep those loyalties alive.

I owe him, Steely thought, I owe him terrific, but I owe Red Hadley, too. And Red Hadley is dead. He's dead and I'm here walking around the streets of New York like I own them. Christ, Jesus, if only I had someone to talk to.

He thought of Kathy then. He had to call her, tell her he had found what they were looking for. What did they call it, a smoking pistol? He had a Gatling gun right in his back pocket. The trouble was, he didn't know what to do with it. He knew what she would say: Take it to the board of inquiry, take it to the Inspector General. It was the only thing that would save her neck. She wouldn't understand that Jack Haggerty was a friend. Still, he knew he had to call her. But she was probably on duty now and he couldn't talk to her at the firehouse. Tonight. He'd call her tonight.

It was then that he remembered the card the priest had given him at the Holy Name racket, Frank Flynn, the Department's new chaplain. He found the card in his wallet. He went to the public phone on the east side of Broadway and dialed the number. The rectory housekeeper answered the phone, a young Spanish voice. "The monsignor will be back at supper time," she said.

Sure, Steely thought, they never miss a meal, the priests. But he was a good guy, seemed to be, I remember. He cared. He seemed to care even if his sermon at Red's funeral was off the mark a bit. "I'll call back," Steely said, hanging up the phone.

Looking down Broadway, he saw the high center arch of the Municipal Building and began to walk toward it, limping, his swelled ankle feeling as if it were wrapped in nails. I wish I had a drink, Steely thought, as he lighted a cigarette. Or anything to take the ocean out of my stomach.

He walked under the arch and through the doors of the Municipal Building. In the elevator he pressed the number 12, and rode up, his cigarette still smoking. He dropped it on the floor and stepped on it when a woman riding in the elevator with him gave him an angry look.

There were boxes in the hallway of the sixteenth floor. The Fire Department's headquarters were about to move again to new quarters up on Sixty-seventh Street, the third move since they left Brooklyn several years before. A sign hanging on the marble cor-

ridor wall pointed to the Fire Commissioner's office, to the left, and
to the office of the Chief of Department, to the right. Steely turned
right and began to walk down the long, echoing corridor to Jack
Haggerty's office.

But then, suddenly, he stopped. Christ, he thought to himself.
What the hell am I going to say to him, that I know he's covering up
something? How can I even be sure of that? For all I know, Steinf
himself might have written that memo to discredit Haggerty. There's
obviously no love lost between them. But no, goddammit. Steinf is
too smart to give me a bogus memo. What would it prove? I've got
to stop reacting, like reacting to that cop on Fifty-ninth Street, the
bosses at work, Kathy Angelli, any number of bar brawls. React.
That's all I ever do. Maryanne says something just a little out of line
and I react, jump like a curled snake. I shouldn't react here, though.
No, not now. There's nothing really I can say to Jack Haggerty,
nothing I know of. Jesus, if only I had someone to talk to. Flynn is
all, the monsignor, and he's out until dinner.

Steely left the Municipal Building and took a cab to Coenties
Slip, where he had parked his bomb in a bus stop. He drove then
over to the South Street Seaport, and up the East River Drive, past
the great smokestacks of City Gas and Electric, past the United
Nations building, and out at Sixty-first Street to Second Avenue and
to the Fifty-ninth Street Bridge, saving the toll to get across the
river, going out Queens Boulevard, the traffic stopping and starting
like the pain in his ankle. He was about to turn down into one of the
side streets that would take him to the poverty pad when he changed
his mind.

I don't want to be in that junk pile, he thought. Not with just
me and the awful aloneness there. Not until I do something, anything. To be alone there, and to think of the things Red might be
doing at the same time. What else would there be to think about? At
least Red would be with people, out on the streets with the dregs
even. But, goddammit, it was something. Red Hadley would be
doing *something*.

Just keep moving, he thought. That was enough. It didn't matter
where. He drove now with as much determination as he had walked
the streets of Manhattan earlier, but without focus, without destina-
tion, out on the Long Island Expressway to the Van Wyck, to the
Belt, to the Sunrise Highway, back along the Van Wyck again.
Then, he continued along Queens Boulevard, toward the city, past

the Tudor bricks of Forest Hills, past the big department stores in Elmhurst and the tall, proud elk that was green with age, planted in concrete before the Woodside Elks' Club.

He passed the old firehouse on Sixty-fifth Place and began to brake the car. I could stop there, he thought, I know some guys in there, in the rescue company. Maybe have a beer, coffee, something, maybe make a few phone calls. Call Parnell Farrell again. Farrell. God, was that phony or what, a woman called by her last name? All right for a man, but who cares? She won't want to see me. Forget lunch. A month or so she'll come around.

He accelerated the car then, remembering that St. Veronica's parish was down just a way, past Calvary Cemetery and the frank-furter stand. Maybe Monsignor Flynn was back by now. Old Frank Flynn from the neighborhood. He'd know what to do, probably. He said he wanted to spend time with the Fire Department, and he finally got to be a chaplain. You get a car with the job, and calls from firemen like me, firemen with problems.

He turned off Queens Boulevard at Forty-third Street and parked the car on Skillman Avenue. Walking up the narrow red brick entryway to the parish house, just as he passed the overgrown holly bushes that rimmed the path, he heard the high, staccato voice of the parish maid. "When you be back in the rectory?" she called from the front door as Monsignor Frank Flynn walked down the brick stairway.

"An hour or two," he said over his shoulder, running flat into Steely.

"Whoa, Monsignor," Steely said.

Monsignor Flynn smiled, holding Steely by the arm. "Oh," he said. "Steely, right?"

"Byrnes," Steely said, "Steely Byrnes. I talked to you at the Holy Name racket, remember?"

"Sure," Monsignor Flynn answered. "I read about you in the newspaper, and, of course, I saw you at the funeral."

Steely knew that the monsignor must have seen him break the ranks of the formation at the funeral. He was suddenly embarrassed. Reacting again, he thought, always reacting.

"Father," Steely said, looking down at the priest's shoes, "I just want to sit and talk to you a little, about a lot of things that are happening. You said to call you, remember?"

"Sure, Steely," Monsignor Flynn answered, beginning to move

259

past him on the narrow pathway, "I remember. But right now I have an important meeting with the local Community Board. I'm the vice-chairman, you know, and we're looking at computers today so we'll have better organizational controls. You should have called."

"Please, Father," Steely said. "I mean, Monsignor. It's pretty important. Not just for me. For the Department."

Monsignor Flynn hesitated. "All right, Steely," he said finally. "We can take some time now, a few minutes."

They sat in the parlor of the priest's residence. It was a small room, overstuffed with furniture, a room that might be called a living room in any place other than a rectory. There was a stale smell in the air, Steely thought, a slightly sweet smell, as if the room had recently been filled with flowers.

"I know you're a chaplain now," Steely said, balancing his cast on the narrow wooden arm of a cane-backed chair. "Good going."

"Thanks," Monsignor Flynn said, sitting opposite Steely on a square-cornered couch. "It came as a complete surprise. Now, what can I do for you?"

Steely picked the envelope out of his back pocket, handed it to the priest, and then waited.

There was a print of the Hans Holbein portrait of St. Thomas More on the wall, the same portrait that hung in the center hallway of St. Aloysius where they had all, Steely, Haggerty, and Flynn, gone through grammar school. He had never forgotten the way the light reflected from the folds of velvet of the martyr's shirt, and had always marveled, even now, at how the painter managed to do that. He remembered that he used to stand before the portrait as a child, looking up at it, wondering why St. Thomas was there and not St. Aloysius, and wondering too what St. Aloysius might look like. He had asked a nun about it, and she told him that from time to time throughout life, he would always find questions without answers. Sister Mary Pious. He still remembered her name.

Steely turned his attention to the priest, and watched the expression on his face change from a kind of polite curiosity to a look of serious concern. "I'm not sure what this means, Steely," he said. "Particularly in terms of Department policy on correspondence."

"It means, Monsignor," Steely said, "that they knew the rescue-V-rig was inadequate at least five days before the . . ." His voice sounded strange in that small room, even to himself.

"So it would seem," Monsignor Flynn said. "But in terms of

Department procedures, I'm sure everything is done always to get the best possible equipment for the firefighters."

"The thing tore, Father," Steely said, speaking now just above a whisper.

"But it had been tested properly," Monsignor Flynn argued. "This memo says the problem was found in secondary testing. Isn't that proof that the initial tests were made properly?"

"Not in firefighting, Father," Steely said, leaning forward in his chair. "There's a building on fire, the firefighters go in and do a primary search for victims, in the fire, risking their. . . . You know, people can get hurt in fires. When the fire dies down a little, though, the firefighters then do a secondary search, a little less risky, but as important as the first. In other words, the job isn't done until both searches are complete. That's the way it is. Part A and Part B together, otherwise bodies can show up and cause a lot of trouble for everyone."

The housekeeper entered the room and looked inquiringly at the monsignor. "Can I get something for you?" she asked. He did not answer, but waved her away.

Steely was staring intensely at the priest, hoping he would understand, would see that he was not seeking comfort, but guidance. Instead, he noticed that Monsignor Flynn had become uncomfortable, moving a little uneasily on the couch.

"What kind of trouble do you think this memo could cause, Steely?" he asked.

"It could cause a lot of trouble for Chief Haggerty, for the Fire Commissioner, the Mayor even. All I'd have to do is send it to the Inspector General or somebody like that."

"That would be unfortunate," Monsignor Flynn said.

"You think *unfortunate* is a good word to use in a situation like this?"

"I mean," Monsignor Flynn replied, "at this time. For you see, Steely, the Chief of Department is very near to being named the Department's new commissioner."

Steely tried to conceal his surprise. Jack Haggerty the Fire Commissioner? Ol' Johnnie Gimme is finally going to make it right to the top. Well. Why not? He's worked hard enough for it, kept his nose clean.

"I think he would be an excellent man for the job, Steely." Monsignor Flynn went on. "An excellent choice for the Department."

"Then how do you explain this memo?" Steely said. There was no hostility in his voice. He was genuinely hoping Monsignor Flynn could answer that question. "How do you explain the Department going with failure of procedure instead of failure of equipment? You know it was a woman firefighter who lowered me, Father. What do you think that's going to do to her if people think she was responsible?"

"I understand there's an official inquiry under way," Monsignor Flynn said.

"That's right," Steely interrupted. "So how come nobody's asked me any questions?"

"These things take time, Steely. You mustn't jump to conclusions."

"The only conclusion I'm jumping to, Father, is that the Department knew these rigs were no damn good and nobody did anything about it. Jack Haggerty knew and he's keeping quiet about it, even if it means hanging somebody else. Excuse me, Father, but the whole thing stinks. And I want to know why."

Monsignor Flynn was standing now in front of the picture of St. Thomas. "I can see you're upset, Steely. But there's got to be some answer, some logical explanation—"

Steely cut him off. "There's a man dead," he said, again in a low whispery voice. "What's the logical explanation for that?"

"I know," Monsignor Flynn said, "a great tragedy, but—"

"There's no *but* about it, Father," Steely said, picking up the memo and rising to his feet. "There is just one question. What is the right thing for me to do? I have two kids, an estranged wife, a mortgage, apartment rent, car insurance, the whole cradle of crayons, and I have this memo. I can blow the whistle, and maybe blow the whole job, the family stability, whatever there is left of it. Or I can forget it. But how can I forget it, especially here in what I guess is a house blessed by the Bishop? Tell me what to do, Monsignor."

"I can't tell you that, Steely. That's between you and your conscience. But let me ask you to promise me one thing. And that is you won't do anything until you talk to Jack Haggerty. You owe that to the Department, to have a talk with him. It's like family, and maybe there's something else he knows that will make everything clear and understandable to you. Promise me that."

Steely started toward the door, limping slightly. "Sure, I'll promise you that, Father," he said. "Thanks for talking with me. Thanks a lot for your time."

He left the rectory, walking down the plant-bordered pathway and along the street to his car. The car rattled as he started it and drove down Queens Boulevard. Between me and my conscience, he thought. Why do priests always say that? He was tired and there was a pins-and-needles feeling in his left arm. He wished he could move his fingers, make a fist, crash it through a window or a mirror. He felt frustrated, like a blind man with a story to tell among deaf people. He felt like lashing out.

Stop reacting, he thought, chastening himself. Like Maryanne said, smashing windows and breaking down doors. Just see what happens, think about it. Be smart, controlled. Things will work out.

He turned off Queens Boulevard in the direction of the poverty pad. God, he asked himself, how long has it been since I've slept a night through? Just a few hours' sleep would be like a weekend in the mountains. Cool and clear. But how the hell could he sleep? He knew every time he closed his eyes he would see the look on Red Hadley's face as he lunged out that window. He thought I'd saved him and the next thing he was dead. He never knew what happened. Red had a conscience, Steely thought. He was always talking about his good friend Jesus. What would he do if he were alive now, if I had been the one who hit the pavement first?

What would Monsignor Frank Flynn do? Suppose he caught another priest hitting the parish till, or shacking up with one of the sodality sisters or something like that, something that would reflect on the church. Would he blow the whistle or would he keep quiet about it, sweep it under the rug? In a way, the Department was like the church and you had to be loyal, no matter what. Like family, Monsignor Flynn had said, and the family always comes first. But Red was part of that family, and somebody in the Department killed him. Maybe not intentionally. But what they were doing to Kathy *was* intentional. What the hell kind of family was that?

He decided to call Kathy then, and hoped she wasn't working. Sure, for God's sake, she's smart. She'd tell him to go public with the memo, he was certain of that. And why not? But then, he had been certain Monsignor Flynn would tell him the same thing. And he got the picture, no doubt about it, that the monsignor wanted him to keep his mouth shut, conscience or not. He knew Flynn and Haggerty were friends. Haggerty probably even got him the job as Department chaplain. Was that the reason? Family. One big happy family.

"Steely?" Kathy said when she heard his voice on the phone. "What's the matter? You sound funny."

"I've just been talking to a priest. We've got a problem, Kathy. Can we talk? I mean, not over the phone. Can I come to your place?"

He realized then she would probably think he was trying to make another pitch, another come-on. But she said yes without hesitation, and told him where she lived.

It was Waverly Place, right off Washington Square, and Steely had to put his car in a lot. Her apartment was small and neat, and if she had a roommate or a regular boyfriend, there were no signs of it. There was a fireplace, but no screen or broom and shovel. The bookshelves were made of pine planks piled upon bricks, and the long, low coffee table in front of the couch was made from an old door stained a deep walnut. The rest of the furniture was of rattan, inexpensive, but made to look classy with a lot of small pillows scattered around. Kathy seemed to have things very together, he thought. Not like the poverty pad. Not like my life.

"You look tired, Steely," she said as he sat on a rattan chair.

"Been a long day," he replied. She looked good, even in loose sweat pants and a NYFD tee shirt. She was wearing no make-up, not even lipstick, and her lips had a fresh, pink color which was new to him. A lot of things about Kathy seemed new now that he was in her apartment.

"Drink?" she asked.

"Water," he said. He wanted a beer and a ball, but thought better of asking. She probably didn't even know what that was.

Kathy brought him a tall glass of clear New York water without ice cubes. "Hope it's cold enough," she said.

"As long as it's wet," he said. He drank the water and put the glass down carefully on the coffee table. "I found out what we wanted to know about the V-rig," he said. "That's why I called. That's why I wanted to talk to you." He pulled the memo from his pocket and handed it to her.

She unfolded it and began to read as Steely watched. It felt strange, different, being here alone with her in a Village apartment.

In this situation with any other woman, he would probably have made a move. But not with her, not now.

"Then the rigs are defective," she said, refolding the memo and putting it back in the envelope. "And they knew it, Steely, before the accident. Why would they do something like that, issue defective equipment? *Who* would do something like that?"

Steely shrugged. "Somebody screwed up and they're trying to keep it quiet. The Commissioner's up for a big new job and Jack Haggerty's in line to become the next commissioner."

"Your friend," Kathy said, "right?"

"We grew up in the same neighborhood. We started out in the Department together."

Kathy exhaled softly and let her shoulders drop. "Well, this gets me off the hook. And I guess I should be happy, Steely, but I'm not. I can't ask you to go against Haggerty, against the Department, for me."

"Christ, Kathy," he exploded. "I thought you'd be overjoyed. I thought you'd be dancing in the streets."

"Did you, Steely?" she said.

He got out of the rattan chair and stood before the empty fire-place, his elbow on the mantel. "Let me tell you about Jack T. Haggerty, Kathy. Let me tell you about what kind of a guy he is."

He paused then, trying to focus Haggerty's face in his mind. "He's a goddamn stand-up guy, the kind of guy who's always there when you need him. I got in some trouble with a cop a while back, and he was right there. I wanted a transfer years ago from Ladder 57 and he was right there. I cursed at some Johnnie-come-lately lieutenant once and faced Department charges, but Haggerty was right there. If I need anything, I know he'll be right there, because he values old friendships, the old ties."

"What's he up to, then?" Kathy interrupted.

"I don't know, hiding something. Sure, maybe he's trying to cover for somebody else, maybe even the Commissioner. But this memo was written to him, Kathy. He is responsible. And this could ruin him, knock him right out of the Department. I'm afraid to do that to him. And I'll tell you something else. It's a lousy, selfish thing to say, but I'm afraid of what will happen to me."

"Steely Byrnes afraid," Kathy said. "I don't buy it."

She was trying to make him feel good, he thought, trying to make things lighter, less burdensome. "It's true," he said. "Let me tell you a story, one that I was a part of. Back in Ladder 57, Nifty Fifty-seven, when Captain Buber, a pretty decent man, wrote a letter to the Fire Commissioner, saying that the firefighters of Harlem deserved better from the job, a better firehouse, one where the boiler didn't break down once a week, where the mice and the roaches didn't end up in the pockets of your turnout coat, and better, safer equipment. We had an old, spare ladder truck, one that had a sideboard you couldn't stand on because of the rust. Imagine that. Beat up, holes throughout, brakes that screeched like a subway train in a curve. A piece of junk like that in one of the busiest fire companies in the whole goddamn world, not just the job. Buber went through the channels first, looking for changes to be made. They ignored him. So he wrote the letter."

"Yes," Kathy said. "And?"

"And they transferred him to Brooklyn," Steely said, reaching into his shirt pocket for a cigarette. "He carried the mark of the transfer with him, and it broke him. He lasted a year, and retired, just faded away unheard-of, a man who led a great fire company, a man who believed in truth."

"But that doesn't have to happen to you, Steely," she said.

"Goddamn right," he replied angrily. "I can't let it happen to me. Sure, I could get another job, a chauffeur, a store clerk, anything, but the Department is the only thing I'm really connected to, Kathy, the only thing I have."

"You have yourself, your family."

"If I don't have the Department, I don't have anything."

He lit his cigarette and stared at the burning match for a moment before he blew it out. "It's crazy, isn't it, to love this job. You've got to be crazy to crawl through the heat and the dripping paint and the falling plaster, searching around through the goddamn smoke, choking maybe, looking for a life, any life, it doesn't matter whose life it is. But it makes you feel special. You may be scared out of your drawers, but you're in there in that fire, you're doing the job, looking for that life, and there's no other feeling like it."

He ground out his cigarette in an ashtray on the coffee table. The memo was laying there on the table where Kathy had left it. "So what do I do with this?" Steely said, picking it up.

"Maybe you don't have to do anything," Kathy said. "Maybe there's another copy somewhere, or some other papers that will turn up in the inquiry."

"Nothing else is going to turn up," Steely said. "Believe me."

"Then send it to the Inspector General or even the Mayor. Nobody has to know it came from you."

"And nobody would pay any attention."

"How about the papers, the *Times*? Who was that reporter at the press conference? Send it to him."

"Burns," Steely said. "The same name as mine only spelled different. F. X. Burns. It's a thought."

"I've got an even better one," Kathy said. "Let me do it. I'll take it to the Mayor or Burns, in person if I have to. They'll pay attention to me, Steely. I don't have anything to lose, at least not like you. I came on this job because it was a salary. A job, that's all, one I thought I could do. I never looked at it like a mission, never thought I had to prove anything to anyone. They don't want me in the Department anyway, and I'm not sure I want to stay. Not after this. But you have your family to think of. I could wait tables and make as much money."

Steely smiled and shook his head. "You're a lousy liar, you know that? Remember what you told Red the very first day you showed up at the firehouse? If you don't, I do. You said you always earnestly wanted this job. Earnestly, that's the important word, you said."

"I remember," Kathy said. "I also remember you weren't too happy to see me that day."

"Hell, no."

"Have you changed your mind about that?"

"Probably not," Steely said. "But I've changed my mind about you."

"No more centerfolds on the housewatch table? No more quick feels when you're shoving me into a fire?"

"Oh Christ," Steely moaned, "don't remind me."

They began to laugh. Kathy was sitting on a low stool, her knees up, her hands hanging between her legs. She looked like a resting dancer, Steely thought. At that moment she looked like anything in the world more than she looked like a firefighter. But that's what she was, what she had always wanted to be.

"I can't let you take this memo to the Mayor, or anybody else," he said. "You know that. And as long as we're taking this stroll down memory lane, maybe you remember something else. Remember we were up on the roof and Jackson wanted to lower me down?"

267

"I'll never forget."

"Then you remember what I said. I told Jackson no, because the rope was in your pocket. It was your rope so it was your job to do. Well, this memo is in my pocket. It's my job to do." He got up. "Thanks for the water. Thanks for letting me shoot my mouth off. And I'm sorry about, you know, the way I acted."

"Oh, Steely," she said. "You don't have to apologize. I'm the one who should apologize for some of the things I thought about you."

"Like what, may I ask?"

"Ladies don't use words like that. We may think them, but we don't say them out loud."

"Some lady," he said with a grin.

They were standing at the door of her apartment. "Where are you going now?" she asked.

"Home, I guess, such as it is. I've got a lot piling up in my head. And then tomorrow I'll see Jack Haggerty. That's a start anyway."

"Whatever you decide to do, Steely, I know it will be the right thing," Kathy said. "But I don't want you to feel you're doing it for me. Or even for Red. It has to be the right thing for you."

She put her hands on his shoulders and pressed her cheek lightly against his. He drew back, feeling awkward and foolish. He wanted to embrace her, to hold her in his arms if only for a moment. But he knew that wasn't what she wanted, what her gesture meant.

"Take care of yourself, Steely," she said, opening the door.

"Sure," he replied. "I'm famous for that. You know, I came down here to ask you what the hell I'm supposed to do in this situation, and I guess I'm still wondering what St. Aloysius looks like."

"I don't understand."

"Just that some questions don't have answers."

Kathy was framed in the doorway, the bright, cheerful light from her apartment behind her casting her face in shadows. "There are always answers, Steely," she said. "We just have to know where to look for them."

CHAPTER 30

THE Chief of Department held the nameplate carefully between his hands, searching it for fingerprints. Sometimes the cleaning women picked it up, leaving behind their finger smudges. CHIEF J. T. HAGGERTY, it read, in gold block letters mounted on silver. Josie had it specially made up for him at Bulgari's of Fifth Avenue when he was appointed to the highest uniform rank. He polished the name lightly with the back of his blue cotton uniform tie, thinking Josie will be happy to order a new one of these for me. Or maybe all we have to do is take the title off and save the name on this one. Just another week and old Neutral Nicholas Gore can manage City Gas and Electric with his mouth wide open and a question mark stamped in the middle of his forehead. It was hard to believe that an incompetent like Gore had been recommended to head a major utility, but Godspeed to him. He would never have gotten the Mayor's nod if it weren't for Bishop Donato, and E. P. Dolan, and old Dougie Ratnor working their independent magic. Goodness, he said to himself, it is a grandly ironic thing to know that Gore owes his elevation to the Peter Principle level to no one other than the likes of me. It's a great country, this New York, a great country to get ahead in.

Haggerty replaced the nameplate on the desk and picked a thick folder out of his *out* box. Better not to wait for the mail pickup to get this delivered back down to the legal bureau. It was the daily packet of information being developed by the various divisions in response to the Department's internal investigation into what was now known as the Ninety-ninth Street job. Reports from the training division, fire prevention, research and development, from the Manhattan Borough Command and the medical division, all commenting on the procedures and equipment used, building construction, training preparedness, firefighting personnel counts, responding apparatus and special units, injuries, deaths, and any other salient information relating to Alarm Box 1082. Nothing there to tie him to the V-rigs and the Ratnors, thank goodness. Absolutely nothing. Every division was pointing a finger at every other division. And that was good, too. The woman firefighter, what was her name, would be exonerated eventually, but women on the job were finished as far as he was concerned. He'd see to that when the time came. Everything was going to work out just fine, with the exception of Katra Hadley, which was a great pity. She had called and told him she was going to sue the Department. It didn't surprise him. When litigation came, he thought, the Department would be ready for it. He hated the idea of having to give Katra up, but he had to be ready for that possibility, too. Goodness, she was so supple, so soft, but the job came first. Every little item, every possible question had to be covered. All the pins had to be in place.

He carried the folder to his outer office, where a young lieutenant, a light-duty man, was sitting at Steinf's desk. Sickly Steinf, Haggerty thought, taking a few days' medical leave with a feigned pain in his knee, just when I need him most. There are lots of preparations to be made for transition when Gore leaves, and Steinf gets home free on medical leave. Well, I won't have to put up with his nonsense for much longer.

"Get this down to legal," Haggerty said, dropping the folder before the fire officer.

The phone rang, and the secretary sitting behind the lieutenant answered it. "Chaplain Flynn for you, sir," she said.

Haggerty returned to his office and picked up the phone. "Frank, how good to hear from you," he said. He listened for a few moments, the happiness, the control, falling from his face. "Goodness," he said.

He was sitting on the edge of his chair, thinking that he must not alarm the Department's new chaplain, but reassure him. "That's not really a troublesome piece of news, Frank," he said. "There's nothing that isn't normal Department procedure and business in that memo. But I do thank you for calling me about it. If you were just a little older, you'd remember how Steely always made a big thing of everything in the old neighborhood. He's jumping the gun, but I'll take care of it, calm him down."

He sat back in his chair, hands together, fingertips tapping against fingertips. "How could this be possible?" he said half aloud. "How could Steely Byrnes end up with a personal memo from the Chief of Research and Development?"

"Sir," he then heard. It was a tone of voice that reminded him of a Marine Corps response, the kind of voice that came from a chin that was folded into the throat.

"Sit down, Lieutenant," was the next voice he heard, just before Nicholas Gore strutted into his office, in quick step, as if he were trying to make the bank before it closed.

"Commissioner," Haggerty said. It was more a declarative statement than a greeting.

"I suppose you've heard the news?" Gore asked, stopping just a foot from Haggerty's desk.

"I heard that the executive committee of CG&E was meeting this afternoon," Haggerty said, smiling, "and I said a small prayer for you." There was no point in not developing a stronger friendship if Gore was to head such a big utility company.

"The Mayor himself showed at the meeting," Gore beamed, "and he recommended me. I can't imagine why the Mayor has been so helpful, but it is now officially a shoo-in. We've only to wait until a week from today when the full board can meet to endorse the decision of the executive committee."

Haggerty rose from his chair, his hand extended. "My congratulations, Commissioner, to you and your family. The street lamps in this city will glow more brightly under your leadership."

He was a little embarrassed in saying that, but, he thought, the past will be the past. I'll have to create a new era in the Fire

Department, and I might as well start with a smile on everyone's face, everyone except Steinf, anyway. It must have been Steinf who copied that memo. There was no other explanation.

Commissioner Gore smiled in acknowledgment. "I don't know what a change in administration will bring, Chief," he said, "but I assure you that I will do everything in my power to effectuate a harmonious transfer of authority."

Effectuate, indeed, Haggerty thought. If old neutral Nicky could effectuate anything, he'd be a much easier man to like. But he was just one of those chosen few who manage to succeed with each failure.

"Yes, sir," Haggerty said, "certainly."

"We owe that to the Mayor," the Commissioner winked, and walked briskly out of the office.

Goodness gracious, Haggerty thought, not a single word about who his successor might be, not a hint of good luck to the traditionally most obvious candidate, the number-one uniformed man of the Department. And after everything he doesn't know I've done for him. Not that it matters that he is an ingrate, but simple courtesy would dictate a word of good luck to me. My heavens, the man has no manners whatever.

Suddenly, he heard the lieutenant's growling voice again. "Hold it a minute," the lieutenant said.

"Just say Steely Byrnes is here."

Already, Haggerty thought? Thank goodness Frank Flynn called me. It's a definite advantage to know what's on a man's mind before he tells you. But I'll have to handle this just right, for Steely has the explosive possibility of an LNG tanker. Good people, though, Steely is, a good neighborhood guy. He'll be okay with some coaxing, some friendship.

Haggerty greeted Steely at the door, shaking his hand, not giving him an opportunity to speak. "Nice to see you," he said, gesturing Steely into the office. "How's the hand? How's the foot?"

Steely sat down on the hard wooden chair next to a red corduroy-covered couch that was squeezed into a corner of the office, and Haggerty saw him looking around, at the citations and awards hanging on the walls, the photos with the Mayor and with the Cardinal, the collection of miniature fire trucks given to him by the Chief of the Copenhagen Fire Department that was positioned like a convoy on the glass coffee table in front of the couch. "See you have the old halls of ivy," Steely said, nodding toward a photo of the St. Aloysius School that was in a leather frame on his desk. Haggerty realized then that Steely had never been in his office before.

"Right next to that picture of Josie," he said. "I like to keep them together because that's where I met her. If it wasn't such a good school, strict, her father would have sent her to someplace more ritzy, Marymount or one of those places. But I don't suppose you're here to talk about St. Aloysius, are you? I understand why you left ranks at the funeral, Steely. You felt your place was with your company."

"You don't understand at all, Jack," Steely answered. His voice was laden with confrontation.

Goodness, Haggerty thought, I will have to approach this gingerly, at least keep him on the defensive, on his toes. "It was a terrible thing you went through, a great tragedy, but thank God you're alive, still with us. It's a miracle."

"Right," Steely said, "I'm here."

"I've been thinking so much about you lately," Haggerty said, sitting down on the couch. "So often. Patrolman Murphy keeps calling here wanting to talk to me, but I thought I should talk to you first. You know, it could be quite serious if he presses charges formally. But I wouldn't worry about that, if I were you. There are still a few things I can pull."

Good, Haggerty thought, that will keep him attentive. I don't have to tell him he could lose the job if that cop does press charges and there's nothing I could do about it. He's a good man, this Steely, though he looks very mixed up, strange.

"Look," Steely said suddenly, standing up directly in front of Haggerty, "I don't give two craps about a traffic cop on the Fifty-ninth Street Bridge, and I don't believe in miracles."

Haggerty also rose to his feet. He did not want to be sitting with a firefighter towering over him. It was not a good negotiating position, symbolically wrong. "Something eating at you, Steely?" he asked.

"Why do you want to dump on this woman, Jack?" Steely asked, his shoulders drawn back in defiance.

"Woman," Haggerty said, "what woman?" Don't let him feel, he thought, that his terrible event is in the front of my mind. It's not, really, or wasn't, anyway, until Frank Flynn called. What does Steely want, I wonder? Of what interest is this woman to him? A diversion, perhaps, like Katra was a diversion for me. Too bad she's

273

going to sue the Department and cause me countless hours of grief. Is that it? Does Steely have a girlfriend in the firehouse?

"Angelli," Steely snapped, "Kathy Ryan Angelli, the firefighter who hooked onto the rescue-V-rig and lowered. She did everything right, Jack. I told you that in the hospital."

"And I told you, Steely," Haggerty soothed, "that we have a Department inquiry into that tragic accident."

"No one talked to me, Jack, not a soul. Some goddamn investigation."

"We talked to the girl," Haggerty said.

"Firefighter," Steely shot back. "Remember, Jack? And she's a damn good one. I've heard the rumors going around, I heard what you said at the press conference. Failure of procedure, my ass. If that V-rig failed, it wasn't because of anything Angelli did. It was because it's a piece of crap."

Haggerty walked to his desk and sat on its edge. He was worried now. Calming Steely down might not be as easy as he thought. He was out for blood. "As a matter of fact," he said, "I'm convinced that Firefighter Angelli operated within correct procedures, and the truth will be known to everyone in a week or so when the board of inquiry submits their findings to me. Just relax, Steely. I know you have concerns, but everything will be put straight in a week or so."

"That's crap, too," Steely yelled. "The goddamn inquiry means nothing. There's no truth, Jack, not anywhere except here in my back pocket." He took the memo out of the envelope and unfolded it. "Here's the truth," he said, and began to read it aloud, starting with the date.

The young lieutenant stuck his head into the office to see what the yelling was about. Haggerty dismissed him with a nod. But he could feel his face begin to flush with anger. Calm, he told himself. Keep calm, let him read the memo, then explain it, make him believe he's barking blather.

"All right?" he said abruptly, before Steely had finished. "So there's a memo to me from Chief Johnson. I must get sixty or seventy memos every day from chiefs all over the city. I don't read all of them. It means nothing, except I have to ask you how it came into your hands."

"That's my business, Johnny," Steely said.

Haggerty realized he had not been called by that name in a long time.

"And it does mean something," Steely continued. "It means you knew about the V-rig *before* the accident."

Haggerty moved to the door of his office and pulled the doorknob to make sure it was completely shut. "No, Steely, you're entirely mistaken about that," he said. "Look, somebody in purchasing sent those things out into the firehouses, some lieutenant or captain who read the initial test reports, thinking that the testing had been complete. We don't know who, it could have been any one of fifty people, the board of inquiry tells me. And the rig bypassed training school because it came with a training book for each rig. I got the memo from Chief Johnson, Steely. I'll admit that. But it got hung up somewhere in the office mail. You don't know what the paperwork is like in this office. I didn't read that memo until after the accident, you've got to believe that. You think I'd leave a defective piece of equipment in the field if I'd known about it? What kind of a man do you think I am? It was a mistake. A mistake, Steely, and now give me that memo, if you will."

"A *mistake*," Steely yelled. He shot his arm out and pointed an accusatory finger at Haggerty. "A good man is in the silk-lined box, and you tell me it's a mistake, a man who gave his life for me, so that I could be in this room to hear you tell me it was a mistake?"

"Steely," Haggerty said, approaching him with his hand out in a gesture for quiet. "Please. Don't raise your voice to me. Just give me the memo."

"Why, Jack?" Steely asked. "So you can forget about it, hide behind your inquiry, and hang it on a woman who's just a probie and an easy target for everyone in the Department?"

"Nothing is easy in this Department. Listen to me, Steely," Haggerty replied quickly, his voice carrying with it his command experience and authority. "We work hard for everything we've got. And we have to work hard to keep it. A firefighter is dead because somebody in the Department made a mistake. It doesn't matter who did it, it could make the whole Department look bad. And I'm Chief, I'm responsible. But my first responsibility is to the Department. I don't have to tell you that. You'd give your life for the Department. You're ready to do it every day you're on the job. Well, maybe I don't fight fires anymore, but I feel the same way. The Department is more important than any one firefighter, especially a woman. It's more important than me, it's more important than you. That's why you've got to give me that memo and let me handle this thing my way. It's an internal Department matter, and we'll solve it. You've got to trust me, Steely. I don't think you'd be here now if you didn't trust me."

Haggerty was pleased with himself. No matter that he always said something like that every time he gave one of his team spirit speeches. It always worked with firefighters. They have to think they're part of something bigger than just themselves, or what's the point? Maybe Steely had always been a little hot-headed, a bit of a maverick. But he was a team player.

Steely had slumped back in his chair and Haggerty could see that the anger in his eyes had given way to doubt and confusion. "I do trust you, Jack," he said. "But there's something just not right there. If somebody made a mistake, why don't you just eighty-six him? Get rid of the bastard. Wouldn't that be better for the Department in the long run?"

"I know what you mean," Haggerty said. "One bad apple can spoil the whole barrel. But sometimes it's not that simple. I'm Chief, sure, but I've got a lot of people over me, telling me what to do. I've got a bureaucracy riding on my back. Politicians and pencil-pushers, most of them, feathering their own nests. What do they know about fighting fires, what do they know about this department? Well, all that's going to change, Steely. And I'll tell you why. Just you, and in confidence. Commissioner Gore is leaving, and it's probable that I will be the next Fire Commissioner."

"Congratulations," Steely said.

He did not seem surprised, and his congratulations seemed half-hearted, even mocking. I wonder what's on his mind, Haggerty thought, searching Steely's face for clues. "Do you know what that means?" he went on. "It means for the first time in heaven knows how long a uniform will head up the Department. I've got ideas, Steely, good ideas, and there are going to be changes made from top to bottom. You know where I came from. I came up through the ranks, and I'm never going to forget that. I'll be in a position to make this a better job for you and every other firefighter in the Department."

He waited for Steely to respond, to bring the conversation forward, but there was just silence. "I'll make you a promise, Steely," Haggerty said. "When I'm Commissioner, I'll pursue this inquiry wherever it might lead. I'll find the man responsible and something like this V-rig thing will never happen again in my Department."

"*Your* Department?" Steely said. "I thought you just told me the Department was more important than any one man. It was Red Hadley's Department, too. And Kathy Angelli's. You could always talk circles around me, Jack. Old Ivory Mouth. But it isn't working, not this time. You're lying to me, and I'm not buying it. Because I happen to know that the Commissioner doesn't want to make any waves. Your beautiful board of inquiry is a white-wash, a cover-up. And even if Angelli wasn't responsible for the accident, you'll kill every chance she might have in the Department. You're going to make her carry the weight of somebody else's mistake, but whose? You're covering for somebody, and I don't know who. But I do know that equipment as important as those V-rigs doesn't end up in the field without you knowing about it."

"Then you're accusing me," Haggerty said narrowly. "You're accusing me of the death of a firefighter."

"Christ, Jack, it's not up to me to accuse anybody," Steely said. "I came here to ask for your advice. For your help. I came here as a friend because I didn't know what this memo meant. I figured you could explain it, tell me what to do. And all you say is it was a mistake and you want the memo back. You want to bury it. Well, I can't let you do that, because I'm beginning to think that maybe this memo isn't the only thing you want to bury."

"I am your friend, Steely. And I'm asking you for the last time, just give me that memo and let the issue pass."

"Not on your life, Johnny," Steely said, refolding the memo and sliding it back into his hip pocket. "I'm going to send it to the *Times* and let them figure it out."

Haggerty was momentarily stunned. Monsignor Flynn never mentioned that Steely was thinking of that, of making the memo public. The *Times*, for heaven's sake. The Mayor would leave a blood trail in this Department if that happened. Get tougher. I have to get tougher with Steely.

Haggerty stood up straight and tall. He put his hands on his hips, and made sure his chest was pushed out. "Don't do that, Steely," he said in a low and controlled voice. "You do, and I'll make sure that Patrolman Murphy presses charges against you from here to China. You'll be thrown off this job in a week's time."

Steely stood, too, and approached Haggerty until they were almost nose to nose. "I'll tell you something, Johnny," he said. "Guys like me aren't afraid to stack shelves for a living, or drive a truck, or whatever."

"You could go to jail," Haggerty sneered.

"But I won't, Johnny," Steely shot back. "Not even murderers go to jail in this city, and all I did was ruin a cop's shoes."

Haggerty relaxed a little bit, changing his demeanor as he knew he had to change his tactics, looking for a new approach, a new appeal.

"Steely, look," he said, folding his arms across his chest, "we've been through so much together, you and me, sneaking into movies, basketball games, trips to the beach. We shared sandwiches, guinea heros in Central Park, remember? We're friends, Steely, from the old neighborhood, friends like it's hard to make anywhere else. I've always been there when you needed me. And now I need you. You've got me wrong, Steely. I would never do anything to harm this Department or any of the firefighters in it. I'm very hurt that you would even think such a thing of me. But you're right about one thing. That memo makes me look bad. People might think the same things you've been thinking, and that could spoil it for me at this particular time. I've worked too hard, Steely, I've worked too long to let that happen. I deserve to be Commissioner, I've earned it. And you can't take it away from me, not now. Not if you're my friend. For the sake of all the good times we had growing up together, just give me that memo. For the old neighborhood. Don't you remember the things we stood for then?"

Steely seemed to be breathing heavily, the anger again building in his eyes. "The old neighborhood taught me a lot of things, Johnny," he said. "Mostly it taught me that you don't have to take an awful lot of crap from anybody, not if you really believe you're doing the right thing. But you always got what you wanted, and it didn't matter if you were right or not. Gimme, was the way you approached things, and you could always bully and bluff your way to the front of the line. You never gave a damn then, and you don't give a damn now."

Steely was just inches away from Haggerty. Haggerty could almost feel his breath. His eyes were locked into Steely's, and he did not see Steely's good arm moving up and around, the power of his body behind it. Not until it was too late, until he felt Steely's fist smash into the side of his face.

Haggerty was propelled backward, landing flat across the top of his desk. His eyes never left Steely's and he watched Steely lose his balance and try to regain it. He watched as he shifted his weight to his left ankle, and as the foot seemed to collapse beneath him. He felt just a touch of sorrow for Steely as he saw him fall to the floor.

The young lieutenant rushed into the office. Steely got to his feet quickly, and limped to the door. The lieutenant put his hand out to grab him by the arm. "Hey," he said.

"It's all right, Lieutenant," Haggerty said, picking himself up off the desk, straightening the jacket of his uniform, bringing his hand up to the side of his jaw where he had been punched. "Steely," he said. "Wait a minute. Please."

Steely stopped and turned. And Haggerty could see that he was shaking, that he was on the border of control. The lieutenant backed quietly out of the room.

Haggerty began to laugh. "Okay, Steely," he said. "Maybe I deserved that. Maybe you've been wanting to take a poke at me for a long time. So now you've got it out of your system and that's good. Because maybe now you'll stop and think. You've always been pretty quick to fly off the handle, to react. That's why you're a good firefighter. One of the best."

Haggerty's voice was grave now, almost pleading. "But a firefighter needs more than just guts, we both know that. He needs brains, or he doesn't stay alive long on this job. You've got both, Steely. Guts and brains. The Department needs a man like you in the ranks, just like it needs a man like me as Commissioner. And when I move up, I'll see to it that you move up right along with me."

Haggerty walked slowly across the room and put his hand on Steely's arm, just above the cast. "Don't blow it, Steely. Don't blow it for both of us. All I'm asking is that you use your brains. And I know you will, because we go back a long time together. We agreed and we disagreed, but we always got along."

Steely flinched a little as he touched him, but Haggerty felt he had reached him. Whatever else he was, Steely was loyal.

Haggerty watched him walk wordlessly through the outer office, and then he turned back to his desk. Sitting there, in the oversize leather chair, he again put his fingertips together, and he remembered how rotten Steely had felt that day when they stole soda bottles out of Henny the Hebe's father's store. "It just isn't right to take from one of your own," Steely had said then. Yes, he was all neighborhood. He would come through.

CHAPTER 31

THE sun shot through the small slits in the venetian blind and pushed down on his eyelids. Steely got up and pulled the sheet-like curtain across the window. He was wearing a pair of plaid boxer shorts. The room darkened as the curtain slid awkwardly across its rod. He looked at the luminescent numbers on the round-faced clock. Past noon already, he thought. But at least I slept a few solids.

He sat on the edge of his bed, brought his ankle to his knee, and began massaging it with his one working hand, slowly, letting the pressure of his fingers circulate the blood in the mass of black and blue. It felt good. Like the sleep he had, it was an alleviative. One look at this ankle, he thought, and Dr. Titlebloom would sell me a pension, no questions asked. He'd sell the welfare rolls back to the poor, too, McFatty always said.

Steely looked up from his foot and around the room. He smiled, then, just a little smile, realizing he was thinking about himself. It was a wasted effort to think about himself, like carrying a bucket of sand along with the hose into a fire, pointless. Not when he was still walking around with that memo wearing thin in the pocket of his chinos.

Steely took a container of milk out of the small freezer section of the refrigerator and ran it under the hot water of the stained kitchen sink until a cupful had liquefied. He poured it into a bowl with some puffed rice, the cereal he had loved more than all the others when he was a kid. He thought about the coming day as he spooned the cereal into his mouth, sitting there covered only by his boxer shorts and the cast that wrapped around his left arm and hand. There was nothing much to do, no doctors to see or appointments. Just the day, he thought, and me.

He dressed and left the apartment. He had strength enough to lock only one lock. The second lock, the bottom one, needed another hand to pull the door tighter against the jamb. Even with his casted fingers he could grip the doorknob, but he couldn't pull. It felt like ice pick stabs when he pulled.

He looked up and down the street for his car, forgetting completely where he had parked it. Like mornings with mean, unforgiving hangovers, he couldn't find his wheels, although he had had nothing at all to drink the night before. He had watched the black and white television, the news, the reruns, the news again, smoked a pack of cigarettes, and drunk four or five cups of coffee, but he never even touched one of the four cans of Miller's in the refrigerator. Yet, now, he couldn't find his car, and he wondered what was wrong with his mind.

When I left Haggerty's office, he said to himself, I came right here, drove up the Drive to the Sixty-first Street exit, and then over the Queensboro to save the tunnel toll. Wasn't much out of the way from Thirty-fourth to Fifty-ninth Street, I remember thinking that, and that I just wanted to rest, to rest and to sleep. Where? Where did I turn off Queens Boulevard, by the Greek Coffee Shop, or by the Mobil Station?

He walked up the street, away from the Midtown Tunnel, and stopped at the corner, his ankle still smarting, passing Chevies and Plymouths and the Japanese cars, parked one after the other as if they were chained. There were no Buicks or Oldsmobiles or Cadillacs, no Mercedeses or Jaguars on his block. You can gauge the wealth of a neighborhood, he thought, by the kind of cars on the street, except on the Upper East Side, where they park all the cars inside.

He spotted his car then, around the corner, half of it over the yellow line of a Borden Avenue bus stop. There was no ticket on the window, anyway. Maybe the union card had worked with a sympathetic cop. Steely sat in the car, started it, and drove into the traffic, still unsure of where he should go, what he should do. He headed toward Manhattan.

It was a clear day, cloudless, and not too hot. It would be a beautiful day at the Jersey shore where the waves came crashing in like they meant business, and Steely wished that he was driving out to pick up Tara and Jeffrey, and Maryanne, and that they would be heading out to Ocean City for the day, or the week, or the month. Just to get away, to be peaceful, to watch the children. Something, anyway, to replace the feeling of emptiness that he sensed within him, the absence of some strong attachment to those he loved. It was not enough to love them, he thought, turning now up the Harlem River Drive exit at 135th Street, to say that he loved them without the connections of time and place. If he could be with them today on the shore of the Atlantic, he could connect with them, that was for sure, but he couldn't even call. Maryanne didn't like it when he called unexpectedly. He'd go out on Sunday when he was expected, go to church again. And maybe they could all drive down to the Jersey shore.

Steely heard sirens as he crossed Lenox Avenue at 137th Street, and then saw the trucks pull out of the firehouse. Ladder 57, Nifty Fifty-seven. It was the first firehouse he had worked in. "Harlem's Pride," they used to call themselves when the companies took to ordering specially designed shoulder patches for the blue work shirts and sweatshirts, and each company needed a title or a slogan. "Harlem's Pride," he thought, that was appropriate. More lives in Harlem had been saved, probably, because of that one firehouse than all the hospitals from the Hudson to the Harlem rivers.

The fire trucks disappeared up Broadway, but Steely decided to go to the firehouse instead of following. Why had he come here? he asked himself, parking the car in the red-painted fire zone. He hadn't come intentionally, like you would decide to go to a diner to get a hamburger or to the corner bodega to get milk. He was just driving, and he ended up here where he had so many great and pleasing memories.

He used his alarm box key to enter the empty firehouse, the key that would open any firehouse door in the city. Maybe that's why he came here, because he knew he could get in, some place he was known, although all of his old friends were gone now.

Steely stepped up into the small, railed housewatchman's area, smiling, thinking they were still calling it "housewatchman." Would it change to "housewatchperson," now that women had finally made it into the firehouse? Or would they simply leave it at "house-watch," he asked himself, sitting in a soft, wide plastic office chair that someone had probably expropriated from a burning warehouse.

He looked around at the dull gray bricks of the apparatus floor, and at the coats and boots and helmets on hooks and hangers that stuck out from the walls. It was a dingy enough firehouse, but there had always been a lot of warmth here, he remembered. Men like Jerry Ritter and Dixie Duggan and Icehouse McPherson, who got his name by chopping through two feet of cork in an icehouse fire. It was a together firehouse here on 137th Street, with the men of the engine and the truck companies working alongside each other at the same pace, nobody slacking, at a fire, or cooking the meal, or playing softball, they were always together. It was where he had learned to be a firefighter, where all the references of probationary school came to life and became real confrontations. They were not just talking any longer about how quickly a fire traveled, how it could blow back or drop down, but watching, feeling, living it, in the sweat and the pain of it, and he couldn't have done it without the acceptance and the enthusiasm of the men of this firehouse, guys who would lie low with him under the flames, hands touching him, prodding him, challenging him to go deeper, faster, pushing him like he had pushed Kathy, making him aware that the fear in the fire is not the fire itself but of being alone, for there is courage as well as comfort in companionship. This was where he received his baptism of water and fire and long freezing winter nights.

It was a bonded firehouse; the parts, the personalities were the glue that kept it together. And then came the Columbia tenement fire. A tenement building designed to house eighteen families had been redone to provide forty-two housing units for students, and with the restructuring that much more per unit potential for fire. And the fire came, late one night as the snow fell.

Steely was tired that night, he remembered, awfully tired. He had gone without sleep the night before, working a side job in the Post Office, pushing gray canvas bags during the Christmas rush to make it a little richer holiday under the tree for Maryanne and the babies. Captain Buber had sent him back to the truck to get an extra ax. They had been working the saw on the roof of the tenement, but there was so much smoke the machine couldn't get enough oxygen and kept stalling out. He had been at the side of the truck when it happened, when the roof caved above the fire, and five firemen, three from the truck and two enginemen, plunged down into the jumping flames. He had run for the ax, but maybe not as fast as he should have. He was so tired. What would have happened if he had really run? In the years since, he had asked himself that question a million times.

After that, after the funeral on Fifth Avenue, the personality of the firehouse changed, as it does in all firehouses where there is a great tragedy, where the dark memories linger. Where the possibilities loom too large. Then Captain Buber wrote that letter to the Fire Commissioner, complaining about the equipment and the firehouse, and all the rest. Downtown, maybe it looked like he was blaming the Department for the deaths of five of his men, which he wasn't. If anything was to blame, it was the city ordinances that permitted that kind of cracker-box construction, along with the inspectors who looked the other way, and Captain Buber had a few words to say along those lines, too. The next thing they knew, he was out in Brooklyn, and the talk was, at least among the men who didn't know the truth of the situation, that maybe *he* had made some error of judgment at the Columbia tenement fire. He was finished in the Department. And so was "Harlem's Pride." One by one, the men in the firehouse tranferred out slowly but surely until, in a year's time, most of them were working in new companies, or in other jobs like Jerry Ritter's.

He hadn't told Kathy that part of Captain Buber's story, Steely remembered now. Bad as it was, a forced transfer wasn't the worst that could happen to someone who blew the whistle on the Department. It was that lingering suspicion that clung to you like a piece of lint wherever you went. That's Steely Byrnes, you remember. He was on the Ninety-ninth Street job. No matter what the Department came up with by way of an explanation, people would still think that he had screwed up, that because he had pointed the finger at somebody else, he was the one who had done something wrong.

ALL HANDS OPERATING AT BOX ONE-TWO-EIGHT-FOUR, the voice-alarm system sang out, its squeaky, static-filled sound reverberating from the bare walls, forcing Steely to jump so that his casted fingers struck the arm of the plastic chair. His wrist felt as if it had been hit with a saw blade. BROADWAY AND ONE-FOUR-ONE STREET.

Maybe it would go to a second alarm, Steely thought. Maybe not. He left the firehouse and climbed into his car. Why not take a look? But then he decided he wasn't going to buff the job, not today. He didn't want to stand helplessly out in the street, watching the flames lap from the windows. Not now, not while he still had that memo in his pocket.

Instead, he turned south and again drove aimlessly, back and forth through the streets of lower Harlem and El Barrio, until he was on the corner of Park Avenue and Ninety-ninth Street. God almighty, he said to himself as he was stopped there, waiting for the traffic light to change. But then he realized that this time it wasn't an accident. He knew why he was there. He had been drawn back to that burned-out abandoned building on Ninety-ninth Street like water sucked into a sewer.

He double-parked the car and walked to the front of the building. Someone had nailed tin over the door and the windows of the lower floors. But the windows of the top floor gaped opened like the hollow eye sockets of a skull. Steely's stomach began to churn and he felt that same dizzy sensation that he had felt as he and Red were falling. Then he saw Red sprawled out on the pavement, his body covered with the unconscious form of another firefighter. Christ, Red, Steely thought. He kicked out his foot then, his left foot, trying to kick the firefighter away. Get off him, for Christ's sake. Get off.

"Yo, sucka," he heard, and he looked around quickly. Two young boys were standing behind his parked car and then began to run down Park Avenue along the granite walls of the New York Central overpass.

Goddammit, Steely thought, turning from the building and walking back to his car. "I need a drink," he said aloud. "I'll give you *hey sucker.*"

The car lunged forward, its wheels making a whining noise, and Steely thought that the old heap was probably the only thing he seemed in control of, and it wasn't going to last much longer. "Bag it," he said aloud, making a U-turn under the overpass, "forget it all. Have a drink, find a babe maybe. Laugh it down and out with a drink and a broad."

Eamon Doran's Fine Irish Food Establishment was crowded and noisy at that hour of the late afternoon, guys in three-piece suits with their imitation-leather briefcases on the floor at their feet, girls in light summer dresses sitting on bar stools with their legs crossed.

286

Steely sat alone by the window overlooking Second Avenue, a boiler-maker on the bar in front of him, hoping he would see Brenda Starr rush into Doran's vestibule. We wouldn't have to go anyplace, or do anything. God, he thought, I just need someone to talk to. If only there were a place called Fine American Woman Emporium, or something like that. One thing for sure, and that was, nobody in this place was interested in talking to him.

He ordered another boilermaker, and then another. Sometimes Steely drank the beer and whiskey side by side, other times he mixed the two together. Then he ordered just a beer without the whiskey. He was conscious of his mind beginning to float in the booze, and he did not want to get drunk. Just a buzz was enough. The beer alone was a safety.

He summoned the bartender. "Let me ask you a question, pal," he said.

"What's that, my friend?" the bartender said.

"You Catholic?"

The bartender cocked his head suspiciously. "That's right. Why?"

"You ever hear of St. Aloysius?"

"Sure."

"What did he look like?"

"Is this some kind of joke?" the bartender said. "How the hell am I supposed to know what he looked like?"

Steely shrugged. "No joke. I just wondered maybe you'd seen his picture somewhere, that's all."

Maybe I should've asked Jack Haggerty that question, he thought. He's got all the answers. But what the hell did I do? I threw a punch, just like always. I came out swinging as if that was going to solve all the problems in the world. Jesus, I hit my best friend. And he got up laughing. Think, Steely, he had said. For the first time in your life, use your brains.

Sure, maybe that was the answer he was looking for. It made a lot of sense. The trouble was, all he could think about was Red. No matter how I figure it, Steely thought, the answer still comes out minus Red. Red is not part of us anymore, dead, like the saints and prophets. And they'll forget him, even in the Department. No-body will care why he died. Nobody will remember what he looked like. Shit, Jack, Johnnie Gimme, never once yesterday in all the talk, *never once*, for Christ's sake, did you mention his name. If only you had mentioned his name, Jack. Just talked about him as if he was a person and not part of an *it*. The *it* was a great tragedy. Bullshit. Not *it*, Jack. Red. Red Hadley. *Him.*

Steely signaled the bartender again. "I think maybe you've had enough, my friend," the bartender said.

"You're damn right," Steely said. "I've had it up to here." He pushed the pile of dollar bills on the bar in front of him toward the bartender. "Take what I owe you and let me borrow a pen, will you?"

The bartender returned with his change and a ball-point he picked up from the ledge of the cash register. Steely put his hand in his back pocket and pulled out the memo. The envelope looked a little the worse for wear, but the stamp was still on it. All he had to do was address it and lick the flap. Squinting in the dim light of the bar, he wrote the name of F. X. Burns just as he remembered it, and *The New York Times*, Times Square, New York City, on the envelope. He looked at it and didn't recognize his own handwriting.

He drank the last swallow of his beer, left a tip on the bar, and walked out into the fried-food air of Second Avenue. He looked around for a mailbox, holding the envelope by the corner, as if it were something dirty, a piece of filth he wanted to get rid of in a trash basket. No, I can't do this, he said to himself. Think, Steely, think. What would it prove anyway? Is it going to make it any easier for Kathy in the Department? No, they'll figure some other way to get her out. It won't bring Red back. And what the hell good will it do me? Everybody suffers, including Jack Haggerty, and he'd probably make a damn good commissioner. How many times has he looked the other way when I did something to hurt the Department? Well, I owe him. It's my turn to look the other way. If I don't, I'm dead. And they won't bury me like Red with brass and bagpipes. They'll dig me a hole so deep I'll never be able to crawl out. Because I betrayed a friend, betrayed the Department. He slipped the envelope back into his pocket.

He bought a copy of the *News* at a newsstand, remembering all the other nights when he was a kid and bought a copy of the *News* on his way home.

"Did you get a hand job, Steely?" one of his friends would have asked the next morning.

"Naw, I went home with the *News*," he would say, almost always.

Now it was a warm summer night. Still plenty of time to look around, hit another couple of bars. But he didn't have enough money for that. Walking to his car, Steely took the roll of bills out of his pocket and counted the two tens and the singles. Twenty-three bucks, he thought. Twenty-three bucks was just enough. He could squeeze it out, like the last of the toothpaste in the tube. If he didn't put more than three bucks worth of gas in the car in the morning, he could meet a South Park Avenue Princess. It was common knowledge it could be done for twenty. Jesus, he'd come to that.

He drove down Lexington Avenue like a madman, careening in and out around slow cruising taxicabs, braking and gunning at the red and green lights, until he got to Thirty-ninth Street. Then he let the car begin to roll almost at idle, searching the faces of the short-skirted women standing in groups at the corners, red-lipped, rouge-cheeked women, the blond-wigged women, the net-stockinged women, all black.

He crossed on Twenty-fifth Street and turned up Park Avenue South. Christ, he thought. I can't believe I'm doing this. Why the hell don't I just go home? But he made a left off Park and went west to Madison, and up Madison to Thirty-second, where he saw three very high-class-looking white women standing in front of a lunch-eonette sign which blinked on and off: Soup and Sandwiches.

He stopped the car. "Going out, baby?" one of the women said, the shortest of them, with a red leather jacket and leather skirt. She looked like a well-to-do disco dancer from a Jersey suburb, Steely thought.

"Could I talk to the tall one?" he said, pointing toward a full-bodied woman with wavy brown hair, a tight sweater, and a pair of dungarees that could have been molten lead before she wrapped them around her legs.

The woman walked to the car, her hands in her dungaree pockets. "What would you like?" she asked.

Steely was surprised. Not "Whatcha want, baby?" or "How muchya wanna spend?" What would you like? That's class. A little finesse.

"I'm not a cop," Steely said. After his separation from Maryanne, when he tried to pick up unescorted women in bars, he always used the opening line, "You know what I do for a living?" They all thought he was a cop, for some reason. He looked like a cop. He talked like a cop. The front wave of his hair fell casually over his forehead like a cop's. The gleam of experience in his eyes was like a cop's gleam. The smile, the self-assurance were like a cop's. But he was a fireman, he would announce, and the women would always feel safer.

She leaned down to take a look at him, and he smelled her perfume. It was not cheap toilet water, but something you might smell when you passed a woman on upper Fifth Avenue or in the East Seventies. "So you're not a cop," she said. "That makes me feel good. Now what shall I do to make you feel good?"

"What *shall* you do?" Steely repeated, as if he were talking to the hostess of a Levittown Tupperware party. "Shall you use the paper napkins, or shall you use the linen?"

She threw her head back in laughter, genuine laughter. "Whatever you say," she said.

"I've got twenty dollars for a pipe job," Steely said. "I could say fifteen and offer you a five-dollar tip, but what's the point in lying, you know what I mean?"

"I understand," she said.

"That's it," Steely said, "that's all I got."

"What's the matter with your arm?" she asked.

"I had a little accident."

"You sure you can drive?"

"I got here, didn't I?" Steely said.

She backed away from the window, then walked around the front of the car, opened the passenger door, and pulled her dungarees up so she could sit in them.

Steely started up Madison. "Where to?" he asked, perhaps too expectantly, too innocently.

"If you had more money, we could go to a hotel," she said.

"No stories here, you got to believe me. Except for the twenty, I'm tapped."

"So it's on the street," she said, "somewhere along Thirty-third then, I guess."

"Not on the street, miss," Steely said. "I can't hack it on the street. It's just, like, it's just like a guy with a raincoat, you know what I mean?"

"Well, there's a parking lot on Thirty-third between Madison and Fifth," she said. "You can pull in there, but make sure you turn your lights off first and back in."

"It's safe?"

"It's safe. It's dark."

"It's dark? Can't we go somewhere it's light?"

"For twenty dollars you want a water bed and a movie?"

"Whatever you say," Steely said. He suddenly felt distressed, unsure.

He backed the car into the parking lot against a side wall at the rear end. There was some light streaming faintly from a street lamp, just enough to see her sitting there with her hand out. Steely took the roll of bills out of his pocket, peeled off the two tens, and gave them to her. She looked at the bills, folded them, and then tucked them into the change pocket of her tight dungarees.

"I'm loosening my pants," she said, "just to give you something to feel around with, but I'm not taking them down."

She reached over and began to unbuckle his belt. "You want to give me some help here," she said. "You've got one good hand at least."

Steely squirmed a little, resisting. "Could we wait just a minute, miss?" he said. "I mean maybe just talk a little bit first."

He heard her sigh. "I don't get paid for conversation," she said. She took his hand and placed it on her breast. "Could we just get this over with, please?"

Steely drew his hand away and studied her face in the dim light of the street lamp. She was a young woman, a girl really, twenty, twenty-one. And pretty. God, he thought, if I could only talk to her, maybe take her out somewhere, walk down the street holding her hand.

"What's your name?" Steely asked.

"Angel," she said impatiently.

"Your real name," Steely said. "It's important."

"Okay, so it's Veronica. You sure you're not a cop?"

"I'm a New York City firefighter." He could have taken Veronica to the Holy Name racket, Steely thought. He would have been as proud of her as he had ever been proud of anyone in his life. Except Maryanne. Maryanne.

"Look," she said. "I've got better things to do than hang around a parking lot with you, whatever the hell you are. You want a pipe job, okay. Or I'll give you a hand job. But that's all you get. You interested or not?"

Steely slumped back against the seat. What was he doing here with a woman who looks closer at the faces on ten-dollar bills than at the faces of the drivers of the countless cars she steps into every night? You don't need a woman like this, he told himself. You need sex like a strung-out junkie needs sex. Forget it. Forget everything.

"Is there something the matter with me?" Veronica demanded. "You picked me, mister. I didn't pick you."

"There's nothing the matter with you," Steely said. "It's me. I'm sorry. I just made a mistake, that's all." He reached over to touch her hand but stopped short. What the hell is wrong with me? he thought. This girl doesn't need my apology, or my approval.

"Yeah, well I'm sorry too," Veronica said. "I don't know what your problem is, mister, but it's not my problem. You don't like me, that's tough. I'm just doing what I've got to do to keep alive."

"I'll drive you back," Steely said. "And you can keep the twenty."

"You're damn right I can keep the twenty, because it isn't my fault." She opened the car door. "And thanks a lot but I'll walk."

Angel Veronica slammed the door of the car and walked out of the parking lot, adjusting her pants. Steely watched her pass through the bright arc of the street lamp. She was probably from some small town somewhere, he thought. She might have been somebody's wife, a couple of kids, maybe, and a husband whose big ambition in life was to own his own mobile home. Instead, here she is in New York. It doesn't matter the reasons. She's just here on the street, doing what she's got to do to keep alive.

He liked her in a way, but he was disgusted with himself. His eyes were heavy and liquor was making him feel sick. No, it's not the liquor, he thought. It's me picking up a hooker to give me a pipe job. Me crawling around in the mud. Me saying I'm sorry. *Here.*

Who cares, he thought? Who gives a damn what I do, so why should I care? Go home. Get some sleep. In a couple of more weeks I'll be back on the job and I'll have that to think about. Sure, that's the answer. We all do what we've got to do to stay alive. Then he remembered the envelope in his back pocket. He took it out and laid it on the seat beside him. It was crushed and wrinkled and he smoothed it with his hand. Red's death changes nothing, he thought. I've got the job. Maryanne and I will get back together when I tell her what she wants to hear. Who cares?

He started the car, turned the lights on, and drove out of the dark, semen-stained parking lot. But he kept going west on Thirty-third Street, past the Empire State building, instead of swinging down Fifth and heading east, then up toward the bridge and his apartment in Queens. He didn't know where he was going. He only knew there was something more he had to do, something that still wasn't straight in his mind, some emptiness he had to fill. We all do what we've got to do to stay alive, he thought again to himself. Jack Haggerty. Maryanne. And me. But Christ, wasn't there something else? There had to be. Some reason to be alive. Some reason to be proud.

He turned up Sixth Avenue, the Avenue of the Americas, to Thirty-fourth Street, and stopped next to a telephone stand. The night shadows of Macy's across the wide expanse of Herald Square were broken all around him by the bright street lamps. He got out of the car, found a dime in his pocket, pushed it into the phone, and dialed the operator. He gave her the 516 area code and the number, the digits a part of his life like his signature. "Make it collect from Steely," he said.

Maryanne answered the phone, awake, not yet sleeping. Probably reading a book, Steely thought. "What is it, Steely?" she asked. "What's wrong?"

"Nothing wrong, Maryanne. Not much. I . . ."

"You what, Steely? You what? You just can't call at midnight like this for no reason."

"Maryanne, I just want to . . ."

"Yes?" Her voice was ice-cube hard.

"Just to connect, connect with something. Maryanne, do you know what I mean?"

"What do you really mean, Steely?"

"I've been asking myself a lot of questions," he said. He was talking very quickly, almost as if it were a speech he had memorized. "Red Hadley is dead, and I'm here, maybe just to give me the opportunity to ask some questions. And the big one is, Maryanne, the one on the billboard, the one in lights, the one I don't know the answer to like I don't know what St. Aloysius looks like, is what went wrong? I know why Red died and I have to do something about that. But first I have to know about us. What went so wrong, Maryanne, that I'm in the hospital and you're unable to give me a kiss of friendship? Maybe you can tell me what happened, now that I have this air and this body and this voice that Red Hadley left me."

"Steely," she interrupted, "don't. All I know is that I wanted the best for you and me and the kids, but every time I tried to bring out the best, it came out as criticism or nagging or a complaint. Any faults I had, I wanted to hide. I only wanted you to see me as good as I can be. I only wanted you to be as good as you can be."

There was a long pause as Steely searched for the right words. "I can change," he said finally. "I remember what you said in the hospital about me not caring about you and the kids, not caring about myself. I care, Maryanne. You've got to believe that. As Jesus Christ is my witness, I do care."

There was another long pause, and he wondered what she was doing, what she was thinking. Please don't hang up on me, he thought. Please. He held the phone so tightly that the knuckles of his hand turned white.

Finally she spoke. "Sunday, Steely," she said slowly, "when you come to pick up the kids. Maybe we can find some things to talk about."

"Right," Steely said, smiling. "Sunday. We can talk Sunday."

He closed his eyes as he heard the phone click, and he felt as if a great weight had been lifted from his shoulders, the weight of Red Hadley as he had lunged at him out of that window. Only this time they weren't plunging down toward the pavement. They were floating together like magic in midair.

For some reason, he remembered that feeling, the exhilaration, the strange yet oddly familiar freedom of falling. When had it happened before, he wondered, how many years ago? Then it came back to him.

They had been swimming off the Forty-ninth Street dock when Steely thought it up. They called him Robert then, Maryanne and Josie and Henny the Hebe, and Jack Haggerty. They had been sitting around the dock, bored with the sun. "Let's jump off the Fifty-seventh Street park," Steely challenged. He had heard that other guys in the neighborhood had done it some years before.

"You're crazy, Robert," Haggerty said.

"How high is it?" Henny asked. He was the kind of guy who never chickened out on anything, but he always made sure he knew completely what he was getting into before he fully committed himself.

"I don't know," Steely shrugged. "Like from the roof of my building."

"That's six stories," Haggerty said, "ten feet a story not counting the parapet. Something like seventy, eighty feet."

"That's pretty high," Henny offered. "You could break your stomach open if you belly-whopped by accident."

"Yeah, but you jump," Steely countered. "You don't belly-whop. If you got balls, you can do it. Steel balls."

Steely pinned them there. What was there left to say, especially in front of the girls, who giggled and looked at the boys expectantly?

They walked along a narrow concrete catwalk parallel to the river, up the FDR Drive, until they reached the emergency stairwell that gave access to the Fifty-seventh Street park from the highway below. They ran up the six flights of bare steel steps. At the top, Steely held the gray metal door open as the others passed into the park. It locked as it slammed shut. The two girls would have to walk down Sutton Place to get back to the dock. The three boys would swim, or they would walk with the girls.

Kids with oversized hats and Roy Rogers guns seemed to be everywhere. Fancy baby carriages rimmed the wooden slat benches around the park. There were no men in the park, and the women, the maids, young mothers, and a few older women, looked apprehensive and searched for their charges and children as the group of teenagers passed the sandbox.

The boys looked through the black cast-iron bars of the fence along the park's edge. It would be easy to climb over, the easiest part.

"Man," Henny said, "that's as far below as from the Brooklyn Bridge, and only Brody lived to talk about it."

"Not that high," Steely said, feeling his stomach begin to tighten as he looked down at the water. "Fifty feet or so."

"More," Haggerty said, looking down. "A lot more."

"Who's going first?" Henny asked.

"Doesn't matter," Steely said. He clapped his hands and jumped up and down, trying to shake loose the knots that were tying up his stomach. It was high, but not high enough to make him want to turn around and walk down Sutton Place.

"You think I'm jumping," Henny said, "only to look up and see you guys wave at me, you're crazy."

Steely grabbed Henny's shoulder and dug his fingers into the poached white skin. He watched the surprise cross his friend's face, and felt his own face redden with anger.

"You really think," he said, "that I could do that to you, let you jump and then walk away?"

Henny laughed even though Steely knew the pressure of his fingers digging down into his shoulder must have hurt.

"Okay," Henny said, "okay. I know you got a big pair and if I do it you gotta do it."

Henny climbed over the cast-iron bars and stepped carefully down into the thin edge of the stone fence support. He held onto the fence behind him for just a moment. Then he leaped out into the air, yelling *"Adios muchachos."* It was a line, Steely remembered thinking, that must have come from a movie.

They watched Henny's slim body crash into the water and disappear. Counting the seconds, the two girls began to say the Hail Mary, aloud, Maryanne starting it, Josie joining quickly in the rat-a-tat-tat of the prayer. "Hail Mary, full of grace, the Lord is with thee . . ." and they prayed for him until Henny's thick curly head popped way up above the water.

"I'm not jumping," Haggerty said.

Steely remembered thinking that there was no point in questioning or arguing with him. Even then, as kids, when Haggerty made a decision, you were supposed to go along with it.

"Your choice," Steely remembered saying.

"It's not much of a choice," Haggerty replied.

"Not to you, maybe," Steely said, looking over at Maryanne.

"Don't," Maryanne said, but then put her hand to her mouth.

He began to climb over the black bars. Looking down, he froze as he brought his foot to the narrow stone ledge. He saw Henny swimming madly against the tide, his arms like little fish surrounded by small waves of attacking whitecaps. God, it seemed a lifetime between him and Henny, between the park overhang and the rushing waters below. He felt his stomach turn, something rushing to his mouth, spittle probably, but acid tasting and burning.

Jump, he told himself. Jump.

"Oh God," Maryanne said, "Jesus, Mary, and Joseph."

Henny was there. He had done it, splashed into the water, and his arms were flailing. Was he okay? Did it hurt? God, it's a long way. Make sure not to hit a glass sheet of water. Hit the rough water, it's already broken. A glass sheet, he once heard, can be like a wall.

There are some things a city kid carries within him all his days, Steely remembered, like stepping on the lines in the sidewalk. Consciously or unconsciously, he still avoided the lines when he walked the streets, stepping across them, measuring the cadence of his walk according to the distances between the lines. Maybe it was like a country kid who never forgets the smell of cut hay. A city kid never forgets the lines. They are a part of him like a definition is part of a word in a dictionary, like memories that pop up in the middle of the night making sleep sweaty and restless. Like the voice of his father, the thick, hairy voice yelling at him when he was just a little boy, six or seven years old.

An older boy was being tough with him during a game of Kick the Can. His father was sitting on the slate stoop of the old tenement as the older boy slapped Steely, hard, across the bridge of the nose. He was being smacked around right before his own father's eyes, and he felt his stomach tighten then as he always would feel when afraid, tighten into a knot that pushed everything up to the chest, to the throat. "Hit 'im back, goddamn it," his father yelled from the stoop. "Your reputation is on the line."

Your reputation is on the line. The words shot through his memory, made his mind reel as he bent over the edge, the whirling waters of the East River directly below him. It was his choice to jump, but jumping wasn't enough. Henny had already jumped, and now it was up to him. He knew what he wanted to do, but was unsure if he could bring himself to do it. Go on, he said to himself. You've got the steel pair. Your reputation . . .

He pushed off. Not feet first, but head first, and the warm summer air rushed against his face as he threw his legs up and as his body sailed out over the river. Then, his hands cupped together, he bent over and touched his toes. Everything seemed to blur as he hurtled downward, but the knot in his stomach was gone. Having made a choice, he felt an exhilaration in his heart that he had never felt before, an exhilaration that made him want to dance. "Goddamn great," he remembered saying to himself, as his head rushed toward the water, his feet kicked up toward the sky, and as the breeze enveloped him like an aerodynamic stream sweeping around the wings of an airplane.

It felt so natural, hurtling down toward the water, as natural as walking down stairs, or opening the *News* to the center page. And free. Haggerty was right, he was crazy. But he had never before been so free, so sure of himself.

Afterward, Henny the Hebe and Haggerty told everyone they met that Robert Byrnes had balls of steel. Steely Byrnes, with steely blue eyes and balls of steel.

Standing next to his car in the mottled darkness of Herald Square, Steely realized now he would never have jumped if he had stopped to think about it. Just like you can never stop to think when you're fighting a fire. There's no time for that. You know what to do, and you do it because you know you have to. Haggerty hadn't jumped. He never jumped. Everything he did had a reason, and the reason was always Jack T. Haggerty. Sure, he was smart. But he would never have that feeling of freedom, of pride, that comes from doing what's right even if you don't know what's going to happen next. Even if you belly-whop, fall flat on your ass, when you pick yourself up, you've still got that feeling.

Steely reached in through the car window and picked up the envelope from the front seat. He held it against his chest, trying to smooth it out again, remembering what Red's body looked like crushed beneath him on the pavement, wishing he could smooth that out, too, somehow save him, bring him back to life. It was too late for that. But there was something he could do. Something he knew now he had to do. He had no choice. The answer to his questions had been right there all along. Not in his brains, like Haggerty said, but in his guts. It was part of him, like knowing how to fight a fire was part of him.

Steely wasn't going to mail this goddamn memo. Hell no. He was going to deliver it to Francis Xavier Burns in person. *The New York Times*, where was it? Somewhere around Times Square, right? Forty-third Street, just a few blocks away, nine, maybe ten. Not far. Not a big jump, not like diving off the Fifty-seventh Street park, he thought, and touching my toes before I hit the water. This one's going to be easy because I'm not trying to prove anything to anybody but myself.

The long blue and white *Times* trucks were parked at all angles on Forty-third Street, and Steely backed his old bomb in between two of them. He looked for an imposing entrance, but saw just a couple of doors that were lighted between two truck bays. It looked like a service entrance. Unimposing. He entered the building, and was struck by how small the lobby was. There were a few palm trees in brass pots, and a single newspaper machine backed up against a chino-colored marble wall. The place looked bare, institutional, like the lobby of a courthouse in a small town, or of a welfare office in a bigger city. A security guard stood behind a black lacquered information desk, and another was standing at the entrance to a bank of elevators off to the left.

"I want to see a guy called F. X. Burns," Steely said to the security guard, a tall, wiry black man. "He works here, right?"

The guard glanced down at a printed sheet on the desk and nodded. "You got an appointment?" he asked. "You supposed to meet him here or something? It's the middle of the night."

"I know what time it is," Steely said patiently. "But this is important." He pulled his badge and the envelope out of his back pocket. "I'm a New York City firefighter," he said, showing the guard his badge. "Now, just call him up, please, and tell him I want to talk to him."

"He ain't here, sir," the guard said.

"How do you know that?" Steely demanded, his temper beginning to rise.

"Because I know who comes in and out of here this time of night. That's my job."

"Well, then tell me where his office is. I just want to leave this envelope on his desk."

"Nobody gets upstairs without an appointment," the guard said, casually looking over at the other guard.

Steely felt himself getting red-faced. "Listen, pal," he said. "I'm trying to do this guy Burns a favor, you understand? And I don't even read his goddamn paper. Has he got a phone number, someplace I can call him?"

"We don't give out that information," the guard said. "Come back tomorrow."

"Tomorrow," Steely exploded. He felt loose and free, ready for anything. "Don't tell me tomorrow, because I'm a fireman and maybe someday your place is going to be burning, your building wherever you live, and I'm going to ask you if you've got an appointment. I'm going to tell you to come back tomorrow."

"Mister," the guard said, this time nodding at the other guard, "you got a breath on you like a brewery. And we don't care around here if you're the mayor himself. So come back tomorrow with or without your badge."

"That's it," Steely said furiously. "You can bust my horns if you want to, but don't embarrass the badge, you know. Because I'll have to take a poke at you."

The guard lifted a panel of the desk and walked out of the cubby-hole just as Steely felt the second guard's arms clamp around his chest, pressing his cast and arm tight into his body.

He was careful not to drop his badge or the envelope as the guards edged him to the door. "Okay, that's the way you want it," Steely said. "Let's go outside. Either one of you, or both."

"Not us, mister," the guard said. "Just you."

Standing out on the street, the two guards glancing at him from behind the lighted door of the entrance, Steely did not feel defeated at all, not in the way he felt when Jack Haggerty had held him in a bear hug. I really am crazy, he thought. Ready to take on two guards, both of them bigger than buildings, with a game ankle and my arm in a cast. The cast. The cast is the icing on the cake. Okay, so I'll play the game their way. Come back tomorrow and maybe even wear the uniform. Command a little respect.

The men hurling bundles of newspapers in the back of a *Times* truck stopped to watch him as he limped toward his car. He got in and laid his badge and the envelope carefully on the seat beside him. There was nothing more he could do now, no place to go but home. And maybe he should think about it some more. No. Jesus Christ, no. He had to do something now or he'd never get to sleep. Mail the memo, he thought. Sure, that's it. Send it to the *Times* and let Francis Xavier Burns call *me* for an appointment.

The noisy mufflers of the *Times* trucks split the air as he backed his heap into Forty-third Street and turned toward Eighth Avenue. He went with the lights, east on Forty-fourth Street, north on the Avenue of the Americas, looking for a mailbox. He stopped on the west side of the avenue in front of the Time-Life Building, just across the street from Radio City Music Hall. Three pimps were standing idly around a mailbox on the corner. They were wearing white suits with silk handkerchiefs gushing out of their breast pockets. And fur-covered hats. Mink fedoras, like they were expecting a blizzard in August.

Steely got out of the car and walked toward them, huddled there, he thought, like bookmakers at a track, as pleased with their own hustle as with anything else in life. They looked at him apprehensively. He was a cop, no doubt that's what they were thinking.

He was holding the envelope in his right hand obviously intending to mail it. And they weren't going to move for him, he could see that. But he was ready to take them on, all three of them, to get to that mailbox.

He went directly into them, that great sensation of freedom and exhilaration still with him, lingering like a potent drug. He pushed one and shoved another, feeling the wind against his face, the sweet night breeze of New York.

"Hey," one yelled.

But they separated for him, backing up quickly on the soles of their feet.

Steely opened the lid of the mailbox. Okay, Francis Xavier Burns, he thought. I hope you know what to do with this, because I sure as hell didn't, except to send it to you. Now you can start asking the questions. He looked at the envelope one last time. Jesus, no return address, nothing to indicate that I sent this. He patted this pocket and found the pen he had borrowed from the bartender to address the envelope. He had picked it up along with his pack of cigarettes. I owe you one, pal.

He placed the envelope down on top of the mailbox, holding it with the fingers of his casted hand. He thought for a moment, and then printed in large, careful letters across the back: "This comes from Robert F. Byrnes, Firefighter, Ladder Co. 7, NYFD." He opened the lid of the mailbox again and flipped the envelope into the receptacle.

"Thank you, gentlemen," he said, bowing slightly in the direction of the pimps. "I have enjoyed your company no end."

He walked back to his car jauntily, like he had climbed out of the river that day, wet and shivering, but smiling, trying to pretend that his exhilaration was everything, that he hadn't been afraid to jump. That he wasn't still afraid. He opened the car door, slid in behind the wheel, and turned the key in the ignition. But he just let the engine run in idle. He closed his eyes. Sleep, that's what he needed now. He would sleep if only he could catch his breath, if his heart would stop pounding.

Steely put his cast and good hand on top of the steering wheel and thought of Maryanne, and of that sunny day he drove her and Jeffrey home from the maternity ward of Elmhurst General Hospital, the baby still wrapped in a small white hospital blanket. It was a city hospital. It was the city health plan. She had been in a ward, six to a room. That's what you got if you were the wife of a firefighter.

But so what? The baby was healthy, just like their first one, like Tara. And Maryanne looked so accomplished, so pleased and happy as if she had played on a great stage, and was being applauded. She had given birth. A child of love. A child that was born of the love between two people. The way it should be. She had given the world something. Life. Just like Red Hadley, he thought, feeling the tears well in his eyes. The life Red Hadley gave me.

Steely lay his head down on the steering wheel. The weight of his arms and shoulders connected with the car's horn, and it beeped first, and then blasted, without interruption. Steely didn't care. He just let the horn go, the deep electric sounds awakening the still morning air between the tall and lonely steel and glass rectangles that rimmed the Avenue of the Americas.